BUILDING STORM

A HAWKE FAMILY NOVEL

GWYN MCNAMEE

Shannon —
Hawkes will always
rise!

— ♡
Gwyn

Building Storm
by
Gwyn McNamee © 2018

Cover Design: Michelle Johnson at Blue Sky Designs
Cover Model: Rachael Baltes
Photographer: Christopher Correia at CJC Photography
Editing: Kathleen Payne

❀ Created with Vellum

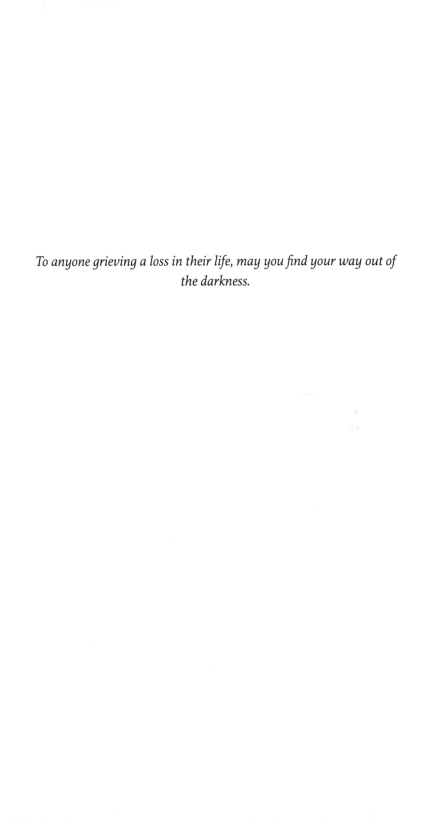

To anyone grieving a loss in their life, may you find your way out of the darkness.

ACKNOWLEDGMENTS

Another huge thank you to my two most important people in my life—my husband and my daughter. This book took a long time to complete because of some medical issues and also because of the content. It was very emotionally taxing to write Storm's story, and I couldn't have done it without their support.

To my trusty beta readers, as always, you ladies helped me polish this story into what it is today. Thank you for always being brutally honest and kicking me in the ass when it is needed.

And finally, thank you to all the fans who emailed and sent PMs asking when Storm's story was finally going to come out. I hated having to put off the release, but hearing how much everyone was excited about it coming kept me motivated to work even through some difficult times.

I love you all!

one

*D*amn!

I didn't even think you could *fit* two cocks in a vagina at the same time. Sure, in pornos, but in real life? Real people?

Heat creeps over my cheeks, and I try to turn away from the raunchy display, but debauchery surrounds me. To my left, a woman with a silver mask hiding her face rides a man's cock like he's a bucking bronco she can barely control. To my right, two men tag-team a woman in a red dress—one plowing into her from behind while the other has his cock rammed down her throat.

Maybe this was a bad idea...

"Remind me again why I let you drag me here?"

Caroline manages to pull her attention away from the scene before us and grins at me. "Girl, because you need to get the fuck out of the house. And don't pretend to be shocked and offended. You know you love watching people have sex."

The matter-of-fact way she makes the statement has me cringing. It's a fact I now regret confessing to her that drunken night. I'll just add it to the list of ways I've failed...the ways I *continue* to fail. The ways I've let my sorrow drown me and turn me into this person I don't even recognize.

Mistake #1,576—telling Caroline that Ben and I had enjoyed a little voyeurism.

In retrospect, it was unwise to spill such an intimate thing to her. But in my defense, when I confessed that uber personal fact,

I was a sobbing, blubbering mess, and Caroline was my "babysitter" for the night back when everyone thought I was so unstable, I shouldn't be alone.

In those first few weeks after I lost Ben, things were so...up in the air. Uncertain. Agonizing. We were trying to make sense of not only his loss but also everything that happened with Dom and Stone.

The simple act of breathing—pulling air into my lungs and pushing it out again—was so excruciating, I had wished I could stop. I just wanted the pain to end.

Who am I kidding?

It's still excruciating to wake up every day with the knowledge I'll never see him again. To know he's gone due to the actions of a man who was supposed to be like family, a man who was supposed to love and care for us. And even worse, that he's gone because of what Stone did...

So, I wouldn't have thought I would want to talk about the things Ben and I shared. But Caroline had insisted that a nice bottle of wine, or even a cheap one for that matter, and talking about the good times with him would somehow help ease the pain of losing both the love of my life and Angelina's father.

I hadn't meant to let it slip what we had been doing, but Caroline has a way of prying things out of you, whether you want them exposed or not. It's the reporter in her. She's more dangerous with a question than Stone, and I was powerless to stop the words from falling from my mouth once that bottle was empty.

Huge mistake.

"I can't believe I told you about that."

Seriously, what the hell had I been thinking?

I guess I wasn't back then...and barely am now. But now I'm here and have to deal with the consequences of Caroline knowing that far too private information.

At least she's not judging. So many people don't understand it. We only attended parties like this a handful of times. It was all about watching and being watched. There was just something so thrilling about knowing someone else was getting off on seeing you get off, even if it was strangers.

We weren't swingers. Both Ben and I were too fiercely loyal to ever touch anyone else. But their eyes on us made the sex...otherworldly.

My body heats just remembering it...the way he touched me, kissed me, loved me...even in front of total strangers.

"You'll always be mine, Storm. Always."

The tears well in my eyes, and my chest tightens.

I can't lose my shit here.

Which is why I have to push him out of my head now, push out the memories of the parties we attended together...what his touch, what his kiss did to me. How safe and loved I felt in his arms. The way the world just disappeared when we were together, even when people watched us. How the parties made us feel alive...

Something he will never be again.

Caroline's laugh interrupts the tears brimming in my eyes. She narrows her vision on a couple banging on a lounge to our left. "But I'm so glad you did tell me, honey, because coming to this party by myself would have been super awkward for me. I had no idea what to expect, but I have to say, I'm certainly enjoying it so far."

I follow her line of sight to the hard, flexing ass of the man on top of a writhing woman, and I can't help but chuckle even if I don't really feel it. It helps loosen the tightness in my chest and banish the rest of my tears. "You would have been fine on your own, Caroline."

The woman is so damn outgoing and adventurous. Not to mention how stunning she is tonight in her floor-length sequin black gown. Her pale, highlighted brunette bob shimmering under the muted lights and her bright green eyes practically scream *come get me.* Even if she had come alone, she would have been the life of the party. She doesn't have a shy bone in her body.

Dragging me along was likely just a pity invite, and now that we're here, things just feel so...different than the parties before. Dirtier. More illicit. It's probably because I was with Ben. But being here, essentially alone, and watching this just feels...wrong.

Care sighs and scans the room. "Yes, I probably would have been fine, and I probably could've guilted one of the other girls into coming with me. But the Hawke men aren't exactly known for being open-minded and generous about other men seeing their women, and I have a feeling they wouldn't be cool with their women being here and watching other people fuck without them here, too."

She does have a good point.

Savage, Stone, and Gabe are rabid when it comes to Dani, Nora, and Skye. They would freak the hell out if she had mentioned it to the girls.

Shit. Now I get it.

"So, I was the last resort?"

That's even worse than a pity invite. It should piss me off, but I have more important things to worry about than Caroline's motives...like maybe finding an excuse to get out of here early. This whole thing just feels wrong. I can't be here.

Her head jerks back toward me, her mouth agape. "What? No! It's not like that. I just thought that since you came to these things with Ben, you'd be more comfortable here than any of the girls. Plus, like I said, you really need to get out."

She's not wrong about that, but I would never admit it.

The house Ben spent so much damn time renovating to make it perfect for me, for us, has become a tomb. A place I hide. A place of despair. A place void of laughter and joy. A place I merely exist.

Angelina is the only thing that matters now. There's no need to go anywhere else other than family engagements, and even dragging myself to those is difficult. Being around everyone should make me feel better, but I only end up thinking of Ben— him laughing with Gabe and Savage; him swimming with Angel in Mom's pool; him arguing with Stone about something asinine simply because Stone loves to argue. Even the office has been a struggle, and God knows I'm screwing my business royally with my almost total absence. But I just...can't.

So, I sleep. I eat—sometimes. I work—far less than I should.

Life is simple. It has to be. I can't do complicated.

And this...this party is bringing up memories I hadn't planned on confronting tonight.

"We could've gone to dinner, Care. Why does it have to be coming to watch people bone?"

Caroline smiles and waggles her eyebrows. "But that's the greatest thing! We don't have to just *watch*. We can join."

I have no intention of diving into meaningless sex with strangers simply to ease the ache between my legs or the gaping hole in the center of my chest. I will spend the rest of my life being the lonely widow and put my energy where it's needed— into Angelina and what's left of my pitiful life.

The only reason I even let Caroline drag me out is because that house was just too much tonight. Too empty. Too full of memories of Ben. With Angel at Mom's for a sleepover, it was just all...unbearable. I had already cried enough to give myself puffy, red eyes before she called.

I couldn't deal with the gut-wrenching loneliness anymore. Not tonight.

Going out was the lesser of two evils, even if it meant accompanying Caroline to this bawdy affair. It hasn't lessened the pain, but at least it got me out of the dark pit of gloom that is my bedroom...if only for a short while.

"So, are you planning on partaking, Care?" I scan the room. Caroline doesn't really have a type, but I feel like I'll know it when I see someone who would pique her interest.

A familiar face stops my survey.

Saint?

The massive bouncer from TWO flashes me a white smile and nods in my direction from where he stands across the room. A warm flush spreads across my face.

Shit. What the hell is he doing here?

It's bad enough Caroline dragged me along, now I have to run into someone I know? If he comes over here, I may die of embarrassment.

But instead of making his way toward us, he turns and disappears down a back hallway.

Caroline grins after him like the Cheshire cat. "Partaking? Well, I do have to do the professional thing first and interview Jennifer, but once I get that done and have everything I need for my article, then why the hell not?"

I'm not entirely sure if she's referencing Saint or not, and I don't bother asking. It's not my business, and there are plenty of other options for her scattered around the room.

An Intimate Affair hosts amazing risqué parties, and the couples and singles here tonight are interested in enjoying things on the spicier side. While Caroline came to conduct an interview with the owner of the company, I'm not naïve enough to believe it's the only thing on her to-do list.

With a lick of her lips, Caroline scans the room again. "If somebody catches my eye, why should I not have a good time? Especially now that my friends are settling down. It feels like I'm the only one who likes to have fun anymore."

Fun.

I don't even remember what that word means.

When is the last time I did anything I actually enjoyed?

Surely not in the last six months. They've been nothing short of excruciating for me and Angel. Not only have I been trying to pick up the pieces of our personal lives, but I've had to deal with everything going on with Ben's business that I'm now a reluctant half-owner of.

Some days, the weight of it all on my shoulders feels like being crushed by a semi, and there are even days I've wished for that very scenario. It would be an escape from the suffocating despair that's overwhelmed my life.

So, as much as I may be uncomfortable at the moment, a night out is probably a good thing for my mental health.

"Thank you, Caroline, for inviting me, but don't get your hopes up that I'm going to get involved in any of the shenanigans."

Not that I could even if I want to. The last-minute invite meant there wasn't time for me to undergo the required health screening, let alone the necessary personal grooming before I could engage in any extracurricular activities. So tonight, I'm wearing a red bracelet given to me at the door indicating I'm an observer only. I didn't fail to notice Care's green wristband.

Fair game.

"Shenanigans? Did you really just say shenanigans while watching adults fuck?"

That draws a laugh from somewhere deep in my chest. I have to hand it to Caroline...she certainly has a way with words. And she always manages to break the tension and put a tiny crack in the wall of pain surrounding me. So, despite the way she can sometimes get a little overzealous, she truly *is* the kind of friend everyone needs.

"Yeah, I guess I did. What would you call it?"

She gives me another grin and reaches up to adjust the mask covering her face. "I call it open season."

The raven-haired woman in the sparkling green dress and green and silver mask standing near the entrance calls to me like a beacon in this storm of flesh and sin.

These things are so often a heathen mess. I was a little reluctant to even come tonight, but Chris insisted I might actually enjoy this place since the company that organized it is very reputable.

He knows how badly I need to forget Chicago. How badly I need to just forget. Everything. And he knows I've spent the last several weeks there at parties just like this, trying to fuck away the pain. Somewhat successfully.

Still, how awkward is that? My brother suggesting I get laid at a random sex party...

But it's been working. Sort of. A hot, sweaty fuck can do wonders even for someone like me whose entire life imploded in a single moment. The similar parties I attended gave me brief respites from the vile truth that invaded my perfect life and ultimately forced me from Chicago to New Orleans.

So tonight, in a new town, the start of a new life, the woman across the room can do the same—give me the release, a way to forget. Plus, the party is actually spectacular—music, dancing, food, beautiful people.

Masquerade balls always make things more interesting. Of course, participants are free to disclose their identities if they choose, but there's something incredibly erotic and enthralling to be with somebody without truly knowing who they are. The required health screenings and the buckets of condoms ensure everyone's safety in that respect, so as long as you're willing to take a chance and play, you really can have an orgasmic time. I certainly have at the other parties...

But tonight has been different. The sultry women throwing themselves at me haven't managed to stir any interest. They're the kind of women I've gravitated toward at these parties before— beautiful, forceful, more than willing to engage in pretty much anything anyone has in mind. The perfect escape from the world and harsh reality. Yet tonight, I've found myself rejecting their advances without much of a thought.

"Hey, handsome." A low, sultry voice whispers in my ear, and a small, soft hand with long red nails slides down my arm. I turn my head toward the woman beside me, and come face to face with a stunning blonde with hooded brown eyes and red lips on a mouth designed for pleasure. She grins at me from below the black mask covering half her face, and her tongue snakes out and across her bottom lip. "What are you doing standing over here all by yourself? Why don't you come join the fun?"

She's what I would have jumped at merely a week ago, but my cock doesn't even stir at her offer. All I want to do is turn away from her back to see what the dark-haired woman is doing.

"I'm sorry, doll. I'm spoken for."

A pitiful, unattractive pout pulls at her lips, and she squeezes my arm. "You sure I can't convince you? My friend over there is dying to meet you." She nods toward another blonde sitting on a couch to our left in a dress so short, it clearly exposes her bare pussy as she crosses and uncrosses her legs seductively.

Every man's wet dream, yet tonight, I couldn't care less. My focus is elsewhere. "Thanks for the invitation. Maybe next time."

She pouts again but scampers off to her friend, probably to scout another target. Some lucky bastard will have a wonderful evening with them.

But not me.

Ever since *she* walked in, flanked by the petite brunette who can't stop licking her lips and eyeing up every naked man in the room like she's at a fucking smorgasbord, no one else has even been on my radar.

While I can appreciate the brunette's obvious enjoyment of what's being offered, it's the relative silence and almost indifference of her dark-haired friend that draws my attention and my curiosity.

She doesn't want to be here.

That much is obvious. Her rigid shoulders and the tight set of her lips scream *get me the hell out of here now.*

I've never seen someone at one of these things so utterly and completely miserable. It's almost like she's here physically but somewhere else entirely in her head. Sometimes people can be a little overwhelmed their first time, but this is more than that. Something deeper. Something darker and heavier is weighing on her.

The chivalrous thing would be to go over and see what I can do to turn those luscious lips up into a smile instead of a frown. Certainly, something needs to be done so this woman doesn't spend the night looking so forlorn in a sea of so much ecstasy.

It would be a shame to waste an evening like this. And while I've turned down every other woman who has approached, this one is finally stirring something I haven't felt in a long time. Interest. And not just sexual.

A short, curvy woman approaches them—the owner of the company who I met when I arrived. She greets the brunette and draws her away from the object of my attention.

Game on.

I swirl the Scotch in my glass and take a sip. The liquid burns down my throat and warms my stomach as I make my way around the dance floor toward the woman standing alone near the entrance.

Jazz music floats through the air, enveloping the room in the cool sounds of saxophone, piano, and bass. Couples who aren't busy engaging in other endeavors dance. The combo on the stage is quite good. I haven't heard a live band perform like this in years, and my feet itch to dance, specifically with the mystery woman in my arms.

She isn't like the other women here, the ones flaunting their sexuality and throwing themselves at anyone with a cock. Those women are easy—easy-going, easy to please, easy sexually, easy to keep happy...or so it would seem. I've done easy women, and I can spot them from a mile away—fake hair, fake nails, fake smiles...

This woman is anything but easy, and she's one hundred percent real.

She's stoic. She's contemplative. She's...stunning in her sad beauty.

Something deep inside me recognizes that kind of grief. I've been there. Too recently to want to relive it. But a pang in my chest refuses to let me walk away from her without at least *trying* to ease some of that sorrow from her.

A waiter circles toward me, and I down the rest of my drink and drop the empty glass on his tray with a mumbled, "thanks."

The woman scans the room, pulling her plump bottom lip between her teeth and wringing her hands together at her waist.

She's nervous. And sad.

Not a good combination for anyone, but especially someone at a party like this. These are meant to be fun and freeing. They shouldn't stress you out. And this striking woman is most definitely stressed.

Her tense body and harsh, straight spine scream *leave me alone*, but I am always up for a challenge, particularly one this agonizingly dark and beautiful. The air of mystery and melancholy surrounding her draws me to her, despite the obvious signs warning me away.

It won't be the first time I make a bad choice in women.

Which is exactly why sex at these parties is the best option right now. No attachments. No drama. Nothing more than a release and a good time. Something this woman needs.

I move slowly around the dance floor and reach her as the band wraps up the song and starts a new one. She doesn't see me approach. She's too busy focusing on everything going on around the room to notice me sliding up next to her.

"Your first time?"

She jerks, and that lip falls from between her teeth, drawing my attention to the place my mouth is almost watering to taste. "What?"

I grin at the bewilderment on her face. Her wide blue eyes search mine for an answer to her question.

Adorable.

"Is this your first time at one of these parties?"

"Oh…" She turns back toward the room and scans everyone before returning her focus to me. Her eyes meet mine again. "Uh, no, actually. But it's been a long time."

Given her demeanor, I would have bet money she hadn't set foot at one of these things before. Something is definitely up. Why come if you're not interested? Why come to only be miserable?

What's your story, beautiful?

"I'm Landon." I hold my hand out to her and wait while she considers it, almost as if she doesn't know what to do.

She's cautious. Probably smart in a place like this.

I shift my weight while I wait for her to make a move.

Maybe I've made a massive mistake coming over here. Maybe whatever she's so wrapped up in inside her head is too much to try to overcome with a little flirting.

If anyone had approached me in the days or even weeks after my world ended, I wouldn't have been too interested either. So, maybe she just wants to be left alone.

But she finally reaches out and clasps my hand with hers. "Storm."

I grin and bring her hand up to place a kiss to the back of it. Her soft, pale skin feels like velvet under my lips.

Will the rest of her feel like this?

The soft, flowery scent of honeysuckle invades my nose, and I peer up at her as I pull my lips from her skin.

Storm fits her. The cascading mane of jet-black hair, the cloud of darkness in her blue eyes peering out from behind the silver mask, the swirling uncertainty surrounding her, it all reminds me of a massive hurricane threatening on the horizon.

And I am more than willing to let that storm crash down around me. Because those eyes are hypnotizing me even as she diverts them back to the room and tugs her hand from mine.

Maybe the kiss was a bit overkill?

I didn't mean to make her uncomfortable. Before she died, Mom did her best to teach me and Chris to be chivalrous, and the kiss seemed like the right thing to do at the time. But my perception may be skewed by what happened back home, or maybe the atmosphere here has warped my ability to think clearly. Or it's just this woman. Because up close, she's even more breathtaking. My heart thuds wildly just being close to her.

Her mask can't hide the blush that's crept into her cheeks and also spread across her exposed breasts in the plunging neckline of the green number she's wearing. I don't know anything about designers or dresses, but whoever made this created it just for Storm and her body. It's like it's been painted on her with an expert brush, perfectly accentuating her every luscious curve and tempting me to do things that would only be appropriate in private under normal circumstances.

But these are anything but normal circumstances. This party is designed for pleasure. And I want nothing more than to erase everything that haunts Storm and show her the greatest pleasure of her life, at least for one night.

Because I need to forget. Because I'm leaving my troubles in the past. Because I'm moving forward. And one amazing night together is what we *both* need.

One night.

two

Storm turns her attention to the dance floor where a handful of couples are swaying to the bluesy tunes. She's trying not to watch what's going on outside the dance floor, and that brings a smirk to my face.

I cover my mouth with my hand. I don't want to offend her and have her think I'm laughing at her, but it's kind of cute. She said this isn't her first time at one of these, but she's clearly embarrassed about what she's seeing or maybe she's just embarrassed by her reaction to it. A lot of newbies come in and are shocked, but not at seeing the public displays. They're shocked at the way their bodies respond to watching other people have sex.

My first time, I was a little taken aback, but it wasn't long before I relished the opportunity provided at these parties. Still, that was only a few weeks ago, and I'm definitely in the "test the waters" stage to see if this is the atmosphere I really want to be in for any sort of long-term. It's fun, but I'm not sure it's something I see myself continuing with forever. There have to be better ways to find someone to engage in a little recreational activity with who isn't looking for anything serious.

But for tonight, I'm here. With this woman.

The dark enigma.

Perhaps her interest in the dancing is my way in. I can use it to my advantage here.

I hold my hand out to her, and she raises a slim, dark eyebrow in my direction.

"Thank you, but I'm really not sure I'm interested in partaking this evening." Her words come out shaky, and the unease in her eyes is evident, even behind the mask. She holds her left hand up, and the red bracelet there tells me I won't be having sex with her tonight. But for some reason, it's not disappointing.

The mystery of this woman is enough to entertain me right now. The need to figure her out. Figure out why she's here and why she appears so...lost.

I chuckle and tip my head toward the dance floor. "I'm just asking for a dance."

A small smile curls the corner of her lips, and she glances across the dance floor again. Something dark and sad crosses her face. Her bottom lip quivers slightly. Then she shakes her head and seems to refocus before she turns back to me and accepts my proffered hand. "Okay, one dance."

Her warm, smooth skin in my grip sends goose bumps skittering up my arm.

What the hell was that?

I don't react this way to women. At least, I haven't any time in recent memory. It's mostly been hot and heavy sexual attraction and good-byes. Which is exactly what I wanted and needed. What I still want and need.

There's something about her, though...

Something...different.

A bright, fast-paced song starts up as we enter the floor. I spin her around and tug her back toward me, sending that light floral scent wafting over me again. She lets out a laugh that lights up the entire room. It's the first time I've seen her carefree and happy since the moment she arrived at the party, and it makes her even more beautiful. The melancholy clouding her eyes since the moment she arrived disappears for a split-second. All that's there is...life.

But just as quickly as it's there, it's gone. She stiffens slightly in my arms, and her focus darts around the room almost like she's searching for someone or something—maybe an excuse to end our dance?

I'm not letting her get away so soon.

"So, Storm, why do I have a feeling you'd rather be somewhere else tonight?"

She sighs and averts her eyes for a moment before returning her attention to me. "Well, my friend dragged me along. She's interviewing the owner of this company for a newspaper article and didn't want to come alone."

That explains the eager brunette, not Storm's reluctance to enjoy herself or the stand-offish attitude she's sporting. "But you did say this wasn't your first time."

She stills momentarily in my arms, and something dark flashes across her eyes, but before I can question her about it, she shakes her head. "It's not. It's been a long time, and that was under very different circumstances."

Color me intrigued.

I want to press her, but it's clear from the rigid set of her body that she's not interested in talking about it, especially with a stranger. It's fine. I won't pry. I'll focus all my attention on ensuring she has a good time this evening, even though she's clearly not here for what I came for.

There's more than one way to enjoy ourselves.

"Well, I don't know what the other circumstances were, but I can tell you that these things can be a pretty good time."

She nods and glances over to a couple banging against the wall—the woman's head thrown back in ecstasy as the man powers his cock into her. Mine hardens between us, and I shift my hips away from her so I don't rub against her. The last thing I need is her freaking out because I have a hard-on after assuring her this was just a dance.

No matter what my original intentions may have been... things tonight are definitely going a different direction.

"Oh, I know they can be quite entertaining." Her bright blue gaze finds mine again and this time, there's a bit of heat and humor there for a moment before it returns to a darker somber color. "But it's not really my scene anymore, if you know what I mean."

I nod as we sway to the sounds of Duke Ellington. "I can understand that."

This lifestyle isn't for everyone, and people who participate do so on many different levels. There's no one way to enjoy one of these parties. "You're a good friend for coming along to something you're not interested in."

She shrugs and moves with me flawlessly, gliding around the floor with the grace of someone who has clearly had some professional lessons. Having a woman in my arms like this instead of in a bed brings a rush of memories I'd rather not relive.

Another time. Another woman. Music. Laughter. Love. A future.

"I guess you could say that." Her eyes scan over my shoulder. "You haven't seen where my friend ran off to, have you?"

No, my entire attention has been on you.

I shift and survey the room, but the throngs of people make it hard to pinpoint anyone, and the masks make it impossible to really catch anybody's faces. "No, sorry, I didn't. Why? Are you thinking of leaving so soon?"

Hopefully not. Things were just getting interesting.

The quick flash of recognition in her eyes makes me confident that's precisely what she was thinking.

Far too soon. I haven't had enough time.

"You just got here."

She frowns, and I shift a little closer to her now that I've got my body back under control. "Like I said, it's not really my scene, and I have things I need to take care of at home."

That's certainly cryptic. Does she have a husband or other family?

I squeeze her left hand in mine, searching for a ring.

A thin band of cool metal rubs against my skin.

Damn. There it is.

I guess maybe she really did only come with her friend for moral support.

These parties draw all different kinds of people—married couples interested in swinging, singles looking to hook up, people searching for a little kink they can't get at home...

Everyone is open with their sexuality here, and unless they pay for a private room, most are engaging in all sorts of debauchery for anyone else to see.

If she doesn't want to be here, I can see how the entire atmosphere may be a bit too much for her.

"I appreciate you staying for a dance, at least."

That tiny smile returns and speeds my heart. She inclines her head. "It's my pleasure. It's been a while since I've danced like this."

"That's a shame." I spin her around and then yank her toward me. She laughs again and tosses her head, sending her cascade of onyx locks flowing down the center of her exposed back. The contrast of the dark against her alabaster skin has my cock hardening again.

Despite my reservations about scaring her off, the words slip from my lips, unbidden. "You know you're absolutely stunning, don't you?"

She pauses, and her eyes widen momentarily as if she's surprised that I would say so. Then a blush creeps up across her chest and over her neck to her cheekbones. "Oh, wow. Um, thank you."

Doesn't her husband tell her how beautiful she is every damn day? I sure as hell would.

"You're very welcome."

Her bottom lip disappears between her teeth, and she glances down at her shoes and away from me. She's clearly contemplating something, and I'd give anything to know what's going on in that mind of hers.

Finally, her head snaps up. "I don't know how to say this without sounding bitchy, but I'm not going to sleep with you."

I toss my head back and laugh, the sound disappearing into the loud music flowing from the band.

Damn. Beautiful. Mysterious. Feisty. And honest. Why does she have to be married?

With another gentle squeeze, I grin. "That was not on my agenda when I asked you to dance with me. I just wanted to have a beautiful woman in my arms, swaying to this lovely music. That was my only intent."

Even if I do want more, like to be buried inside her.

Eventually.

Her blush deepens, and she can't meet my eyes. "I'm sorry if what I said offended you. I just thought I'd make myself clear, given where we are."

I nod my understanding and spin us around the floor again.

I'd be lying if I said having Storm under me wouldn't be at the top of my to-do list, but it really wasn't my intention when I asked for her hand. Given the menagerie of sex surrounding us, I can understand her need to clarify her position, and I want to put her back at ease. It's the only way our evening can continue. And I need it to if I have any hope of getting Storm to agree to see me again. If I have any chance of moving this horizontal in the future.

"You didn't offend me, I promise."

Way to put your foot in your mouth, Storm.

I can't believe I actually said that to him. He's a nice guy who asked me to dance, and I immediately assumed he was trying to fuck me.

Mistake #2,321—thinking I know how to converse with a member of the opposite sex without sounding like an idiot.

It's been over a decade since I was single and had to interact with a man in anything other than a purely professional manner. And I *suck* at it. Everything was so comfortable with Ben, even from day one. He put me at ease with a quick smile and soft caress. I've completely forgotten what it's like to have to interpret what a man's words *really* mean.

Although, surveying the couples in the room, I guess it wasn't totally out of the question for me to think sex might be on his agenda.

There's no denying Landon is a handsome man. The mask concealing a large portion of his face can't hide his high cheekbones and strong jawline. And his sandy blond hair, smoldering bourbon eyes, and strong, broad shoulders would be appealing to any woman.

But not to me. Not now.

They can't be.

Even at a party like this, I can't be swept away in how easy it was to fall into Landon's arms and forget the world in favor of mindless pleasures.

These things were always a bit hard to prepare yourself for, even when I came with Ben. Couples swapping partners. Singles looking to meet new people, whether it be for a relationship or just a one-night stand. You never really knew what you were getting when you attended.

I guess that's part of the mystique for some people, but that was the part that always made me feel uncomfortable. Now, being here alone, it makes me wish even more that I had told Caroline no. Getting out of the house is good for me. I can't deny that, but this is probably the last place I should be in my current mental state.

My constant mental state since Ben died.

In bed in my pajamas with Angelina is where I belong.

Not that I'm not enjoying my dance with Landon. It's just being in a different man's arms, especially in a place like this, feels...all wrong.

Liar.

That's not true. It feels different, but there's something about Landon that's captivating and reassuring. Something that makes guilt claw at my heart because Ben has only been gone for six months, and the last place I should be is tangled within another man's arms on a dance floor...at a sex party.

His crisp, clean scent lulls me into a calm I haven't felt in months, and I relax against him.

Bad idea.

The very real feeling of his body pressing against me is just too much. Too much heat. Too much need. Too raw.

I push away from him, putting some much-needed distance between myself and his hard, lean body.

Focus on something else. Anything else.

A muscular, dark-haired man in an immaculately tailored tux stands at the edge of the dance floor with a glass of amber liquid. Our eyes meet, and the corner of his mouth turns up into a sexy half-grin. There's something vaguely familiar about him, but I can't quite put my finger on what it is or how I might know him. He nods and raises his glass to me, and another blush rushes across my skin.

Wrong place to look.

It's time to get out of here. Away from all of this. I'm about to offer my apologies for having to leave when Landon catches my face with his palm and turns me to face him.

"I promise you didn't upset me, so don't go running off

thinking you offended me in some way. I'm probably the most easy-going, unlikely to be offended person in the world."

The heat of his hand against my cheek spreads out through my body and centers between my legs. Those soft amber eyes flare with passion.

Holy hell.

A simple touch. A simple look. Innocent enough. Yet, it makes me miss a step and almost trip over his foot.

Shit. You klutz.

Shaking off his hand, I try to regain my composure, but his warm eyes continue to bore into mine. "That's not it. I just..." I struggle to find the right words. I barely know this man, and I don't want to reveal everything my shredded heart is going through right now, but I feel like I owe him an explanation for my sudden desire to depart. "I really need to get going."

Back home where I can be alone with my memories.

He squeezes my left hand again, something I noticed him doing earlier, and his finger slides down around my wedding ring. I can't bear to take it off. Ben is and always will be my husband, the only one who holds my heart.

Shit. I'm so oblivious.

That's why Landon did it in the first place. He was checking for a ring.

"To your husband?"

My blood runs cold, and I shiver, my gut instantly churning and acid rising in my throat. I place my hand over my stomach and step away from him. The music continues and couples twirl around us as we stand motionless in the middle of the dance floor.

His eyes search mine as he waits for an answer.

"That's none of your goddamn business." I don't know where those words came from or why they came out like that, but the second they're out of my mouth, I regret the way I snapped at him.

He didn't know what he was doing or what he was asking, and my reaction likely seems a bit extreme to him given we've been having a nice, cordial conversation.

Shit. Shit. Shit.

I'm such a neurotic mess. This poor guy didn't sign up for my crazy when he asked me to dance.

"I'm sorry." I shake my head and offer him a small smile, the only thing I can manage when thoughts of Ben twine with what's happening in the present. The last time Ben and I danced like this was Dani and Savage's wedding. They even played our wedding song. It felt like we were young again, just married and completely blissfully unaware of what was to come.

Tears burn my eyes. I can practically feel his arms around me. Hear his whispered words in my ear. His warm breath across the sensitive skin of my neck.

I twist my ring around my finger and try to fight the water-works. With a quick swipe, I brush them away before they can fall.

Crying at a damn party, how embarrassing. I never should have come with Caroline tonight. What the hell was I thinking?

He holds up his hands and assesses me carefully. "No apology necessary. You don't owe me any explanations." He reaches out a hand again.

Do I take it?

Maybe it's best to end this tragic interlude now, before I do something even more stupid. But the hopeful look in his eyes and small smile tugging at his lips has me closing the distance between us, and when I place my hand in his, he pulls me back against him. I'm too shocked by his reaction, or should I say non-reaction, to my breakdown to really contemplate that I so easily fall into his strong embrace.

The warmth of his body permeates my dress and soothes my frayed nerves. Even his very obvious erection pressing against me doesn't faze me in the moment. I close my eyes and let myself get lost in the jazz music and the soft movement of our bodies together. We sway to the music until the final notes ring through the air, but when the notes of the next song start up, any semblance of control leaves as my heart shatters.

Fly Me To The Moon.

Of all the goddamn songs in all the world, they had to play this?

I've listened to it a million times and replayed the video of our wedding and reception more times than I can count, yet even now, the tinkling notes bring back memories of being in Ben's arms for our first dance. Of swaying with *him* to this song. Of all those things I will never have again. Of all the things I lost.

I suck in a deep breath and pull my hands out of Landon's. He observes me, and before he can say anything, I turn and run from the dance floor.

Anywhere but here.

three

"*L*andon, what do you think?"

The water of Lake Pontchartrain ripples in the morning light of a new Monday morning. Floor to ceiling windows make the space bright and inviting, and the solid wood floors gleam despite their weathered age. It's spectacular.

I turn back to Conrad, realtor extraordinaire, and spread out my arms. "What's not to like? The location is great, the views are spectacular, and you said they are willing to do a short-term lease, right?"

He nods and thumbs through the stack of papers on the kitchen island in front of him. "Absolutely. The owner is ultimately looking to sell, but he's willing to do as short as three-month leases as long as it's all paid up front."

Perfect.

The hotel I've been crashing in is nice, but there's a lot to be said for having a place that's *mine,* even if it's only temporary.

Who knows if I'm staying in New Orleans long. When I left to make the thousand-mile drive here, I fled like a thief in the night. I had no plans other than getting the fuck out of there and away from what my life had become.

Only one thing was clear in that moment. I couldn't stay there. I tried. For almost six weeks, I slogged through the crumbling remains of my life searching for a way to get back to some semblance of normal, but that city was too full of memories and people I couldn't bear to look in the eye anymore.

This city offers me what Chicago can't—a place free of obligations, histories, betrayals; a place where I can start over without fear of judgment or guilt.

Without things eating away at me every fucking hour of every damn day.

Staying in New Orleans permanently wasn't on the agenda, but Chris is the only one who understands what went down and can help me work through all this shit.

I never thought I'd be hitting *reset* on my life at barely thirty, but life can be a real bitch sometimes.

"I'm going to take it, Conrad."

A huge grin splits his face, and he claps his hands together. "Wonderful. I have all the paperwork here for you to sign. As soon as I receive the check, I can work on getting you the keys. Are you going to be moving your furniture and belongings soon?"

Not fucking likely.

The last thing I want is this place filled with things from my former life. Even a simple damn piece of furniture holds too many memories—bad and good. I don't want to see anything that will bring up reminders of what used to be. As far as I'm concerned, it's dead and buried. And as soon as Barry wraps everything up for me, there will be no reason to think about the windy city, or anyone there, ever again.

"No. I'm going to be replacing everything. Can you give me some information on stores for furniture and appliances? Maybe somewhere I can rent and if I decide to stay, then buy?"

"Of course. Anything you need, I'm here to help." His smarmy, used car salesman demeanor would normally annoy me, but today, I'm completing a major step in restarting my life, so I can overlook it.

I'm sure his bill will reflect all his "help" too. Not that I mind. Frankly, I'd rather pay someone to do all this for me than do it myself, but starting over means doing it all from scratch. The condo is just the first major step. There are so many other things to do, including finding a new assistant for the office. I will miss

Eileen's ability to know what I need and handle the day-to-day things so I can concentrate on what I do best—build. Finding another assistant like her will be difficult.

Assuming I get the job, that is.

Chris seems pretty confident he can convince the co-owner to invite me on-board, but on the off-chance I don't get hired, I will have to either scramble to find other work, or I will have to move on from New Orleans.

That's why this three-month lease is ideal. It gives me a little time to figure shit out in a place I can call my own. And if things don't work out, I'm not tied down to anything. I won't make that mistake again. Ever.

Attachments. Commitments. Feelings. All things that pull you under and drag you down to the murky bottom to drown you.

I turn back to the water. So blue and calm and shimmering right now, it can turn into a raging tempest in blink of an eye. I've seen it happen to Lake Michigan back home with the massive storms that blow through. I can only imagine what it must be like here when a hurricane hits. Not something I'm looking forward to, but I need to take the good with the bad.

This town is filled with opportunity. A new place. A new job. A new life. Even the possibility of a new woman to enjoy some extracurricular activities with...maybe.

Despite everything offered at the party, Storm managed to captivate me. Something happened to that woman, something tragic. That much was clear in the anguish in her eyes and the way she ran out of there on Saturday. She was searching for something, and if it's the same thing as me—sex without any commitments—then she's exactly what I need right now.

The fact she was even at the party suggests to me that she may be not be completely opposed to the idea. She said it wasn't her scene anymore. Yet, it was once, and that means the door may not be open, but a window may be cracked on the possibility.

Still, I don't know how I would track her down in a city this vast. I don't even know her last name. And is it really worth the effort when meaningless sex can be found at any bar on Bourbon Street?

Maybe not.

But the memory of her eyes...the way she felt in my arms...the way my body responded to her...that damn sweet scent of hers that I keep smelling...it hasn't left my mind.

Maybe the party organizer has contact information for everyone who attended?

Fuck.

It doesn't matter. Even if she did, I'm sure it's confidential, and she's not going to hand it out to anyone, especially someone she doesn't know, like me. But maybe I could find Storm through that friend of hers.

What was her name?

Crap.

I don't think Storm ever gave it to me. She works for a newspaper, though. Maybe I can find the article and track her down that way.

Does that make me some creepy stalker?

I would like to think no, but it is borderline. I won't harass her, though. I just want to make sure she's all right. She was so sad. The darkness in her eyes spoke of a deep heartache, something weighing on her that I wanted so badly to help with and make go away, even if only for one night. But she fled before she gave me a chance.

It's probably not my place anyway, but I guess I'll never learn.

I've always been a sucker for women who need help. It's not a knight-in-shining-armor complex. Far from it. It's more a desire to see people let go of the things that drag them down.

Just like I finally did for myself. It took me far too long to realize I wasn't living my own life that way. I stayed for weeks when I should have left right away, the moment it happened.

I won't make that mistake again. Live in the moment. The

here and now.

Let Storm go. You don't need the chase, as alluring as it may be. You don't need to solve that mystery. You don't need to be the one to save her from whatever is weighing her down.

I sigh and turn back toward the water. The new start begins today, with this condo.

The water calls to me, and with it being so close, it will be easy to stroll down there whenever I want to smell the clean, crisp, salty air and feel the spray from the waves crashing along the shore.

"I think I'm going to love it here, Conrad. I really do."

As long as I can shut the door on my old life.

Wham!

Something slams, and I jerk awake. Footsteps sound down the hallway, and I struggle to push myself up onto my elbow.

The overhead fixture flips on, and I squeeze my eyes shut against the offensive blinding light.

"What the hell?"

Who is in my room?

I shake clear the lingering scent of ocean and something crisp and clean that occupied my dream. So different than the other dreams that usually plague me. So...

"What the hell is right, Storm. Get the hell up and out of bed."

"Skye?"

I blink against the light until my eyes focus on her standing at the foot of the bed with her hand on her hip and a scowl on her lips. Even my sleep-fogged brain recognizes the look of annoyance and determination on her face. She's here on a mission.

Fuck.

"What the hell are you doing here?"

She waves her hand over me and then scans the room. Clothes sit in piles on the floor and draped over the furniture. The trashcan overflows with used tissues. "Helping you get your shit together."

I sigh and run my hands back through my tangled hair. "What are you talking about?"

With an exaggerated huff, Skye storms over to the side of the bed and pulls the covers off me. "Look at yourself. And take a sniff. When was the last time you even showered?"

I rack my fuzzy brain. "Saturday."

It was Saturday because it was before I went somewhere...

Ugh, the party.

I've tried so hard to forget it. To pretend it never happened. To act like it was someone else who went and acted like a total fool.

How could I have a meltdown like that in public and then run away?

I wouldn't have thought I could move that fast in stilettos and such a tight dress, but I managed to book it out of there with record speed.

Cheetah style.

To make it even worse, I almost knocked over a couple coming in the door as I rushed out, and I didn't even tell Caroline I was leaving. I just sent her a lame text message excuse from my cab as I made my getaway.

So damn embarrassing.

Landon, and anyone else who saw me, thinks I'm a total psycho. And I guess I am.

If one damn song can make me melt down, I'm definitely not in as good of a headspace as I managed to convince myself I was when I agreed to go out. It was too soon. I should have known. I should have stayed here and wallowed rather than subject other humans to my shitshow.

God, I'm such a fool.

I drop my face into my hands. The first notes of that damn song play in my head. Will I ever be able to hear that song without sobbing like a child?

Probably not.

Just like there are a million other things I can't do on a daily basis without thinking about Ben.

"Get up." Skye's demand rankles me. She's always been a bit abrasive and bossy, but to come into my house like this is above and beyond even her normal style. It screams of Savage or maybe Stone, but Savage is occupied with Dani and Kennedy these days, and Stone wouldn't dare after what he did.

"Why are you here?"

She sighs and crosses her arms over her chest. "Storm, you bailed on family dinner last night with no explanation, and now, it's nine o'clock on Monday morning and Angel isn't at school because you haven't gotten your ass out of bed."

Shit.

The clock on my nightstand confirms I've majorly fucked up. Again.

Mistake #3,245—thinking I had my shit together even for an instant.

I should've known someone would call me out on skipping dinner. No matter how bad things have gotten during the last couple months, I've always managed to drag myself out of bed and get myself and Angelina together enough to go to Mom's.

But Saturday night...it was just too much.

Being held, being touched by another man, and then hearing *our* song.

Why did it have to be that damn song?

It broke me. It took all the progress I made by even agreeing to go out to the party with Caroline in the first place and flushed it down the damn toilet. Instead of treading water and barely keeping my head afloat, I was suddenly drowning again.

All I could do when I got home was change and sit on the back porch with Mittens, sobbing. That damn cat has become almost like a therapist to me since Ben died. The thing refuses to live in the house even though we bought him as a housecat, but at least he comes to me and Angel if we go outside. For some reason, stroking his soft fur and snuggling with him seems to ease some of the loneliness most nights.

It wasn't enough to get me going yesterday though, or today, apparently.

"You can't do this anymore, Storm." Skye's eyes bore into mine, her anger and frustration mixing with concern. Then they soften and she sighs. "Stone is getting Angelina ready right now. I'm going to take her to school."

Shit. Stone's here?

She walks out of my room without a glance back at me. If she brought Stone with her, she must really mean business. Savage is demanding and has a king complex, but Stone...hell, Stone is something else altogether. Law school took his natural talent and honed him into a machine who can dominate any argument and win.

And, I am in no mood to show down with baby brother today...or any day, for that matter.

We've spent months walking on eggshells around each other ever since he returned from rehab. From where I sit, there's nothing more to say. He made his choices, and those choices impacted all of us in Earth-shattering ways.

They brought me to where I am today, sitting in my bed, having not showered in two days, in my pajamas when I should be at work, and with a daughter down the hall who has had to watch her mother disintegrate into nothing after already losing her father.

Shit. I'm a terrible mother.

I shouldn't be letting Angelina see me like this, living like this. Or should I say, not living.

Mom wasn't like this. At least, not that I remember.

She was strong. She raised the five of us completely on her own, and I don't think I saw her break down once or shed a single tear for Dad after the funeral. Maybe I'm romanticizing it or not remembering properly after all these years, but damn...

How the hell did she do it?

Therapy didn't help, and God knows, talking to the rest of the Hawkes only further muddies the waters. Everyone has an opinion about everything and thinks they know what's best for everyone else. It's a goddamn madhouse being in the same room with everyone. I can't listen to them placate me when they don't even know half of what's happened. When I can't tell the true depths of my loss.

And now, it's invaded my own home.

I slide out of bed and right the t-shirt I was sleeping in. Ben's shirt. One of the last ones that still smells like him. The thin, worn fabric glides between my fingers, and I tug it up to my nose to inhale his scent. Tears pool in my eyes, but I brush them away as Skye pushes Angel past my open bedroom door.

"Say good-bye to your mom, Angel."

"Bye, Mommy!" Her voice carries to me from down the hall before the front door opens and slams shut.

A second later, Stone appears in the doorway and leans casually against the jamb. He's softened some since he came back. That harsh "destroy you with one look" thing he had going has morphed into something a little less hostile, but the tension between us is palpable.

This is the first time he's set foot in this house or that I've been alone in a room with him in three months.

At least I'm on home turf. Whatever he's here to say is going to start a battle one or both of us may not walk away from unscathed.

four

*S*tone's eyes move up and down, assessing me in a way only a trained litigator, or a little brother, can. "You look like shit."

Asshole.

My first inclination is to lunge across the space between us and deck him. Even though I may have been young when Dad died, he did teach me to throw a punch. But when I take stock of the ratty old, dirty T-shirt and combine that with my unwashed state...

Fuck. He's right.

I do look like shit.

Boiled, rancid, old, smelly shit.

Shit that's been baking in the Louisiana sun for days.

Crap.

I heave out a sigh, and instead of bashing baby bro's face in, I return my gaze to his. "What do you want, Stone?"

He levels his cold blue scrutiny on me. "To help you."

Help me? He can't be serious.

I scoff and push past him into the hallway. Tension builds in my shoulders, and I clench my fists at my sides as his footsteps follow me out into the living room. He settles on one of the stools across the kitchen island while I reach for the coffee maker.

"I'm probably the last person you want to hear this from, Storm, but you can't keep going on like this. I know I can't understand what you're going through, but it's been six months, and you can't keep staying in bed and shutting out the world. You've barely been working, and Angelina has already missed way too much school. You need to get it together."

Rage boils in my veins, and it takes every ounce of strength I have not to slam the glass coffee pot against the marble counter. Or toss it at his head. "You have some fucking nerve coming here and saying that to me, Stone."

His blue eyes, the Hawke eyes we all share—for better or for worse—soften and something akin to regret shimmers there. It doesn't matter, though. No amount of regret can erase what he did, what his actions set in motion.

"I know you blame me—"

I shove the pot into the machine to remove the temptation from my hands. "I blame you because it's your damn fault Ben is dead!" And so are so many other things I can't even talk about.

My angry words echo against the lofted ceiling, and they sound harsh even to my own ears. But they *are* the truth. A truth I've been too nice or too afraid to say to Stone for all these months.

His stoic expression doesn't change. He just sits and watches me fume. It's so like Stone to keep a poker face. Whether he's questioning a witness or being hammered by his big sister, it doesn't even faze him.

"Say whatever you need to say, Storm. Do whatever you need to do to let go of everything you've been bottling up. It's not healthy."

Arrogant mother fucking prick.

"Fuck you, Stone! You, of all people, shouldn't be lecturing anyone about what's *healthy!* You're a coke addict who worked for a damn mob boss. You killed your girlfriend and sister-in-law's father and then got my husband killed. You are in no position to be giving any advice."

Not in any fucking world.

That gets a reaction. He recoils slightly, and his eyes narrow.

Maybe it *was* over the line, but every word of it was the stone-cold truth, and finally saying it feels so fucking good.

He sucks in a deep breath and spreads his palms across the counter. "I know you blame me for what happened, but there's no way I could have known what Dom would do, how insane he was. I had no idea all that shit went down with Dani and Savage and Gabe. If I had, you have to believe, I never would have come back to work for him. Never."

I want to believe him. I really do. The burning and tightening in my chest begs me to walk around the counter and embrace him. For better or worse, he's my baby brother, and he's hurting too. That much is readily apparent, but I can't just forget. I can't pretend his actions didn't have disastrous ramifications for all of us.

Especially me.

Hot tears trickle down my cheeks despite my best efforts to hold them in. I don't want to hurt Stone. I don't want to hurt anyone. But those words have been festering inside me for months, just waiting to explode out. It's like one giant weight has been lifted off my shoulders while another has settled on my heart.

I flatten my palms on the counter and drop my head down. Looking at him right now only makes this harder, so I won't. "I believe you never intended for anything bad to happen to anyone in the family. But I can't just overlook the fact that you *knew* what Dom was and what he did when you went to work for him. You knew he was hurting *other* people, and you still did it."

Silence lingers, and I force myself to raise my head to regard him again.

A single tear falls down his cheek.

Fuck. I've never seen Stone cry.

Not even when he was revealing the entire sordid history with Dom.

It twists the knife in my chest even harder.

"I'm sorry, Storm. For everything. There's nothing I can do to change what choices I made, what I did. But I *can* do something about what's happening now. And at this moment, *you* need to see what you're doing. To yourself. To Angelina. This isn't healthy. Are you even going to have a business anymore? You're never at work. It seems like the only time you leave the house is when you manage to get Angel to school or drag yourself over to Mom's. When was the last time you did something fun? Something for yourself?"

Images flash through my head. The party. Sex. Music. Landon's arms around me.

I felt free for a few brief moments. I felt alive.

But it came crashing down so fast, it left me spinning.

Maybe Stone is right. Maybe I need to be doing more for myself, more for Angelina. It's not like I didn't know this deep down. Hell, even that damn therapist I saw for a few months told me the same thing, but I never realized how true it was until this moment.

Tough love works, apparently.

Even if it does rip your heart out.

I shake my head and dash away the tears falling in earnest now. "I don't know what to do anymore, Stone."

"None of us do. Do you think I had any fucking idea what I was doing when I left rehab and came back here? I left here without a word, with Nora hating my guts and not even wanting me to touch her. I never in a million years could have anticipated coming back to find her pregnant. It was like my entire world changed in an instant. All the plans I had...the things I wanted... none of it mattered anymore." He sighs and runs a shaking hand back through his dark hair. "The only thing that mattered was her and the baby. This is going to hurt to hear, but you need to think about Angelina, not just your own pain right now. Do what's best for her, but also, make sure you are taking care of yourself."

Damn.

Who would have known the drug-abusing, mob lawyer of the Hawke family would be the one with all the words of wisdom?

A sardonic laugh slips from my lips. "It's not that easy."

He shakes his head, and a humorless smile tips the corner of his lips. "Nothing in life is easy, Storm. I've learned that the hard way."

I have to give Stone credit. His words sting, but there's a lot of truth in them.

"You're sure you want to do this?"

Chris analyzes me from across his desk, his fingers steepled in front of his mouth. It's the same look he's given me our entire lives whenever he thinks I'm making a big mistake. Big brother prerogative, I suppose, but it still makes me grit my teeth.

He's judging. Whether he knows it or not, he is. And he has no damn right to.

If he had been in my position, he would have done the same thing. Anyone would have. Anyone sane, that is.

So, he can cut the attitude. I wouldn't have come to New Orleans if I thought he would give me shit. But now that I'm here, the prospect of working with him again, in this business Dad taught both of us, has a certain appeal.

Success without the old man. Success in *spite* of him.

"I can't go back there. And I'm here. So, why not try to see if we can make this work?"

He sighs and drops his hands. The age is starting to show on his face—lines around his eyes and mouth and a tiredness to his eyes I never noticed before. "And you're sure you don't want to reconsider? Have you talked to Dad?"

Fucker.

It would be wrong to hit Chris, but my fist clenches all the same at the mention of the man who sired us. "No. And I don't plan on ever talking to him again. Drop it."

He has some real fucking nerve to even suggest it. It's like he's completely forgotten what and who drove me here in the first place.

His hands fly up in surrender, and he shakes his head. "Okay, okay, forget I asked. If you're one hundred percent sure you want to stay here and work with me, then I'll talk to my partner. She doesn't really get involved with the day-to-day operations of the business, but I don't want to bring you on, in such a major role, without her approval."

Fair enough.

I don't know much of anything about this woman, other than she was Ben's wife, and she inherited his shares of the company when he died in the fire. But Chris really seems to respect her and wants her to have a say in me coming on-board. If it means waiting a few extra days to start, it's no skin off my back.

There are other things I can do to occupy my time, like get my condo furnished and arrange to have the very few things I did leave that I still want sent to me.

Very few.

"Call her. Tell her what's going on. If things don't work out here, I'll be on my way."

He frowns. "To where?"

Good question.

I shrug and look to the right out the window at the trees blowing in the afternoon breeze. The tropical climate is certainly something I can get used to. Going back north to the cold and snow and sleet this coming winter just doesn't have any appeal, even if it isn't Chicago. The world is wide open, though, when you have no commitments. "No clue."

He scoffs. "Doesn't that bother you? Not having a plan? Not knowing where you are going?"

It would have, a few months ago. Not anymore. If I've learned anything, it's that plans mean nothing. Intentions mean nothing. You can do everything right and still have it blow up in your face and rip you apart.

So, the answer to his question is a huge, resounding...

"Nope."

I may end up in California, or Vegas, or maybe the Southeast Coast somewhere like Florida. It doesn't matter. Not anymore. I have the skills to start over anywhere. Getting licensed in another state won't be an issue with my background and work history. And there are willing women everywhere. Maybe not one like Storm, but she's a lost cause at this point anyway. As much as I would love to roll around the sheets with that woman, there's no way I'm going to find her. Not in a city this size. And not without coming across as a creep. There's something to be said for the thrill of the chase, but I have to find her before I chase her. And that feels like an awful lot of work right now just to solve the mystery and appease my cock.

If I have to leave, I'll make do wherever I land.

Being close to Chris would be great. He's the only family I have left as far as I'm concerned. But it does have its drawbacks... like the fact that he still talks to Dad. Maybe the distance and time has made Chris forget what a shit father Dad is. Maybe the fact that *it* didn't happen to *him* makes him unable to truly grasp the gravity of the situation. Maybe he just loves the old man despite all his horrible bullshit.

That man could fall into Lake Michigan and drown, and I wouldn't throw him a life vest, let alone jump in after him.

Maybe if Chris were in my shoes, if he'd been betrayed the

same way, he would get it. As it stands, I'm just going to have to keep reminding him when he brings up Dear Ol' Dad.

"Son...this isn't what it looks like. It has nothing to do with you."

Those words. The look on his face...complete calm, like he wasn't doing anything wrong. Oh, no! The illustrious Alistair McCabe could never do something like that to his own blood...

Deceitful motherfucker.

I shove myself up to my feet to pace. Moving is the only thing that's going to keep me from exerting all this pent-up anger and energy into something bad. The sound of my fist hitting his flesh echoes through my head, and I press my palms over my ears.

No. Not now.

I can't keep reliving that day over and over in my head, or in my heart. It's not healthy. It's in my past, and I need to leave it there. That's why I left. Why I had to.

Start over.

Leave it behind.

"Landon? Earth to Landon?"

"Huh?" I whirl back to face Chris.

Concern lines his face, and his eyes narrow on me. "Are you okay?"

My hands drop to my sides, and I heave out a sigh. I've been asked that question so many times over the last couple months, it's become meaningless. Just something people say to be polite, not because they really care how you feel or how you're processing things. No one wants to hear the truth. No one wants to hear the gory details of a demolished life. "Yeah, just fucking peachy."

"Tell me what you need."

Like it's that fucking simple.

A way to turn back time? A way to erase all the things and people I obviously misjudged in my life from my history? A way to make the sting of betrayal go away?

But that's not what he means.

"Have your secretary set me up with an office and get all the supplies I'll need ordered. I brought a box of my important paperwork shit, but I'm not going to bother with much of anything else from my office there." Maybe a few awards I earned, my diplomas hanging on the walls, but everything else, anything tied to Dad or my work with him, that can go into one of our industrial-sized dumpsters for all I care. "And give me a list of current projects you want me to take over and where each one stands. As soon as we get the okay from Mrs. Matthews, I'll dive in head-first."

Chris rises and strolls around his desk to stand in front of me. The same eyes I stare at every morning in the mirror assess me. "I really am glad you're here, Landon. I need the help. But for what it's worth, I don't think leaving Chicago was the answer, especially the way you did it. You're going to have to address what happened at some point."

Not if I can help it.

Yes, there are...loose ends that need to be tied up. Things that couldn't be taken care of overnight, but that's why I have a high-priced lawyer. If Barry can't sort things out for me, then no one can.

I shake my head and flash him a tight smile. "You know as well as I do that we're never going to agree on this. So instead, let's agree to never discuss it again."

His brow furrows, and he frowns and crosses his arms over his chest. "You're putting me in a very awkward position."

"No, Dad put you there." I step forward and place my hand on his shoulder for a moment before I head for the door. "Now, come show me where my office will be, assuming I can win over Mrs. Matthews."

It shouldn't be too hard. My work experience speaks for itself, and despite my recent history, I've never had a problem charming a woman when I have a goal in mind.

five

*P*iles of half-finished design plans cover my desk, making it almost impossible to see the beautiful wood grain of the massive piece of furniture Ben designed and built for me.

Fuck.

I've really made a mess of everything.

Mistake #5,535—thinking I could keep this business going when I was barely getting out of bed since Ben died.

I can't seem to concentrate on anything. The plans all blur together. I'm lucky to have any left to even work on.

Skye and Stone were right. I've pretty much killed my business. The clients were understanding at first. Of course, they were. I lost my husband in a terrible, brutal way. But after the two-month mark, the calls started coming in...

"We're sorry, Storm. We just need to move forward on the project..."

"It's nothing personal. Let us know when you're back at work..."

"Maybe we can use you for the next project..."

The only customers left are Savage and Gabe and a handful of long-standing, loyal clients who weren't in any time crunch. I've managed to come in a few times to get essential things complete, but barely. The Hawkes will never desert me, but the others...

Who the fuck knows?

All I do know is, I'm so far behind on work, I may never catch up. And I can't blame the clients who bailed on me, or the ones who have stayed but have one foot out the door. I left them hanging when they needed me. I failed and have no idea how to get back on track.

Mistake #6,458—thinking I can ever have a normal life again.

How am I supposed to just go back to my days as if he's not dead, as if my entire life didn't go up in flames with that building? How am I supposed to pretend Angel's life hasn't been destroyed? She's going to grow up without a father, just like I had to, and I'm going to spend the rest of my life alone, pining away for a man who is six feet under, just like Mom has for the last two decades.

I've spent years hoping she'll find someone to fill that void in her life, someone who can make her as happy as I remember her being with Dad. But that hasn't happened. The only other man she's ever had in her life was Dom, and that turned out to be catastrophic for all the Hawkes on an infinite level.

I can't end up like that. I can't let Angel see me suffer and live as an empty shell for the rest of my life. Mom hid it well, but there was a loneliness in her eyes she couldn't cover up all the time. A longing.

But maybe moving on is impossible. Just dancing with another man this weekend was enough to send me running. There's no way I'll ever be able to be in another relationship. I can hardly work without the crushing weight of misery dragging me under. It's like I'm drowning in a black abyss, and no matter how hard I kick and push toward the surface, I only end up choking down more water and diving even deeper toward nothing.

It's pathetic, really.

I'm a grown-ass woman who can't get her life on track.

If Ben were here, I'm sure he would tell me to get my shit together and move on, get back to life, but I can't do that. I can't just pretend like nothing happened. I can't pretend there's not a gaping hole in my chest that burns with every breath I take.

It's a good thing I will never see Landon again. I need to forget him and forget that night ever happened. It's time to concentrate and get some work done, otherwise Angel and I will end up begging on the street corner.

Or on the pole at the Hawkeye Club.

The thought of me up on that stage has a laugh bubbling up and out into my office, and I shake my head at the absurdity of it.

Neither me nor Angel will ever end up there.

But the pile on my desk rivals Mount Everest, and sorting through it, I'm terrified it may tumble onto me and suffocate me. My hand lands on a design I was working on but kept putting off finishing. My heart just wasn't in it, and when that happens, it shows in my work. I can't give a client subpar work. That's as bad as not finishing at all.

This job requires creativity. A clear mind that allows ideas to flow. And mine hasn't been clear for so damn long, I've almost forgotten what that feels like.

The long, straight lines and arched dormers on the page would normally comfort me. There's something about the exactness of architecture that's always appealed to me on a very base level. Things are definite and set. They have to be a certain way or buildings aren't structurally sound. You know what to expect, and you know what you're going to get when you design it. There is no chance. There is no room for error. It's perfection and stable. No surprises.

If only life were like that.

The best laid plans...

I dig into my work, trying not to think about Ben, and with determination to get the revisions to the client today, but I don't work very long before my phone buzzes.

"Yes?"

"Sorry, ma'am. I have Mr. McCabe on line one for you."

I sigh and shove my hands back through my hair, yanking out the hair tie I used earlier to try to tame the wild mess. "Okay, thank you."

Dealing with Chris wasn't on the top of my to-do list today, but I'm still half-owner—actually fifty-one percent owner—of the company he had with Ben. For a while, he gave me some space, but his need to run things by me hasn't dissipated even though I told him that essentially the company is his to do with as he sees fit.

I don't have the time, energy, or emotional wherewithal to be invested in the construction company that Ben spent so much time building. It was his baby. It was his dream. And with him gone, I can't bear to even think about assisting with anything having to do with it.

Please make this quick.

"Hey, Chris. What's up?"

"Hi, Storm. Sorry to bother you, but I'm wondering if you can come in tonight or tomorrow for a quick meeting."

What could he possibly need from me that we can't do over the phone?

Usually, we're able to take care of anything that needs to be decided with a simple call. "Can't you just tell me what this is about right now?"

"Well," he sighs, "I've been so goddamn busy lately, I barely have time to think. So, I'm thinking of bringing someone in to help with the business, to manage more of the day-to-day operations and split up some of the projects so I'm not having to handle everything myself."

My chest tightens slightly at the thought of someone else having their hands in Ben's business, but I quickly push that feeling away. Ben's gone and he's not coming back. Chris is doing his best, but I can't expect him to run everything on his own. Ben was always so hands-on and spent a lot of time at all the different locations, whereas Chris spent most of his time in the office. Now that Ben's gone, I can see how he would be overwhelmed with all the work he has to do.

Their project managers take care of a lot, but it's not the same as being there to check it out yourself. Or having someone you can trust do it.

"Who are you thinking about hiring?"

"My younger brother. He's been in town for a couple weeks kind of taking a little vacation. I asked him to meet with us about joining the team instead of returning to Chicago. He's worked with our dad in the family construction business for years and really knows his shit. I think he'll be a good addition to the company, but I don't want to do anything without running it by you first. So, I would really like you to come meet him. We can sit down and have a talk."

The fact that it's Chris' brother eases some of my apprehensions. The McCabes have a long history in the construction business in the Midwest, and if Chris says his brother knows his shit, I believe him.

But meeting with him is something else altogether.

I don't have the time or energy.

"Look, Chris, I'm just swamped right now, and I like to be home when Angel gets back from school, so meeting is really going to be difficult in the next couple days."

There's a momentary silence on the line, and I can almost picture him twirling his pen anxiously like he always does while he waits for me to give in or considers what he's going to say next.

He clears his throat. "I get that. I do, but you're the primary owner of the company, and while I appreciate that you trust me to make this decision, I would feel a lot more comfortable if you would come meet with us. This is still Ben's company. This is still Matthews Construction. His name is still on it. It's your company as much, if not more, than mine."

Well, what can I really say to that?

It *is* Ben's company. And now, it's mine, whether I want to be involved or not. "Okay, I'll swing by tomorrow night around five. I'll just have to make sure that somebody can pick up Angel."

"Sounds good. Thanks, Storm."

I hang up and stare at the phone for a minute. A shiver slides down my spine, and my stomach twists. I don't understand the unease. There should be no problem with his brother coming into the company. In fact, it's probably going to be great for business.

So, why does dread sit like a damn rock in the pit of my stomach?

I cut through the cool water like a ship through the ocean waves. My legs and arms burn already, but I keep pushing myself to go harder, faster, longer. I need this after the weekend and my meeting with Chris yesterday.

The truth of the matter is, maybe everything that's happened has rattled me more than I'd like to admit.

What went down back home...

Fleeing in the middle of night...

Starting over here...

...and then that night with Storm.

I shouldn't even still be thinking about her. It was one night. One dance. And she made it clear how she felt when she turned tail and ran from me. She wasn't there for the same reason I was. For the same reason pretty much everyone was. She wasn't there for sex.

But she was there for something. Searching for something. Maybe a way out of whatever darkness surrounded her?

Maybe she couldn't admit it to herself, but sex can do that, even if only temporarily. Maybe she subconsciously wanted to be there, wanted what that party offered. Maybe she couldn't deal with the depths of her own feelings about it.

Or maybe I'm just overanalyzing something I don't have a fucking clue about.

That's more likely.

She's not my problem. She's not my anything. Plus, she's married, and even if they have an open relationship, is that really the kind of thing I want to get involved with when all I am looking for is someone who would be nothing more than a fuck buddy?

No. Not worth it.

Yet, the mystery that surrounds her occupies my mind more than it should. Her sadness. Her odd reactions and behavior.

Something deep inside me needs to know the answer. Needs to help. Even though I keep telling myself it's not any of my damn business.

Why can't I just let it go? Let her go?

Maybe because she's nothing like any woman I can remember ever meeting. Maybe it's the thrill of the unknown or the thrill of the chase. Maybe it's the chivalry Mom taught me creeping up again, demanding I help someone whenever I can.

Whatever it is, I need a way to get over it before I drive myself mad. Even though I recognized something in her, a sadness I am all too familiar with, it's not my place to intrude on her life.

There's no way to find her. I don't even know her last name. And it shouldn't bother me so much. Yet, here I am, at the pool, trying to work out some of my frustration over her and everything else I'm trying so damn hard to leave in my past with a thousand laps.

And as if I don't have enough on my mind, today could make or break me in more ways than one way.

Between the meeting with Mrs. Matthews and the call I'm expecting, my life could be changing in huge ways. That has my heart racing as much as the physical exertion of my much-needed time in the water. Ever since I first dipped my toes into the pool as a child, it's been my safe place. My haven from the world. Through high school and college, swimming on the school teams not only gave me a chance to feed my competitive nature, but it also gave me an outlet for all the pent-up stress and energy I collected.

When I can't get in the water regularly, I can feel the tension building in my body.

I needed this so damn bad.

The anticipation of my call with Barry, and the meeting about the job, had me so wound up, I thought I would break. But the stress isn't going to dissipate until everything's firmly resolved both at home and here. It's hard to move on when strings keep you tied to the place and people you want to forget. They keep pulling me back when all I want to do is break away completely. Today might be that day. The final nail in the coffin on my old life. At least, I hope it is.

Then I can concentrate fully on what's happening here. The projects Chris showed me last night got the juices flowing again and my hands itching to get back to work. I belong on a site. Building is in my blood, and two weeks of just sitting around here have left a restlessness in me that needs an outlet.

So, today is beyond important.

I reach the end of the pool and turn for my final lap, pushing off the wall and straining with my last big kick. It's damn good to be back in the water, but my burning muscles don't have much more left to give, and I need to get out and go get ready for the day. A day that could mean the difference in where my life goes from here.

God, let everything work out.

My fingertips touch the end of the pool, and I pull my head out of the water and suck in several deep breaths before I tug off my goggles and shake the moisture out of my hair.

When I drag myself up out of the pool, an appreciative hum

sounds to my left. I turn my head to find a young woman watching me greedily from the side of the pool where she's about to climb in. She ogles me openly, licking her lips and grinning from ear to ear.

Obvious much?

I return her smile while I make my way to my towel. Any other time, I might've gone over there and tried to strike up a conversation with somebody who's so blatantly interested in me, but right now, the only thing that's on my mind is what an important day I have. And no woman has held my interest since the moment I saw Storm.

Christ, move on already, Landon.

The woman's gaze follows me as I grab my towel and begin to dry off. Even at thirty, the fact that women still check me out and find me attractive makes my chest swell with pride more than it probably should. I keep myself in good shape, and the appreciation of the woman is making my stressful day better.

A shiver hits me in the chilly air, and I finish drying and make my way to the locker room to shower and change. The day ahead of me is both daunting and exhilarating. So many things may change in the next twelve hours. Some, I've been praying for. Others, like the opportunity to settle here, have come as a huge surprise and will turn my life upside down overnight. I never expected Chris to offer me a job. I meant New Orleans to be temporary, but in the end, all of it will be worth it—the challenges, the sacrifices.

It's a completely new life I never imagined I'd be living at thirty.

A house. A wife. A white picket fence. Two point five kids. A dog. That's what I always saw having at this age.

I chuckle darkly to myself as I reach my locker.

You were a naïve asshole.

That perfect life doesn't exist for anyone, especially me. And it never will.

Sex. Release. Carefree living. That's my future. One that doesn't give me any stress. One that can't hurt me.

Yet, those stormy blue eyes flash before me again.

Jesus.

I'm losing it if I can't get a woman I don't even know out of my mind and am ignoring a very real flesh and blood woman out by the pool who is clearly interested. The way my cock was straining against my pants Saturday night was a stark reminder of how long it's been since I had sex.

That party back home was weeks ago. After my life imploded, the city that has been my home for my entire life had started to feel foreign, more like a prison, and no amount of trying to fuck away the pain changed that in the weeks I stayed, living in limbo. That's precisely why I needed to leave. A fresh start.

I never expected I'd meet someone like Storm. Or what a number she would do on me in such a short time.

six

The elevator dings, and I step out on the second floor of Matthews Construction. Polished wood floors gleam in the overhead lights, and the high ceilings and nature landscapes lining the walls welcome me.

I used to love this building. I should. It's one of my babies.

So beautiful and strong. Regal.

It doesn't have the appearance of a typical office building. Ben didn't want that. He wanted unique. A place that not only showed off his skills as a contractor, but also mine as an architect.

But now, I can't stand to set foot in here. My throat tightens and breaths come harder. Everywhere I look, I see him. I see us.

It's one more reminder of everything I lost, and being here puts me on edge. I swipe my sweaty palms along my skirt and swallow back the bile threatening to rise in my throat just by being in the hallway.

Hold it together, Storm. Get in. Get out. Never come back.

Climbing back in my car and driving home to Angel as fast as I can sounds like the ideal plan, but I told Chris I would come even though I knew it meant entering here for only the second time since Ben died.

I didn't have the heart to clean out his office myself, and I asked Chris to do it. But I know he hasn't touched anything other than to go in and grab a few things for me. The only time I've been in the building at all was to pick up the box Chris put together for me of a few family photos and some paperwork I needed.

Now the door at the end of the hallway beckons me, but I can't go in. Ben's office is just too...personal. I can't bear to be in there without him, to be enveloped by his scent, by everything that's his. I wouldn't be able to keep it together, and I need to make it through this meeting so I can get home to Angel. I already feel bad enough leaving her with Dani while I'm here. There's no need to drag anything out.

Get in. Get out.

The door to Chris' office stands ajar, and I make my way to it, using every single ounce of my willpower to stop myself from again staring at the door at the end of the hall where I spent so much time with Ben.

I knock and push the door open all the way. "Hey, are you ready for me?"

Chris spins around from his computer and offers me a huge smile. "Storm! Yes. Thank you so much for coming."

He rises, and I take in his khaki pants and button-down shirt. He always did dress just as casually as Ben even though he spent most of his time dealing with clients in the office and not out at sites. One of the perks of being self-employed.

When Ben told me he wanted to offer Chris part ownership in the business, I was leery at first. He worked for Ben from day one, and he was reliable and a crazy hard worker. But this was *Ben's* baby. Sharing it with anyone else felt so wrong. Now, I can't imagine Chris *not* being a part of it. He's been a godsend since Ben died.

"Where's your brother?"

I want to get things rolling here.

Chris envelops me in a tight hug and then motions toward one of the empty chairs in front of his desk. "He just stepped down the hall to take a phone call. He should be back in a minute or two."

Too long.

He gives me a soft smile that says more than words ever could.

The pity and the concern are there. After this much time, it's so easy to spot them. "So, how have you been?"

That's a loaded question, and he knows it.

Nothing has been easy the last six months. Even breathing feels like a chore some days. But people don't want to hear that. People want you to smile and tell them things are fine and that you are doing well. They want to hear that you are picking up the pieces of your life and trying to move on from the tragedy.

Mistake #7,435—not doing that.

It's not that I'm not trying. I am. I really, really am. It's just not that easy. And I know Chris knows that. He's been Ben's best friend since college. The three of us spent four years together, drinking, studying, working.

Chris has suffered a loss, too. So, the question, coming from him, means a hell of a lot more than it does coming from just about anyone else. He wants the real answer, and talking about what's going on is almost as hard as living each day without my husband.

"It's been..."

His amber eyes watch me expectantly.

"...hard. If I'm being honest."

He frowns slightly and nods. "I understand completely. How is Angel handling things?"

The last time Chris and I talked, it was almost two months ago, and Angel still wasn't sleeping at night. She kept asking for her daddy and wanting him to tuck her in.

How do you get a five-year-old to understand her daddy is never coming back?

It's been a constant struggle to keep her on track every day and moving forward while also distracting her from my grief.

She doesn't need to see her mother breaking down on an endless loop. And I haven't hidden everything. It was impossible.

I do my best to keep things positive for her. She spends time with Mom and Dani and Kennedy—people who are always so upbeat and happy. She needs happy, and the Hawke family has rallied around us like I knew they would. Anything we need, someone is there with it almost before I ask. The only problem is, that doesn't bring her daddy back.

"She's doing a little better. She doesn't ask for him as much anymore, and the sleepless nights are to a minimum. But she doesn't have that sparkle in her eye like she used to. She misses him."

I miss him.

Chris nods solemnly and clasps his hands on top of his desk. "You know you can call me at any time if you need anything, don't you? If you want me to take her out or something. I know you have your brothers and Gabe to help, but if you need anything..."

I appreciate his gesture. I do. Having a male role model and father figure in Angel's life is important to me, and I've been going out of my way to make sure she spends time with Savage and Gabe.

Things with Stone are still a bit...tense. I love him, and I regret the harsh words I used the other day, but his actions can't be so easily forgotten. Deep down, the logical part of me knows he didn't cause the fire. Dom would have done it to send a message to the Hawkes even if Stone hadn't been working for him. But knowing Stone kept such a huge secret from us, and that he chose to work for Dom through all the bullshit that was happening, has left a sour taste in my mouth and a crack in my heart.

How can I trust him after everything he did?

I can't. Not yet. So, Angel hasn't been seeing much of Uncle Stone, even though I'm sure he's more than willing to step up and help.

None of it replaces Ben, though. No one could.

"I appreciate that offer, Chris. Really."

Footsteps echo down the hallway, and Chris looks up to the open door. "Oh good, you're here."

"Yes, sorry to keep you waiting."

That voice.

Goose bumps pebble across my skin, and my face heats. The familiar scent of something crisp and fresh, like clean linens and the ocean hits my nose along with a tidal wave of memories.

Warm, strong arms around me.

Laughter.

A moment of joy.

A few seconds when the world...and all the painful parts of it...melted away.

It can't be.

I shift in my chair until I'm facing the door, and all hope I'm mistaken flies out the window when my eyes land on the one man I hoped I'd never see again.

Bourbon eyes that have haunted my dreams stare back at me, and my lungs seize in my chest.

"Landon, this is Storm Matthews. Storm, this is my brother, Landon. You two haven't met before, have you?"

His eyes flick between me and Storm, probably trying to figure out the bewildered look that must be on my face. The same one Storm sports.

You have got to be kidding me.

Of all the ways I had imagined trying to track down Storm, I never, in a million years, thought she would end up being Chris' business partner. Over the years, he always referred to her as "Ben's wife" if he was talking about them, plus, I really didn't pay much attention. But I would have remembered a name like Storm. And if I had known her name, I'm sure things would have clicked into place the other night.

As it is, I'm standing with my mouth agape, like a total moron, while Chris stares at me, and Storm tries to avoid making eye contact. She twists her hands together on her lap and shifts in her seat.

I shake my head at Chris and do my best to school my features. I need to let Storm lead here, and there's no way she will want Chris to know she was at that party. That goes without saying the way her body language is screaming *please no.*

"Uh, no. We haven't met."

Talk about fucking awkward.

Although, I've been through far, far worse not so long ago. It's one of the reasons I had to get out of that city I loved so much. People knew. Everyone knew. And the looks of pity I got were just too damn much. I didn't want their pity. I wanted to be left the fuck alone to try to rebuild my life on my own terms.

Was that too much to ask?

I can only imagine it's the same here for Storm. I won't put her in an even worse situation by revealing what we shared.

I step forward and offer her my hand. She turns her head my direction without meeting my eyes and places her palm against mine. Images of our hands entwined on the dance floor flash through my mind as a jolt of electricity zings up my arm at the contact.

There it is again.

That charge. That energy vibrating between us that promises to combust if we were ever together. The thing that's kept her at the forefront of my mind despite my best efforts to bury the memory.

My eyes drift to her left hand still resting on her lap.

Oh God. The ring. I'm such an asshole!

No wonder she freaked out and ran. I grilled her about her

husband and home life. Of course, she wanted to get away from me and that conversation.

Although, that was *after* the whole husband line of questioning. Something else set her off and made her flee. Something that put a dark cloud over her blue eyes again after I had managed to remove it for a moment. I wish I knew what that was so I could make sure it never happens again.

The strange tingling in my arm finally alerts me I've been holding her hand inappropriately long, that and her surreptitiously trying to tug hers away.

Dammit.

I release her hand and plaster what I hope is a nonchalant smile on my face as I take the seat next to her facing Chris' desk.

My knee bounces rapidly, and I cross my ankle over it to try to contain the movement. The last thing I need is for either Chris or Storm to catch on to how damn nervous I am. It was bad enough knowing this meeting will decide whether I relocate to New Orleans permanently or shove off to parts unknown to restart my life. Now throw Storm into the mix, and I'm a fucking wreck.

Keep your shit together and forget about having her in your arms.

Easier said than done.

All I can think about is how soft and warm she was cradled against me as we swayed to the music. How perfectly her body molded to mine. How her honeysuckle scent invaded my nostrils and lingered there for days after.

My cock stirs with the memories, and I shift back in my chair to ensure my wholly inappropriate response isn't obvious.

Down boy.

Chris breaks the uncomfortable silence lingering in the room by clearing his throat. "Well, let's get started, shall we?"

Storm seems to snap to attention, and she offers him a tight smile but doesn't even peek my way. "Yes. So, you want to bring Landon in?"

Christ.

My name on her lips isn't doing anything for this damn semi I have. I haven't felt this out of control with my libido since I was in high school.

Dial it back, Landon.

I take a deep, cleansing breath and turn to Storm. "Yes. Ideally, I would come on to help manage all the projects so Chris can focus on the business end of things here."

Her blue eyes flick over to me before she settles them back on Chris. "And you feel like you need him in order to keep things running smoothly?"

Straight to the point. No nonsense.

Fuck, that's hot.

Chris nods and points to me. "He's an amazing contractor. He oversees all our dad's projects in Chicago, and I know he would do an amazing job here, too."

"What about your dad? Doesn't he need Landon there?"

Why does it feel like they're talking about me and have forgotten I'm in the damn room?

Probably because Storm is doing everything in her power to ignore me.

"My father is just fine on his own." My words come out a bit harsher than I intend, but it's impossible for me to talk about him without wanting to tear something apart or rip his throat out.

I just hope Storm gets what I can do here and doesn't let what happened between us affect her decision.

She finally permits her gaze to drift over to me, probably due to my outburst, and she frowns. My stomach tightens.

A light sigh slips from her lips, and she regards Chris again. "There isn't anyone else currently employed here who can take over these responsibilities?"

Ouch.

She doesn't even have the decency to look embarrassed by her question.

How could she want me gone that badly? Was the other night really so terrible?

I embarrassed her with my questions—ones I *never* would have asked had I known who she was—but I thought we were having a nice time dancing together before she ran out like her dress was on fire.

Shit. Bad term to use.

Honestly though, I'm just confused about what's happening here. Is she really trying to get rid of me? Or is she just being cautious about her late husband's business, as she should be?

Am I reading too much into this?

My fate literally sits in her hands, and the woman can't even make eye contact with me.

Shit.

That damn honeysuckle scent lingers in the air with her question. I inhale deeply, taking it in and savoring what is unquestionably the sexiest thing I've ever smelled. Everything about Storm is sexy, even when she's sabotaging my career path. I can't find it in my heart to be angry with her. She's embarrassed about the other night and thinks having me thousands of miles away is the way to ensure she won't have to address what I think is a very real connection we shared. She knows as well as I do that if we ever came together, the sex would be off the charts.

Well, I'm not about to let her torpedo this meeting.

Chris saves me from having to step in and defend myself. "No one who can do what Landon can. Are you uncomfortable with this?"

Storm takes longer than she should to consider his question, and I can practically see the cogs turning in her head. Her bottom lip disappears under her teeth, and she fidgets with her ring, spinning it around and around her finger.

Please...

Finally, she releases a sigh and shakes her head. "No, I'm

just...I want to make sure we are doing what's best for the company."

And you.

I bite back the words. Storm is in self-preservation mode. And I guess I can't blame her, considering everything. Having your life destroyed, no matter the means, leaves an indelible mark on you. She will never embrace me with open arms after what she's been through.

I just wish my life and career didn't hinge on a woman who apparently now hates my guts.

seven

What the hell was I thinking?

Two days later, I still I can't believe I said yes to Landon McCabe joining Matthews Construction.

It's like inviting a thief into your house to ransack your things. The man is nothing but trouble for me, and I knew it the moment I stepped into his strong arms on that dance floor. It was confirmed when I placed my hand in his during the meeting and a jolt of *something* shot up my arm and straight down to my core.

I don't react to men like that. I don't react to men, period.

I can't...

But I found myself blushing and unable to meet his eyes the entire meeting, like some shy schoolgirl sitting next to her crush instead of a widow who was there to do business.

Grow up, Storm.

Now, he's going to be around. A lot. The only saving grace in the situation is that I am almost never at the Matthews Construction office. The only time I may have to see him is on projects I design and they build...like the new club building. But that's almost complete, so if God is on my side here, I won't have to come face to face with Landon anytime soon.

"Hey, Storm, are you with us?"

Caroline's voice breaks through my thoughts. I've been staring at the open fridge for far too long.

The group scattered around my kitchen has undoubtedly noticed my bizarre behavior. I shift away from the fridge and let the door close so I can face the women who have been my rocks.

Skye stirs a pot of sauce on the stove while Dani slathers

garlic butter on the loaf of bread in front of her on the counter. Caroline tosses back the wine in her glass and reaches for the bottle to refill it. Nora just examines me from her perch on one of the bar stools, her hand resting over her protruding belly.

She offers me a smile and raises her blonde eyebrows. "You okay?"

Without them "babysitting" me and forcing me out of the house, I'm sure I would be a shut-in by now. Probably one who doesn't bathe and ignores all personal hygiene in favor of Netflix marathons and vats of ice cream.

Actually, that's not far from the truth.

At first, I resented them constantly hovering around me, but it helped keep my pit of despair from turning into an abyss. It kept me afloat when all I wanted to do was drown in the sorrow of my loss. I can never thank them or repay them for everything they've done for me. Hosting once a month Friday girls' night dinners was the only way I knew to show my appreciation.

The wine is always flowing, and the lips are always loose. Frankly, I learn way too much about them and my brothers during these dinners, but they are a much-needed time to unwind. And I really need it after the last week.

This thing with Landon has thrown me off my, albeit, not that great game. I was trudging through life, doing pretty okay, and he had to come crashing in like a runaway freight train.

How he managed to get under my skin in only a few dances is beyond me. Maybe it's because I've been so starved for affection that the first man who shows any interest in me has this effect.

Or maybe you really like this guy?

The thought has me shaking my head and forcing a smile back at Nora. "I'm fine. Just got distracted."

She eyes me suspiciously but doesn't say anything. Nora is by far the quietest of the group. Sometimes, I think the Hawke women and Caroline overwhelm her into silence even if she wanted to say something. Which makes her kind of perfect for

Stone. Even though he and I aren't on the best of terms, I *am* happy that he's finally found someone who supports him and pushes him to be a better person. If it weren't for Nora's intervention and involvement in his life, I doubt he would have uncovered the truth about Dom, or himself. He certainly wouldn't have accepted he had a problem and gone to rehab. And now, they're expecting a baby, and Stone will have to figure out the whole father thing.

Terrifying, really.

Still, it's good news for the family, even if the thought of him caring for a child makes me cringe.

I need to give him more credit, and eventually, forgive him for everything that happened. But, that's easier said than done. Having Nora around helps me see the other side of him, though —the loving, caring side he hides behind his wall of control and tough machoism.

Skye turns to me and winks. "I was just asking Nora when Stone was going to make an honest woman out of her."

Oh Lord.

I feel bad for the poor girl. My well-intentioned Catholic family keeps pressing Stone to propose so they can marry before the baby is born, but even in the very limited time I've spent with them since Stone came back, one look at those two together tells me they are nowhere near ready to tie the knot—baby on the way or not.

I give Nora an apologetic smile. Skye can be a real jackass when she wants to be, but she means well, and she has dialed things back considerably since settling down with Gabe. He calms her somehow and brings out the best in her we used to see when Star was still alive. "Leave the poor girl alone. We could ask the same thing about you and Gabe."

Skye points the wooden spoon in Nora's direction. "I'm not knocked up."

Dani chuckles, and Caroline barks out a laugh. "God, I love

this family."

Nora rubs her stomach and smiles softly. "I appreciate your concern about my virtue, but Stone and I are not getting married any time soon. Really, we're still learning a lot about each other. Things happened so fast, and yes, I love him, but it hasn't even been a year. We don't want to rush into anything."

Skye rolls her eyes and coughs dramatically. "Yeah, like parenthood."

"Skye!" I fling the package of Parmesan cheese I'm holding at her, and it smacks into her back. "Shut up!"

She grins and returns to stirring the sauce. No one dares bring up marriage with her and Gabe. It's pretty much accepted they're content the way they are. If it happens, it happens. If not, it doesn't really matter.

Nora blushes and giggles. "It's fine. Really. We're all adults here."

I'm glad she's being a good sport. The Hawke girls can be difficult to handle, especially in large groups, and Skye isn't helping by giving her a hard time.

Caroline swirls the wine in her glass and sends me a grin. "Speaking of being adults. Did Storm tell you guys what we did last weekend?"

Dani stops her work and drops the knife. "What? No! You actually got her out of the house?"

Oh, shit.

My heart races, and I shake my head. "Caroline, don't..."

Please, for the love of God, don't go there.

"Oh, I more than got her out of the house! I got her to go to a sex party with me!"

A collective round of "what?" is shouted, and Skye abandons what she's doing to examine me. "*You* went to a sex party? I don't believe it."

Caroline grins and sips at her wine.

This doesn't bode well for me.

That woman has zero filter. No wonder she's Dani's best friend. They are two sides of the same coin. A foul-mouthed one.

I open my mouth to cut her off, but it's too late.

"Not only did she go, she actually *danced* with a *guy*."

Shit. Shit. Shit.

There goes any chance of getting out of this with any semblance of my privacy intact.

"Ooooo," trickles from the ladies, all except Skye who watches me skeptically with her arms crossed over her chest.

Her eyebrow raises. "A guy?"

Acid churns in my gut as guilt claws its way up my esophagus. I shouldn't be dancing with a guy this soon after Ben died. They probably all think I'm some sort of heartless slut. I definitely need to defend myself here. "It was just harmless dancing and then I left."

That's the truth. They don't need to know how much I enjoyed it or how natural it felt being in Landon's arms for those few minutes. They don't need to hear about the pull I felt toward him when I saw him again at the meeting, or the fact that I'm technically his new boss, either. They don't need to know *anything*.

"Oh no!" Dani slams her palm down on the counter. "You aren't getting off that easily. We need details. All of them!"

I move to pick up the cheese package from the floor, hoping to buy myself some time to consider my response.

How much can I say without giving too much away?

"There's not much to tell. A guy asked me to dance. I said yes. We danced to a few songs. Then I left."

Not a lie.

Skye taps her foot on the tile floor. "And does this mystery man have a name?"

Shit.

There's no way I can tell them it was Landon. It's only a matter of time before they meet him in his new capacity at

Matthews Construction. I can't have that connection known. It's awkward enough as it is without anyone knowing we met before and under what circumstances. These women won't let it go if they understood the full extent of the situation.

Lie.

"I actually didn't get his name."

Caroline narrows her eyes on me and shakes her head. "I don't believe you. No way you danced with someone without asking his name."

She's right.

Dammit. Why do I have to be such a shitty liar?

"Tell us!"

"Yeah, tell us!"

There's no getting anything past these women. It's like the Spanish Inquisition and a witch hunt all rolled into one. I used to join in the fun. I used to enjoy playfully ribbing them right back, but somehow, when the attention focuses on me, it's a whole other ballgame. I can't fight it. They will push and push and push until I break, so I might as well give in now.

"Fine. It's Landon, okay."

At least it will take them a while to make the connection. I have a small reprieve here to figure out how I'm going to deal with the situation.

Dani grins at me. "Ooo, and did you and *Landon* make plans to talk again?"

I shake my head, toss the cheese on the counter, and move to stir the pot Skye abandoned. It gives me a reason to avoid eye contact with everyone in the room. "No, we didn't."

That's the absolute truth, too. After the meeting, I raced out of there before he could corner me or make it any more awkward by having a one-on-one conversation.

Hopefully, I can convince the ladies to lay off me by telling them I'm never going to see him again. And if God smiles upon me, I can make that come true by avoiding him the rest of my life.

She can't avoid me forever.

At least, that's what I keep telling myself as I unpack the few boxes I have at my new office at Matthews Construction. The rest of my things are coming next week, but Eileen overnighted my office items so I would be ready to start right away on Monday in an office that was already set up.

Her efficiency and quick smiles will be missed. But leaving the bad behind also means giving up some of the good things, like an amazing assistant who kept things in line and made sure I stayed on track.

I hate disorder, and my life has been anything but orderly lately. It's been more like a tornado, whirling and spinning and sucking things and people into it, mixing them up, battering them, and then spewing them, and me, out across a wasteland it created.

How the fuck did this happen?

With a sigh, I drop into the large, leather chair behind my new desk and survey my new work home. The office is stunning. Storm designed the building, so it shouldn't surprise me. High coffered ceilings, gleaming oak built-in shelves lining the wall, floor to ceiling windows that let in the natural light. It's perfection.

But not exactly where I ever imagined I'd be spending my Friday night. Unpacking my office in a new city, starting a new life.

When did my social life become so damn boring?

I'm in a city with a million things to do, and instead of being out on Bourbon Street, enjoying the nightlife, I'm in here, arranging books and pens.

And it's all because of Storm.

Any desire I had to explore the city went out the window when I saw her sitting in Chris' office. I want to spend some horizontal time with *her*, not with some random woman I meet out on the street or at some bar.

Even the party tomorrow night is sounding less and less appealing. Especially because I know Storm won't be there.

There's no way she's going to show after what happened last time. Not when she knows who I am now and that I'll likely be there. But she's not going to be able to avoid me forever. Not when she owns the business and there are so many connected projects.

My heart swells slightly. There's hope there for maybe an opening to get to know her better. To see if she's interested in pursuing this sexual attraction between us to our mutual benefit.

Chris said Savage and Gabe want me to take over the rebuilding of the third Hawkeye Club location, which everyone calls THREE. They lost a brother and an employee in that fire, and Storm lost a husband. To go ahead and rebuild on the same property must have been an excruciating decision for the family.

But it gives me a major project to work on right from the start, and it's an excuse to see Storm since she's the architect. I'm sure I can come up with a hundred reasons to consult with her and see where we stand.

It's unfathomable what she's going through, having just lost Ben, and I don't want to push her into anything she's not ready for. But we had a connection, and it's not like I'm looking for a relationship. Some Earth-shattering sex would be good for both of us. And I know I wasn't the only one feeling it.

Maybe she's not ready to explore whatever it is between us, but that doesn't mean I can't try. I just need to spend time with her for her to realize we could be good for each other, even if it's only for sex. She's been alone for six months, and there's no doubt in my mind we would be combustible in bed together. The energy buzzing between us when we danced, and again when we touched at the meeting, is undeniable. I can't even remember the last time I experienced anything like that. It would be mutually advantageous, kind of a friends-with-benefits situation.

It's probably all either of us are capable of right now.

I certainly wasn't searching for this kind of arrangement—random sex partners served their purpose just fine for a few weeks back home, but I barely hit town before *she* came thundering into my life. Fate really has a fucked-up sense of humor to throw Storm at me right now. But as long as we both go into it eyes wide open and both want to keep it casual, it will be the perfect arrangement. No randoms. No worrying about hang-ups or feelings getting involved.

The shrill ring of my cell phone sounds in the room. I glance at the screen and growl.

Not today, Satan. Not today.

I send it to voicemail and toss my phone onto the desk. It skitters across the top and stops halfway over the edge.

It could fall off and shatter for all I care. There's only one person who has this number who I ever want to hear from again, and that's only because he's the man who holds my future in his hands. I don't need anyone else to contact me. They're dead and buried.

To keep myself from grabbing the offending device and smashing it against the wall, I jerk open a drawer and start organizing my various office supplies inside.

The beep alerting me to a new voicemail slices through the silent room.

Of course.

I grab the phone and stare at the voicemail indicator. My thumb hovers over the "delete" button, but something gnaws at my stomach and makes me hit "play" instead.

"You're probably avoiding my call."

No shit, Sherlock.

"I went by your hotel room. Someone else answered the door, so you're obviously not staying there anymore."

Stalker much?

*"*sigh* I don't understand why you won't see me or talk to me. It doesn't need to be like this."*

It sure as shit does.

I wasn't given any choice in the matter, and no amount of begging or pleading is going to change how I feel.

"I need to see you. There's so much to talk about."

The voicemail ends, and I immediately delete it.

So much horseshit in such a short series of sentences. It really is a learned art-form. But I've developed the ability to sniff it out from a mile away. Maybe I couldn't always. I guess that's been proven. But things have changed. I've changed. For the better. I was too soft. Too open. Too easily manipulated.

Well, never again.

Those days are gone.

This is a new city.

This is a new life.

This is a new Landon.

There are plenty of other things to worry about right now. Like trying to establish myself in this job while also trying to get in good with the woman who is essentially my boss.

Maybe nothing will come of this spark between me and Storm, but I can't let a good thing walk away without putting in a little effort. Otherwise, I'll spend the rest of my time here, however long that may be, wondering "what if" while fighting my desire to bend her over a desk and fuck her brains out.

Sometimes a spark just needs a little fuel to ignite.

eight

"*H*ave you ever noticed that seals look like giant sperm?"

I clap my hands around Angel's ears and glare at Caroline while Dani laughs next to me.

"Jesus, Caroline, can you reel it in a little around my daughter?"

She feigns innocence and swipes her hand out toward the giant window in front of us where white seals slice through the water. "What? Come on, they do look like sperm. Or maybe it's been so long, you don't even remember what sperm look like?"

Bitch.

I roll my eyes. "You can't see sperm, Caroline. They're microscopic."

Caroline scoffs. "You know what I mean." She wiggles her eyebrows. "This may be as close as you'll ever get to seeing one again."

I drop the earmuffs and point to the next exhibit where the penguins are swimming. "Angelina, why don't you go look at the penguins? We'll be right behind you."

She squeals and darts off to the big glass window a few feet down the hallway. At least I got her out of earshot for whatever else may slip out of Caroline's mouth.

Caroline huffs. "Really, Storm, I never thought you were so uptight, especially after some of what you've told me."

The implied reference to what I revealed to her, what led to me being at that damn party in the first place, has a flush rising to my cheeks.

Dani laughs while she pushes Kennedy back and forth in her stroller, trying to get her to fall asleep. She doesn't have a clue what Caroline is referencing, unless Care betrayed me with that very private info. But I don't think she would. She might joke about it and encourage me to open up and share it with Dani, but she wouldn't spill my secrets.

I hope.

"I'm not uptight, Caroline, but you'll understand once you have children." I never thought it would bother me, especially since I swear all the time in front of her, but when someone else says it, it seems to rankle me.

Dani's laugh echoes obscenely in the hallway. "Caroline? Kids? Yeah, right."

Caroline joins right along with her. "She's right, Storm. I'll leave the whole mommy thing to you and Dani."

She says that now, but I know how easy it is to forget the no-baby stance once you find the right person. Baby fever is *real*. Not all suffer from it, but it is definitely a force you don't see coming. Ben and I never thought we'd be parents so young. We were just a few years out of college when Angel was born, but we somehow figured out the whole parent thing pretty quickly. We had no choice, and we had Mom to help. With his parents long gone, she stepped into the role of sole grandparent with gusto and hasn't looked back since.

And now, I'm floundering and failing miserably at the mom thing.

It's a whole different ballgame doing it on my own. It doesn't help to have Caroline making crude comments. "Please just watch your language in front of her."

She holds up her hands in surrender. "All right, all right. I'm sorry."

We move toward the next exhibit to catch up to Angel, and Dani casts me a strange look.

"What?"

She leans forward to check on Kennedy. "I mean, she does

have a point. Have you even thought about starting to date again?"

I stop walking for a moment to make sure I heard her question right.

How can she even ask that?

Dating or a relationship is off the table. I can't give my time to someone when I barely have enough to spend with Angelina or on work as it is. I can't give my heart to someone else when it's buried with Ben and will always be his.

They don't understand. They can't. Mom is the only one with any semblance of an understanding what I'm trying to juggle right now. Everyone else is just talking out of their asses offering advice based on absolutely zero personal experience.

Date again...yeah, right.

I restart my walk toward the next exhibit and catch up with Dani. She knew how to do it. How to enjoy life. Sex without connections. Enjoyment without pesky feelings.

So, maybe Caroline may have a point.

Am I really gonna stay celibate forever? Just because I can't have a relationship doesn't mean I can't have sex, right? People do that these days, don't they?

Friends with benefits, or fuck buddies, or whatever they want to call it. It works for a lot of people.

Can I really have sex just for sex's sake?

Landon's bourbon eyes flash in my head.

Even if I could manage to turn off my emotions long enough to have sex, it certainly can't be with him. Not when he's working at Ben's company. Not when I have to see him professionally, and maybe socially, and pretend there's nothing going on between us.

Sneaking around isn't my thing, and I don't particularly want to try it. Still, a life without sex forever? Do I really want that?

Dani and Caroline might be the only ones who would actually understand the need for mindless sex. Well, and Gabe. Maybe Stone.

Oh, hell, who am I kidding?

The whole Hawke family was full of whores before they found their respective significant others. Pretty much everybody but Savage slept around. But I won't judge their life choices. Those choices led them to where they each are today—happy.

Maybe I should follow their lead and give it a try?

No.

I shake my head. That's a stupid idea.

I'll resign myself to spend the rest of my life alone and so sex deprived that my vagina dries up like a barren wasteland.

I have my job. I have Angel. That's my life now, not sex and romance, and I'm okay with that.

Really, I am.

"I'm not ready to date, Dani. Even if I were interested in someone, I'm in no position to get emotionally involved."

She sighs and turns to check on Angel and Caroline where they stand pressed against the glass. At least she cares if Angel is out of earshot before she says something that might not be appropriate for little ears. "I get it, I really do. But..."

"But what?"

She glances back my way and shrugs. "Just because you can't get emotionally involved doesn't mean you can't have some fun. Go out on a few casual dates. Have some sex. There's nothing wrong with that."

"Maybe that was true for you before you met Savage, but I just don't think I can do it. Separate sex from love. Ben is the only one I've ever slept with."

Dani's eyes almost bug out of her sockets. "You're joking."

I shake my head. "Nope."

"Holy shit! How is that even possible?"

"Because I was a good girl in high school, and Ben and I met freshman year of college. He's the only boy I ever seriously dated."

And the only one I've ever loved.

The first time he kissed me, I knew I was a goner.

"You're beautiful, Storm. What did I ever do to deserve you?"

His words the first time we made love will remain forever etched in my heart.

How can I go from that to banging some random dude just to scratch an itch?

That's just not me.

Caroline moves over toward us, and Angelina follows. "Mom, can we go see the fish?"

"Yeah, baby." I grab her hand and lead her down the hall toward the exhibits with the fish. When I check back to make sure Caroline and Dani are following, a tall, muscular man in a suit with dark hair steps from around the corner and stops at the penguin exhibit.

Do I know him?

There's something familiar in his profile, but I'm too far away to really see any details, and he's turned facing the glass. Kind of odd to be wearing a suit to the aquarium, too.

Dani and Caroline brush past me, and Angelina tugs on my hand.

The mystery man forgotten, we walk to the tank with the blue surgeonfish. Angel drops my hand and rushes to the glass. "Mom, look! It's Dory!"

Seeing her happy and excited makes my heart swell. She's been suffering since Ben died, and bringing her here today was what she, and I, needed.

Caroline sidles up next to me. "You know there's another party tonight, right?"

The music and the feeling of being in Landon's strong, warm arms comes rushing back to me. Then the memory of the song...

Tears well in my eyes, and I dash them away.

Knock it off.

There's nothing to cry about. It was a song, one you're going to hear the rest of your life. And Landon...he's just someone you had a nice dance with once. Nothing more. Nothing less.

"I'm not going back to another one of those parties, Caroline."

"Why the hell not?"

"It's...just not for me."

She sighs and glances at Dani, who just raises her eyebrows. "I really wish you'd reconsider. I had a *great* time at the last party, after I got my interview done, and I know you would too, if you just went with an open mind."

I can only imagine what kind of "great time" she had. I'm sure it involved a whole lot more than opening her mind. "It's not my mind I'm worried about opening, Caroline."

She rolls her eyes at me and loops her arm through mine. "Girl, you need to lighten up. Enjoy life. Live a little."

As if it's that easy.

Living is just about the hardest thing right now.

The Roman theme for tonight's party means plenty of flowing togas that grant easy access. Everyone still wears a mask, but this time, they're made to match the historical style of the dress.

A group of gladiators works over two women in the corner, their cries of pleasure audible even over the band music, while a female dressed as Cleopatra has a man worshipping at her feet—and between her legs—to my right.

I sip at my whiskey while I scan the room.

Why did I even bother coming tonight?

There have to be a hundred beautiful and very willing women

at the party, yet my interest hasn't been stirred once, nor has my dick.

In fact, the only time it's risen to the occasion at all since last Saturday was when I've thought about Storm and her body pressed up against mine while we danced in this very room. Or when I was sitting next to her in Chris' office.

More than once, I've taken it in my hand and stroked myself, imagining it was her small, soft hand or hot, wet mouth wrapped around it. The orgasms did nothing to quell my desire for her, though.

Just thinking about her dark hair brushing against my hand as we danced, her scent floating around me, her warm breath against my cheek...it has my cock stirring to life now.

Looks like another night of self-appreciation is in the plans for me.

I should just get out of here. There's no point in staying when I know no one here is going to interest me the way Storm has. Then again, maybe I could get her out of my head if I just took one of these ladies up on what they're offering so generously tonight. It's probably best to do what I can to wipe this interest in Storm from my head.

"Having a good time?"

The deep voice next to me has me jerking, and my drink sloshes over my hand.

Shit.

A dark-haired man in an immaculately draped toga grins at me, holds up his drink, and offers an apologetic smile. "Sorry, I didn't mean to startle you."

I wipe away what spilled over my hand and return his smile. "No problem. I guess I was just deep in thought."

About the same damn thing that's been occupying my mind for the last week. No matter how much I try to focus on the new job and everything I need to do to complete my move here, I can't seem to shake Storm.

He chuckles and takes a sip of his drink, his eyes scanning the crowd. "About your plans for one of the lovely ladies here tonight?"

I let my attention drift over the mass of bodies engaged in various carnal activities before returning to him. "Nah. I don't think anything is going to happen tonight." He nods his understanding, and as I stare at him, a memory floats up. "Hey, you were here last weekend too, weren't you?"

I remember him clearly. He had been standing along the side of the dance floor, watching. Our eyes met more than once, and he nodded to me. I assumed he had been checking Storm out, but maybe I read that all wrong. I never actually saw him talk with anyone, let alone engage in any of the sensuous activities we are all here for. Maybe it wasn't *Storm* he was checking out at all.

"Yes, I was." His right hand extends. "I'm Steele."

I shake his hand and try not to grimace at his firm grip. "Landon."

What kind of a name is Steele?

His parents must have hated him to curse him with a moniker like that. But the guy is built like a boxer, so I don't think commenting on his name would be wise for my well-being.

The man's dark eyes leave mine momentarily to search the dance floor and the main room. "Where's the woman you were dancing with last week? I assumed you two were here together."

I wish.

I shake my head and return my attention to the dance floor. "No. I just met her that night. We are most definitely not together."

He sighs, and I peek over at him to find a grin occupying his face. "That's too bad. It looked like you two had a lot of chemistry."

"Yeah. We do." And we would have even more in bed. I just know it.

"So, why isn't she with you?"

I sigh and take a big swig of my drink. I consider my response as the alcohol burns its way down my throat and warms my gut.

How the hell can I explain Storm and the situation?

It's impossible when I don't understand it. No doubt, she's been through Hell. I can't even imagine what losing a husband would be like, especially when it means your child loses a father too. I'm sure the last thing she wants is a relationship. I get that. Hell, I don't want one either. But she didn't even give me the chance to explore something less...committed. She took off before we could even have an in-depth conversation.

Surely, it could be mutually beneficial and enjoyable. Without strings. Without emotions. Just sex for both of us. If she'd only give me a chance.

"It's complicated."

Steele narrows his eyes and holds up his glass to me. "Then uncomplicate it."

I bark a laugh. The band starts up a slow, sensual song that only reminds me of how much I loved having Storm in my arms, and of how much I want her there again. "If it were only that easy."

Nothing will ever be easy with Storm. If I had known who she was that night, I never would have even *thought* about approaching her. But now that I've met her, that I've held her in my arms, I can't seem to shake the need to touch her. To be with her.

If I had a psychiatrist, he would likely tell me this obsession with her stems from some deep-seated damage I suffered in Chicago. And maybe that's true, but maybe it's as simple as a chemical attraction. The thrill of the chase and the need to unravel everything that makes her tick. Her sadness and actions that night are no longer a mystery, but there's still so much to learn about her.

Steele shrugs and laughs lightly. "I tend to think people make things more complicated than they need to be. If everyone just acted with their heart instead of overthinking things, the world would be a much better place. We'd have a lot less stress."

Whoever this guy is, he sounds more like a philosopher than someone who would come and engage in one of these parties. I have to snicker to myself. And in that robe, he might as well be Plato, or would it be Socrates? I never was very good at remembering the ancient wise men or where they were from.

Were they even Roman? Shit. They might have been Greek...

"I appreciate the advice, man. Wouldn't you rather be spending your time entertaining the lovely women here rather than talking to me?"

Steele flashes me a devious grin. "I've already taken care of my plans for tonight. I wish you the best of luck with your lady friend."

"Thanks. I appreciate that."

With a nod, he saunters off into the crowd. I lean back against the wall and contemplate his words.

Uncomplicate it.

It can't really be that easy, can it?

Is there way to uncomplicate things with Storm?

I'm not so sure. Maybe it's worth a try.

It's sure better than beating off and wishing I was with her.

nine

"Come on, Angel. We're already late." I grab her hand and drag her up the front walkway to Mom's door.

Today of all days, this kid had to throw a tantrum. She usually loves Sunday night dinners and seeing everyone, but for some reason, she was stomping and screaming and planting her feet, refusing to get in the car. Manhandling a five-year-old having a meltdown is not on the top of my to-do list.

Mistake #8,683—thinking this would ever get easier.

The door opens just as I reach for the handle. Dani gives me a sly grin. "I was wondering when you were going to show."

I shove Angel into the house in front of me. "Sorry, you know...kids."

Dani waves at someone over my shoulder. I turn back as a black sedan with tinted windows rolls past, the male driver barely visible.

"Who was that?"

She waves her hand in the general direction of the street. "I don't know. Just being friendly." She grabs my upper arm and drags me inside. "So...is there anything you want to tell me?"

I raise an eyebrow.

What the hell is she getting at here?

"Uh...no? Should I?"

She walks me toward the dining room, and a cacophony of chatter from the entire family hits my ears.

"Oh, I don't know, something about that mystery man you danced with at the party, perhaps?"

Landon? Where is she going with this?

We turn the corner, and my eyes find familiar warm amber ones.

Shit. What's Landon doing here?

I freeze, and a hot rush flows through my body. Mom's house is supposed to be the safe zone. Landon here is very *not safe*—for my libido or my sanity. I thought I'd have more time to prepare myself to see him again, to come up with some way to handle the awkward tension between us.

Guess I was wrong...

Dani squeezes my arm, and I glower at her. She smiles at me knowingly. "Apparently, Savage and Gabe invited the newest member of Matthews Construction to dinner tonight. Imagine that. Landon...such a unique name. And wouldn't you know, I saved you a seat right next to him."

Dammit.

I guess it was only a matter of time before they figured it out once they knew his name, but damn. So not ready for this.

Yet, I can't seem to keep myself from peeking over at him and his panty-melting smile.

He grins at me from across the table, and Chris turns around and waves from his spot right in front of me. Nora and Skye both wear knowing smirks. I sure as hell hope they haven't said anything to Gabe and Savage.

My eyes meet Stone's, and he gives me a tight, grim smile. The tension between us at these dinners is always palpable, but tonight, it will be suffocating. We haven't spoken since I hurled those harsh words and accusations at him. Since he threw back those things I didn't want to hear, even if they were the truth.

At some point, we're going to have to work out everything that stands between us. He's my brother, after all, and despite everything that's happened, I do love him.

Dani drags me over to the empty chair next to Landon, and he pulls it out for me. I force myself to smile as I sit. Angel follows us around and plops down on the other side of me.

Landon leans in, his hot breath tickling my neck. The scent of his crisp, clean aftershave and that underlying ocean smell envelops me. "It's nice to see you, Storm."

I gulp past the knot in my throat. Having him this close isn't good for my self-restraint. Not at all. The heat rippling across my skin and the way my fingers itch to reach out and touch him scream *danger* to me in a very clear language.

"Hello, Landon."

Keep cool.

Be friendly.

Nothing more.

Skye kicks my shin under the table.

Damn, that hurt.

I reach down and rub at it as surreptitiously as I can.

She grins at me. "Nice of you to join us."

Smartass.

No doubt, she's reveling in knowing the secret I'm keeping about Landon and how uncomfortable this is for me.

Mom appears from the kitchen carrying a massive bowl of spaghetti. "Oh, Storm, you're here! Perfect timing. Hi, Angelface!" She sets down the bowl and rushes over to hug Angelina.

"Hi, Grandma!"

When Mom returns to her seat, she waves her hands at everyone. "Eat! Eat!"

Leave it to her to get right down to business. It saves me from having to engage in small-talk with the enticing man next to me. But I can feel the eyes of all the women on me, just waiting for something to happen between me and Landon.

Bitches.

They set me up. I'm sure Dani and Skye knew Landon was coming, yet they never warned me. And they certainly could have saved a seat for me somewhere else. This was very intentional.

Payback's a bitch, ladies.

I give them my best "I'm so going to get you back for this"

smile while I heap pasta and some meatballs onto my plate and then serve some to Angel.

She digs in, and I turn my focus to my food. Anywhere but on Landon. His presence beside me is unmistakable, though. My body practically leans his way without me even realizing it.

His left arm brushes against mine, and I close my eyes against the little shock of electricity that travels through me.

Ignore it.

The bright flavors of Mom's sauce hit my tongue, and a little moan of appreciation slips from my lips.

Landon stiffens next to me, and his hand drops below the table.

What's he doing?

It doesn't take long for the light brush of his fingers to run along my thigh.

Holy hell.

A shudder runs through me, and I shift in my chair against the desire to move closer to him and his touch. His hand shifts until his palm flattens over my thigh, his fingertips grazing the inside.

I should pull away, get up, and leave.

I should say something.

But the light, sensual caresses feel so damn good. It's been far too long, and my body is desperate for it even if my mind isn't ready.

My eyes drift closed as he runs his hand up and down my sensitive skin.

"So..." Mom's voice has my eyes flying open. I scan the table to ensure no one witnessed my momentary lapse into bliss, but everyone is absorbed in conversation or eating and no one seems to be paying any attention to me.

Thank God.

"Landon, are you enjoying New Orleans?"

He squeezes my leg, and I almost choke on the half a meatball in my mouth. "It's great so far. I'm meeting a lot of very interesting people."

Dani snort-laughs and glances to Skye and Nora, who are both covering their mouths with their hands, trying to hide their laughter.

I'm going to need to have a talk with them about discretion. They might as well be waving a sign that says *"Storm met Landon at a sex party"* across the sky.

"That's wonderful." Mom smiles at him and glances to Chris before returning to gush over Landon. "Are you enjoying working with your brother? You worked for your father in Chicago, didn't you?"

Landon's hand tightens, and his body tenses beside me. He sucks in a deep breath. "I'm enjoying it here, and yes, I did work with our father."

There's a deep tension in Landon's voice.

Chris casts a wary look his way, then straightens and clears his throat. "Our father isn't the easiest person to work with, so I think the move was good for everyone involved."

Hmm. I wonder what that's all about?

Seems there's a story there with their dad. Maybe why Landon is here now instead of working for the family company?

Angel leans into the table to see Landon. "Do you build stuff like my daddy does?"

Oh God...

The question is like a bucket of ice water poured over me, and it kills the warm, fuzzy feelings Landon's ministrations created. He pulls his hand away and returns it to the top of the table, and his worried dark eyes flash over to meet mine.

Shit.

How the hell am I supposed to answer that?

The poor kid probably barely understands her father is dead, if at all. *Like my daddy does.* Not *like my daddy did.*

I'm pretty clueless at handling these situations. Kids aren't really my strong-suit.

Looking to Storm for guidance does no good. She's a deer caught in the headlights, her fear and distress soaking her blue eyes with unshed tears.

I suck in a deep breath and smile at Angelina. "Yeah, honey, I do, but your dad was much better at it than I am."

There. I hope that wasn't too bad.

Storm's hand on the table shakes, and when I dare to check on her, her head is dropped down, and she swipes at her cheeks with her other hand.

Shit.

I reach out to touch her again, take her hand in mine or somehow offer some support, but she shoves her chair back and rises to her feet before I can.

"Excuse me. I need to get a little air."

All eyes in the room follow her as she disappears down the hallway toward the back door. Dani leans over and whispers something to Savage. Skye looks to her mom, who frowns and shakes her head slightly.

Nora scans the room. "Should someone go after her?"

I sure want to. Seeing her so distressed just reminds me of the way she fled from me that night at the party. Something set her off then, no doubt me prying into her personal life, and tonight, *again* it's my fault she's so upset.

Fuck. I said the wrong thing.

Stone reaches out and wraps his arm around Nora's shoulder. "Let's give her a little space."

Nods of agreement from around the table settle that debate, and everyone returns to their plates and conversation.

I shovel food into my mouth mindlessly, but what had only a moment ago been so delicious is suddenly devoid of any flavor. It sits like lead in my gut with my regret over my comment.

Apologize.

Everyone seems to think Storm needs or wants to be left alone, but I want her to know how sorry I am for what I said, for upsetting her.

As casually as I can manage, I shove my chair back from the table and rise to my feet. All eyes follow me. "Excuse me for a moment. Bathroom?"

Savage motions over his shoulder. "Down the hall, on the left."

I nod my thanks and make my way out of the room. Chris catches my eye as I brush past him, and he raises a suspicious eyebrow.

He doesn't know anything about me and Storm, but he clearly doesn't believe my bathroom excuse either. Sometimes having a brother who can read you like a book really sucks. I can only imagine what it's like for Storm with this entire crew in her business all the time.

I ignore his look and wander out of the dining room and down the hallway. Instead of making my way toward the bathroom, I head toward the back door that overlooks a concrete patio and a beautiful pool.

The sliding glass door opens silently, and I close it behind me to ensure no one inside can overhear any conversation I may have with Storm.

Where is she?

All the deck chairs are empty, and I step out from under the patio overhang.

She's on my far left, leaning against the siding of the house with her head tipped back and her eyes closed. The tears running down her cheeks shimmer in the light from the moon and the patio light. Her arms wrap around her chest, and her lower lip trembles.

Maybe I should just leave her alone?

Watching her makes me feel like a real creeper, but there's just something about her, even when she's distressed and completely off balance, she's still the most beautiful woman I've ever seen. Her thick, dark hair falls in waves over her shoulders, with loose strands blowing around in her face in the early evening breeze.

I take a step backward toward the door when her eyes open, and she turns her head my way. The tempest churning in her eyes draws me to her when I should walk away. Each step brings me closer until she's right in front of me, dragging me into her orbit.

Even in her anguish, she's magnificent.

Does it make me an asshole to still want her when she's like this? To want to hold her? To want to comfort her and make her feel...alive again?

I can do that for her. If she'll let me.

Her eyes never leave mine as I close the distance between us, stopping when our lips are mere inches apart. I rest my forearm against the house beside her head and lean into her.

"I'm sorry. I didn't mean—"

"No." She shakes her head, freeing more dark tendrils around her face to dance in the wind. "Don't apologize. It wasn't what you said. That was...perfect. It just breaks me when Angelina says things like that, and I hate that she's constantly seeing me having meltdowns."

I shouldn't touch her. It's a terrible idea, but my hand moves of its own volition. The soft strands of onyx I catch between my fingertips might as well be pure silk. They float between my fingers, and I reach out to tuck them behind her ear, letting my thumb brush across her damp cheek.

She doesn't pull away, and her lips part, her breath blowing out in a long, slow sigh.

"And I'm sorry about the other night. What I said...my questions. If I'd known who you were—"

"Stop."

The word, nothing more than a heavy breath, freezes my hand and stills my pounding heart.

It's not unexpected, though. I've stepped over the line more than once with Storm. It was only a matter of time before we had to confront what happened and she can send me packing officially.

"You have nothing to apologize for. I had no business being there, at a party like that."

She can't be more wrong about that.

I know what it's like to lose something... someone...you thought would always be there. Not in the way she did, of course, but in a way that gutted me and made me rethink my entire life. Finding joy in anything was hard...*is* still hard. But sex... indulging in that very natural act of release and pleasure...that's never wrong.

I move a step closer, until her breasts press against my chest and the thudding of her heart beating in time with my own vibrates through me. "You're wrong, Storm. You have every right to do whatever you want to do, whatever feels good. Whatever makes you *happy* and takes away a little bit of the pain that's weighing so heavily on you."

My thumb grazes over her open lips, and her hot breath against my fingertip sends goose bumps traveling across my heated skin.

The distance between us disappears in a split-second, and my lips find hers. Her arms wind around my neck, and she moans against my mouth. The sound goes directly to my crotch, and my pants are suddenly ten sizes too small. Metal presses painfully against my cock as I taste her for the first time.

Sweet.

Salty.

And all Storm.

My tongue slips along her soft, yielding lips, requesting entrance. She opens for me, and her hot tongue tangles with mine, warring for control.

Yes. Take what you want from me, Storm. Take it.

Her tight curves mold against me, and I dig my fingers into her hips, drawing her even closer.

Small fingers twine into my hair, holding me in place, so she can continue to kiss me back with the same fierce desire I have coursing through my veins.

This.

I knew it would be like this with us. She just had to give it a chance.

"Storm?"

Fuck!

She jerks back from me, panic in her lust-hazed eyes, and I retreat from her just before Dani appears from under the patio. When she sees us, a grin spreads across her face, and she motions toward the house.

"Angel is asking for you. We are about to pull out dessert unless you two want to eat some more. Then again, it looks like maybe you guys have already filled your mouths."

She chuckles at her own joke and turns toward the house, leaving us staring at each other—her breathless and chest heaving and me with a raging hard-on and impending blue balls.

Double fuck.

ten

My office phone buzzes, and I look up from the plans on my drafting table to hit the intercom. "Yes?"

"Mr. McCabe is here to see you."

Shit. Did I have an appointment with Chris that I forgot about? Were we supposed to review the plans for THREE?

It wouldn't surprise me. I've been dragging my ass and haven't exactly been on my game lately. Especially when it comes to THREE. I know we're doing the right thing by rebuilding and keeping it at the same site. It was a hard decision, but now, it will not only be a business. It'll be something to help us remember Ben and Caleb and what happened, and not necessarily in a bad way. It's what I know Ben would want for us, to move forward on the project, and that's the only thing that's kept me able to work on it even though I have yet to set foot there again.

What I want to do is bury my head and pretend none of it ever happened. I don't have that luxury, though.

Just like I don't have the luxury of acting on the attraction I feel for Landon. Last night was...I don't even have words for it. My cheeks heat just remembering the way his lips felt melting to mine and the press of his *hard* body.

It's a fantasy, Storm. One you cannot have.

I have to keep reminding myself of that. Angel's comment at dinner coupled with the panic I felt when Dani caught us together only cemented my need to keep things professional with Landon.

And Chris can never find out.

Christ, that would be even more awkward.

"Send him back."

I run my hand through my hair and try to tame the mess I created throughout the day, then I return my attention to the plans in front of me. They're almost done, and I can finally mark one more project off my massive to-do list.

My door opens as I finish drawing one final line. "Chris, I'm so sorry. I totally forgot we had a meeting today. You should have reminded me at dinner last night."

"Hello, Storm."

Son of a bitch.

I freeze with my hand still poised over the plans. That is most definitely not Chris. I would know that voice anywhere. The deep rumble is the same one I felt through my entire body when his arms were around me.

Landon. Shit. Shit. Shit.

I hadn't even considered it might be him. It hasn't fully clicked in my head yet that he's going to be around...a lot. There will be no avoiding him, no matter how much easier that would make everything. I take a deep breath and brace myself before I turn to face him.

Game face.

He's devilishly handsome in his dress slacks and white button-down shirt open at the collar. A day of stubble dots his face, giving him a rugged appearance so much in contrast to what he sported at the party or even at dinner.

God, he's hot.

My blood heats, and I shift on my heels to control the dull throb between my legs. Going so long without being touched, without finding release, has left me a quivering mess around this man.

The corner of his mouth quirks up. "Sorry to show up unannounced, but I was in the neighborhood and thought we could discuss some of the plans for THREE now that I'm taking over the project."

A glint in his eye tells me that's not the only reason he's here, but he doesn't say anything else, just moves toward where I stand with the ease and grace of a man completely in control of his body.

Butterflies fill my stomach, and I press a hand there to try to quell them.

Goddammit. How am I ever supposed to work with him and pretend nothing happened?

Do I even want to?

Not now.

Wrong person.

Wrong place.

Wrong time.

He places his briefcase on the drafting table and opens it. His long fingers wrap around rolled up plans, and images of what he can do with those fingers flit through my head and send another wave of heat through me.

I bet he's good with his hands. So, so good at so many things. Things I shouldn't be thinking about. The way he touched me last night, held me to him, caressed my cheek, it's all just too much.

I shake my head as he leans over to unroll the plans across the table. His arm brushes against mine, sending a spark traveling through my body and straight between my legs.

My gasp is loud enough that I'm confident he heard, and I step back. Either he didn't feel it or he pretends not to notice as he clips the plans for THREE in place.

Stop it, Storm.

It's time to get my head in the game. I need to learn to work with Landon on a professional level without letting his charm or outright sexiness get to me.

I'm a grieving widow for Christ's sake, not a wanton slut.

"What is it you want to discuss?"

Still bent in front of the plans, he turns to peer at me over his shoulder. "There are a lot of things I want to discuss with you, Storm. But let's start with the design for the champagne rooms. I was wondering about making a little change over here."

He extends a long finger to point to the back of the building where the three large, private party rooms will be.

I shift closer next to him so I can see what he's indicating, and his shoulder brushes against mine. He presses into me slightly, and I catch a faint tip up of the corner of his mouth even though he's still staring down at the plans.

He's doing it on purpose.

Part of me wants to be mad that he won't just let this go, but the part of me that was wrapped around him last night revels in the fact that he wants me.

Keep it professional.

"What do you want to change?"

"I'd really like to see a little more division of the rooms. Would it be possible to have a private entrance for each one, so the more discreet clients could enter without having to walk through the main floor of the club to get there?"

"Hmm."

It's not a bad idea. In fact, it's pretty smart. Savage and Gabe always do their best to accommodate those clients who want to fly under the radar at the various club locations, but the nature of security at the buildings requires them to use the main entrance where the security officers are located. No one will mess with Rocky or Tubbs at the main club, and there's no *way* someone would be dumb enough to try to pull anything after they see Saint at the door at TWO.

"I guess if Savage and Gabe are willing to pay for extra security, adding a private entrance for VIPs that would lead them straight into the back hall where the champagne rooms are would work." There are also private rooms upstairs for smaller parties but those will have to be accessed by the elevators or main staircase.

I'll have to resubmit the plans to the Safety and Permits Office and get them approved before we could do any work, though. It could set us back significantly if we can't get things pushed through fast.

His head tilts. His eyes flash with humor, and he grins. "I have a good idea every once in a while."

That earns him a chuckle. "I'm sure you do. Have you discussed this with Savage and Gabe? They haven't mentioned it to me."

He rises to his full height and turns into me. "No. It came to me after I met with them and Chris last week, so I haven't had a chance. I wanted to run it by you to see what you thought and to find out if it would cause any major delays with the city if we made the changes to the plans?"

I shift slightly, away from the temptation of his wide, strong chest and soft lips. "I don't think the delay would be very long. I have contacts in the office and could get things moved through pretty quickly...hopefully."

Sometimes it pays to have friends in high places. And while the Safety and Permits Office isn't exactly a "high place," having people who like you and are willing to do you favors, like get you moved up the top of the list, always comes in handy. Hawkes have been greasing the wheels for times just like this.

He nods, and I turn back to the plans and lean over to examine the specifics of where the rear door would need to be added.

A wall of heat meets my back, and Landon's hot breath flutters against my skin. "I have full confidence you can handle this and get the plans pushed through."

Fingers brush my hair off the back of my neck and down over the front of my left shoulder. Wet lips find exposed skin, and I bite my lip to keep the moan from escaping.

This is wrong.

Mistake #9,407-Letting Landon get close enough to touch me.

"Don't think, Storm. Just feel. Let yourself enjoy this."

His whispered words go straight to the heart of the matter and to my needy center.

Need for touch. Need for release. Need for connection.

Just...need.

God, it's been so long. How can something that feels so good be so wrong?

Her body trembles against mine, and she pushes her ass into my hard cock. I grit my teeth and suck in a breath through my nose, trying desperately to control the desire to tear her clothes off like a fucking madman.

Christ.

I wasn't sure what to expect when I got here today. Last night ended rather...abruptly. She fled inside without another word, and I went home with one of the worse cases of blue balls in my entire life.

But Storm needs this just as much as I do.

A way to forget.

A way to just feel.

What we lost may not be the same, but what we need is.

I brush my lips against her exposed ear. "Don't overthink it. You're allowed to take what you want. If that's me, I'm more than happy to give it to you." My cock presses into her ass.

A little moan escapes her lips.

My hand shifts off her waist and down and around her tight pencil skirt to caress over the place she needs me. Her splayed hands on the drafting table bend, the fingers crinkling the plans under them.

She's fighting a war. I just hope the right side wins here.

There's no way I'll ever push her into something she doesn't want or isn't ready for, but I see the desire in her eyes, in the way she reacts to me. The loss of Ben has been devastating for her, and she may not even realize how badly something like physical contact is needed as human beings.

Being touched, being held, being fucked...it can make all the difference in the world when you feel like things are crumbling and spinning out of control.

It has to me after everything that went down. If I had holed up and turned away from things like those parties and what they offered, I probably would have gone insane. Sometimes sex just for the sake of sex is exactly what a person needs. And given everything Storm's been through, I think a release is exactly what the doctor ordered.

I press my lips to the sensitive skin behind her ear, and her hips roll backward into mine. "Tell me to stop."

Her head shakes back and forth.

It's all the permission I need.

I shift my left hand down to the hem of her skirt and slowly drag it up, letting my fingertips graze along the pale, flawless expanse of her thighs. Goose bumps explode across her exposed skin, and when I reach her ass, my breath hitches in my throat.

Christ.

"A thong, Storm? Fucking sexy." The whispered words have her moaning and arching into the palm of my hand cupping her firm cheek.

She groans, and I slide that hand until I can slip my fingers under the thin fabric of the black lace barely covering her pussy.

The wet fabric and the folds of her core slick with her need assure me she's completely on-board with where this is going.

A low whimper accompanies my touch, and she turns her head to peer over her shoulder at me. The blue eyes that have been so full of pain and unease are now clouded with lust and desire.

There's no denying it. She's finally given in to what she wants, what she needs, and she's even *more* beautiful.

My finger finds her clit, and one swirling motion has her eyes rolling up and her head dropping toward the table. Her hips rotate and thrust against my hand, and I use the other one to shift the skirt fully up around her hips before I dig in my pocket for a condom.

I pull away from her to unbuckle my pants and shove them down. She peeks over her shoulder at me, still bent over with her luscious ass in the air, and her eyes drift to my freed cock as I roll the condom down over it.

Her pink tongue snakes out and over her lower lip, and I groan and stroke myself.

Fuck, that's hot.

If I'm not careful, this will end long before she gets off. And that just won't do at all. This is more for her than me. Her pleasure is what matters, not mine.

Her hands move to her hips, and she slides the thong down around her ankles but doesn't kick it off. The creamy white skin of her exposed ass beckons me forward.

Sweet mother of God...

She is everything pristine and sinful rolled into one.

I step up to her and drag the head of my cock through her wetness. She mewls and leans forward, splaying her hands out across the plans for THREE.

"Landon...please." The soft, breathy words are scarcely audible over the thundering of my blood in my ears, but they don't have to be loud to spur me on. I've been dreaming of this moment since I first saw her at the party.

Her heat engulfs my cock, inch by inch. I grit my teeth, biting back the urge to drive into her in one hard thrust. She's so damn tight. So damn fucking tight. Every shift of my hips pushes me deeper, and she moans and rolls back, driving me all the way up to the hilt.

"Fuck!" We both gasp the word in unison, and she squeezes my cock with her pussy. I still inside her and lean over, pressing my chest into her back. I can't get close enough to her. All I want to do is kiss her senseless, but her face is down, forehead pressed to the table.

My lips explore her exposed neck, and I pull back and drive into her again. The force rocks her forward against the table, her thighs pressing into the edge. She reaches up and grips the top edge, and her knuckles whiten with the strain of holding on as I start a relentless rhythm designed to send her soaring.

Every drive of my hips meets her backward thrusts, and the sound of skin slapping against skin echoes in the room, mingling with the pants, groans, and gasps tumbling from both our mouths.

She clamps down on my cock with every retreat, letting the head drag along the walls of her pussy, and sending me into a tailspin of pleasure. The slow burn of an impending orgasm tingles in my balls. I dig my fingers into her hips. It won't be long now.

No way I'm coming first.

I slide one hand off her hip and down to find her clit. She gasps and bucks against me. Every slip of my fingers elicits a moan or gasp until her entire body is vibrating under me. Her pussy ripples and clenches. She tenses, and then she explodes.

"Oh, GOD!" She gasps and clutches at the design plans, crushing and crinkling them as she claws for purchase.

I continue to drive into her, drawing out her pleasure and

chasing my own release. My teeth grind together, and a bead of sweat trickles from my temple.

It blindsides me. A rush of heat and light and ecstasy tumbling down on me and overtaking my entire being as I empty myself into her wet heat.

She moans and sags against the table. Dark strands of her hair cling to her dampened skin. I lean over her and press a kiss to her temple.

Her eyes flutter open, and she pushes back against me, forcing me to right myself. My still-hard cock slips from inside her.

I shudder at the loss of the connection, and when she deliberately keeps her back to me instead of facing me, cold dread freezes in my chest.

Shit.

She's already regretting this, second-guessing what we've done. She can't even let herself enjoy the afterglow of great sex.

I can't let that happen.

eleven

"Storm, look at me."

I can't.

Not with the threat of tears burning my eyes.

Only, I don't even know what they're for—the incredible ecstasy I just experienced for the first time in so goddamn long, or the fact that I feel like I somehow betrayed Ben, by not only doing it but also enjoying it.

A lot.

God, I'm a fucking mess.

Ripples of pleasure still jolt through my body from my core, and a post-orgasm fog still envelops my brain. It makes it impossible to get a firm grasp on anything I'm feeling right now.

One big cluster of a mess.

As sneakily as possible, I swipe at my eyes. I can't cry in front of Landon.

I won't.

It's bad enough he witnessed me break down at the party and then at Mom's. If he sees me crying after sex, he'll definitely be questioning whether I'm batshit crazy or just plain nuts. And somehow, I've managed to fool everyone into thinking I'm not. A mess...definitely. But not crazy. I can't blow my cover by letting the waterworks stream out today.

Despite his eerie silence, his presence behind me—the heat radiating off him and the tension in the air—is unmistakable.

Somehow, I naively thought having sex with him might somehow change the dynamic between us. Every time I'm in a room with him, it feels more like being on stage at The Hawkeye

Club. Utterly and completely exposed. And I always manage to turn into a quivering mess with even the slightest touch from him.

People talk about being able to fuck someone out of your system. I guess that's a thing, just apparently, it doesn't work for me. If it did, I wouldn't be so tempted to turn around and fall back into his embrace and ask him to come home with me to do it all over again.

Mistake #10,956—thinking having Landon McCabe inside me once would ever be enough.

I pull up my thong and right my skirt. I can't believe I let this happen in my office.

Good God, what was I thinking?

Landon's arm stretches around me to grab a tissue from the box near the corner of the table, and a few seconds later, he tosses it into the wastebasket. The sound of a zipper sliding up and his belt buckle clinking makes me cringe.

This is so awkward.

What do I do? What do I say?

It almost makes me wish I had slept with someone other than Ben before, maybe had a one-night stand. At least I'd know how to handle this situation. As it is, I feel more like a virgin on prom night than a thirty-year-old woman who's been married and had a baby.

This shouldn't be so embarrassing. People do this all the time.

His hand falls on my shoulder, and he tugs at me, urging me to face him. After a momentary pause and a deep breath to try to gain some semblance of composure, I turn and meet his eyes.

So much lingers in their depths. Lust. Concern. Longing. Understanding.

It's too much.

That damn sting returns to my eyes.

I break free of his loose hold and hurry to my desk.

Safety in distance.

He releases a loud sigh, and when I glance up, he's bent over the drafting table rolling the plans up...the plans that are now crinkled and crumpled and probably ruined and unusable because I couldn't control myself and let him fuck me over the table like some hussy.

Shit.

I'll give him another copy. Just not today. Today, I need him out of my office before I say or do something else entirely stupid.

My dry throat makes it hard to swallow, but I need to force out some words. I can't leave, and he's going to turn to face me soon. Those eyes will see right through this façade of put-togetherness to what a total basket case I am.

I clear my throat. "I'll draft those changes we discussed and talk to Savage and Gabe about it. If they're on-board, I'll bring it to my contact so we hopefully don't have any delays."

Landon stuffs the plans into his briefcase and approaches to stand on the other side of my desk. Only a few scant feet of wooden surface separates us, yet the pull he has over me already has me wanting to lean across it toward him.

But no.

This shouldn't have happened, and I can't let myself fall into his arms again. No matter how incredible it felt.

"I know what you're doing, Storm."

What am I doing?

Besides having a total mental breakdown while my pussy and legs are still quivering from the mind-blowing orgasm he just gave me.

"Don't let all the static in your head cloud what really happened. Two consenting adults had sex. Nothing more. Nothing less. If it was as good for you as it was for me, and we both know it was, it's something we should definitely do again."

He gives me a moment to process his words.

Of course, it was good. Actually, good isn't even the right word.

Existential.

It made me almost believe in God again, and I never thought that would happen after Ben was taken from me.

"Given everything that happened, I'm sure you're not looking to get emotionally involved or in a relationship, and neither am I. So, we're on the same page. There won't be any hurt feelings or broken hearts. We'll both get what we want."

"What we want..."

What do I want?

I don't think I've known the answer to that question for a very long time. The only thing that echoes in my head in response is *Ben back.* But I know that's not what he's asking. He doesn't want to hear the dirty truth about what I feel deep down, about the secrets I have to hold onto, the pain...

"Don't let social constructs and guilt get in the way here. I sure as hell won't." He doesn't raise his voice, but there's a tension and dominance there I haven't heard before. He really wants this, and the thought I might simply say no because of what other people might think really upsets him.

That's kind of endearing.

He leans across the desk, and before I know what's happening, his warm lips press to my cheek. When he pulls back, he offers me a grin that matches the twinkle in his eyes.

The easy-going, carefree attitude he exudes is so different from Ben's more reserved nature, yet it somehow makes me feel as if I've known him forever instead of only such a minuscule amount of time.

His knuckles rap against the desk. "Let me know about the plans. And you know how to get a hold of me for anything you may want...or *need.*" He turns toward the door and glances back at me for a moment before opening it and pulling it shut behind him.

What the hell just happened? Was that a booty call?

I don't know the terms being used these days since it's not

something I've ever engaged in. But back in my day, I'm fairly certain that was what people referred to as a booty call.

Christ...

Never in a million years did I think sex would make me feel cheap afterward. Logically, I know it shouldn't. He's right. We are two consenting adults who acted on an attraction. But that feeling lingers...like what we did was just...*wrong.* And it has absolutely *nothing* to do with Landon. He's pretty damn incredible, and apparently, we *are* on the same page with the desire to avoid any emotional attachments.

Loving someone, giving your heart and soul to another person and letting them hold your life in their hands, is only setting yourself up for heartbreak and devastation.

I won't do that again.

I can't.

Mistake #11,343—opening my legs to Landon McCabe.

By the time I settle into my chair at the office, the post-orgasmic buzz has started to fade from my body, replaced with the tension I've been carrying around for months.

Finally being with Storm hasn't managed to free me from it. I don't know why I thought it would. Leaving home didn't. Burying myself in this new job didn't.

There's only one thing that will...and as of my last conversation with Barry, the day I discovered who Storm really is, it's nowhere near happening. Every effort he's made on my behalf has met with failure. It's not completely his fault, yet things should have been wrapped up by now. Some phone calls. Some paperwork. It *shouldn't* be hard.

And the delay is only aggravating me more.

How can I close the door on Chicago when there's something wedged in there, keeping it open?

It's in his hands. There's nothing I can do from here, and I am not going back, not even for that.

At this point, I can't do anything except to get back to work and hope the universe sorts everything out in my favor instead of anally fucking me with no lube.

I fire up my computer screen and start to open my emails when a light knock on the open door has me turning in my chair.

Chris leans against the jamb with a grim set to his jaw.

"Hey, what's up?"

He nods toward my computer. "You busy or do you have a couple minutes?"

I turn all the way to face him. "I got a little time. What's going on?"

A few quick steps bring him to the chair across from me, and he drops into it with a sigh. "Well, I just got off the phone with Dad."

Mother fucker.

My hands curl into fists, and I practically snarl at Chris. "What does that asshole want?"

The eyes that are so similar to mine narrow on me.

Chris was always closer with Dad growing up, probably because he was the first-born and the golden child who excelled at everything and always toed the line. I preferred to question authority and do my own thing. I got that from Dad, yet he always resented me for being a younger version of himself somehow.

"He wanted to discuss the business and you."

"There is no 'me and the business.' I left."

He's lucky I didn't kill him.

"He wants you to come back."

I snort and shake my head. "Why the hell would I ever do that after what he did? I don't have any plans to set foot in Chicago, and I sure as *hell* won't ever work for him again."

The man is the epitome of a narcissist. But surely, even *he* has to know I won't ever be caught dead in the same room as him. No doubt, he called Chris in an effort to try to guilt me into it by appealing to some sort of family obligation. I put a lot of time and energy into helping Dad build on the already stellar McCabe name, but nothing is worth having to deal with what waits for me back home.

Nothing.

"Look, Landon, I understand where you're coming from. I really do. What he did...what happened was...well, I don't even know what to say. But for better or for worse, he's our father."

"That man is *not* a father. He's a self-centered, egotistical bastard who could never keep his dick in his pants."

The continuous stream of women who flowed in and out of the house and in and out of our lives after Mom died is far too many to count.

No one stayed long, and it's not like we would have wanted them to anyway. They weren't the type of women you would consider motherly figures. Most had IQs of 50 and had undergone more plastic surgery than Michael Jackson. But that seems to be what Dad wanted, at least for a while.

Age, it seems, hasn't granted him any more self-control...as recent events have proven.

"Landon. Look at the big picture here. The company has been in our family for a hundred years. If you don't take the helm when he retires, what's gonna happen to it? He's either going to shut it down or sell it off to someone who will probably fire all the employees, change the name, and erase any trace of the McCabes. Everything our family has worked so hard for will disappear."

He's not wrong there. A lot of blood, sweat, and tears went

into McCabe Construction. I don't want to see it closed or sold off to the highest bidder. But some things aren't forgivable.

They can't be.

"Why are you trying so hard to convince me? You were the one who insisted I come here to work with you."

He shakes his head and leans forward. "I know, and I don't want you to leave, believe me. Having you here has been a godsend already, but I want you to really think about what you're giving up by not going back to Chicago."

"You could go back. Why does it have to be me who takes over from the old man?"

Chris chuckles and waves his hands around the room. "This place is as much my baby as it was Ben's. It's been too many years and hours to walk away. I've created my own business here. This is my home, and it has been for a long time. You just got here. It would be a lot easier for you to go."

Easier.

Absolutely nothing would be easy about going home, and he knows it.

"It's not gonna happen, Chris. Unless you're telling me that you're firing me, I plan on staying right here." Even if he *did* fire me, Chicago wouldn't be my next stop. For the first time in a long time, I'm free to do whatever and whoever I want. And I'm not going to let Dad's guilt-trip get in the way of that.

He sighs and shoves his hand through his hair. "I figured you'd say that, but I had to try for the old man."

"Why do you care about what that asshole wants or needs? What has he ever done for you?"

He shoves to his feet and glowers. "He may have issues, but he taught both of us the business, and we never wanted for anything growing up. I know it's hard to see the good right now, but it's there. I just want to make sure you're staying here for the right reasons."

"The right reasons? What would the wrong ones be?"

His palms flatten on the desk, and he looms over me. "How was your meeting with Storm?"

The accusation lacing his words is evident. Either I came back looking a little more disheveled than I thought, or he's a lot more observant than I give him credit for. He can read me well, but even so, the only times he's seen us together was our brief meeting and Sunday dinner.

"It was good. I think she's on-board with making the changes, and she's going to run them by Savage and Gabe. Unless that's not what you meant by your question."

I know full well what he meant, and he knows that I know.

"She's the wrong girl at the wrong time, Landon. Between the two of you, what you've both been through..." He shakes his head. "Just please, leave her alone."

"I will if she wants me to."

He scowls. "Don't do anything to piss her off. One day, I may want to buy her out or hell, you may want to buy her out and become full partner in this business with me, so let's not make her life any more difficult than it already is."

That's the exact opposite of what I'm trying to do. She needs to escape her life for a while. My cock can do that.

"I would never do that, Chris."

"All I know is that woman looked just as distraught if not more so when she came in from outside last night, and you were hot on her heels. She doesn't need more drama and neither do you."

He's right about that. I don't need more drama or angst in my life, and Storm certainly doesn't either.

That's why this thing between us is perfect.

Casual. Nothing more.

twelve

"*A*ngel, let's go. We're gonna be late."

She trudges to the door slowly, with more sass than I thought a five-year-old was capable of, yanks it open, and storms out onto the front walkway.

The older this kid gets, the more attitude she develops.

Was I like this when I was her age?

If so, I've just developed even more respect for Mom. She had five of us to deal with, and I can barely handle the one without pulling my hair out. It's a wonder I'm not bald.

A light drizzle falls as I pull the door closed behind me and lock it. "Okay, let's get..."

Angelina stands staring at the car in the driveway. "Mom?" Her voice wavers slightly, and she turns back to me.

"What is it, baby girl?"

Her little arm extends out, and she points at the car. "Something's wrong with the tires."

Quick steps bring me to her side.

Holy shit.

The rims sit on the concrete.

Not one.

Not two.

I walk around the front of the car to the other side.

Four. All four tires.

I lean in to examine the one on the driver's side. Clear, clean slash marks are ripped through the rubber.

Who the hell would want to slash my tires?

I spin around and scan the immediate area. My eyes land on the black sedan I've seen a few times over the last couple weeks, now parked a few blocks down the street.

Maybe Savage and Gabe's security guys saw something. They've certainly been around enough. Though I'm not sure they stay overnight. That would seem excessive.

"Come on, Angel."

She stares at the car until I grab her hand and give it a tug back toward the house. "What happened to the car?"

I don't want to scare her. It's likely nothing, just some kids pulling a prank. "It's nothing, baby girl. The tires are just flat."

"Does that mean I don't have to go to school today?"

Her hopeful eyes, the exact same ones I stared into when I looked at Ben, peer up at me. I should make her go. I should call somebody and have them give her a ride. She's missed enough school since Ben died. But honestly, a day at home snuggled in bed watching movies with Angel sounds pretty incredible right now, especially with the dreary weather.

"Not today, baby girl. It's gonna be a mommy and me day."

"All right!" A grin splits her face, and she jumps up and down at the door as I unlock it. "Can we watch My Little Pony?"

"We can watch whatever you want as soon as Mommy makes a couple phone calls."

She drops her bookbag on the floor and races back toward her room to change out of her school uniform. My briefcase slides to the floor next to it, and I make a quick call to the school and then work to let them know I won't be in today before I dial Savage.

"Storm? What's up? If you're calling about the suggested plan changes to the club we talked about the other day, Gabe and I are meeting with Landon at the site today to take a look at a few things."

Simply hearing his name sends heat spreading out from between my legs.

Aww hell.

That is *so* not a good sign.

"Great, but that's not why I'm calling. I'm wondering if you can talk to your security guy sitting outside my house and see if he saw anything suspicious last night or early this morning."

Silence greets me on the other end of the line, and a cold unease slithers up my spine.

"Storm, what do you mean?" Savage's voice is hard and concern laces each word.

"I just went outside with Angel to take her to school and the tires were slashed on the car. I'm still parking outside because I haven't had time to clean out the garage. I'm sure it's only neighborhood kids or whatever, but I thought maybe your guy saw something."

"What do you mean *my guy*?"

Goose bumps pebble my skin. "You know, the security guy you've had following me the last couple weeks."

He mumbles something low and unintelligible to someone. Probably Gabe. "Storm, I don't have anyone on you."

Huh?

"What do you mean? You told me you were hiring security for everyone after Dom died."

He sighs, and my hand clenches around the phone. "We did, but after a couple months, when nothing happened and everything seemed calm, we called them all off. So, that begs the question, who's been following you?"

Shit.

Maybe it's nothing. Maybe I'm merely imagining it.

I walk to the window and pull back the curtain. A glance up and down the street reveals the black car is gone now.

"Why do you think someone has been following you?"

"There was a black sedan. I've seen it a couple times."

"How many times? And where?"

I wrack my brain, trying to go over everywhere I've been the last couple weeks and where I remember seeing the car.

"I'm not entirely sure. Maybe four times. Near my office once...maybe when I came to the club to talk to you a couple weeks ago. There was a black car that drove past Mom's as I arrived the other night. And now this morning parked on the street."

Savage growls. "Is it still there?"

"No. It was about two blocks down from the house but it's gone. One other time was when I was dropping Angel off at school. It was behind me for a couple blocks but then drove past me when I stopped to drop her off. So, maybe they weren't following me at all? All I know is I noted a black car and remember thinking I'd seen it before, and I assumed it was someone you'd hired. Again, maybe I'm overreacting. There are probably a hundred black sedans like that in town."

Nothing about it stood out. I'm not even sure why I noticed it in the first place. If Savage and Gabe hadn't warned us to be more vigilant, I probably wouldn't have noted it at all. Before the fire, before everything that went down with Stone and Dom, we were living in a damn bubble, totally oblivious to what was happening right under our noses. The danger was so close, we even let it into our homes.

I shake my head at the memory of Dom holding a giggling Angelina and handing her a birthday present three years ago.

God, we were so clueless.

"Everything that's happened is making me a little paranoid and jumpy. It's nothing, Savage. Don't worry."

"You're not being paranoid. You're being observant. It's a good thing. Gabe and I are going to look into this more. Did you see the driver?"

I think back again. "It had tinted windows, but I know I saw a man at least once."

"Okay. You call me right away if you see the car again. Make sure you're watching for it or any other car following you or anything else suspicious, and report the tires to the police."

I release a long sigh. I don't want to deal with the cops today, but he's probably right. It's better to document it in case something else happens.

"Okay, I will."

"Are you and Angelina going anywhere today?"

"No, I called her in sick to school."

"Good. If there is something more to it, being at home is probably the safest place for you."

That damn chill returns, and a shiver rolls through me. Savage tends to overreact and be a little overprotective at times, but his concern here rankles me. After Dom betrayed us and Gabe ended him, no one knew what the fall-out would be, how his minions would react, so I understood the worry. But Savage's obvious distress here, with something that could just as easily be a coincidence, only reminds me of the very real dangers out there.

"Do you think I should be worried?"

He's silent for a few moments before he finally responds. "Honestly, I don't know. Everything's been so peaceful. Gabe and I are pretty sure none of Dom's men are dumb enough to act out against us after what happened. I don't know why they would start up now with you, and not me or Gabe or even Stone."

Exactly what I'm wondering. They are the logical targets. Not me.

"Just be observant and let us know if anything comes up."

"I will."

I end the call and drop onto the couch.

Shit. What the hell is going on?

It's nothing more than some neighborhood kids being hooligans.

I have to believe that. I don't think I could handle it being anything else. Not right now.

Mistake #12,456—ever getting out of bed this morning.

The light rain that's been plaguing us continues, despite the weatherman insisting it was going to clear up by mid-morning. Of course, that means I have to do a site visit.

Karma fucking hates me.

I lean into the backseat to grab my umbrella and step out onto the street in front of what will soon be The Hawkeye Club THREE. A strange tightness forms in my throat, and a melancholy settles over me. This is where Ben and that club manager died.

What was left of the building after the fire has long since been cleared, leaving only the concrete foundation on the lot. Only the basic walls of the structure have started going up, but my mind still creates a picture of how it must have appeared that night. An inferno hot enough to melt glass and destroy lives.

Chris told me he came over the next morning once he heard what happened. He said it was the most devastation he'd ever seen, like a bomb had gone off. And in a way, I guess it did. It was a conflagration that disintegrated everything and everyone in its path and left a wasteland of ashes.

No wonder Storm has completely shut herself off from the world.

Somber, heavy steps carry me to the center of the foundation, and I try to imagine what the new club will look like based on the plans Storm designed and the artist's rendering Savage and Gabe had done of the interior.

It's going to be pretty fucking epic. They truly have gone out of their way, above and beyond, to create a brand for the Hawke clubs, restaurants, and bars. These clubs are about as far from the smoky, trashy joints on Bourbon as can be, and THREE will not be the exception.

Only minor changes are being made to what was originally standing here before the fire, and once we settle on this Champagne room issue, the project should move forward quickly, with the exterior going up in a matter of weeks.

A car door slams, and I turn to find Gabe approaching through the drizzle.

"No Savage?"

Gabe shakes his head. "Can't today. He had something he had to take care of."

Those words are ominous. Savage and Gabe go together like cigars and good Scotch. I haven't been here long, but whenever I've had to speak with them, they've always been together, and from what Chris tells me, they are more or less attached at the hip unless Savage is with his wife and kid.

"Is something wrong?"

Gabe considers me for a second, like he's deciding whether or not I'm a douchebag or someone trustworthy enough to discuss whatever is happening with. Those green eyes tear into me, delving somewhere deep into my soul.

A shudder rolls through me, and not from the slight chill of the rain. No, it's the cold, calculating look in Gabe's eyes—the one that promises he could kill me in less than two seconds flat without even breaking a sweat.

How the fuck does he do that?

When he releases me from his gaze, I heave out a sigh of relief. He gives me his back as he examines the foundation. "Storm's tires were slashed on her car this morning."

What the hell?

Every fiber of my being screams for me to go to her to make

sure she's okay, but it's not my place. And Gabe doesn't know anything about us. That's the way she wants it.

So, instead of racing to my car and flooring it across town, I school my features and wait for him to turn back to me.

"Oh, my God. Is she okay? Does she know who did it?"

Gabe brushes past me toward the back of the concrete slab. "She's fine, and no. She doesn't know. She decided to keep Angel at home today just in case something was going on."

A tiny bit of relief floods my system.

"You think this has anything to do with...well...you know?" Mentioning the man who was like an uncle to the Hawkes, who then tried to kill almost all of them and did kill Ben, by name seems sacrilegious, especially in this place.

Those shrewd eyes assess me over his shoulder. "I sure as hell hope not." He turns away from me and heads toward the rear of the building. "Show me exactly where the new back entrance would be. I know you pointed it out on the plans, but I like to visualize in person."

"Yeah, of course."

His abrupt change of topic clearly screams that any discussion of the Storm situation is closed.

The patter of rain drops fall harder on my umbrella, but it doesn't seem to bother Gabe. We wander around, and I point out a couple different options to him.

"I think your first suggestion is the best. That's pretty much where I had visualized it and where I think it's the least conspicuous and easiest to staff with security so they could still be utilized in other areas as well."

"So, you're giving me permission to make the change?"

"Yeah." He nods. "Make sure Storm knows so we can get the permits ready."

I nod my agreement and follow him back toward our cars on the street.

Good, that gives me an excuse to see her.

Climbing into my car without getting soaked is almost impossible, but when I get my umbrella tossed in the back and right myself in the seat, I dig my phone from my pocket, pull up her number, and hit "send."

It rings a few times before her voicemail picks up.

"Hello, you've reached the voicemail of Storm Matthews. I can't answer the phone right now. Please leave a name, number, and the reason for your call, and I will return your message as soon as I can. Thank you."

So direct and professional. So unlike the Storm bent over the table the other day.

That's her problem. She's forced herself to detach so she'll never feel hurt again. Maybe so she'll never feel anything again.

I understand that inclination more than anyone—the need for separation. The need to build up a wall to protect your heart. But that doesn't mean ignoring how good it is between us. I just need her to understand and accept that having sex doesn't have to mean having a relationship.

Maybe what I said to her the other day got through to her, but the fact I haven't heard from her since means I'm not holding my breath.

Beep.

"Storm, this is Landon. I just met with Gabe out at the site. He told me about your car. Hope you're okay. Please let me know if there's anything I can do. I wanted to update you on the project. He approved the design change officially, and he wants to go with the door and hallway immediately in the middle with the champagne rooms on either side along with private entrances in the back as well. Give me a call to confirm...and again, call if there's anything I can do...*anything at all.*"

My final words have me cringing slightly as I slide the phone back into my pocket. I hope the innuendo wasn't too strong. I'm really trying not to pressure. She just has to know I'm here and willing to take whatever she's going to offer.

Storm is a force, a strong-willed woman, and she's not going to let me talk her into anything she doesn't want.

But I can already tell she's going to be stubborn about accepting what's right in front of her.

Good thing I like a challenge.

thirteen

Storm? Mr. McCabe is on his way back to see you."

I jerk up from the plans spread out before me on the drafting table and glance to my open office door behind me. "Which Mr. McCabe?"

"Landon."

Double shit.

My position over the table suddenly seems completely inappropriate. It's only been two days, but I must've thought about what he did to me here a million times already and wanted it again just as many times.

"I'm sorry, Storm. He just walked right past me with a wave."

I don't even have time to respond to her before he appears in the doorway looking sexy as hell in dark blue jeans and a light blue button-down shirt. And wearing that damn smirk.

"Hello, Storm."

Shit. Shit. Shit. I'm so not ready for this.

You would think a couple days would have given me time to consider what happened and rationally come up with a way to handle the inevitable awkwardness that will forever exist between us, but instead, I spent that time remembering the feel of his hands, his lips, his cock...

My vibrator got more work the last two nights than it has the last six months.

And now he's invading my space again, making my office feel a quarter of its size.

I need some sort of barrier between us, so I walk to my desk and drop into the chair. He saunters over toward me and stands in front of the massive piece of furniture. At least over here, with the desk between us, he can't get to me with his light, brushing touches. The only thing that can reach me is that damn smile.

Although, that might be enough.

No.

"I'm sorry, Landon." My eyes immediately track over to the table. "We can't do...what happened the other day...it can't..."

He grins and holds up a large paper bag I hadn't even noticed he was carrying. "I just thought you might like lunch. But it *is* nice to hear that you're thinking about what we did. I sure have."

He brought me lunch?

That's so sweet.

If he were a total dick, it would make saying no to him again that much easier.

He sets the bag down on my desk and reaches inside, coming out with a black plastic take-out container and a bundle of plastic silverware. "I went to The Trolley Stop Cafe. I got you a reuben." He holds it out for me.

How in the hell did he know that's my favorite?

I reach out to grab the container, and my fingers brush against his. Every single touch of his hand from the other day comes flooding back to me. My skin heats, and my clit throbs. I shift to press my legs together and look away from him before he can catch the instant lust one simple, innocent stroke of my skin can apparently create in me.

"Thank you. I appreciate it."

He shrugs and winks. "You're welcome."

Christ. Why is that wink so adorable?

He reaches into the bag and pulls out another container then drops into the chair across from me.

"You're staying?"

Humor flickers in his eyes, softening the amber brown with flecks of gold. "Don't look so terrified. I promise not to try to seduce you."

I scowl.

That's exactly what he did at Mom's house and here.

Although, I didn't really fight him either time, nor did I want to. Not really. The two sides warring inside me are threatening to tear me apart. Being with him the other day...being touched, being kissed, being fucked...it made me feel *alive* for the first time since Ben died.

And all the feelings that's brought up—the pleasure and the guilt—are so tangled together in my head, I don't know if I'll ever unravel it all. It would be easier to close the door on what's going on with Landon than to confront it all.

I pull out my sandwich and take a bite.

Mmm. Fuck, that's good.

It's always been my favorite place to sneak out to for lunch. And in fact, I was just there Monday before Landon showed up. He must have seen the take-out container in the garbage can and figured it out. Sneaky. And really rather sweet.

He takes a bite of his salad and chews while I work on my sandwich.

The comfortable silence is finally broken when he clears his throat. "I met with Gabe yesterday at the site, and he okayed the changes to the plans we talked about. I left you a message, but I didn't hear back so I thought I would just drop by today to get things straightened out."

Does he mean the plans? Or what happened between us?

Best to go with the more professional answer here. "Yeah, sorry I didn't call you back. I had kind of a weird day yesterday."

He nods and takes another bite of what appears to be a Caesar salad. "Gabe told me about your car. You okay?"

I shrug off the concern in his voice. "Yeah, I'm fine. I'm sure it was just some neighborhood kids getting into trouble. I'm really not that worried about it." I have enough things on my mind. The man sitting in front of me being one of them. What some stupid teenagers decide to do for fun doesn't need to be another.

Don't worry until there's something to worry about. That's my new motto.

One of his light eyebrows rises. "Is Angelina okay? That must've been scary to see."

His concern for Angel makes my heart swell and has one side of the war inside my head suddenly advancing. The side that's all about hooking up with Landon again.

"She's all right. She didn't realize what happened and just thought that the car was broken. We stayed in and watched movies and made popcorn and had a mommy daughter day so she thought that was pretty great, actually."

A tiny smile lights up his face. "That's nice. What did the police say when you reported it? Are there any other incidents in the neighborhood?"

I shake my head and swallow the bite in my mouth. "No, they said that mine was the only incident that has been reported, but that doesn't necessarily mean other things haven't happened. Some people choose not to report. Honestly, I might not have if it wasn't for everything else that happened."

The things I am never going to talk about, especially with Landon.

But it appears I don't have to go into the specifics. He gives a knowing nod. Chris has probably filled him in on everything about Dom and what went down over the past two years. I'm sure he doesn't know some of the particulars, but he knows enough to understand the very real danger to all of us that once existed.

"Well, I'm glad you at least reported it to the police. Make sure you're vigilant and on-watch for anything else."

"Of course." I snort-laugh. "Like Gabe and Savage would ever let me forget that."

He smirks and takes another bite of his salad. "Yeah, Gabe seems a little...what's the word? Intense?"

I grunt out a laugh. "Intense is an understatement. He's a former Army Ranger. He was one of their best snipers. He is hypervigilant about everything. I don't blame him after everything that happened."

I take another bite of my lunch and toss the empty container into the bag. I was so hungry, I basically inhaled it while talking with Landon without even noticing it.

Real ladylike.

Landon finishes his salad and sets the empty container on the chair next to him. He watches me intently, though I'm not sure what he's waiting for.

I clear my throat. "Is there anything else we need to discuss?"

He chuckles softly and leans forward, putting his elbows on his knees and dropping his face into his hands. The position is so relaxed, so comfortable, so completely opposite of how I'm feeling right now.

How can he act so casual after what we did?

Mistake #13,589—thinking I could ever be in the same room with him again and remain professional.

My eyes drift toward the drafting table again, and when I drag them back to him, he offers me a knowing grin.

Shit.

Busted.

She's thinking about what happened just as much as I am. Reliving every kiss. Every touch. Every movement of our bodies together.

And that's a good sign.

I would hope I'm not forgettable and it's not every day she

gets fucked like that. If I am or if it is, then I've greatly misjudged her and the spark between us.

The sex was...incredible. I haven't been able to stop thinking about how hot and tight she was, the drag of my cock against her clasping body, her moans, the way she responded to me so magnificently.

So unlike the women I've been with recently. It was a real connection and coming together of two people who moved as one.

My cock wakes, and I have to shift to avoid strangling it with my zipper.

Shit. Thinking about it again isn't the best move right now.

All I want is to take a little bit of the stress off her, to give her a way to release and enjoy something in life. To find that little bit of relief I did through carnal pleasure. She's so tense, I sometimes wonder if she ever remembers what it feels like to let go.

She certainly did the other day, but will she do it again? Will she *let* herself have some damn fun?

Letting go has been the only thing keeping me sane the last couple months, so I speak with authority when I say I know it would help her. Sex is so primal, such a basic human need. The connection. The release. Without it, we wither into shells of pent-up sexual need and frustration. Coupled with the anger and emotional baggage she must carry after how Ben died, I'm confident she's a woman on the edge of a total breakdown.

I can help her. If she'll only let me.

Storm holds her bottom lip between her teeth as her gaze returns to mine. A war rages in her blue eyes. I can't remember a single time I've seen them where they didn't remind me of watching a hurricane come crashing to shore. I haven't experienced one in person yet, but watching them on television was enough to understand their power, to feel their force.

Those eyes search mine, and she releases her bottom lip. "Can I be honest?"

Yes! Finally!

"That's all I want, Storm. Honesty. I've been one hundred percent honest with you about what I want. I think I know what you want, too. But I don't think you're being honest with yourself, or me."

She considers me for a moment and twirls a strand of her dark hair around her finger. "This is all a little awkward for me. I've never done...anything like that before."

I chuckle and glance over my shoulder to the drafting table. "What? Have sex in your office?"

Her head shakes back and forth, and she releases a sigh as a blush creeps slowly up her neck. "This is going to sound crazy. Yes, have sex in my office. But also..." She trails off and takes a deep breath. "I've never had a one-night stand or random sex before."

Damn. I wasn't expecting that. Should I be proud?

"Really?" I straighten back up. Storm's a gorgeous woman. I can't imagine boys weren't chasing after her like crazy in high school and college. Not that I thought she was a slut, but she must surely have been with at least a handful of people. "I can appreciate that you've been careful with your sexual partners in the past."

She sighs and a longing sadness overtakes her face. "I wasn't just careful. Ben's the only other person I've ever slept with."

Well, shit.

Any air left in my lungs just got knocked out by her confession. That sure puts a whole new light on how she's been acting. I can see now how what happened here the other day would throw her off totally. "Jesus. You should've said something."

She furrows her brow and runs a hand back through her hair. "Yeah? When would have been the appropriate time to tell you? When you were kissing me outside my mom's house? When I was bent over the damn table with your cock inside me? I mean, there are so few people I ever told that to. And I certainly don't think it's appropriate to bring up when you're about to get fucked."

For some reason, I laugh. It just flows out of me before I can stop it. She scowls at me, and I hold up my hands. "I'm sorry. I'm not laughing at you. It's just the whole thing...I don't know. It's hard to wrap my head around it."

I've never been promiscuous. Until recently, I was anything but. When I was with someone, I was with someone. But only *one* partner at age thirty? It's just...unique in this world.

"I'm sure it is. For someone like you who has probably had a hundred sexual partners, anything other than random sex is likely a foreign concept."

Ouch. A hundred partners? That hurt.

I guess meeting at a sex party could give her that impression, but the fact that she thinks I'm incapable of commitment or love still stings. Not wanting something is a whole lot different than not being capable of it.

"You're not the only person who has lost someone."

Her eyes narrow on me as she tries to disassemble my words. I have no intention of getting into my sordid history with her. It's in the past...mostly...and I don't want to relive it. Nor is it relevant to what we could have together.

Being burned has left me jaded, but it doesn't affect my ability to engage in some hot, mindless sex with a beautiful, willing woman.

"From where you sit, it probably looks like I'm some sort of playboy gallivanting around and banging random women left and right. But the truth is, I'm just at a point in my life where I'm not looking for anything serious. That doesn't mean it's a foreign concept. I've just made a choice to avoid emotional attachments. And frankly, I don't think you are looking for anything serious either, right?"

She doesn't answer immediately, and her eyes drift down to something on her desk instead of at me.

The silence draws out to the point that it's uncomfortable.

Maybe it was a bad idea to push this conversation, but I'm not the type of person to sit back. Storm seems to have had her head in the sand and has ignored life since she lost Ben. I can understand that reaction, but it isn't healthy. It's why I left home. I knew what I was doing there, who I was becoming, wasn't right. It wasn't me.

I tap my fingers on my leg and glance at the clock.

Is she even going to say anything? Or am I going to have to get up and walk out of here with everything left unsaid hanging between us?

When she looks up, the blue in her eyes has softened, but the sadness and uncertainty still lingers there. "Is it really that easy?"

"What?"

She glances toward the open door then returns her eyes to me. "Casual sex."

I shrug and hold my hands out. "It is for me. I want you to know that I've been tested, and I'm totally clean. And despite how it looks, I *have* been careful about my partners. I wasn't picking up random women in bars and fucking them."

The sex parties were my only foray into the commitment-less sex arena in recent years, and they were always classy and well-managed. I never once felt like things weren't in total control at them, and the partners I chose were fewer than she thinks.

Storm goes silent again and twirls her hair around her finger. A nervous habit I doubt she knows she has.

Damn, she's adorable.

It reminds me of the girls from high school when they were crushing on someone and too shy to do anything about it.

I rise to my feet. "Look...you know what I want. You know what you want. Figure out if what we want can be mutually beneficial. And let me know when the revised plans are completed and you've talked to your guy with the city."

Don't push her, Landon. She has to come to you when she's ready.

I'm tempted to lean across the desk to give her a kiss, but I don't want to force anything, not when she's on the verge of making the decision to dive into this...let's just call it "friends-with-benefits" situation.

The bag crinkles when I grab it off the desk. I take a quick peek back as I walk to the door. She isn't expecting it, and she can't manage to hide the fact that she's watching me with great interest and the tiniest of smiles at the corners of her mouth.

I've got her.

fourteen

Heat licks at my skin, enveloping me and sending sweat trickling between my breasts. An inferno rages around me, cocooning me, searing me. Yet something cool accompanies it...a scent. Crisp. Clean. Fresh. Familiar.

Large hands wrap around my waist and haul me back against hard flesh.

My core throbs and clenches, desperate for something...for him. My hands grip at strong muscle. A lean, solid body. Something so real.

My body screams for me to turn around; to take his face in my hands and inhale every single breath he offers; to kiss those perfect lips; to stroke that perfect...

"Mommy?"

Huh?

I jerk awake and blink into the dark room. My chest heaves, and I struggle to suck in a deep breath.

Angelina stands at the foot of the bed, the ragged bunny Ben gave her right before he died clutched under her arm. The pinkish streaks down her cheeks from her tears might as well be knives being driven straight into my heart.

Shit.

"Yeah, baby. What's wrong?"

"I had a bad dream."

Most nights, I can sympathize. The burning of my skin is usually due to being surrounded by flames and the sweat from running for my life through an inescapable conflagration. The dream never changes, not once since Ben died. I jerk awake when the fire finally reaches me, my skin searing, the agony consuming me and stealing my final breath.

But tonight...

God.

It was so different.

So real.

So damn good.

About as far from a nightmare as possible. I have to shake off the lust-induced fog from my brain and push myself to a sitting position. "Come on up."

Angel climbs up the foot of the bed and crawls over. She still looks like a baby to me. Even though she's five, all I can see is that tiny pink bundle we brought home to our first shitty little apartment.

The baby we were wholly unprepared for. The daughter I was terrified I was going to fail with.

Who I am failing with.

I flip back the covers, and she slides in, snuggling down next to me with her head against my shoulder. Soft black hair falls across her forehead, and I brush it back with my fingertips. "Are you okay? Want to tell me about the dream?"

Her pain breaks me. Eyes so much like Ben's stare back at me in the dim moonlight streaming in from the window. She shakes her head. "Nuh-uh."

I can't say I blame her. There's no way I'd want to talk about my nightmares with anyone either. Or the not-so-nightmare I just had.

What the hell do I do with that?

Nothing right now. The only thing that matters is Angel and what she needs, not what my traitorous body wants.

"Would it help if we went out on the porch and saw Mittens?"

The corners of her mouth tip up slightly. It's not really a smile, but it's a good start.

There's something about that cat. I swear, for a seven-pound bundle of fur, she has the uncanny ability to soothe whatever ache may be plaguing you.

Angel's tiny head nods, and I return her smile.

"Okay, then. Grab some shoes and let's head out there."

I throw back the covers, and Angel slides out the other side of the bed and races off toward her room, bunny in tow.

The clock tells me it's only 4:15. Getting an early start might not be such a bad thing for me. More time to catch up on all my neglected work, but it means Angel will be exhausted all day in school. I doubt I can get her back to sleep now even if I tried though.

It's going to be another one of those days.

I tug on my robe and slip into a pair of flip-flops before I meet Angel at the back door. The moment I slide the glass door open, she bounds out onto the deck and into the yard.

"Mittens! Come here, Mittens!"

In the darkness of the early morning, everything seems so peaceful, so quiet. So far from what the rush of everyday life feels like. Maybe this is the time of day I should be awake for.

It wouldn't matter.

Mistake #14,534—thinking things will change for the better.

I'm doing my best to push through this wall, to set aside my internal turmoil to ensure Angel and I are both in a good place, but the weight of the responsibility, the sheer will it takes to move ahead every day, is starting to crush me again. It comes in waves like this, threatening to overwhelm me. And between the tire incident and what happened with Landon, the guilt that's been clawing at me since that day, I'm damn near close to going under the surface again.

But Skye and Stone aren't going to let it happen. And I'm positive Savage had a role in that little intervention too, even though he wasn't here in person. He's the driving force behind everything in this family, it seems. Even more so than Mom sometimes.

I love him and hate him for it, but it's kept the family together through a lot of really awful shit over the years. And it will continue to. Even this.

A black shape emerges from the bushes, and if it weren't for the white socks on her paws, it would be almost impossible to see her. She approaches Angel slowly at first, then picks up her pace until Angel scoops her up and turns back to the deck.

She settles into the porch swing with the cat on her lap, and I slide in beside her and set us in motion.

The call of a sparrow rings out, and tears burn in my eyes.

Ben always slept like shit. There were so many nights and early mornings I would find him sitting out here with a book or a cup of coffee. And more than anything, the sound of the sparrows that nest in the yard always accompanied our time on the patio. It was the song that created the music for that tiny portion of our lives.

"You hear them? The sparrows?" His soft-spoken words easily reach me in the still and silence of the morning.

"Yeah."

"Their song always reminds me of home. Of being here with you and Angel."

Yet another thing I'll never be able to forget. Another memory that will haunt me and this place. I swipe away the tears that fall before Angelina can see them.

How do people do this, day in and day out? How do they survive?

Mittens purrs, and I turn my watery vision to Angel. She snuggles into my side with the cat content on her lap, and the lazy motion of the swing lulls any lingering bad feelings from her dream.

Within minutes, she's asleep and so is the fur ball. I wish I could sleep like that.

But something tells me nothing will ever be easy for me again. Especially when Landon is now haunting my dreams and walking around in my daily life.

How do I stop the longing? How do I stop the guilt? How do I stop the pain?

It seems impossible. And maybe it is. But something in his words...the offer of freedom from everything that's weighed me down for so long with no strings attached...it sits at the front of my mind, urging me to push aside the guilt if only for a few moments.

Can I ever really manage that?

I slam the locker door shut just as my phone shrills in my pocket. It's still early, not even seven. "Who the hell would be calling me this early?"

Dealing with problems on a project at the ass-crack of morning isn't on my agenda. The swim helped relax some of the tension from my body, so I don't want it all to return right away.

But a smile crosses my face when I see the number. "Just the man I've been waiting for. Any luck?"

I never thought I'd actually be anticipating and looking forward to a call from a lawyer, but desperate times and all. The man holds my life in his—supposedly—capable hands, so anytime he calls, it's the potential for the closure I so desperately need.

Barry sighs. The old codger is probably sitting in his over-sized leather chair in his office on Michigan Avenue with his feet up just counting the minutes of this call and calculating how much he can charge me for it. "Sorry, Landon. I don't have good news. My investigator can't seem to find her. Do you have any idea where she could have gone?"

My hand shakes, and I growl. "He can't find her? She literally goes three places every day. How can she just disappear?"

I thought this would be taken care of by now. When we spoke last week, things were in motion. An end was in sight.

Now, it's like a sledgehammer has been smashed into my plans to leave that world and the people in it behind.

"I know. She hasn't been at the condo for at least a week. At least, not when he's been there, and he sat on it for multiple hours. She hasn't been to the gym. She hasn't been to the salon either."

"In over a week?"

"Yes."

Shit.

That certainly is strange. She's always been so predictable. It was one of the things I liked about her. Things were...easy. Comfortable. Happy. She was one of those easy women who was quick with a smile and went along with the flow without raising too much of a fuss.

"Did you talk to any of her friends?"

"That's what I have him doing now."

I slam my fist against the locker, then immediately regret it as pain spreads through it and up my arm. "Dammit, Barry. I need to find her."

I can't do anything without her. I can't move forward while she's keeping one of my feet in Chicago. If we can't find her...

No, don't even think about that.

She will turn up. Eventually. She has to.

"I know. I'll keep looking."

"Call me back when you have something."

I stomp past the reception area of the gym and shove open the door into the crisp morning air. This is my favorite time of day, before the sun gets too hot to be outside. I always thought summers in the Midwest were bad, but nothing compares to the heat and humidity here. I'm sure I'll adjust, but right now, being outside during the day feels like suffocating and drowning all at once.

And now this bad news...just when things are starting to look up with Storm.

Mother fucker.

I toss my bag into the backseat and climb into my car. So reminiscent of when I left home. Now, it feels like ages ago instead of only weeks. Settling here permanently has started to sound more and more appealing. I would love to say it's because Chris offered me the job, one I've easily slid into and am enjoying. But mostly, it's because I met Storm. She's what I need. Hot, sweaty sex sessions without attachment or emotion. The parties are great, but having a go-to person—someone who knows what you like and want and you know the same for them—that's when things get good. We can have that. And she's *this close* to accepting that as the truth.

Things back home need to get resolved. Fast. I want that life in my rearview permanently.

I only have fifteen minutes to make it over to meet Chris at the site of the new industrial office building we're the general contractors on over on Tchoupitoulas Street. It's another project he's wants me to take over. I don't mind doing the walk-through with the sub-contractors today. Working gets my mind off all the bullshit going on.

How can she just disappear?

Acid churns in my stomach, and my knuckles whiten around the steering wheel. It's possible this is on purpose. I wouldn't put it past her. But something tells me it's more than that. Something is very wrong.

Chris is waiting outside the building when I pull up to the curb. He frowns and glances at his watch. "Cutting it a little close, aren't you?"

I check my watch as I slam the door. "I'm two minutes early. If you wanted me here ten minutes ago, you should have said to be here then."

He scowls and tosses his hands up. "Where were you?"

"The gym. And then Barry called."

An eyebrow raises as I join him on the walk up to the door. "Good news?"

"I wish."

It feels like all I've had for months is bad news. What does a guy have to do to catch a damn break? I don't think I've done anything to piss off Lady Karma, or God, or whatever force controls the universe. But it's been one thing after another.

He opens the door and ushers me in front of him. The entire building buzzes with the sounds of tools and shouting of the workmen. "What's wrong?"

"She's gone." I stop and turn to face him in the foyer.

His brow furrows, and he shakes his head. "What do you mean gone?"

"I mean Barry's investigator can't find her. She hasn't been to the condo, or the gym, or the salon."

It's like she's vanished into thin air. Whether intentionally or not, it throws a major wrench in my plans.

His eyes narrow on me. "Don't hate me for asking this, but have you considered asking Dad?"

The suggestion has me curling my hands into fists. Only extreme personal restraint prevents me from decking him. It certainly wouldn't be the first time I've done it. We used to fight all the time growing up, but we're adults now, and I can't let my anger at someone else come out as violence toward him...no matter how much I want to.

I pace away from him to let my temper cool. If I didn't know I'd have to repair it, I might throw that punch at the fresh drywall I'm staring at. Instead, I shove my hands back through my hair and tug on the ends.

The jolt of pain helps me focus.

Cool it.

My words come out through gritted teeth. "Hell no. I'm not calling him for help. Ever. As far as I'm concerned, he's dead to me."

The man has never given a shit about me. His actions made that clear. Maybe Chris can overlook what he did, but if he were in my shoes, I doubt he'd be all lovey-dovey with the man.

"I'm just sayin', he may know how to get ahold of her."

He might be right, but acknowledging that only adds salt to an already festering wound. I turn back to him and let my eyes meet his. "Not happening. And you aren't going to talk to him about it either. Stay out of this. It's between me and him."

His hands fly up, and he walks away, giving me his back. "Whatever. Then don't complain to me."

Asshole.

I follow him reluctantly to where he stands talking to one of the subs over a makeshift table made of sawhorses and plywood.

Chris points to a spot on the plans. "So, this will be where the reception desk goes. We need to make sure the electrical guys get extra plugs in the floor and wall."

The other man nods then looks up at me. "You must be Landon. I'm Mark Swensen. It's nice to have you on the project."

His handshake is firm, his hands rough. It's been a long time since I got my hands dirty on a job site, but maybe it's time. Doing a little manual labor might be good for me. "Nice to meet you, too. Show me where we're at."

He motions to the plans, and I walk around to join them on the other side of the table.

Getting back to work is good.

Storm agreeing to our arrangement will be even better.

And if Barry's guy can do his damn job, things will be perfect.

fifteen

The young waiter sets my credit card and the receipt on the table next to me and offers a polite smile. "Anything else I can do for you today?"

Give me more hours in the day and half the stress?

I bite back the snippy comment and instead shake my head and return the smile. He doesn't need to be subjected to my mood today. "Nope. I'm good. Thank you."

He gives me a little half-bow and backs away from the table and into the busy restaurant. Eating alone has been one of the many things I've had to get used to that I never would have been caught dead doing before I lost Ben. Our lunches together during the week were always the perfect break in my day, the time I so desperately needed to unwind and have some one-on-one time with him away from Angelina.

I let my eyes drift around the restaurant. Commander's Palace was always one of Ben's favorite places to meet. This morning was rough. The angry call about another project delay left me craving the comfort of somewhere familiar. Some place I shared with him.

Since he's been gone, on the days I have managed to drag myself out of bed and to work, I've found myself holed up in my office eating a protein bar for lunch instead of taking much-needed "me" time...except Monday when I managed to get out for my reuben and when Landon dropped by over the last few days....

After our lunch and chat Wednesday, I assumed—maybe naïvely—that I wouldn't be seeing him again until I had something to tell him about the plan approval, but then...there he was yesterday, standing in my door again with a bag of food in tow.

The man is relentless in his desire to ensure I eat lunch, and that I'm constantly reminded of what he did to me on my drafting table. There's nothing overt. He's being a gentleman about not pressuring me after we had our little conversation the other day, but it's there all the same...

Just thinking about the effortless smiles he flashes and the way his eyes roam over me in appreciation have heat spreading up my neck and over my cheeks. And that's not all he does.

Somehow, despite my best effort to keep him at arm's length, he manages to break through the wall of pain surrounding me to release little bits of the old me—the one who laughed, the one who smiled, the one who enjoyed life. I'd almost forgotten the sound of my own laugh, but over the last week, it's come often and effortlessly when we've been together. Even when we're discussing project plans, there's a quick joke or endearing comment that momentarily makes the pain and tension disappear.

That's the most terrifying part of it all and the very reason I've spent today trying to convince myself our little office interlude meant nothing, that *he* means nothing. Because the alternative just isn't possible.

Not now. Not ever.

Lunch somewhere that was mine and Ben's reminds me why it can't ever happen. Because I will *always* be his.

I sign the receipt, grab my purse, and make for the door.

It was nice to get out today, a much-needed break from the memories my office now holds, but it's time to return to the suffocating piles of unfinished plans laid out across my drafting table and desk.

"Storm?"

There's no need to even turn around. I'd know that low, sultry voice anywhere. The way he says my name like a reverent prayer goes straight to all the parts of me I should be ignoring in favor of what my head says.

But there's no denying my attraction to Landon, and there's no ignoring the fact he said my name and is standing behind me just inside the door.

Of all the restaurants in this city...what are the chances?

I take a deep breath intended to center me and turn to face him. Any calm it gave me disappears the moment my eyes meet his smoldering bourbon ones, and the corner of his mouth ticks up in a lop-sided grin.

Shit. I am in so much trouble.

A few steps are all that separate us, but even across the tiny space, need and tension vibrate between us.

I clear my throat to remove the giant knot there. "Landon. What are you doing here?"

He grins and steps up to me, stopping a little too close to be appropriate in public. "I just had lunch with a prospective new client." His eyes sweep over me and linger on my exposed cleavage a second before returning to my face. "This is a pleasant surprise."

It certainly is.

I hadn't realized how badly I wanted to see him. And hell, if that truth doesn't make my stomach swim and my heart ache.

It's wrong. I shouldn't be feeling like this about a man I barely know. I shouldn't have let him kiss me...let him touch me...let him fuck me...let him get under my skin and into my head the way he has. It isn't fair to Ben...to what we had.

One of his light eyebrows rises. "Do you have a little time before you have to head back to the office?"

I narrow my eyes on him and the little smirk playing at his lips. "It depends on what you have in mind."

If he suggests finding somewhere private...

Hell. I don't know what I would do.

Half of me wants to throw myself at him and the other half

wants to tuck my tail between my legs and run to go hide in that black hole I've created for myself.

A deep rumbling chuckle flows from his mouth, and he leans in until his warm breath tickles my ear. "I don't know what you're thinking, Storm. But you just turned the most beautiful shade of pink. So, I have an idea."

Christ. Damn my pale skin and inability to hide my reaction to this man.

He pulls back and runs his hand over the light stubble covering his chin. "I was going to take a walk down Coliseum and Prytania to see some of the houses. Would you like to join me?"

Bad idea, Storm.

"Yes."

There was no doubt how I was going to answer. Not only does the man make me melt with his near presence, but he also shares my love of the beautiful architecture in the city.

Does he have any flaws at all?

I sure as hell haven't seen any. The man is offering me sex without strings. Enjoyment in life where there has been so little for so damn long. A way to forget all the pain and longing that's dominated every minute since Ben died.

Why am I fighting it so hard?

Landon holds his arm out to me in invitation, and I slip mine through it and let him lead me from the restaurant and out onto the bustling sidewalk. He turns us to the northeast up Coliseum and pats my arm with his free hand.

"What's your favorite house in the area?"

I release a sigh and scan the street ahead of us. "That's an impossible question to answer. That's like asking a parent to pick their favorite child."

He smirks and shakes his head. "Not quite. You didn't design any of these."

"True, but they are all so beautiful and majestic in their own unique ways. I couldn't possibly choose just one. I love different things about all of them."

Truth be told, the buildings in this town have always been a huge source of inspiration for my designs. The history here is inescapable, the old mixed in with the new, and while many architects are designing modern high-rises and glass and metal structures, my heart lies in the classic designs of the past. And it shows in every single building I've worked on—for better or for worse.

"I feel the same way about Chicago. There are so many gorgeous buildings there. Ones far ahead of their time in size and design. I used to go downtown and just walk to clear my head sometimes. Something about the structures, the art they are, and the way they still stand tall despite all the years and progress around them, has always soothed my soul."

My breath catches in my throat, and I have to force my feet to keep moving. His words could have come straight from my mouth, and they work to further chip away at the armor of fear and pain keeping me from letting him in.

We're the same in so many ways.

What are the chances of finding two men in a lifetime who share the same passion? Does it even matter?

I can't let the way my body reacts to him or the fact I find him incredibly charming, intelligent, and kind overwhelm the one very real reason I need to stay away.

Keeping feelings out of sex may be possible for a lot of people, but I've never done it, and I don't know that I can. I don't know how *anyone* does it.

What if he develops feelings for me? Ones I can never return.

If he ever wanted more than the friends-with-benefits situation he's offered some time down the road, my heart will never be free to let him in that way.

That's not fair or healthy for either of us.

Storm thinks I didn't catch the way she reacted to my confession about Chicago, but it was impossible to miss. Even now, two blocks later, she remains quiet, stoic, her eyes trained on the buildings, the trees, the people...anywhere but on me.

She's fighting it. And I don't have a single damn idea how to break through that last little wall she has up.

I understand her hesitation. She lost the love of her life, the only man she's ever been with. She has Angelina to care for and the entire Hawke family hovering around her, making sure she's okay and questioning the decisions she's making about her life. That kind of love doesn't happen in every family. It certainly doesn't exist in ours, but it has to be suffocating for her.

If they knew about what we were doing, what we've done, there would undoubtedly be judgment. People are so uptight about sex sometimes. It takes something that's supposed to be simple—a biological imperative—and convolutes it into something that's leaving Storm questioning her attraction to me and feeling guilty when she has no reason to.

It wasn't so long ago I was getting the same judgmental attitudes from my friends back home. Even after everything that happened, the betrayal I suffered, they couldn't accept my decision to move on, to try something new, to put the past in the past. They didn't understand how I could do it so quickly. No one can. Not unless they've been through the same thing. So, I know I can never comprehend the depths of what Storm is suffering. But I can sure as hell try, and I can offer her a release from the tension and anguish she's drowning under.

She deserves that and so much more. But it's all I can give right now, and also probably all she's capable of accepting.

Had we met under better circumstances—before she met Ben, before I trusted the wrong people—things would certainly be much different. She's the type of woman I could give my whole heart to if I were capable.

But I'm not. Not now. Maybe not ever.

That sad truth applies to both of us. It's why this arrangement makes so much sense.

We pause at a corner to wait to cross, and her eyes drift over to meet mine. A question lies in their depths, something she wants to ask but is holding back for some reason.

"What is it?"

She shakes her head slightly as we step out onto the street. "I don't understand. If you love Chicago so much, why did you leave?"

It's the one question I hoped she would never ask, because it's the only one I refuse to answer. I told her I'd always be honest with her and that I was an open book, and that's true about everything but this. That book is very much closed, and not to just her. To everyone. It slammed shut the moment I left the city limits and put the skyline in my rearview.

I wish I could tell her, let her know I do understand loss, even if not on the same level as her, but I can't. Even thinking about voicing the truth of what happened makes my skin crawl and my lunch churn wildly in my stomach. It's bad enough things are being dragged out because of Barry's inability to track down that damn woman. Coming clean with Storm and exposing all my own wounds will only make it worse.

Not going to happen.

We step up on the opposite curb, and I let out a small sigh. "That's a long, complicated, painful personal story. I'd rather not discuss it."

Her arm looped through mine tenses a little.

I hate not being able to be completely honest with her. But truth be told, the wound from what happened is still too raw, too real, too much. Storm is new, and exciting, and a breath of fresh air I hadn't expected to find so quickly, especially with someone carrying so much baggage. And this is only casual. She doesn't need to know my whole sordid history to sleep with me. It's irrelevant and would only taint the way she sees me and what's happening between us.

No one back home looked at me the same once they knew. I was forever "that guy." The one who was too blind. Too stupid. Too busy working to see what was going on right under his nose.

I don't want to be that guy to Storm.

She nods slowly and pulls me to a stop in front of a massive two-story tan house with intricate black wrought-iron balconies. Her head tilts back as she stares up at the second-floor windows and a white rocking chair placed near one of the doors.

I can almost see her sitting here, rocking in the cooling evening air, watching the tourists wander the streets. She fits here. In a house like this. Somewhere with a lot of history and details she can appreciate.

This city fits her, but it's also destroyed her.

"What about you? Would you ever leave New Orleans?"

I wouldn't blame her if she did.

Putting the kind of things that happened to her here behind her would be logical. It's worked for me...so far. And I'll be able to completely close the door on Chicago and that life once Barry comes through for me.

A moment passes where I'm sure she's not going to answer me before she tears her eyes from the house and returns them to me. "No." She shakes her head as I lead her on toward the massive mansion on the corner of Jackson. "I couldn't. New Orleans is home, for better or worse."

Her voice catches on *worse,* and I squeeze her arm as my chest tightens at her emotion.

"But so many terrible things have happened here, to you, to your family, to the city. Don't you ever just want to...I don't know...start over?"

Maybe it's overstepping asking that question, bringing up—even if only vaguely—what happened to Ben and the rest of the Hawkes at the hands of Dom Abello. But now it's out there, occupying the space between us.

She continues walking, but her bottom lip trembles. She pulls it between her teeth for a moment before she releases it and sucks in a deep breath. "One of the best things about this town is its ability to start over. I can't even count the number of times it's been destroyed by something—war, fire, hurricanes—and it pulled itself back up and boomed again. That spirit of revival gives me hope when I really shouldn't have any at all."

I pull her to a stop and turn her to face me. Tears shimmer in her eyes, and I want nothing more than to take away that pain, but her words have struck me square in the chest.

"That's why I'm here, Storm. To start over. To pull myself back up and renew a life that...well, got out of control so fast, I don't even know what happened. But don't you *dare* say you shouldn't have hope. Hope is what keeps us going, even when everything is crumbling around us. Hope for something new. Hope for something better."

She contemplates my words, and a single tear trickles from her eye and down her cheek. I cup her face and brush it away with my thumb, letting my hand linger there against her smooth, pale skin. Her thick, dark hair blows around her in the breeze, and her sorrowful blue eyes scream for me to do something, anything to make it better.

Only one thing comes to mind.

I lean in and press my lips to hers.

The kiss is gentle.

Reverent.

An apology.

A question.

A promise.

I just hope she can see what I'm offering her and accept it for what it is. Even if it can never be something more...

It's hope.

sixteen

This is a bad idea.

I should be at home in bed, not standing outside Landon's building, staring up into the night sky as thunder rolls around me and the clouds threaten to unleash a torrent.

What if he doesn't want to see me? What if he does want to see me?

This shouldn't be so hard. We're both adults. He told me what he wanted. Yet, standing here, about to make a booty call, feels so slutty and wrong. But what Landon did to my body felt so right. And I haven't slept since without dreaming of his touch.

With Angel at Mom's tonight, and after what happened during our walk today, it was just too much to bear anymore. That kiss...it was so gentle. So comforting. So completely non-sexual. Yet it ignited a fire in my soul I haven't been able to quench. A burning desire to be in his arms again. To feel his touch and kiss.

Be an adult. Call him. Go up there. Take what you want. Just keep your heart out of it.

The mental pep-talk doesn't help with my shaking hands or racing heart, but Mother Nature spurs me on by opening up the sky.

Rain falls in a deluge. My clothes soak almost instantly and hair clings to my face.

Shit.

Huddling under the tiny alcove outside his building offers little to no protection as I dial his number.

Please be home.

With each ring, my heart sinks a little more. He's probably out. It's a Friday night—late—and he enjoys a certain type of life-style. One that involves hot, mindless sex. He's not sitting around waiting for me—

"Storm?"

Crap. What was I going to say?

"Uh, hi."

"Is everything okay?"

I'm not entirely sure how to answer that. My heart might beat straight out of my chest, and now I'm shivering in soaking wet clothes outside the apartment of the man I intend to make my... what? Friend with benefits?

"Yeah, but I'm outside your place. Are you home? Can you let me in?"

Lightning streaks across the sky, and almost instantly, thunder cracks close enough to rumble the ground beneath me.

"Jesus. You're outside in this? I'll buzz you in. Come on up. Number 301."

The door buzzes, and I tug it open and step into the warmth of the lobby.

I've never felt, or probably looked, more like a wet dog in my life. Or maybe it's more like a drowned rat?

A puddle forms under where I stand waiting for the elevator.

Real sexy, Storm. Good job.

The elevator doors slide open, and I step inside the car and press three.

Drip. Drip. Drip.

That sound might drive me insane if this ride were any longer, but thankfully, the ding alerts me to my arrival, and the doors slide open.

301 and 302 sit on opposite ends of the long hallway, the only two condos on the floor. Before I even take the first step toward Landon's door, it flies open.

His eyes meet mine and widen, and his eyebrows raise. "Christ, you're soaked. You must be freezing."

I nod and move toward him slowly even though all I want to do is close the distance between us as quickly as possible. His warm, strong arms wrapped around me sounds pretty fucking good right now.

He steps out into the hallway and drapes an arm around me, cocooning me in his heat and leading me into the condo. "Let's get you warmed up."

Was that supposed to be a sexual innuendo? Or is that just wishful thinking?

The door clicks shut behind us, and I pull away so I can turn to face him. As hard as it is, I need to be looking at him to say this, to have this conversation. Looking into someone's eyes gives so much away, things I'd rather keep to myself, hidden beneath whatever false front I can put up, but if I'm going to fuck him, I at least need to be able to tell him that's what I want without my back to him.

He brushes a clump of wet, matted hair from my temple. "I wasn't expecting to see you tonight after the way we left things this afternoon."

We didn't part on bad terms. Far from it, but that kiss sent me spinning. I thought life was confusing before I met Landon. Now that he's here, floating around in my orbit, he's thrown me completely off an already unsteady axis.

"I wasn't expecting to be here."

A grin breaks out across his lips, and he grabs my hand and leads me through the open concept living room and down a hallway past several closed doors.

His bedroom is exactly how I pictured it in my head.

Not that I've been imagining him in his bed...

Shit. Who am I kidding? Of course, I have been.

The large, low bed occupies the middle of the room and matching dark wood furniture fills the rest of the space. It's sleek and modern and yet warm, and it's so Landon.

Thunder rumbles outside, close enough to rattle the windows, and driving rain pings off the glass. The storm perfectly mimics what's happening in my body right now—a dark, tumultuous combination of want and need mixed with lingering guilt I'm desperately trying to push into the background.

He ushers me into the huge, subway-tiled bathroom and releases my hand to reach into the shower and crank on the water before turning to face me again. "I'm going to find something dry for you to put on. I'll be right back."

I don't need clothes!

Screaming that would make me sound like a hussy, though. So, I bite back the words and enjoy the warmth of the room as the steam starts to rise from the shower.

His returning footsteps on the hardwood floors send my heart skittering.

Seriously, what the hell am I doing here?

I'm not built for this. Seduction. That's never been my game. I don't play games. At least, I never have before.

Do I just tell him I want him to fuck me?

Do I do a little striptease to show him what I want?

Do I give up and run out of here and hide away from him forever?

He answers my question by pressing his chest against my wet back and pulling my tangled hair to the side so he can nuzzle my neck. "I don't know why you're here, Storm. But I know why I *want* you to be here."

His words take the stress of not knowing what to say and throws it out the window.

I twist my head back until I can press my lips against his.

The kiss is hot. Wet. Demanding. I moan against him as he turns my body into his. Soaked clothes cling to me, but the heat of his chest and the steam from the shower ensure the shivers racing through me right now are not from the cold.

It's pure, unadulterated need.

Warm hands tug the hem of my shirt up, and I lift my arms to let him peel it from my damp skin. The storm rages outside as the warring emotions in my head and heart continue their battle. This feels so right. It can't be wrong.

His mouth returns to mine, while his hands move to the waistband of my leggings. He pulls away to lean down and roll them off my legs. I grasp his shoulder and switch from foot to foot to help him remove them before he tosses them onto the tile with a wet slap. He rises to his feet and reaches around to unclasp my bra. My breasts fall free, exposed to him for the first time, and he releases a low hum of appreciation.

My heart flutters as his eyes rake over me, and I tug down the straps and toss it to the floor.

Pure lust simmers in his gaze as he brushes a thumb across one pointed nipple, then the other. Then his hands slip into the waistband of my panties, and he slowly lowers them down my legs, letting his fingertips brush gently across my goose-pebbled skin.

He leans forward and places a kiss against my stomach. "Let's get you warm."

God, yes...

He stands, yanks his shirt off, and drops it to the ground. His jeans and boxers join the pile, leaving him gloriously naked and hard in front of me.

Oh, my God.

This is what I missed seeing the other day?

My fingers itch to run along the lines of his hard, lean body and beautiful cock.

He's magnificent.

A shudder runs through me, and he steps forward and takes me into his arms again before walking me backward into the shower stall.

Hot water hits my back, heating my cool skin. I groan in appreciation, and my head drops against his shoulder. He slides his hand across my back as he presses himself against me fully—a wall of muscle holding me up on unsteady legs.

Is it wrong to want him to turn me around, bend me over, and fuck me?

Or is it more wrong that what I really want is for him to just hold me?

The former may be morally questionable, but the latter...

It's downright dangerous.

Don't question it, Landon. Embrace the fact that she showed up. This is her choice. Let her make it.

Having Storm in my arms was the last thing I expected tonight. I've spent almost every night since we met dreaming about her, about what she would look like naked and spread out across my bed...and now, it's finally going to happen. The other day in her office was incredible, but it was hot, hard, and fast. There was no finesse. There was no time to do the things I wanted to with her...to her. There was no way that could happen there. It can here.

My hard cock throbs where it's crushed between our wet bodies. Water cascades down over us, and Storm buries her face into my neck and clings to me.

She's more beautiful than I ever imagined, and there's nothing sexier than a woman knowing what she wants and taking it. Her coming here tonight was a massive step for her. I'm not going to do anything to jinx it. She's calling the shots.

I'm hers to do with what she will...to a point. There are things

I've dreamed about, things I'm not sure I can hold back from now that she's here and willing. I need to taste her, to know the flavor of her release on my tongue, to feel her body bend and bow and have her hands tug at my hair as she comes against my mouth.

I slide my hand under her chin and raise her face to mine. "You warm yet?"

A twinkle sparks in her eyes, and the blue shifts into a darker shade. One I've never seen before.

This is Storm unleashed. This is Storm giving in to what she wants. What she needs.

Me.

It's everything I've been waiting for and what I need to forget everything else and leave it in the past. Someone to lose myself in for a brief moment in time.

"I think there's something else we could do that would work better."

Holy shit.

My cock twitches, and I reach around her to turn off the water. This woman needs to be in my bed and under me immediately.

I climb out of the shower and wrap a towel around my waist before holding one open for her. She steps into my waiting arms. I gently dry her hair as best I can, massaging her head and letting my breath flutter against her neck.

She shivers. Goose bumps break out across her exposed flesh. Every slow, soft stroke of the towel along her wet skin has a soft gasp whispering from her lips. My mouth follows the trail of the towel, pressing kisses across her back, her ass, her thighs, then around to the front of her. Water droplets linger on her breasts, and I lean down and suck a wet nipple between my lips.

She moans and buries her fingers into my hair. "God. Yes."

That's all it takes.

We're dry enough. We will only need another shower after we're done anyway.

I let our towels drop to the floor then scoop her up in my arms. Her surprised shriek echoes against the tile, followed by a soft giggle.

In the brief time I've known Storm, I've never heard her giggle. There has been some laughter, but a *giggle?* That's something entirely different. It means she's carefree. She's not thinking. She's not stuck up in that head of hers.

This is exactly how I want her. How I *need* her if she's going to enjoy this as much as I want her to. My cock throbs, and my heart swells knowing I'm the one who can do this for her. Make her forget. Make us *both* forget.

Laying her down on my bed is truly a wet dream come true. Her damp jet-black hair and alabaster skin spread across the soft gray of the bedspread like some sort of masterpiece. If I were an artist, I would want to capture this image forever. As it is, I'll have to take a mental snapshot, because I'm not waiting any longer.

While the storm rages outside, there's only one thing I set my laser focus on—the Storm in front of me and what I'm going to do to her luscious, willing body.

I drop to my knees and grab her ankles and tug her down to edge of the bed.

She pushes up on her elbows, and the eyes that were only a moment ago so filled with lust and need are now filled with something else.

Fear? Reservation?

Her head shakes, and she shifts back, out of my reach. "No. Come up here and lie down."

Part of me is annoyed and frustrated she won't let me go down on her. I've been fantasizing about how she'll taste, what sounds she'll make coming apart on my tongue. But the other part is more concerned about that look in her eye, and the fact that she won't meet my gaze as I climb up onto the bed and lie back next to her.

I need to let her take control. That's what I said I would do, and she needs that to feel safe with this situation, with me.

She shifts up onto her knees at my side, her focus on my cock resting against my stomach. Her eyes on me, examining how hard I am for her, seeing what she does to me, makes my dick twitch.

Her tongue darts out and across her bottom lip, and her eyes momentarily flick over to mine. The lust has returned, whatever else was there now banished.

I can get behind this. Though I'd much rather have her sitting on my face while she does it.

"If you are thinking what I think you're thinking, then I have one condition."

She frowns and sits back on her heels. "What's that?"

I motion her up toward me. "You're going to let me eat you out while you suck my dick. I've been dying to taste you, and I'm not about to let you have all the fun."

The wink I give her might be a bit over-kill or maybe a little cheesy. But it also apparently does the job. A small smile cracks through her façade, and she shifts up and straddles me backward, placing her hot, wet pussy right in front of my face.

Holy hell.

She's fucking glistening with arousal already, and when she takes my cock in her small hand, her entire body quivers. I grasp her hips and pull her backward, centering her over my greedy mouth.

Her hand tightens and glides up and down my hard flesh. I choke back a groan and snake my tongue out to slide through her core.

Christ. She tastes just as incredible as I imagined.

Warm, wet heat engulfs my cock, and I gasp against her flesh. Her tongue trails along my length as I plunge mine inside her, coating it in her need.

She moans and shifts back slightly, giving me even better

access. I spread her open with my fingers and sink two inside her while my tongue lashes at her clit.

The suction on my cock increases, and she twists her hand around me with every stroke.

Fuck...I'm not lasting.

I need her to come. There's no way I'm not giving her the same release that's barreling down on me. She needs it more than I do.

A curl of my fingers has her gasping around my cock and driving her hips against my mouth and hand. I swirl my tongue around her clit and suck it between my lips.

She moans and redoubles her effort on my throbbing flesh. A tingling burn starts in my balls and works its way up my spine.

Now.

I bite down on her clit, and she cries out, bucking against my face and clenching her pussy around my fingers as she finally detonates. The taste of her release floods my mouth, and she regains enough control to latch back onto my cock while she rides out the orgasm I continue to drag on with my tongue and fingers.

Two sucks and I'm a goner. My hips arch up, and Storm pulls every last drop from my cock and all the pain, all the stress, all the regrets right along with them.

When I collapse onto the bed, Storm licks the head of my dick one last time, then rolls off to the side with her head at my feet and sprawls onto her back.

Wow.

The words to describe what just happened can't seem to form in my foggy brain. All I can focus on is the taste of her on my tongue and the soft pants of our breath mingling together with the sound of the pouring rain and thunder filling the room.

I curl my hand around her warm thigh where it's pressed against mine and squeeze. She shifts slightly but makes no move to turn around so she's facing the same direction.

Silence occupies the space between us. I can't remember a time a woman didn't want to crawl up and snuggle after coming like that. Even the ones who knew it was just a one-night thing.

Is she pissed? Was it not good for her? Am I just being a total chick and overthinking this? Why do I even care?

I know the answer to all of that. Because I've never been a selfish lover. Even when the sex means nothing, I need to know my partner got it as good as I did.

That's all this is. Worry about making sure Storm got off and enjoyed herself.

It has absolutely nothing to do with the fact that I actually like her.

Nope. Not that.

seventeen

The pounding of my heart slows, and my breathing finally evens out. Landon's hand squeezes my thigh again, but he doesn't say anything.

How long before this silence gets awkward?

We're getting close. I don't know what to do with this after-coming thing. Not when I'm trying *not* to form a connection to this man.

I shift, and the bed moves under me as he does too. His eyes are on me now. They rake over my skin, leaving a trail of heat in their wake.

But I can't look at him now.

I *couldn't* look at him a few minutes ago.

Not when he wanted to drop between my legs to go down on me and certainly not if I had tried to go to my knees to blow him. The eye contact would have been too much. Him looking up at me with his mouth on me. Me looking up at him with my lips wrapped around him.

Too intimate. Too...everything. The only way I could do it was with my back to him, and the fact he let me do it without questioning why was a relief I wasn't expecting.

"You okay?" His voice comes low and husky, and despite my desire to keep staring at the ceiling, I force myself to rise up on my elbow to face him.

Heavy-lidded eyes examine me. I nod.

I'm okay right now, but I won't be unless we get back to what I came here for.

Sex.

Nothing more.

No talking.

No cuddling.

Just no.

He opens his mouth to say something, but I roll to my side and grasp his semi-hard cock before he can get a word out. His sharp intake of breath goes straight between my legs to where I'm still tingling from my release. There's something so heady about knowing you can do that to another person. That your touch can make them lose their control.

It's been a long time since I've felt it...since I felt anything really. But his touch and his response to mine frees me from so much yet exposes me to even more potential hurt.

This is supposed to be simple. I need to keep it that way.

I slide my tongue along his length, and he comes to attention immediately with a groan.

"Fuck, Storm."

Exactly.

Fucking. That's the plan. Get it in. Get off. Get out of here.

I reach my free hand back in his direction. "Condom?"

He tugs open a drawer on his nightstand. The move sends his cock closer to my mouth, and I take the opportunity to suck the head between my lips. Having him in my mouth makes my swollen clit throb and my core clench.

I need this.

I need him.

And I hate that.

"Damn." Landon drops back and places the condom package in my palm. "You keep doing that, we aren't getting to the sex part, Storm."

That's definitely not an option tonight.

As good as his mouth on me felt, I need more. I need that void to be filled...even if only for a few moments.

I free his cock from my lips with a *pop* and tear into the foil package. I toss it off the bed onto the floor and lick my lips. "Then I better stop."

Slowly, deliberately, I slide the condom down his length with a shaky hand.

His warm palm squeezes my ass, and he tugs on my upper arm. "Come up here."

He wants me to ride him...to sit on top of him and meet his eyes...to stare down at him while I fuck him.

Not happening.

I swing my leg across his waist, putting my back to him, and align his cock. His hands find my hips, and I slowly lower myself down.

Fuck.

The large, broad head stretches me, and I suck in an unsteady breath. He's even bigger this way, and being full, feeling whole, is exactly what I need. Even if it is temporary.

I move and take even more of him in. His fingers dig into my hips, urging me lower. Hot pants flutter across my back. A groan slips from my lips when he's seated inside me to the hilt.

One hand works its way up from my hip to grasp my hair. He twists it around his wrist, tugging my head back slightly and sending little zings of pain through my scalp as well as a jolt of something else to where we're connected between my legs.

"Ride me."

The husky, strangled command and another tug on my hair send me into motion. I push up onto my knees and slam back down, forcing him deep inside and grinding so my clit rubs against the base of his dick. Jolts of pleasure race from my core out through my limbs.

Fuck. Yes.

A mewl slips from my lips as I rise up and crash down on him again. Every movement tightens his grip on my hair and releases a little bit more of what I've been holding onto so tightly for so long.

Who knew that could be so fucking hot?

The fingers of his free hand dig into my hip, and he braces his feet on the bed so he can thrust up on my every down stroke.

Flesh slaps against flesh.

Thunder rolls.

His cock stretches and fills me.

Rain pours.

Every grind of my hips sends me into overdrive.

I can't get enough. Of this. Of him.

Heat builds low in my abdomen, and a bead of sweat trickles between my breasts and down to where he's buried inside me. His hips snap up to meet mine, driving him hard and deep into my pussy.

The slow burn of impending orgasm ripples across my skin.

So close.

I lean forward, pulling against his hold on my hair. The pain radiates across my scalp, but I need more friction on my clit. I need him deeper. I need more. More of everything.

Hovering on the edge is too much. This is too much. *He's* too much.

Landon releases a bit of the tension on my hair, giving me the room to take what I need from him. I grind against him harder, faster, ignoring the burn in my legs in order to reach the end goal.

Every drag of his cock along my G-spot, every tilt of his hips, every grunt and groan sounding from behind, every pull on my hair...it all adds to the building pressure in my body.

It coils tighter and tighter until it finally snaps, drowning me in a tidal wave of pleasure and sending me spasming on Landon's hard dick.

He growls behind me and thrusts up with renewed force and determination. My orgasm rages, erupting on for what feels like forever, until he grunts, and his cock gets even harder inside me as he finds his release.

I collapse across his legs.

Holy shit.

Inky blackness encroaches on my vision, and I don't fight it.

I can't, even if I wanted to. My limbs might as well weigh a hundred pounds each.

Landon slides his arms around my waist and hauls me back over him until I'm sprawled across his body.

No.

This is way too much like snuggling.

This feels way too good.

The rapid beating of his heart under my ear, the gentle rise and fall of his chest, the warm puffs of his breath against my hair...it all makes this so...real.

I can't do real.

I can do sex.

I can do fucking.

That's what tonight was. That's what it needs to stay.

With my palms flattened against the mattress, I force myself up on shaking arms.

Landon's heavy-lidded eyes meet mine before I roll off the bed and to my feet. I wobble on weak legs and have to grab the nightstand to steady myself.

Shit. That's embarrassing.

"You okay, babe?"

Babe?

No one's called me that for a long time. It's so personal. So intimate.

You just had the man's dick in your mouth and rode him like a damn wild stallion.

Yet, a stupid pet name is what causes my stomach to churn and my hands to shake. I run them back through my tousled hair and sigh. "I'm fine. I just need to get going."

For my own sanity.

The bed creaks as Landon shifts. My natural inclination is to want to turn back to him, but that's the last thing I should be doing. He's not the type to let me slink out of here quietly and without question.

Keep your eyes on the floor, Storm. Find your clothes. Get out.

"You don't have to rush out. Come back to bed."

I shake my head and search the floor.

Where the hell are they?

Landon's low, throaty chuckle fills the room, and I force myself to look up.

A slim blond eyebrow raises at me, and he gives me a devastating grin. "Looking for something?"

I twist and scan the room. "Yeah, where are my—"

The loud boom of thunder that rolls through the room brings everything that just happened tonight all flooding back. The storm. The pile of very wet clothes on the bathroom floor.

Shit.

She's trying to run. I understand that inclination better than anyone.

At first, I thought maybe she was just going to clean up, but the frantic panic in her eyes when she pushed up off my chest appeared more gazelle facing a lion than someone just needing to hit the head.

After sex that incredible, the fact she's ready to bolt so quickly screams to me that all sorts of crap is jumbling her thoughts, making her question things that don't need to be analyzed.

A great orgasm can't even clear Storm's head of her fears and insecurities. It always has for me. I wouldn't be sane right now if I hadn't found that way to release all the pent-up tension, anger, and frustration. A way to get rid of all the hurt without hurting anyone else.

Because there were times I wanted to hurt someone. I *did* hurt someone. Dad may have deserved it, but it still wasn't the right thing to do. I see that now, looking back at that fateful day. But I wasn't thinking clearly, all I was seeing was the ultimate stab in the back. The ultimate betrayal. By the only people who mattered.

I've managed to rein in my anger. And I've worked damn hard to let go of that past. Storm needs to do the same. Yet she just can't seem to. Watching her scramble to find clothes that aren't there causes a smirk that probably isn't very nice or appropriate given her borderline distress.

Don't laugh at her, Landon. Be a gentleman.

"I put a t-shirt and some boxers on the counter in the bathroom, but your clothes are still in a wet pile on the floor. Unless you want to go home in my clothes, you're going to have to suffer through my company long enough to toss yours in the dryer."

The epic struggle between fight or flight flashes across her blue orbs before she averts her eyes and glances toward the open bathroom door.

She wants to bolt, but that would mean the walk of shame at almost midnight in my clothes. Waiting for her own clothes means fighting against whatever is making her want to flee. Maybe that's me. Maybe it's something in her. Whatever it is, it's gnawing away and eating her alive. That much is clear.

I don't want her to feel like that around me. I want her to be comfortable. Content. Happy. But what can I possibly do or say at this point? She needs space and time to figure it out on her own without me pressuring her.

With a sigh, she turns back to face me and shrugs. "Where's your dryer?"

The resignation in her words stings a bit, but I can't let it get to me. She's in a shitty place. A place I was in not so damn long ago too.

I climb from the bed and stand only inches from her. Heat still radiates off her naked skin, and my fingers itch to glide across her breasts. It takes all my willpower not to reach out and do just that, but I'll be damned if I'm not going to take the opportunity to kiss her.

My lips find hers before she can protest or turn away. I wrap my arms around her, and she stiffens, but she doesn't pull away.

Please, don't fight it.

A second passes before she sags against me and deepens the kiss. My cock stirs to life between us, and I pull away and press a kiss to her forehead.

"I'll throw your clothes in while you get dressed."

She nods and averts her gaze again.

Why doesn't she want to look at me?

It didn't go unnoticed that she kept us in positions that prevented me from making eye contact with her while we were together. I won't push her on it...for now. As long as she got what she needed, what she came here for, I can let it slide.

This isn't lovemaking. This is fucking. I guess you don't need to look at someone to do that. But a part of me—a part bigger than I really want to admit—wishes I could have been drowning in her deep blue eyes while I was inside her.

I push past her and into the bathroom. The condom hits the trash, and I grab the clothes off the floor and counter.

Storm stands next to the bed in the same place I left her.

The strong, beautiful woman who was just an animal in bed, suddenly became so small and fragile.

Still fucking beautiful, though.

This isn't easy for her. I won't do anything to make it harder. "Here you go."

She turns and grabs the clothes from me with a mumbled, "Thank you." The shirt will drown her, and the boxers won't stay up on her slim hips, but it's the best I can do until these clothes dry.

I drop them in the dryer and turn it on full blast. Storm hasn't appeared in the hallway yet. Maybe she plans on hiding out in the bedroom until she can go?

Not going to happen.

If she's here, she's going to come out and talk to me while we wait. This doesn't have to be awkward like she's so desperately trying to make it.

I grab a pair of gray sweatpants and a t-shirt from the laundry basket on top of the dryer and turn toward the open bedroom door as I tug them on. "Meet me in the kitchen."

I'm fucking starving.

Although, eating means I won't have the taste of Storm's orgasm coating my mouth anymore. I lick my lips and grin at the memory of her riding my face.

There's nothing hotter than a woman taking what she wants and giving in to her sexual needs. Seeing Storm unleashed was something I'll never forget, even if this never happens again.

Her soft footsteps carry down the hallway behind me, and when I reach the kitchen, she slides onto one of the stools at the island facing me. My shirt hangs off her, exposing one slim, naked shoulder.

Christ, that's hot.

I clear my throat and turn to the fridge. "What do you want to eat? I have...leftover Chinese food, leftover pizza, stuff to make salad, and chicken breasts."

My stomach rumbles and screams "PIZZA" but I know this late at night, something healthier would be better for me.

"Pizza, please. And maybe the Chinese too."

A woman after my own heart.

I pull the grub from the fridge and grab two plates from the cabinet. She watches me move around the kitchen as I drop one of the plates in the microwave.

At least she's looking at me now. I guess that's an improvement.

Should I push it?

I lean back against the counter and examine her. Her eyes dart down to something really interesting on the marble counter in front of her. "Where's Angelina tonight?"

Her head snaps up, and she twirls a strand of hair around her finger. "At my mom's. She goes there almost every Friday."

The microwave dings, and I swap the plates and set the hot one down for her.

"Is that why you're here?"

The question is intentionally vague. She's lonely. That much is evident. But was it the loneliness, sexual need, or a combination of both that finally had her tossing off her reservations and appearing on my doorstep? I'd love the truth, but I somehow know calling her out on it isn't the way to approach it.

She ignores my question in favor of taking a massive bite of the pizza. I grab two bottles of water from the fridge and set one in front of her. Chewing gives her a momentary reprieve, but I don't intend to let it go that easily.

I quirk an eyebrow as she swallows, and she sighs.

"I don't know why I'm here."

"Fair enough."

At least she came.

And came.

And came.

A grin spreads across my face that I only manage to hide by turning to retrieve my plate. She may not fully know what she wants, but as long as she's willing to explore sex with me, I'm game.

Being with Storm helps me forget all the bullshit I ran away from, and who's going to complain about hot sex with a beautiful woman?

My door is open. As long as she doesn't want more than that —like my heart.

That needs to stay closed up tighter than Fort Knox. Even if I do like her.

eighteen

The rain that's been plaguing the city for the last couple of days since Storm showed up at my place looks like it's finally releasing its hold on us. Sun peeks through the cloud cover just as I pull up outside THREE.

It's a much-needed break from the dreary feeling that's settled over me with the weather combined with the continued lack of progress from Barry and what's been happening with Storm. Seeing the sun streaming down onto the site is like a beacon saying everything is at a turning point.

I thought Friday was for me and Storm, too.

There's no doubt she was struggling when she showed up. There's no doubt part of her wanted to run as soon as we had finished with the sex portion of our evening. But the necessary time to dry her clothes gave me a chance to show her it doesn't need to be awkward. It doesn't need to be anything. Just two friends hanging out after we had sex.

When she left, I thought she understood that.

When she texted me Sunday night, asking if we could meet at my place Monday, I was *sure* we were on the right track. She initiated things...again. She had obviously been thinking about what we did, about me, about what we could do together. But despite another round of mind-blowing sex, there was still something plaguing her.

She still wouldn't look at me—during or after.

And even though she tried to hide any emotion from me and act like it was a business transaction, she couldn't keep me from seeing the way her body responded to me. How it seemed like the entire world had been lifted from her shoulders when she came. How relaxed and content she felt wrapped in my arms for the brief moment she let me drag her against me afterward before she got dressed and fled again.

All the things she needs so badly are the very things she's fighting so hard against.

You're supposed to be keeping it casual. You shouldn't care how she reacts as long as you both get off.

But I do care. Far more than I should. I care about her as a human being who is suffering. I care about her as a friend and a lover. I care about her as...God only knows what.

Today's meeting will give me the opportunity to assess where's she at while also accomplishing some needed steps to get this place closer to completion.

Since Storm was able to get those final changes approved quickly through her contacts, the crews have been working non-stop when the weather permits, trying to get the club open before Christmas, but it always seems like something crops up that causes little delays here and there. It's just part of the business. I learned early working with Dad that these things are expected and worked into the schedule, but it doesn't make it any less frustrating when they happen.

And frustration seems to be my only friend lately.

Cut me a break, life. Please!

I climb from my car and into the sunshine. My muscles burn from the long swim this morning. I needed it, though. Other than being with Storm, it's the only way I've been able to relax and de-stress since I got here. Barry continues to struggle to secure what I need to wrap things up back home, and until everything there is fully resolved, I won't ever truly be able to just *be*. I won't ever truly be able to give myself one hundred percent to this new life.

And that's all I want to do right now.

Storm pulls up across the street and parks along the curb. She doesn't look my direction. The car shuts off, but her door doesn't open.

Maybe she's on the phone?

The shadow of the building obscures her face, so I lean against my car and wait. The heat of the sun warms my skin, and I drop my head back and absorb the rays I've so been missing the last few days. I won't complain about the weather here. Any misery in the summer in Louisiana is a small price to pay for no longer suffering the winters in the Midwest, but still, I'd love a few days without the constant threat of rain.

When I open my eyes again, Storm still hasn't moved from her car.

What's she doing?

I glance at my watch. We're late for meeting with the foreman. I can't wait for her anymore. We need to get this meeting going so I can get back to meet with Chris on a new project in a couple hours.

With a sigh, I shove away from the door. I pause to let a black sedan drive past before jogging across the street to her car. I didn't want to interrupt her call, but I don't have a choice at this point.

Only, she's not on the phone.

Her forehead rests against the steering wheel. White knuckles clutch the wheel, and her back heaves up and down violently.

Oh, my God.

"Storm?" I tap on the window, but she doesn't move. Whatever's happening—a breakdown, a panic attack—she's in the grips of it. Blood pounds in my ears, and my heart thunders. "Storm? Can you hear me?"

I pound harder on the window. She flinches but doesn't raise her head or otherwise acknowledge me.

Shit.

I grab the handle and pull.

Please let it be unlocked.

The door pops open, and I release the breath I've been holding in a loud *whoosh* as I squat down next to her.

"Storm?" I place a shaky hand on her shoulder, and she jerks away and lifts her forehead from the wheel.

Wide, wet, red, confused blue eyes meet mine, but it's like she's looking through me and not even seeing me at all. I rub my hand down her arm. "What's wrong? Are you okay?"

She's clearly *not* okay, but I'm not sure what else to say at this point. I don't have a fucking clue what brought this on, so how the hell can I help her through whatever this is?

It takes a moment before she reacts to my question—a long moment when my heart stops in my chest. She shakes her head and swipes at the wet streaks down her cheeks. "Shit. I'm sorry. I don't know what came over me."

Her eyes drift over my shoulder to THREE, and her lower lip trembles.

Fucking hell. I'm so stupid.

I squeeze her arm gently, trying to keep that physical connection to ensure her I'm here. "Storm? Is this the first time you've been here since..."

The rest of the words won't come out. Somehow, mentioning Ben's name and what happened feels wrong. Like it's not my place, not my pain, not something I should have anything to do with.

How fucked up is that? I'm sleeping with this woman and can't even bring myself to mention her dead husband?

She gives me the smallest, almost imperceptible nod to confirm my suspicion.

Shit.

It never occurred to me that she may not have been back at the site since they cleaned up from the fire and started rebuilding. When I asked her to meet me here, I didn't detect any hint of reservation or concern from her about it. We just set the time like it was any other project.

How could I have been so inconsiderate?

I flatten my palm against her cheek and turn her face until her eyes meet mine. The anguish there is so real, it makes *my* heart ache, almost as if I were the one who lost so much in those ashes. "You don't need to do this. I'll take pictures. We can do a phone call with the foreman. You don't need to go in there. We'll figure something out."

She closes her eyes and takes a deep breath. Storm is one fucking strong woman, but asking her to do this...it would be too much for *anyone*. Especially going in there with me when she's so conflicted over what we've been doing.

When she reopens them, there's a new resolve there. A don't fuck with me and count me out look that has a tiny smile tugging at the corner of my mouth.

There's the fighter I knew was in there.

"No. I have to do this. It's my job. I can't avoid the club forever."

Pride fills my chest, and I lean in and press a kiss to her forehead. "You sure?"

There isn't even a second of hesitation before she nods. She has to be one of the most impressive women on this planet. Being able to confront this place with the determination on her face now makes me respect her even more. She possesses a courage and tenacity I've never seen in any woman I've ever known before.

She's absolutely remarkable.

Which is why it's getting harder to believe my own words when I tell her we can keep this casual.

I take her shaking hand and help her from the car and out into the sunshine. She brushes her free hand over her dress, smoothing out the wrinkles there before she turns back to grab her briefcase.

When she faces me again, she's a completely different woman than the one who was just crying in the car.

This woman has more strength than she knows.
This woman is slowly working her way into my heart.

I can't believe I let Landon see me fall apart like that...again. Every time I'm around this man, it seems like I can't keep my shit together.

This is a job. I'm supposed to be working...

So damn embarrassing.

And even though I'm trying not to devolve back into a quivering mess, I'm barely holding on by a damn thread. My hands shake. My chest heaves, and every fiber of my being is screaming at me to climb back into my car and drive home where I can crawl into bed and never come out again.

Only I can't do that. Not if I ever want to move forward with my life.

I need to be able to work. I need to be able to be here with Savage and Gabe and do my job without falling apart. When they said they wanted to rebuild here, I should have said no if I couldn't handle it. It's not fair now to use what happened as an excuse to not do my damn job.

No way. I can't give in to the darkness. To the desire to collapse into a ball and ignore the world.

Ben wouldn't want that. He wouldn't want me to completely melt down every time someone mentions him, or anytime I have to come to the club in the future.

So, I'll suck it up and put on a brave face, even if I'm shattered inside.

Landon watches me carefully where we stand next to my car, waiting for me to say or do something. Waiting for an indication I'm *not* going to have another panic attack.

He's so sweet. So supportive. So damn understanding of what a disaster I am.

I take a deep breath and walk across the street to the club with my head held high and my eyes on the front door. If I don't think about what happened here, what I lost, then maybe, just maybe, I can get through this meeting.

Having Landon here with me helps, even though it kills me to admit it. His soft touch and sympathetic words back there were the only thing that dragged me from the dark hole I found myself in the moment I saw THREE.

Because I didn't see it how I see it now. No. When I pulled up, I saw it how it was *then*.

Massive pillars of flames shooting to the blazing orange sky.

Fire trucks. Flashing lights.

Men running around shouting out orders.

And smoke.

God, there was so much smoke.

It billowed up in enormous columns like a black demon rising from the inferno.

I knew what it meant then. The moment I pulled up, I felt in my soul he was gone and my life was over. It was as if half of me had suddenly been ripped away, leaving me bleeding and helpless. And I just stood there watching it, knowing there was nothing I could do.

And it's all I could see today.

Until Landon broke the dark spell and opened my eyes to the light. This will be a new building. A new chance to create something great for Savage and Gabe's brand. An opportunity to show the world, and especially any lingering members of Dom's crew, that we aren't going to back down from a fight or be intimidated. The Hawkes will *not* be broken.

And neither will the Matthews. My name may have changed, but it's Hawke blood running through my veins. It's that blood that keeps me walking up to the front door and tugging it open before Landon can even reach for it.

If I had paused to think before entering, I may have never done it.

Charging ahead is the only way this will happen.

"David!" The foreman turns toward me, and his eyes widen slightly before they flicker over to Landon then back to me. Maybe he wasn't expecting me to actually show today. He knows what happened here. He worked with Ben for years and understands what it means for me to be setting foot in this building. I shouldn't be surprised by his reaction, but it does rankle and send a jolt of anger through me.

I'm stronger than you think.

I force a smile and hold out my hand to him. "I'm so glad we could arrange this meeting today, David. Show us what we need to talk about."

He takes my hand and contemplates me for a moment, his dark brown eyes moving over my face, before he finally nods. "Nice to see you, Mrs. Matthews." He nods to Landon. "Mr. McCabe. I'm sorry you needed to come down here, but the inspector came by and pointed out a few things that need to be addressed now that we have the structure up."

His words rush through my ears but barely register as I allow myself to take in the interior of the club. Or at least the bare bones of it.

This room was so beautiful before.

They've made some serious progress. Things move so much faster when we're able to pre-fabricate sections off-site while waiting for permits. The structure goes up so quickly, but it's nowhere near the stage of completion we were at when Ben died. We were only weeks away from opening when Dom decided to send his deadly message.

My body turns, almost of its own volition, until I'm facing the stairs to the second floor. That's where it happened. That's where Ben and Caleb lost their lives at the hands of the goons sent by Dom. The man who cared for us. The man who was supposed to protect us. The man who was a second father. The man who betrayed us all.

Cold dread spreads through my limbs. I can't seem to suck in breath. The room spins and darkness clouds the edges of my vision.

Strong hands grab me and hold me upright. "Storm? Are you okay?"

I don't know.

The words won't come out. Nothing will. I shake my head, trying to clear whatever strange fog has overtaken my ability to think or speak. I manage to right myself and shrug off Landon's hold on me. "I'm fine. I just got a little dizzy."

More like had another panic attack. But I won't admit that in front of Landon and David.

As it is, David is eyeing me like he's waiting for a full-on meltdown. I'm not going to give him the satisfaction of watching me fall apart. I have to face all the demons this building holds. And I need to do it *without* Landon.

I can't rely on a man. Especially one who doesn't want anything more than sex. It doesn't matter he's kind and supportive and everything a woman could ever ask for. Not when we both want something else. Not when we both want to avoid the pain and complications forming attachments can bring.

"I need to go upstairs. You two start without me. I'll be back."

Landon places his hand on my shoulder and leans in so David can't hear. "Are you sure you want to do this?"

His concern is equally maddening and endearing.

I don't *want* him to have to worry about me. The fact that he can so easily read me and knows what just happened and why has me clenching my fists at my sides.

"I have to. Alone." I add that because the next question out of his mouth is sure to be whether I want him to go with me or not. Even though part of me craves his quiet and supportive presence, I have to do this by myself. To prove to everyone else, and even more so to *me,* that I can.

He nods his understanding even though worry still darkens his face.

My chest squeezes as I ascend the unfinished staircase. Each step is like driving a stake into my heart. I force myself to breathe and make my way toward the spot Ben and Caleb died.

Maybe it was a mistake to rebuild with essentially the same design, to make this place almost an exact replica of the building that killed them, but Savage and Gabe were so in love with the original. It was everything they wanted, and the work Ben and his crew had done to implement my design had created an absolutely stunning club, one that screamed sex and opulence.

Right now, it's just a shell, but as I take the final step up onto the second floor and face the smaller secondary stage and the row of door jambs leading to what will become another set of private rooms, I see what it will look like. Though smaller than the ones downstairs, and lacking a private entrance, they offer the opportunity for more personal and discreet entertainment.

They were also the perfect place to trap someone...

I focus on the middle room. No door hangs in the jamb yet, and only the basic framing and drywall marks it off, but when I blink and reopen my eyes, I see it as he would have that night. Almost complete. Just a few minor details to hammer out. The very reason he was even here with Caleb so late.

Dom claimed they were "unfortunate casualties" of what was intended to be simply sending a message. He *claimed* the men doing his dirty work didn't know anyone was inside the building when they doused it and set it ablaze. But that's horseshit, and we all know it.

I pause in the jamb and lean my shoulder against it to steady my shaking legs. They were barricaded in this room. They were trapped. It was no accident.

The acrid smell of smoke invades my lungs, and I cough against it and step back. Tears burn my eyes, and a familiar heat licks at my skin even though I know it's all in my head.

I stumble back into the main room and away from the spot where I lost my world.

"I'm so sorry, Ben. For everything."

So many things weighing down on me, so much guilt eating me alive.

The things only he and I know. The things I've done since he died. All the things I never got to say. They all choke my breath, and I sink to my knees with a massive sob that echoes in the empty space.

nineteen

*A*ngel's hair floats like silk through my fingers. I glance down at my lap where her head rests, tiny soft puffs of breath floating out from her slightly open mouth as she sleeps. The final scene of one of her movies plays on the screen—the one where the girl gets the prince and everyone lives happily ever after.

I wish.

She's too young to understand it's not the way the world works. That not everyone gets to spend the rest of their lives with the person they love.

My epic meltdown at the THREE site today was proof happily ever after doesn't exist. After I dragged myself up from the dirty floor and did my best to hide the evidence of my complete collapse, I avoided making eye contact with Landon during the rest of the meeting.

I rushed David through showing me the issues I needed to address and then made my excuses and left before Landon could pose the questions he so obviously wanted to ask about what had happened upstairs.

There's no doubt they both heard me. I wasn't exactly quiet. And the unfinished state of the building means sound flows easily throughout the space.

Knowing Landon witnessed that, yet *another* breakdown, even if he only heard it, has had me warring between embarrassment and relief. The last few weeks, and especially the last few days, have made it clear something has been building between us, something neither of us expected or wanted.

It's useless to try to deny it anymore. He doesn't treat me like a booty-call-friends-with-benefits girl, and I have never been able to separate my attraction to him physically from the pull I feel toward him because of who he is—his compassion, his humor, his reverence when he talks about his work, his...everything.

So, his knowing what a mess I am is probably a good thing, even though it *does* make me want to bury my head in the sand and hide from him and the world. He knows why I can never give him more, if that's even what he wants.

If that's even what I want.

I just don't know anymore. He keeps saying *casual*, but his touches, his words are anything but.

The final credits roll, and I slip my arms under Angel and stand. She moans slightly and snuggles into me. I don't know when she fell asleep, but I envy her ability to let the Sandman take her so easily.

I can't remember the last time I didn't lie awake for hours and hours and wake in the middle of the night drenched in sweat from the same nightmare...or recently, really amazing dreams about Landon. That switch has been a surprise, a not all unpleasant one, but fighting the guilt it brings is almost as exhausting as the nightmares were.

Angel sighs as I lay her in the bed, and she rolls onto her side toward me. Her eyes open sleepily as I pull the comforter up over her.

"Goodnight, Mommy."

I lean in and press a kiss against her forehead. "Goodnight, baby girl." I flip off the light on her nightstand and turn away to move to the door.

Her tiny voice stops me in my tracks. "I'm glad you're happy, Mommy."

What?

I turn back to her and drop to my knees next to the bed. "What do you mean?"

She smiles and hugs the stuffed rabbit Ben gave her. "You're happy. You've been smiling more, and I don't hear you crying as much."

Those words break the dam that's been holding back my tears since I left the club.

I knew she saw me crying. I knew she saw what a disaster I was and that I wasn't the same Mommy she had before. I just didn't know how damn perceptive she was, that she's managed to pick up on the little things I've been denying to myself since Landon came into my life.

He's made me happy...or at least...*happier.*

It's as simple as that.

The sexual release is a huge portion of that and can't be denied, but it's more...enough that a five-year-old can see it despite my best efforts to deny it to myself. His quick, easy smiles and soft touches, his passion for the job, his ability to put his past behind him—whatever it may be—and move forward in a new place...it's all worked together to lighten the weight I've been carrying for months.

That's thrilling and terrifying.

I press another kiss to Angel's forehead. "I am happier. You make me happy. Goodnight."

"Night, Mommy."

Guilt sits heavy on my heart as I make my way out to the kitchen. Guilt that she saw all that and that I couldn't be stronger for her. Guilt that I feel something for someone who isn't Ben.

I don't know how people do it...move on after losing their husbands or wives.

How are you supposed to forget that love...that life? How are you supposed to let someone else in when there's no room in your heart?

There's only one thing that can calm my nerves right now—wine, cool night air, and that damn fluffy cat on my lap.

The irony of the fact I'm going out to mine and Ben's spot to contemplate my feelings for another man doesn't escape me. But somehow, sitting out there on the swing just feels right.

I pour a glass of cabernet, then pour a little more, grab the blanket off the back of the couch, and tug open the back-patio door. The crisp evening air hits me, and I step down onto the porch.

My bare foot lands on something wet and sticky.

"What the—"

Red fills my vision. Something dark red...and with fuzzy black and white fur.

"Oh, my God. What is tha—"

A scream claws its way up my throat, and the glass slips from my hand to shatter on the porch. Wine splatters, mixing with the blood already staining the ground and what's left of poor Mittens.

Oh, my God.

My stomach turns, and my dinner rises up my throat. I choke it back and step away from the grisly scene.

Some neighborhood dog or a coyote must have gotten ahold of her. Tears sting my eyes, and I step back into the house and close the door with shaking hands.

"Mommy? Is everything okay?"

Shit. Angel.

She must have heard me scream. I can't let her see the poor cat. She'd be traumatized for life. I swipe away any tears that have worked their way down my face and turn back to find her standing in the hallway at the edge of the living room watching me with sleep-heavy eyes, clutching her rabbit under her arm.

I fight through the pounding of my heart and somehow plaster on a fake smile. "Everything's fine, baby. I just...saw a spider. Go back to bed."

She yawns and nods before turning and disappearing back toward the stairs and her room.

Thank God, she bought that story. I am such a shitty liar.

I need to get that cleaned up. And the blood I tracked in on my foot.

There's no way I can do it, though. I can take care of a lot of things around the house by myself, but I draw the line at scraping a dead cat off my patio. My hand shakes as I pull out my phone and dial the first person I think of.

Landon.

All it took was the word "blood" from Storm's lips for me to throw on shoes and jump into my car. I managed to decipher her garbled, rushed words enough to know it wasn't her or Angelina bleeding and had something to do with a cat, which slowed the racing of my heart somewhat.

But the panic in her voice has me rushing across town and into her neighborhood at speeds that will probably get me arrested on the spot. The quiet of her street is probably comforting under normal circumstances, but given the limited information she gave me about what happened, it has the hair on the back of my neck raising.

These older neighborhoods have a completely different feel from the area where my condo is. There's something darker here, older...you can really sense the history of the city. Good and bad.

I don't know enough about the area to know if it's safe or not, but given the size and historical nature of these houses, it has to be affluent. But affluent doesn't always equal safe.

It's probably nothing. Don't panic her.

I fly past a minivan and a dark sedan parked along her street and pull up in front of the address she gave me.

Wow.

The old house suits her. It's no Garden District mansion, but it clearly holds a lot of history and was undoubtedly built to exacting standards over a century ago. Two stories. Gables. Intricate lattice work and a beautiful wrap-around porch. It's the kind of house I imagined she would live in, and while I never knew Ben, I have no doubt he loved this place too. Either they paid a fortune for it, or Ben spent a lot of time and money on fixing it up.

My car is barely in park before I'm leaping out and racing to her front door. Storm opens it before I even ring the doorbell. Her wide, wet blue eyes and shaking lips have me drawing her into me the second I step through the door.

She shakes in my arms and buries her face against my chest while her hands snake up around my neck.

Christ, she's a mess.

"What happened? Are you all right? Is Angel all right?"

Storm would've told me if they weren't but I can't help worrying about them, especially seeing her this distraught.

She pulls back from me and nods toward the back of house. "I was going outside to sit on the patio and have a glass of wine. I opened the back door and..." She closes her eyes and sucks in a deep breath. "...and our cat...it must've been a dog or a coyote or something. She's just shredded."

I cringe at her description and run my hands up and down her bare arms to try to soothe her. "Did Angel see?"

Please God, say no...

She shakes her head. "No, thank God. I already put her to bed. She came out when I screamed but I told her it was just a spider and she went back to bed."

Relief relaxes some of the tension in my shoulders, and I lean forward and press a kiss to Storm's forehead. She releases a tiny sigh and leans into me.

"Okay, show me where it is. I'll take care of it."

She gives me a tiny nod, and I follow her into the house

through the grand entryway with its immaculate shining wood floors and hand-carved staircase leading to the second floor. I was right about how beautiful this place would be. It's like something out of *Better Homes & Gardens*.

The living room and kitchen are just as immaculate, and I do my best to focus my attention on where Storm is leading me even though the carpenter in me wants to examine every minute detail of the place.

She pauses beside a rear door with her hand on the knob. "It's right outside the door."

"I'll take a look. There's no need for you to see this again."

There's been enough death and loss in her life already.

Her mouth tips up in a soft smile, and she opens the door and steps behind it, effectively shutting off her own line of vision from the massacre on the patio.

Holy hell.

She wasn't kidding about the blood. When mixed with the wine she clearly dropped, it's like something out of a slasher film out here.

I step to the side to let the light from the sconce on the side of the house hit the patio and squat down.

Shit.

Rage surges through my blood, and I clench my jaw. A wild animal didn't do this. This cat was butchered. By something worse than a wild animal. A human did this.

The slashed tires on Storm's car pop to the forefront of my mind, and cold dread slithers down my spine and lodges in my stomach.

This isn't a coincidence. It's a message.

I glance toward the door, but it's still closed. Storm isn't visible in the glass inset, so she must have stepped away.

Good. I don't need her to hear this.

Rising to my feet, I grab my phone and dial Gabe. It's late, but I know he'll answer.

"Landon? What's going on?"

I suck in a deep breath and turn away from the gory scene. "I'm at Storm's. She called me over because she found the cat dead on the patio. She thought a coyote or dog got it, but..."

A low growl slices through the phone. "But what?"

"This wasn't an animal, Gabe. Someone cut this poor cat apart. It sure seems like a message to me, and coupled with the tire thing...I'm worried."

"Shit." Something bangs in the background, and rustling comes across the line like he's moving. "Someone's been following her too."

My eyes immediately move to the darkened yard and the neighboring houses. "What?"

"She said she's seen a black car several times. She thought it was one of the security personnel we put on everyone after Ben's death, but we pulled everyone off the family a couple months ago because things were quiet."

I scrub my free hand over my face and turn around to examine the bloody message again. "Fuck. This is really not good."

"No. It's not. And we need to do something about it."

Damn right, we do.

I'm not going to let anything happen to Storm or Angel. Things may be complicated and up in the air between us, and maybe it's not my place to step in as her protector when she has a very capable Gabe and two brothers to fill that role, but if anything happens to her...

Christ.

A dull ache forms in the center of my chest, and I reach up and rub at it with my free hand.

I couldn't handle that.

Somehow, in the short amount of time I've spent with her, Storm has managed to work herself into the one place I tried to keep her out of—my heart. The thought of her or Angel being harmed is unfathomable. I have to do whatever I can to protect them.

Gabe will know how best to deal with this obvious threat, but it doesn't mean I'm going to let him push me out of my role here. Whatever that role may be. Whatever Storm will *let* my role be.

"Tell me what you want me to do."

twenty

$\mathcal{I}$ scowl at the phone. If Savage could actually see me, there'd be no doubt I'm ready to end this conversation. "For the third time, I'm not leaving the house."

Something about my words just isn't getting through here. I sigh and lean back in my office chair, dropping my head back to stare at the ceiling with the phone pressed to my ear.

He growls and a thump comes through the phone that is undoubtedly him slamming his palm against his desk. "Dammit, Storm. Why do you have to be so stubborn?"

Me? Stubborn?

I let out an annoyed laugh and shake my head. "Coming from you, that's real fucking rich, Savage."

The man is completely blind to the fact he's the worst one in the family by far.

"How can you not see the concern here? Someone slashed your tires. Someone killed your cat. Someone has been following you." He pauses and releases a deep sigh. "We don't have a fucking clue what any of this is about either. Until we have more information to get this figured out, you either need to go stay with Mom or come to the building and stay with me and Dani or Skye and Gabe."

Hell no.

There's no way I'm leaving my house. The house *Ben* built for us. The only home Angelina has ever known. I won't throw off her normal life any more than it already has been by moving her somewhere else, even if it is with one of the family.

"I can't do that." I push to my feet and wander over to the

windows overlooking the river. "I know you're really worried about this, and it's not that I'm not worried. It's just we don't have any evidence who is behind this, and I think there's a chance it really could just be neighborhood kids."

Sickos exist in this world. People who will hurt animals just for the fun of it. Kids who slash tires just to be little punks.

"And the black car?"

Landon did mention seeing a black sedan on the street last night, but when he went out front, it was gone. Still, there are a lot of black cars in this city.

"Maybe it's totally unrelated?"

The silence that greets me tells me Savage doesn't buy my assessment. He can't understand what asking me to leave means. "I'm not going to pull Angel from the only home she's ever known and worry her for nothing."

"Dammit, Storm. I had a feeling you would say that so I made other arrangements."

Shit.

Savage "making arrangements" usually means him taking control and doing whatever the hell he wants regardless of what anyone else says.

"What kind of arrangements?" Anger simmers just beneath my heated skin. The only thing keeping me from going completely postal on him is he genuinely means well and only wants to protect us.

"Saint is going to be, for all intents and purposes, your bodyguard."

"What?" I slam my palm against the glass and growl. "You can't do that!"

I don't need a babysitter. I can take care of myself, mostly. My frantic call to Landon aside. So, maybe I couldn't handle *that* on my own, but I've survived. Not well, but I've managed.

"I can, and I have. Expect to see him soon. He can keep you

safe, Storm. Do you really think anybody's gonna fuck with you when you have a guy who looks like that watching your back?"

No.

And I hate that he's right about that. I hate when he's right about *anything*. I chew on my lip and bite back the retort I want to throw at him—the one where I insist he's *not* right just to avoid admitting I'm wrong.

"Look, Storm, until things get settled, it's just the way it's going to be, whether you like it or not."

There's no point in even responding to him. I end the call and squeeze my hand so tightly around the phone, I'm afraid it might actually snap. It's not that I'm not concerned about what's been going on, because I really am. All these things piling up have unease settling in my stomach.

But after everything that's happened to the Hawkes in the last two years, I don't believe in needless worry. Until I have some information so we can really know who is behind this, I don't want to jump to the worst possible scenario, even if I do understand why Gabe and Savage might go there.

Even Landon looked worried last night. More than worried. He was terrified and angry. When he came in after checking things out, he told me there was no reason for me to see it again and asked where he could find a trash bag and some kitchen tongs. I directed him to the kitchen and leaned against the counter and watched while he rummaged through my drawers and cabinets for everything he needed.

Seeing him in my space, doing something so intimate, tore me in two. Another man in Ben's kitchen, in the kitchen he built for me, going through the cabinets Ben handcrafted...it made me want to scream at him to get out. But the part that has slowly been falling for Landon released a little contented sigh at the way he rushed to my rescue and stepped in to take care of everything without a second thought.

I can admit...he looked good in there. I could get used to

having him around. Like everything since I met this man, it's a total contradiction.

And that's fucking terrifying.

Wanting to need someone is not at the top on my to-do list. Needing Ben and losing him is what broke me. I can't need another man that way, no matter how badly I want him.

And hell...do I want him. When he announced he was staying the night, my body immediately flooded with heat anticipating his touch, but then my mind kicked into gear and the question of where he was going to sleep was at the forefront. I hate the disappointment that sagged my shoulders when he offered to take the couch. I understood it, though. This is complicated enough without Angel potentially waking up and finding him in my bed.

That didn't make it any easier to climb into bed alone. Knowing he was asleep down there, so close yet so far away, kept me awake more than the dead cat did. Plus, I'm not entirely sure what to do about the Angel situation.

If Landon and I are going to keep this casual, then she definitely shouldn't see us together. She may run into him at family functions or work things but she can't see the connection between us. She can't think there's anything more. That would be too confusing for her.

Then again, if there's any possibility of this going anywhere, it would be good for her to start spending some time with him.

God, this is just one giant clusterfuck, and I've got Savage and Gabe breathing down my neck to have a God damn bodyguard.

It's not going to happen.

The intercom buzzes. "I'm sorry, Storm. You have a visitor on his way back."

My heart leaps. "Is it Landon?"

"No, sorry."

Who else could it be?

I check the door just as a mountain of a man appears, occupying the entire jamb with his shoulders barely making it in. He closes the door behind him and flashes me that brilliant smile.

Well, this is awkward. I've managed to avoid seeing Saint since our little non-run-in at the party. I haven't had to go over to TWO, where he primarily works, and I was hoping I wouldn't see him for a long, long time to avoid this very situation.

My only hope is that he ignores it and pretends it never happened like I plan on doing.

"Saint? What are you doing here?"

I move around my desk and sit back in my chair. He leans over the two chairs facing me, putting his giant palms on the backs.

"Did you talk to your brother and Gabe?"

I sigh and shove a hand back through my hair. "Yeah, I just got off with Savage. I'm going to tell you exactly what I told him. I don't need a babysitter."

A low rumbling chuckle comes from deep in his chest, and he rises to his full six-foot five height. "I'm not a babysitter, Storm. Just think of me as an added security."

"That I'm still not sure I actually need."

He shrugs his massive shoulders. "If you don't need it, then great, I'm getting paid to do nothing, but if you do, if something happens and I'm there, then is it not a good thing we were all overly cautious?"

Shit. He has a point.

The same point Savage and Gabe were trying to make, but it doesn't mean I have to like it. Hearing it from someone who isn't family makes it sound a lot more reasonable.

"I just don't like it, Saint. I didn't like it when Savage and Gabe initially put someone on me after Ben died, but I understood the reasoning there. We didn't know what was going to happen with Dom's associates who were still around or if anyone was going to retaliate against us for his death. But things have been quiet. It's been over six months."

Long, hard, agonizing months where I wasn't worried about what Dom's men might do because I could barely manage to keep myself functioning.

"There's no evidence this has anything to do with that, which is why I think it might just be a misunderstanding and some neighborhood kids."

It makes sense. Dom's men wouldn't slash tires and kill a damn cat. They would just end me if that was their ultimate goal. When Dom decided Dani was becoming a threat, he set things in motion to have her taken care of. He didn't mess around. There's no reason to think any of his surviving goons would.

None of this makes any damn sense.

Saint frowns. "What about the car that's been following you?"

"There are a lot of black sedans in the city. And it could all be in my head. It might not even be the same car."

He considers me for a moment, his chocolate brown eyes analyzing with a depth of intelligence you might not expect from somebody in his job.

I've always thought people underestimate Saint. He played professional football, but not all jocks are brick-headed, and Saint has proven time and time again that's he's not only loyal but also incredibly smart.

It's not immediately apparent to some. All they see is a massive man who could break them in half with the flick of his wrist, but underneath all that is so much more. He doesn't talk much, but when he does, the compassion, intelligence, and humor there seem to draw people to him.

He's perceptive. He's a good person to have on your team. No matter how reluctant I might be, I need to remember that.

The corner of his mouth ticks up, and he nods. "Yes, it's possible it's nothing, but do you want to risk that for yourself and for Angelina?"

It's the mention of Angel that has my throat tightening and cold dread working its way under my skin. If anything happened to me, she would be alone. And if anything happened to her, I just...

I shake my head and clear my throat of the emotion currently clogging it. "You're right. But I have some ground rules."

He raises a dark eyebrow and crosses his colossal arms over his chest. "What kind of rules, *ma'am*?" The emphasis on *ma'am* along with comedic lilt in his voice bring up a grin.

"I don't want Angel to see you. I know she knows who you are, but I don't know how I would explain you hanging around, so you can't be in the house. You can follow me from home to work and back, and wherever else we may need to go, but I don't need protection in the house or here."

A muscle in his jaw ticks, and I squirm under his consideration of what I just said. He nods and squeezes his lips together. "I think that's fair as long as you let me check the house and your office before you enter."

I roll my eyes and rise to my feet. "Fine, that's fair enough."

"What about when you go to Landon's?"

His words freeze me in my spot halfway around the desk. I reluctantly meet his eyes and find a spark of humor dancing in their depths.

I should've known he would know. He must've seen us together at the party and figured out who he was. I know Landon has been by TWO several times to examine the design and décor while working on THREE. They've undoubtedly met.

Still, Landon wouldn't have said anything to him.

Would he?

"How did you know?"

He chuckles again. "I know you've been trying to avoid discussing the party, but I saw you dancing with him and the way you ran out of there like a bat out of hell. Gabe also told me that Landon was the one you called last night, not him or Savage. It's not rocket science to deduce something's going on there."

Shit.

I'm not very good at the whole covert thing. "Angel doesn't know, and she can't find out. And I don't think the rest of the family knows either."

This time, he barks out a deep laugh as he moves toward the door. "You really think they don't know already?" He winks before disappearing without a look back.

Mistake #15,328—thinking I could keep anything secret from the Hawkes.

And they're no doubt judging me for being with him so soon after Ben's death. Especially Savage and Gabe. They always think they know what's best for me. What just happened here is a case in point. I'm so damn sick of them thinking I need protecting and that they need to be in control.

I'm in control of my own life. Even if I'm not when it comes to my feelings for Landon.

Storm shudders under me as her pussy clenches and ripples along my cock. I drive home one final time and squeeze my fingers into her hips and the top of her ass before my release washes over me in a tidal wave of pleasure.

She sags down onto her stomach, and I brace myself against the headboard to keep from falling on top of her.

What the hell was that?

I knew something was up the moment she got here. She didn't say a word, just charged in and kissed me and started tugging at the hem of my shirt to get it off. I won't complain about hot, aggressive sex, but there's something on her mind, something she was trying to take out on me, and I don't have a clue what it is.

She wouldn't let me ask either, just led me to the bedroom by my cock and kept my mouth occupied with hers the entire way.

I release the headboard, drop and roll onto my back, and drop my arm over my forehead while I try to catch my breath and let my racing heart slow. She lies next to me with her head turned away, her back rising and falling with her heavy breathing.

She hasn't looked at me since the moment she got naked and climbed onto the bed, offering herself to me in a way that would never require her to make eye contact.

Just like every other time we've been together.

I thought last night at her house we had another break-through of sorts. She called me instead of going straight to Gabe or Savage...

How can that not mean something?

And the fact that all I've done since the second she called last night has been worry about her and Angel means I can't continue to overlook that we are becoming a hell of a lot more than what either of us planned.

That's problematic in so many ways, not the least of which Barry has yet to come through for me.

Even if I wanted to move forward with Storm, my past keeps dragging me back. I'll have to tell her eventually, but there's no point in reliving that nightmare when I can't figure out what's going on in Storm's head or where we stand.

I release a sigh and turn onto my side. The warmth radiating off her flawless skin draws me to her. I wrap my arm around her naked shoulders, and she flinches and shifts away from me to sit on the edge of the bed.

A sharp pang hits my chest at her reaction. "What's wrong?"

She casts a glance over her shoulder before reaching to the ground to grab my T-shirt. With quick, jerking motions, she tugs it on, and then pauses and shakes her head. "It's nothing."

It's not nothing, and we both know that.

I push up onto my elbow. "Don't say that when something is clearly bothering you. You came in here all worked up about something."

She sighs and rises to her feet. "Sorry I took it out on you."

"Don't apologize, Storm. Just tell me what's going on."

I'm not asking for much. At least, I don't think I am.

Why is it so hard for her to just tell me what's going on in that damn beautiful head of hers?

Probably because opening up means admitting to me and herself that this isn't what it started out being. What we both intended.

She tugs on her underwear and runs her hands through her sex-rumpled hair but doesn't answer me.

I bite back a frustrated growl and push myself up until I'm fully sitting. "Is this about last night? The cat? Are you worried that something is going to happen?"

I sure as hell have been.

The kind of fear that's been occupying my thoughts is unlike anything I've ever felt. If I feel like this, how much worse must it be for *her*?

She huffs and turns around to address me. Fire blazes in her eyes, but it's not the one she had earlier, the one that screamed of lust and need. This one is all anger and frustration.

Two things I'm very familiar with. For months, they were my constant companions until I finally decided I had to leave in order to free myself and find a new life. I let that all go—trying desperately to move on—so I don't understand why Storm can't too.

"I'm just...I don't know. I'm sick of my brother and Gabe making decisions for me and what's best in my life. I don't need that. I'm an adult."

I sigh and climb from the bed to throw away the condom and pull on my boxers. "You're always going to be their little sister,

Storm. It doesn't matter how old you are or the fact that you have your own family. You have to know that."

An adorable scowl tilts the corners of her kiss-swollen lips. "I do. I just don't like them sending in a babysitter for me."

Babysitter? Does she mean me?

If that's how she sees me, it would certainly explain the way she's been acting.

Does she think I only spent the night because I had to?

"You know I stayed last night because I wanted to, right? That had nothing to do with Gabe asking me to keep an eye on you."

She shakes her head. "That's not...grrr...they have Saint following me like he's my new goddamn shadow. The only reason he's not in here watching us fuck is because I told him I was going to be with you and that I'd be perfectly safe."

So, I am kind of a babysitter. That bothers me more than it should, and I fight against the anger threatening to rise to the surface.

She closes her eyes and runs her hands through her hair again with a groan. "I'm just so sick of this shit. It's like it's never going to end."

Sympathy quickly replaces my anger. She's been through more than any one person should ever suffer in a lifetime before she even turned thirty. And now, there's this new unknown threat looming over her and disrupting her life again.

"And I'm so sick of relying on other people—you, and Savage, and Gabe. I need to be able to stand on my own and take care of things myself." She drops onto the bed and buries her face in her hands.

Self-reliance is important to her. I get it. But she *has* to know accepting help from family doesn't mean she's weak.

I've seen her growing, moving forward over the last couple weeks. After she met me. It's slow. And sometimes two steps forward and one step back. But she's getting herself back. She's getting her life back.

It may be different than the one she had before, but it's a *life*. I, of all people, understand what starting over is like. I made a promise to myself that I *would* start over. That I wouldn't let myself get bogged down by the ghosts of my past and the pain I felt. I *thought* Storm had finally come to that point too.

But maybe not.

It's like she doesn't even see it. She doesn't even realize that what's been happening between us has made a positive change in her and her life.

Perhaps I jumped the gun thinking her call last night meant she wanted something *more* between us. Maybe it was just the rush of adrenaline surrounding what happened that had me seeing things that don't exist. Because right now, any of that connection I thought we'd finally established, the one that has had me considering tossing the idea of simply being friends with benefits in the dust, seems to have disappeared.

I sigh and drop on the bed beside her. "You don't need anyone to take care of you, Storm. We all know that, but—"

She climbs to her feet and stalks over to where her pants lie on the chair in the corner of the room. "Don't placate me, Landon. I know there's too much unknown right now for Savage and Gabe to feel comfortable about me being on my own. That's the only reason I agreed to let Saint follow me around. But it doesn't have to mean I like it, and it doesn't mean I have to let it continue once we get things figured out."

What the hell does that mean? Let it continue?

Whether she's talking about her brother and Gabe's meddling or *us* is uncertain. What is absolutely crystal clear, though, is that her words drive a painful knife into my heart. I'm so not ready for this to be over. Despite my best efforts and intentions, this has become more.

And I won't let her walk away that easily.

"I don't want to fight with you, Storm. I'm trying to figure out what I can do to help."

She tugs on her pants and shakes her head. "I don't know. I don't know anything anymore except I want my own life. I don't want to rely on anyone anymore for anything."

Including her own happiness...

The words aren't said, but they still hang in the air between us. She's worried that by becoming attached, by letting herself *feel* something for me, she's opening herself up to more hurt, more pain.

It's true. She is. We both are. It's the exact reason all I've wanted is meaningless sex for months.

But things change. People change. Even the best laid plans can splinter and fall apart when the heart is involved.

And we would both be lying to say our hearts aren't involved anymore.

twenty-one

*A*ngel squeals and splashes in the water with Gabe. I slide the door closed behind me and drop into the patio chair opposite Dani and Skye with a sigh.

I ate way too much. All I want to do is roll myself back home and climb into bed in a food coma, but Angelina wanted to swim, and frankly, I need to talk to Dani. Skye may have some insight as well, but anything she says has to be taken with a grain of salt, considering her situation. It was easy for her to distance herself from the men she was with when her heart always belonged to Gabe. My situation is the opposite. My heart belongs to someone who will never be here again, and putting distance between me and Landon is increasingly impossible.

Every time he looks at me. Every smile. Every single touch. Every pant of my name when he's inside me. All of it. It's become a giant, driving force hammering away at my resolve and the wall around my heart. I completely lose all sense of anything else when we're together. The pain. The loss. The emptiness. It's all gone. Until I come back up for air to face the guilt.

Dani watches me for a few seconds, then raises a blonde eyebrow. "You okay?"

That damn loaded question again.

I throw my hands up. "Yeah. Just thinking about some stuff." Like how I totally overreacted and went off on Landon the other night when he wasn't the one I was mad at...not really. This unsettled situation with the threats—if they even *are* threats— has only further frayed my nerves. I took my frustration out on him when all he tried to do was be there for me and give me exactly what I wanted.

What I wanted...

That's the problem. I don't know anymore. Landon occupies far too much of my headspace for this to just be casual. And last night, the realization I hadn't even thought about Ben all day had me breaking down all over again. I can't give myself to Landon if it means forgetting Ben. It's not possible to have both.

Skye takes a sip from her wine glass. "What kind of stuff?"

"Well..." There isn't really a delicate way to say this, not without giving away details they don't need or revealing far too much about how messed up I am about this right now. "Dani, before you met Savage, how did you...well...how did you have sex and avoid *feelings* becoming an issue?"

Dani leans forward with her elbows on the table, her jaw open. "Holy shit. If you're asking that—"

"It means you're fucking someone!" Skye's words float out from under the patio and into the night.

I jerk my head to make sure Angelina and Gabe didn't hear anything, but they seem blissfully unaware of Skye's inappropriate outburst. "Shh. Knock it off, Skye."

My blood pressure slowly returns to normal. Sometimes, I really just want to smack her upside the head.

A giant grin plays on her mouth. "But I'm right...you're boning someone. Who is it?"

Dani nods and smiles. "Yeah, who is it?"

Shit.

Mistake #16,102- thinking it would be possible to ask a simple question without receiving the third degree from them.

I'm not ready to reveal all the details. I wouldn't even know how to begin telling them how he makes me feel—alive again. The way my heart races when he touches me. How the mere thought of him has my body heating and me giggling like a school girl with a crush.

How do I explain that without betraying what I had with Ben?

Skye turns to Dani and taps her finger against her chin while she spins her wine glass in the other hand. "It has to be someone we know. I mean, Storm hasn't exactly been spending a lot of time ou..." Her words trail off and her head spins in my direction. Those blue eyes, the same ones I see in the mirror every day, the same ones we all share, stare back at me, comically wide. "Holy shit. It's *Landon!*"

Crap.

I drop my face in my hands and groan. "Is it that obvious?"

Somehow, I doubt it. We've been very discreet, and other than the first time in my office, we've only been together at his place either during one lunch or on nights when Angelina is gone. If they know, it isn't because they saw anything. But he *was* at my house the night with the cat. Savage and Gabe know. And Saint practically laughed in my face when I suggested the family was unaware.

Yeah, totally obvious.

Dani holds out her hand and rocks it back and forth. "Kind of. I mean, once I figured out that he was the one you met at the party and saw you two outside after dinner, it wasn't a big leap to think you might hook up for real. Then you called him with that damn cat thing the other night." She takes a sip of her wine then nods at me. "Plus, you've been...well, happier? It seemed like something major had changed recently that's helped get you out of your funk. We just didn't know for sure what had happened."

Guilt turns my stomach, threatening to force up the wonderful dinner Mom just prepared. "Is it wrong? For me to be sleeping with him?"

Skye slams her wine glass down on the table a little too hard, sending splatters of red wine across the table. I'm surprised it didn't shatter. "Hell no. After everything you've been through, having a hot man fuck you is *not* wrong. It's a damn necessity."

My eyes dart to the pool again. "Shh."

She rolls her eyes and glances over at Angel. "She can't hear me. Stop worrying."

"Skye is right, Storm. This is a good thing, as long as the sex isn't bad. And I'm going to assume it isn't, or you wouldn't have made it more than once. And I'm assuming you have done it more than once if you're asking about feelings."

Dani's pale blue eyes see far too much. The same thing a damn five-year-old saw yet Landon and I were too blind or too stubborn to admit.

It's only been three weeks since we met, but in that short time, he's changed my world.

I nod my agreement. There's no need to get into details. Those aren't for them and are irrelevant. What is relevant is the warming in my chest and tightness in my throat whenever I think about Landon and the way my body gravitates toward and responds to him whenever we're in the same room.

Being drawn to someone like this is totally new to me. Ben and I always had a connection, an incredible one, both in bed and out. But it wasn't this. It wasn't this physical need for his comfort, for his touch. Or maybe it was, it was just like that so long ago with Ben that I've forgotten what it was like.

"It's just lust." *Keep telling yourself that.* "I know that. He knows that." *Sort of.* "Neither of us want anything more than sex." *A lie.* "But..."

A smug smile spreads across Dani's face. "But you *are* starting to feel something for him you don't want to."

I wouldn't be asking the question if that weren't the case. "No." *Yes.* "Maybe." *Definitely.* "Fuck if I know."

And isn't that a real bitch. Just one more thing I'm totally clueless about and have no idea how to handle. When one part of me wants nothing more than to run to him and throw myself into his arms, but the other tells me to just run...what the hell do I do?

Skye's matching grin makes her eyes spark. "Oh, my God. You *do* like him."

"Of course, I like him. I'm fucking him."

Shit.

My eyes fly to Angel but she's oblivious, although Gabe does give me a strange look. I force a smile and wave until he returns his attention to Angel. Even if he does know about me and Landon, which is pretty obvious at this point apparently, that doesn't mean he needs to hear any of the dirty details.

Skye shakes her head, sending her black hair flying around her. "That's not what I mean."

Dani sighs and reclines back in her chair. "To answer your question, keeping sex separate from feelings was easy...until it wasn't." She shrugs. "I guess sex has never been something intimate or special to me, so it wasn't hard for me to get what I wanted and move right on. But with Savage..." A grin spreads across her face. "God, I hated him at the beginning. He was so smug, but once I got to know him, I couldn't pretend there wasn't something more there, something more than a physical attraction. If there is in your case, I don't know that it's something you *can* ignore."

That's what I'm afraid of.

Giving in to my feelings for Landon means letting go of my feelings for Ben. It means forgetting everything we had. It means handing my heart over to someone else who could break it—intentionally or otherwise. Ben's death crushed me. I can't go through that again. Living alone sometimes seems more preferable to opening myself up to that kind of hurt again, giving someone that kind of power over me.

Skye shifts forward and focuses her stare on me, analyzing me as only a sister can. "Do you like spending time with him outside the bedroom or is this just a lust fogging your brain kind of thing?"

The latter would be so much easier to handle. The former... well, that's complicated in a way I've been trying to avoid.

Landon is sweet, funny, respectful—even when he's hitting on me—and he's good with Angelina too. What he said to her that night at dinner, how he handled that super awkward situation, and his concern over her seeing him in my room the other night, it all demonstrates how much he cares about her too.

Not to mention, he's incredible in bed.

He's the complete package. For someone who's looking.

Which I'm not.

At least, I *wasn't*.

I'd be lying to myself, and the girls, if I said I haven't developed...we'll just call it a fondness for Landon. Despite my best efforts and a shattered heart, he's managed to find a way to make me smile, and laugh, and *feel* something other than miserable.

But there's also the crushing weight of guilt. And that's not something I'm sure will ever fade. I'm not sure I *want* it to. I don't want to forget Ben or how he made me feel. Letting Landon in will do that. It's already started...

"I do enjoy spending time with him. It's just..."

I watch Angel. Sometimes, she looks so much like Ben, it makes my heart seize and breathing impossible. Dani and Skye follow my gaze, and when I turn back to them, the sympathy in their eyes just about breaks me.

Skye grasps my hand across the table. "You feel guilty for having feelings for someone other than Ben? You feel like you're cheating on him?"

Bingo.

"Does that sound crazy?"

Dani shakes her head. "Not at all. It's perfectly normal. I mean, look at your mom and my mom. Neither of them ever remarried after our dads died. Hell, I don't even think my mom *considered* dating. But that doesn't make it *wrong* to move on, Storm. There's no timeline for grief. Do you think Ben would want you to be alone the rest of your life? To keep living how you have been and to never be happy again?"

No.

But I also can't get him out of my head or heart.

His touch. His words. His love.

How do I forget that? Push it aside to let someone else move in...someone who doesn't know everything that's happened, everything I really lost.

"I guess not. It's just not that easy, you know?"

They both nod even though neither could possibly understand what I'm saying. There's no explaining what it feels like to lose the other half of you. There's no comprehending the agony, the loneliness, the physical pain. I know they mean well, and I appreciate the support, but it seems hollow.

This is something I just have to work through on my own. They're correct that there's no *right* answer. But there is an answer that's right for *me*, and right for Angel. I can't let myself forget that this isn't just about what I need, but also what is best for the little girl splashing in the water.

Her life was changed as much as mine. To bring another man into it, not knowing where it's heading or for how long, would only confuse her more. I can't do that to her. I *won't* do that to her.

Which means I have no clue where that leaves things with Landon. I want to be happy again. I want to not dread getting out of bed every morning to face a new day. I want Angelina to have a mom who is fully present. I want to be able to do that for myself, without relying on someone else, without relying on Landon. But the way he makes me feel is undeniable. Those things have gotten so much easier since he's been around. So, where do I go from here?

Mistake #17,862—thinking I could ever figure this all out.

The slam of my car door echoes loudly in my ears. Maybe I did that a little hard. Good thing no one is around to see how frustrated I am or that it's starting to get to me.

Even my swim this morning hasn't seemed to alleviate any of it. It's a constant pressure building in my chest, my shoulders, my throat, my head. A tightness. A force that's threatening to drive me crazy.

I stare at THREE and take a deep breath, trying to gather myself before going in. At least Storm won't be here for this meeting. I'm not entirely sure I'm ready to face her right now.

Not yet.

I hate the way we left things the other night. She was clearly pissed, but taking it out on me doesn't sit well. She's stressed and worried and frustrated. I get it. I'm not going to push her when she's like this, though. That's only going to further push her away, which is the last thing I want to do...despite everything.

I've left it in Storm's hands for now. The whole situation is too much for her to handle right now. Maybe I pushed things too hard and too fast. But she was right along with me for the ride every step of the way. Once she got past her initial roadblock, things changed. For the better.

But, she has a new problem breathing down her neck, and not having answers can frustrate anyone and cause them to lash out.

It has to me.

My former life should be long in my rearview, but it just won't go away. *She* just won't go away, because we can't fucking find her. So, I understand frustration, and I understand the need to take it out somewhere. For me, it's been the pool. For Storm...it's apparently me.

Once we have some answers, things will be better. And I will be there for her when she feels ready to talk it out.

Gabe is working hard to track down anything he can that could clue us in on what's going on. But all we have are the slashed tires, the dead cat, and a black car with a male driving it that may or may not be following her. Gabe's connections on the force have relayed there haven't been any other reports of similar incidents near Storm's neighborhood, which only gives more credence to the belief that this is about Storm, not just random incidents.

That only raises more concern for all of us. Even knowing Saint is watching her doesn't give me the relief it should. *I* should be watching her. Protecting her. Keeping her safe.

The last place I should be is on the job. Being distracted at a construction site leads to accidents. Everybody knows that. But I have to keep the work moving on THREE.

Completing this place will be a massive form of closure for all the Hawkes, Storm especially.

God knows, she needs it.

We corrected the issues the inspector found so we can start moving forward on the next phase of the build. This isn't one of those projects where we just slap everything together as quickly as we can. The Hawkes have way too exacting standards for that. And the design Storm did—both the exterior and the interior— require handcrafted wood elements and other items that just can't be rushed.

Not having her here, not talking to her about what's going on with the build makes my stomach roil. This is her build. Her baby. A place that means so damn much to her as a tribute to Ben, but she doesn't need to deal with this little stuff. It's why they hired me.

Time to get your head on straight.

I scrub my hands over my face and approach the building. I haven't been able to stop thinking about the way she looked when she came down from the upstairs portion last time we were here. I can't get her distress from my head. Nor can I erase the way she makes my heart race just being around her. It's all proved one thing to me...I feel way more for that woman than I should. More than I have any right to.

Storm deserves a man who can give her everything, and I don't have everything left to give. A huge part of me is still tied up in Chicago. And the way things are going, maybe it always will be. If I came clean with her now, she'd use it as an excuse to run just like she's been trying to since the first night we met. And maybe she would be right to run. She needs somebody who can be all she needs, not someone who is just going to try.

But I can't come clean. Not until things are settled.

So maybe it's a lost cause. Maybe it's too much to hope that things are actually going somewhere. Too much. Too fast. Too soon. For both of us.

My phone rings just as I step through the door. A massive part of me wants it to be Storm, but it's the next best thing.

Just the man I've been waiting on.

"Barry, you bald, old bastard. You better have some damn good news for me."

My faith in Barry is starting to wane. He's never failed me in anything else over the years, but this simple task seems to be beyond his capability for some *insane* reason.

"It's nice to talk to you too, Landon."

Here I am, upset about Storm taking it out on me when I'm doing the same thing to Barry. It's frustrating, but it's really not his fault. It's *hers.*

Don't be a dick.

I sigh and lean against the wall just inside the door. "Sorry, I'm just anxious."

He clears his throat and glugs on something—probably old

coffee. There always seems to be two or three cups of it sitting on his desk from throughout the day whenever I had to go meet with him. "I know. I know. Look, we got a hold of one of her friends."

That's definitely an improvement from where we've been. Anything is a damn improvement.

"Which one?" A mental list of all the vapid women she called friends scrolls through my head. Cassandra, Anna, Donna, Angela...the list is really endless.

"Sandra."

I snort and roll my eyes even though he can't see me. I wouldn't call Sandra a friend. She's more of a hanger-on. One of those society women who is only friends with you if you can benefit her social standing or do something for her. I never particularly liked her. I could see through her games. But she wasn't my friend, and I wasn't going to put myself in the middle of that by expressing my concerns about her.

Maybe if I had, things would have been different. The influence of those women clearly played a role in what happened, what Candace did.

Even thinking her name has me gritting my teeth.

"Well, what did Sandra have to say?"

"Sandra spoke to her a week and a half ago but didn't know where she called from."

"Shit. Did she have any idea what Candace was doing?"

"She said she was still trying to get in touch with you."

That's odd. Aside from the call that I let go to voicemail when I first got here, there haven't been any other calls from her number, and I don't remember any blocked or unknown numbers calling recently either. I typically answer those since they could be potential new clients.

"You're sure she was trying to get in touch with me?"

"That's what Sandra said."

I drop my head back against the wall—nothing more than drywall at this point—and laugh. "Shit."

How's that for ironic?

It would be a lot easier if she would just *call* me. When I declined her call weeks ago, I had no way of knowing she was going to go AWOL and Barry wouldn't be able to locate her. Had I known then what a pain in the ass it would be to track her down, I would have answered and spoken with her. Even though hearing her voice and excuses is the last thing I want or need.

My own anger got us here. If I had just answered, this whole thing might be over already, and I could concentrate on work here and trying to figure out what's happening with Storm without the dark cloud of my old life hovering overhead.

Fucking eh.

"What do you suggest, Barry? What else can we do?"

It's been weeks, and we still haven't found her. Candace isn't the type to leave her life behind like this, to stop going to the gym and seeing her friends, to just disappear. It has my chest tightening, even though all I feel for her is disdain.

"I have my men checking everywhere we can think of and trying to track her any way possible. Talking to friends. Going anywhere she frequents. We're trying to track her credit cards, but that's taking a while to access. It would have been a lot easier if it was a joint card you could just log into."

No shit.

It's definitely not like her to up and disappear, but then again, neither was what she did. At least, it wasn't the Candace I knew. But I think time has proven that maybe I didn't really know her at all. Maybe I had seen what I wanted to see, who I wanted to see, instead of what was really in front of me. Or maybe she was exactly who I thought she was, and that was just the *wrong* type of woman to be with. I just couldn't see it until she shoved the truth in my face.

"Just keep on it, Barry. We can't keep striking out much longer."

"Why are we all of a sudden on a timeline? I mean, I know

you want everything here concluded, but you seem more stressed about this than you should be. Whether it's now or a month from now, it won't impact the outcome."

He's not wrong. A few weeks' delay isn't a big deal in the grand scheme of things, but I hate keeping this from Storm. I expect her to open up to me, but I can't do the same with her. Not yet. She just wouldn't understand, nor am I in any position to discuss it without completely coming unglued.

Hypocrite much?

Maybe if Barry knows the truth, it will light a fire under his ass to get things wrapped up. "I met someone."

"You what?"

The shock in Barry's voice isn't a surprise. Given everything he knows, he has every reason to expect me to stay far away from romantic involvement with anyone for a *long* time. Which, of course, was the plan...until Storm.

"I know it sounds crazy with everything that I've been through, but this woman is different."

He snort-laughs. "Famous last words, my friend."

"No, Barry. If you saw her, if you sat down with her, if you heard her story, you'd understand."

No one can hear what Storm has been through and not immediately feel for her. Not immediately be impressed with the way she's managed to hold herself and Angelina together since losing Ben. No man can possibly be immune to her beauty and the power she has to suck you in and drown you with those blue eyes.

"Another blonde bombshell?"

I chuckle as visions of Storm's thick black silk hair flowing all around her as she rides me flip through my head. "No, man, she couldn't be more different. Dark hair, pale skin, eyes the color of the summer sky." Except they darken and swirl with every emotion, revealing everything she's thinking at any given moment. I just wish they told me what she felt about me. Why she's been holding back.

It can't just be about Ben. There has to be more to this.

"Anyway, Barry, I just want this done. I want that part of my life over, so get it taken care of. It's why you get all my money."

"I'm doing my best."

"Do better."

I'm sick of waiting for my old life to close so I can fully pursue my new one.

Back then, I always wanted the two point five kids and white picket fence. That went down the drain so fast, I barely knew what happened.

But, here, with Storm...there's something.

It's standing right in front of me, I just don't know what it is. It's more than what we intended. There are feelings there—a word I never thought I'd use again, floating around in my head, one I'm terrified to even think.

Storm feels it too. She just needs to know she can trust me despite how we started out and what this was intended to be. Things are different now. We are different. This is different.

She needs to see this is it. This is everything we never wanted yet somehow managed to stumble upon. This could really be something.

twenty-two

*CM*y stomach works its way up my throat as Landon pulls open the door. I haven't apologized for how I acted the other night yet, and I'm not sure how to. Even my talk with Dani and Skye only further muddied the waters.

How I feel hasn't changed...I can't let anyone else run my life —not Savage, not Gabe, and not Landon. I need to be able to stand on my own two feet—for me and for Angelina. But that doesn't mean I can ignore what's happening between me and Landon.

This pull...it's too much to fight.

Which is why I'm standing in front of his door while he leans against the jamb in nothing but a pair of gray sweatpants looking absolutely fucking sinful with a raised eyebrow.

He's waiting for me to say something.

I clear my throat and take a tiny step closer to him. "I'm sorry. Okay? I was frustrated. That wasn't your fault the other night. It was the situation."

A situation that hasn't resolved. Saint is still attached to me like a damn shadow almost twenty-four/seven. The only time the big man isn't on my ass is when I'm in the house, the office, or here. At least he's managed to stay somewhat discreet about it, though. Angel hasn't seemed to notice. But there haven't been any other incidents either. So, either whoever is doing this has seen him despite him staying in the background and backed off, or there was never a threat to begin with...like I thought.

The corner of his mouth quirks up in a half-grin, and he reaches out and pulls me up against his warm, naked skin.

"Apology accepted." He brushes my hair off my shoulder and leans forward to press his lips to my neck.

Oh, Christ...

Heat pools low in my belly and spreads between my legs. It would be so much easier to sort through my feelings for Landon and everything else if I didn't turn to absolute Jell-O under his touch and mouth.

My fingers dig into the hard flesh at his sides, and he groans against my skin and presses his very hard cock into my stomach.

"I'm glad you came tonight. I hated not talking to you, feeling like there were things unsaid and anger between us. I never want that."

I don't either.

The problem is what I *do* want and how to reconcile that with my love for Ben and that life. This miserable downward spiral I've been on since his death never would have ended if Landon hadn't arrived and dragged me from the dark depth of the abyss.

Why do I keep running from what makes me happy?

He nuzzles my neck and then pulls away and drags me into his condo. The door clicks shut behind me, and his mouth is on mine before I have a moment to think.

That's probably for the best. Thinking seems to get me in trouble these days. Overanalyzing everything. Second-guessing every single decision. Running scared from the feelings boiling over inside me.

I return his kiss, letting go of all the shit whirling through my head and just feeling his lips, his hands, his erection pressing against me.

He walks me backward across the living room and down the short hallway to his bedroom without taking his mouth off mine. Every sweep of his tongue. Every nip. Every suck. It all winds me tighter...builds me higher. So, by the time the back of my legs hit the bed, I'm almost ready to combust.

"Please, Landon." My mumbled words against his lips draw a

chuckle from him, and his rough palms skim up under my shirt and over my heated skin.

This. This is why I can't walk away.

This...and the way he makes me forget everything else even when we aren't naked.

Those talented hands work into the cups of my bra, and his fingers find my pebbled nipples. He twists them sharply, and a jolt of pleasure goes straight to my clit.

"Fuck!" I drop my head back and arch into his touch. The man is a master. And his control over my body is complete.

His warm breath flutters the hair next to my ear. "There are so many things I want to do to you tonight."

Yes.

That's an offer I can't refuse. I push him back, and he raises his blond eyebrows at me. My shirt is up over my head and on the floor and my fingers find the clasp of my bra before he can get a word out.

He pushes his sweats down and frees his hard cock as I toss my bra to join my shirt. The only thing separating us is a few inches and the thong covering my aching center.

"Fuck, Storm. You're so damn beautiful."

Those words...

"You're so damn beautiful...and all mine. Forever." I freeze as Ben's voice floats through my head. Visions of the white lingerie I wore on our wedding night hitting the floor and Ben's wide eyes as he pushed into me for the first time as Mrs. Matthews are too much for me to take.

I can't look at Landon when Ben is in my head.

How can I keep doing this?

It's not fair to Landon. It's not fair to Ben.

I turn to face the bed.

If I can't give myself to Landon completely, then I need to end this. Tonight. This was never meant to be more than sex. We can go back to just being professional friends. We can chalk this up as a failed experiment in the friends-with-benefits department. We can eventually forget. Learn to ignore the feelings there.

Eventually.

His strong, warm arms wrap around me, and he tugs me back against him. Warm lips make their way over the back of my neck and settle just behind my left ear. He works his fingers into the top of my thong and moves it down my legs. I raise my feet to let him slide it off.

One more night.

I'll give him that. I'll give *us* that.

Because I'm selfish. And the way he makes me feel, those moments of pure bliss and complete calm...I need that more than I need to breathe right now.

I reach back and grasp his cock. My clit throbs, and I press my thighs together.

Why does he have to make me feel this way?

Brushing my thumb over the silky head has him groaning in my ear. He tugs on my shoulder, urging me to turn back to face him.

I can't.

Tonight, of all nights, I can't look at him. I can't have those molten bourbon eyes seeing through me, seeing everything I'm trying to hide. My feelings for Ben. My feelings for *him.*

I pull away and climb onto the bed. The mattress dips as he climbs on behind me, but he tugs on my shoulder, forcing me to flip onto my back to stare up at him.

His normally soft gaze is dark and hard. There's no use. He saw through me despite my best efforts to hide it. He knows me so well already. Better than he should in such a short amount of time.

He knows, and he isn't happy about what I'm trying to do.

I shouldn't be avoiding this conversation with him. I shouldn't be avoiding the connection that's there, the one he seems so eager to make even deeper. I shouldn't be avoiding the very real fact that I'm falling for him.

There's no way he will let this go on any longer. He's not going to let me use sex as a way to distract him from what really needs to be said.

This is going to hurt.

Storm peers up at me from under her thick, dark lashes, trying to hide behind the only thing separating us now.

She can't hide anymore.

The shift in her was so clear, so dramatic, it was like watching a dark cloud wrap around her and drag her down from the high she was floating on only a moment ago.

Only, I have no idea what happened to cause it, and she has no intention of telling me. She thinks she can get away with turning her back on me and letting me fuck her without questioning her. She thinks she can keep this just about sex. She thinks she can keep me out.

Not anymore.

She's not pushing me away again. Not if we ever want to make this work. But only absolute honesty will ever clear the air between us, and we've spent too much time keeping things from each other, denying how we feel.

I need to come clean with her too...

But I need finality before that can happen. I wouldn't even begin to know how to tell her what happened when she's already dealing with so much on her own plate.

Once things are over, she'll know everything. Right now, it's about *her* and the way she's pushing me away every time I get even an inch closer to her. I've accepted how I feel about Storm, and it's time she does the same.

"You think I don't know what you're doing, Storm?"

Anger and something that looks an awful lot like fear darkens her eyes, and she shifts out from under me and off the opposite side of the bed.

She squeezes her hands into fists at her sides before wrapping her arms across her naked chest, as if that will somehow protect her from the conversation that's coming. Her eyes stay focused on her feet.

"I don't know what you're talking about."

I growl and slide off the bed so I'm standing in front of her. "Yes, you do." I swallow past the emotion suddenly clogging my throat and rub at the burn in my eyes. "Do you think I haven't noticed you won't have sex while looking at me? That you always put yourself or me in a position where you don't have to meet my eyes?"

Saying it out loud while she's standing naked and vulnerable in front me...while *I* am naked and vulnerable in front of her, is so much worse than thinking it. My chest aches, and I reach up and rub at the spot while I wait for an answer, or any reaction for that matter, from her.

Storm lives her emotions, and a war is waging inside her right now. She tugs her bottom lip under her teeth and curls her arms around her even more tightly.

She regards me, and the shimmer in her eyes almost looks like churning waves on the ocean outside my windows. Her bottom lip slips from between her teeth and quivers, and she shakes her head. "Why can't you just fuck me?"

Anger roars through my veins, and I take several deep breaths to try to quell it before I say or do something I will regret later. It's amazing how words can sting so much. Especially words most men would kill to hear.

A beautiful, willing woman here begging to be fucked...any man's dream.

And it was mine not so long ago. But not anymore.

Not with her.

I scrub my hands over my face and let out a deep sigh. "I don't want to fuck you, Storm. I want to make love to you."

She releases a sob and slaps her hand over her mouth while shaking her head.

Not the reaction I was hoping for when finally expressing how I feel.

I can see her crumbling. The carefully constructed walls she's used to keep me from getting into her heart are falling away with each tear that trickles down her cheek. She's been holding so much back. So much that I don't understand, that I *can't* understand if she won't tell me.

"What is this, Storm?" I motion between us. "And don't say we're just having sex, because we both know that's absolutely not true. At least, not anymore."

She wanders to the other side of the bedroom, giving her back to me. If she thinks I'll let her walk away without having this discussion, she's wrong. She can't ignore it anymore. Neither of us can.

It was never like this with Candace. Things were always so... easy. Too easy. I was comfortable. It had become routine. We didn't even have the passion to fight. With Storm, everything is passionate. Everything is fire.

And it will burn us alive if we don't do something about it. We need to control the flames. Rein them in and send them in the right direction. Holding them inside will only destroy us both.

"Storm. Answer me."

Her shoulders heave, and my gut clenches. The last thing I want is to cause her pain, but there's no way to avoid it right now.

Ignoring this and continuing or ignoring this and ending things —either one does no good for either of us. We have to play our cards on the table before we can decide how to move forward. Before we can decide if there is a possible future here.

She turns slowly, wiping at her cheeks, and meets my eyes. "I don't know what this is. I wish I did."

I scoff and take a step toward her. "Bullshit. You know. You're just too scared to admit it and say it out loud." She recoils slightly at my words, and regret immediately cuts at me. It needed to be said, though. "Why, Storm? Why are you fighting this so damn hard?"

The pain in her eyes tells me everything.

Ben.

His name doesn't need to be uttered for him to be in the room with us. I knew Storm came with a lot of baggage. You can't go through something like that, lose someone like that, and not come away scarred. But I can't believe Ben would want her to be like this, to be miserable, to be fighting a war with herself every single time she's with me.

"I don't know what you want me to say, Landon." Her words are barely a whisper, but they fill the room.

I move toward her again, giving her all the time in the world to step back if she doesn't want me close. She holds her ground and watches my approach with uncertain eyes. I reach out and tilt her chin up to look at me.

"I don't want you to say anything. It's not about what I *want* to hear. All I want is the truth."

A bit hypocritical of me to be demanding it from her when I haven't been fully honest. Maybe I'm not strong enough to own up to my own truth, to tell her everything. Maybe I'm not strong enough to be the man Storm really needs. But I sure as hell am going to try.

She pulls away from my touch as another round of tears pours down her cheeks. "I don't think I can..."

Christ.

Her struggle breaks me and shatters my heart into a million pieces. This is so not how I saw this night going when she texted and said she was coming over.

"Please, Storm, just tell me the truth."

Please.

twenty-three

Storm's shoulders sag, and her lip trembles. She wraps her arms tightly around her naked chest and shakes. "You don't want to know."

How can she really think that? By now, how does she not know how much I care?

"I wouldn't ask if I didn't want to know."

She closes her eyes and paces. Her hands shove back and tug on her hair. She's fighting everything inside her telling her not to answer me.

I give her a moment to compose herself. Watching her struggle, watching the pain in her eyes, her jerky movements, the way she worries on her bottom lip, it all tears me apart more than what Candace did.

Fuck if that isn't eye-opening.

I care more about the woman in front of me who I've known barely a month than the one back home who was supposed to be my happily ever after.

After what feels like an eternity, she stops pacing and lifts her head up to face me. "You want the gory details? Fine. You asked for it." Her words waver, and her entire body shakes as she speaks. "You want to hear about how every single day, I struggle to even take a breath. How that simple act of sucking in oxygen feels like drowning. That most days, the only reason I get out of bed at all is because of Angelina coming in and crawling into bed with me and telling me I need to get up. That more than once, I've contemplated taking the entire bottle of sleeping pills and anxiety meds the doctor gave me."

Christ.

I knew it was bad, but to think she was considering taking her own life. It's like a bullet going through my heart.

She fights back a sob and shakes her head. "You want to know the thing that I haven't told anyone, not my family or my friends or even the damn shrink my mother made me go see?"

The tears are streaming down her face now. I want nothing more than to close the distance between us and take her in my arms, but I can't interrupt whatever she's about to say.

"Ben and I had been trying to get pregnant for two years. I was eight weeks along when he died, and then a week later, I sat in the shower sobbing while I miscarried our child and never told a single fucking person about it because all I could do was wonder what I had done wrong and blame myself, because I hadn't eaten for a week, because I had done nothing but cry and be an emotional basket case, because I didn't take care of my body or that baby...it was my fault it died."

Oh, God.

I never expected that. How could she have kept something like that from everyone? Losing Ben was bad enough, but losing a child they'd been trying for so desperately, for so long, was just another brutal blow to her. One she kept from everyone so she never got to work through her feelings about it.

No wonder she's been struggling. It's not just about Ben's death. It's her own guilt over the loss of the baby.

She can't really believe she caused the miscarriage, can she?

I take a step toward her. "Storm, I'm so sorry. I had no idea."

She raises a shaking hand up to stop me from advancing further. "Don't. I don't want your pity."

"Pity? Is that what you think this is?"

It's the furthest thing from what I'm feeling. I could never pity her. She's so fucking impressive and inspiring. She's everything a man could want—intelligent, hard-working, a wonderful mother and sister, and so beautiful, it takes my breath away. There was never pity there. Never.

A sob breaks free from her mouth, and she covers it with her hand. I need her in my arms. I need to comfort her, but she doesn't want me to touch her. Even the words I'm saying to try to break down her walls aren't getting through.

The tempest swirling around her has been buffeting her from all sides for months, the winds and the rain lashing at her relentlessly and shredding her skin. But despite what she may think, what others may think, she's not broken. Far from it. Storm is a rock. Life may do its best to beat her down and weather her resolve, but she stands strong. She's just too caught up in her own grief right now to see the truth of the situation.

I lower my voice, ensuring it's soft and gentle and that she'll understand I'm here for her and only want the truth. "Why didn't you tell anyone, Storm?"

Her wet, red eyes meet mine, and she releases a sigh choked with another sob. "Because it wouldn't change anything, and the family didn't need more grief. Then we found out Nora was pregnant and...at that point, even if I wanted to, I just couldn't. I couldn't drag my family down when we finally found something good out of everything that happened."

Always so selfless. Storm *would* think about what they needed and not what *she* needed. Keeping this all bottled up inside has been eating away at her, and no one knew.

Jesus.

She told me when she didn't tell anyone else. That *has* to mean something. Why can't she see that? Why can't she see I'm what she needs?

"You didn't need to go through this alone. No one can ever understand the losses you suffered, but we can all be here for you to support you."

"What if I don't want you to support me? What if I just want to be left alone?"

The words are so heavy with despair and resignation, it's almost as if she's given up. On life. On me. It shatters my heart and has a lump of emotion clogging my throat.

"Why? So you can crawl into bed and curl into a ball and pretend the world doesn't exist and let yourself slowly waste away? What about your brothers and sister and your mom, your employees and your friends, what about your goddamn daughter?"

What about ME?

Another sob wracks her body, and she collapses in on herself. "I'm failing her."

"No, you're not."

"He was her entire world, and she lost him. And then I disappeared too."

I step toward her again, and this time, she doesn't back away. But I don't dare touch her yet. I don't want her to bolt, and pushing her too far, too fast is sure to do that. "You didn't disappear."

"Yes, I did. My body may have been there, but I have been anything but present for Angel." She scrubs her face, wiping away her tears and rubbing at her red eyes.

"Storm, she loves spending time with your mom and that gives you a break you need. There's nothing wrong with asking for and accepting help from people."

Fuck it.

I step forward and wrap my hands around her biceps, holding her in place. She tries to twist out of my hold but stops almost immediately and drops her head down, shaking it as she sobs. I don't want to hurt her, but I need her to look at me. She needs to hear this.

"Stop." I squeeze her arms gently. "Look at me."

Reluctantly, her head rises.

"You need to listen to me right now, whether you like it or not. You are *not* failing. You're doing everything you can to make it through what has been a truly awful situation."

Something none of us could ever fathom. Something no one should ever have to endure.

"You've been through two tremendous tragedies. No one can question your love for Angel or say that anything you've done to function through this is wrong. Nothing you're feeling is wrong. Nothing you've been doing is wrong. Everyone processes grief in a different way."

"But—"

I shake my head. "No, no buts."

This part will hurt. I suck in a deep breath and brace myself for the impact my words will surely have. "Ben is gone. He's never coming back."

Her bottom lip quivers, and she tries to twist out of my hold.

"He was your life. I know that, and I know I can never take his place, nor would I want to."

But I do want something I never expected, because I feel something I never anticipated was possible again.

I fucking love her. I'm falling in love with Storm Matthews.

"He's gone, and I am right here right in front of you, asking you to let me love you. You deserve to be loved. Don't let your own guilt prevent you from taking what's being offered. Don't let fear and regret stand in the way of your future happiness, Storm." I hold her face between my palms, forcing her to look at me. Forcing her to hear my words. "Ben wouldn't want that for you. You know that. And you deserve to be happy again. Maybe the timing is shitty. I don't know if there's ever an appropriate time to move on from something like that. But what I do know is that if we walk away from this, if *you* walk away from this, it will be something that you'll regret for the rest of your life. Don't let his death end your life."

Seven months ago, hell, even seven weeks ago, if anyone had told me I'd be standing here naked, pouring my heart out and baring my soul to a man, a man I am *sleeping* with, I would've told them they were batshit crazy. Ben was my entire world—he and Angel. When I lost him, I lost a piece of myself. One I never thought I'd get back. I never thought I could feel a connection like this again.

And Landon's right.

This is more than just physical. I've been kidding myself thinking it's not. I've been intentionally ignoring the fact that it's more than just fucking away my sorrows. It may have started that way for both of us. But now...it's so much more. He is so much more.

As awful as it was to hear those words said so bluntly, I needed to hear them. People have been walking on eggshells around me since Ben died, like anything they say could shatter me completely. Little do they know, it wouldn't have mattered. I've been shattered since the moment I knew he was gone, but it's only recently I started to wonder if perhaps those pieces can be glued back together, and that's all because of Landon. Because of everything he's given me and shown me could exist again.

I meet his warm amber eyes, and the understanding I see there steals my breath and words.

Even if I knew what to say, I can't seem to get anything past the giant lump in my throat. So instead, I press my face in his neck and let him wrap his arms around me, cocooning me in his strength and warmth.

He buries his face in my hair, inhales deeply, and squeezes me. He doesn't say anything. He doesn't have to. Everything we should have been saying to each other the last couple weeks is out in the open now.

Almost everything.

I still can't voice how I feel about him, but I know he won't force me to do anything I'm not ready to.

He pushed hard tonight, but I think he knew as much as I did deep down that I needed to tell him everything.

He understands and sees so much more than I ever gave him credit for.

I was so blind.

He pulls back and presses a soft kiss on my forehead. His fingers find mine and twine together, and he tugs me gently toward the bed.

It's going to happen.

This time, I'm not going to fight it. This time, I'm going to let myself feel everything I've been suppressing and trying so hard to fight. This time, I'm going to be one hundred percent present the way Landon deserves. No guilt. No regret. No hesitation. No Ben. Nothing between us.

Oh God, this is it.

It's been there, just out of reach for so long, and now, it's finally going to happen. Landon is going to make love to me. He's going to hold me the way I've been craving for what feels like forever. He's going to give me everything.

He helps me climb up onto the bed, and I spread out on my back across the vast expanse of the king size mattress. He crawls toward me, his muscles rippling with every movement.

He really is beautiful.

Long and lean and also powerful but capable of being so damn tender and loving. Given the chance to go all-in, my body vibrates with anticipation of what he has in store for me.

He slowly lowers himself onto me, propping himself up on

his elbows, and warm breath flutters across my skin. His right hand rises and brushes some hair off my forehead, then he leans in and kisses me. The moment his lips touch mine, the agony of what I just told him floats away on a cloud of need. Blood rushes through my veins and straight to my core. My clit throbs, and I shift to press my legs together against the feeling.

His hand makes its way down, across my breast, over my stomach, and between my legs. I shift under him, opening myself and giving him better access. Fingers glide across my wetness while his tongue demands entry against my lips.

God, yes.

I open for him completely, letting his tongue and his fingers into me. A moan falls from my lips into his mouth, and his fingers curl inside me, finding the exact right place to drive me wild.

How can a man who has known me for such a short amount of time know exactly how to touch me? How to kiss me to drive me completely insane?

He releases my mouth and pulls back. "Storm, open your eyes." The softness and caring in his voice breaks through the remaining resolve I have.

I hesitate only momentarily. Not because I don't want to see him, but because I'm afraid when I do meet his warm bourbon eyes, I'm going to say something I'm not ready for.

But I'm weak, and I can't deny his request. My eyes open and meet his. They simmer with need, compassion, longing, and something else that scares me and has my stomach flopping around worse than it did on my wedding day.

Don't say it, Landon. Please don't. Not now. Not tonight.

I don't think my heart can handle it tonight.

Landon either reads my mind or had other plans all along, because he doesn't say the words I can't bear to hear right now. Instead, he removes his hand from between my legs and shifts to grab his hard cock. He drags it through my wetness, sending a shudder through my body and wrenching a moan from deep in my chest.

His lips find mine again briefly, and then he enters me for what feels like the first time. Weeks of fighting this connection, of refusing to look at him while we're together, of pretending this meant nothing, have all led to this moment. His cock stretches me, filling the black void I've felt for so long and making me feel whole for the first time in what might as well be a lifetime.

I gasp and shift under him, wrapping my legs around his waist and driving my heels into his lower back, urging him even deeper. He draws his hips back, then pushes into me with a deliberate stroke.

Christ.

The drag of the head of his cock along my G-spot makes me clamp down around his hard flesh. He grunts and captures my mouth in a searing kiss. Panting breaths mingle and tongues tangle in a duel we've been building up to for weeks. But it's not hard. Not aggressive. Not the desperate race to release we've been so intent on. It's slow, lingering, unhurried. Every swipe of his tongue. Every thrust of his hips. Every single movement steady and deliberate.

It's everything I've needed. Everything I've been searching for without even knowing it.

Landon's strokes quicken, and he cups my face in his palm. He refuses to look away, and this time, I don't want him to.

Sex is amazing—the push, the pull, the sweat, the heat, the gasps, and moans.

But sex with *feeling* is something else altogether. Staring into the eyes of someone who holds such a deep passion for you, and you for them, the connection it creates. The depths of the soul that are laid bare for the other to see. It's transcendent.

I forgot what this was like...

He shifts, and his hands grip my hips, angling them up. The change of position has me biting my lip to keep from screaming.

"Don't do that, baby. Let me hear you." The words are more order than request, and almost without thought, my mouth opens and the pants become strangled moans and begging.

"Please...Landon. Harder."

He's kept the pace slow, trying to draw out our pleasure and no doubt savor this pivotal moment in our relationship, but I can't take it anymore. The coiled tension in my body screams to be released. Every fiber of my being demands he go harder, faster, deeper.

A low growl is the only answer he gives me before he slams into me and sets a rhythm designed to drive us both to orgasm faster than a virgin on prom night.

"Oh, God, yes!" I dig my nails into his shoulders, and my hips rise to meet his every thrust. His lips find my neck, and he kisses his way up to my ear. Hot breath flutters across my sweaty skin, only enhancing my need for this...for him.

Heat blooms in my core, spreading out through my limbs.

So close. So damn close.

His thrusts meet mine. He sucks and kisses at my neck, and then his tongue slides along my ear, sending a bolt of lightning down my spine.

One nip of his teeth, and I'm gone.

It hits me so hard, the world goes black before thousands of brilliant colors explode across my lids. Cascading waves of pleasure course through my body. Weightless and floating, the heat spreads and undulates until I can't even breathe.

Landon's cock continues to drive into me, spreading me and dragging out my orgasm longer than I knew possible.

He groans beside my ear and slams his hips into me so hard, I bang my head against the headboard. The tingling euphoria of my orgasm still consumes me when he presses his lips to my ear and comes.

"I love you, Storm."

twenty-four

The whispered words still ring in my ears as the faint light seeps through the crack in the blinds and hits my eyes. Lying here cocooned in Landon's arms, it's still hard to wrap my head around it.

He loves me.

It shouldn't be such a surprise. Not after what we said, what we finally let happen last night. It was never casual. Not really. He has a history, something in his past he still can't or won't talk about that kept him from wanting to make that connection the same way my history kept me from accepting it was true.

But hearing the words makes it real. It makes it something I now *have* to deal with. Feelings can't be ignored anymore.

I've spent so long trying *not* to feel anything. The pain consumed me so completely, I couldn't bear anything else invading my brain. Landon changed that. In such a short amount of time, he reminded me why *feeling* was so good. How feeling could be *better* than good.

His words were harsh but accurate. I can't let Ben's death end my life. That's what I've been doing, and it's wrong. It hurts not only me, but Angel as well. I don't want her growing up thinking it's healthy to withdraw from the world and wallow in misery.

We'll always miss Ben. We'll always *love* Ben. But that doesn't mean there isn't room for other things that make us feel or even love.

Christ, I do love him.

There's no denying it anymore. I squeeze his hand where it

lies against my naked chest, and he hums and shifts, tugging me even closer against his hard, warm body.

Once I purged the truth to him last night, it was only a matter of time before those three words were going to spill from my lips. I don't know how I managed to keep them to myself last night, especially after his declaration. It must have been by sheer force of will, or maybe self-preservation. Either way, a clock has started ticking down the time until I have to admit and confess it to him.

Why is that so terrifying?

Maybe because I've never said those words to anyone but Ben, never even felt it for anyone else. Maybe because I can't bear the thought of losing someone I love again, and somehow, by not saying the words out loud, I've convinced myself it will make things easier if anything *were* ever to happen to him.

Crazy. You're batshit crazy, Storm.

I know how insane that logic is, but it doesn't change the part of me deep down that still believes it. And now I will have to figure out how to work him into my life and Angelina's, leaving *her* open to more pain in the future should anything happen to us, to him.

How the hell do I tell her? How do I tell the family?

Landon's light snoring fills the otherwise silent room. I squeeze his arms gently, then slowly peel my way out from his grasp. I finally open my eyes to glance at the clock. It's still early. I can get home before Angel wakes up and get her off to school myself so Mom doesn't have to do that. Maybe we'll stop by the coffee shop for a pastry if we have time, too.

It's been far too long since I did anything special for her for no reason.

Mom fail #3,679.

Despite Landon's reassuring words last night, I know I haven't been excelling in the mom department lately. It's time I *made* time for her, even if it's just something little like a stop on the way to school.

Angel will appreciate it. She always does.

She has so much of Ben in her. He was always smiling and happy with the little things in life. Angel was too. Until he was ripped away from us. Now, I struggle to find that part of her. When I look at her, I see Ben, but what used to be on the surface with an easy smile or giggle is now buried beneath the hurt of never seeing her father again. I have to drag it out of her most days. And a stop for something sweet will be just the ticket to see that smile that always manages to light up my day, even in my darkest hours.

I slide from the comfort and warmth of Landon's bed and spend a minute gathering my clothes from where they lie strewn on the floor. There's always been such a rush to get out after we're together, so I don't know whether he's a light sleeper or not.

There are so many things I should know about Landon that I don't because I've intentionally avoided knowing, because I always tried to convince myself it was only about the sex. How he takes his coffee. Whether he drinks whiskey neat or on the rocks. When he had his first kiss. Shit, I don't even know anything about the rest of his family besides Chris other than a few off-handed comments about his shitty relationship with his father.

Girlfriend fail.

If I even *am* his girlfriend...

I don't have a clue what last night meant. I just know it was a massive shift from where we had been—like tectonic plates moving and rumbling the Earth, this will alter the landscape of our lives. For the better, or the worse.

With a quick glance over my shoulder to ensure he's still sleeping, I slip into the bathroom and close the door gently behind me. The click of the latch engaging sounds.

Please stay asleep.

There's no way I'm ready to face the aftermath of last night. Not yet. I know I can't put it off forever, but just a little time will help me gather my thoughts and will put me in a better place to deal with the ramifications of those certain words.

How can three little words shift the entire world off its axis?

I pull my phone from my jeans pocket. I need to check in with Mom and let her know I'm on my way. I turn it on and freeze.

Shit.

Four missed calls from Mom and two text messages. It's not like her to call when I go out. I think she's just so happy I'm leaving the house that she doesn't want to interrupt. She knows something is up. I've been asking her to watch Angelina several nights a week since Landon showed up, far more than she ever did before. Yet she hasn't said a thing when I told her I needed some more "alone time." The woman has to suspect I'm meeting someone, yet she smiles and agrees to take her without asking questions.

Thank God for that.

I can't imagine having to tell Mom that I've been off fucking the new employee of Ben's business.

Talk about awkward.

I open the most recent voicemail.

"Storm, first, don't panic. Everything's fine. But I had to take Angel to the ER. She had a really high fever and was complaining her ear hurt. She just has an ear infection. It's no big deal. We're still at the hospital but I'll have her home soon. Call me when you get this."

Oh, my God...

My baby is sick and in pain, and I was here, fucking my brains out and being the shittiest mother in the entire world. I should have been with her. She must have been so scared...

Tears pool in my eyes, and my hand shakes as I try to call Mom.

"Storm!"

"Is she okay?" I bite back a sob that threatens to make its way out.

"She's fine. She's sleeping now. I assume you won't send her to school today. Are you coming home soon?"

I manage to swallow through the tears and lump in my throat. "Yes, I'm coming now."

"Okay, see you soon."

No questions. No comments.

But a world of judgment there. What kind of mother not only leaves their child but also doesn't answer urgent phone calls and texts?

A shitty one.

My phone clatters to the counter, and the sob finally breaks free, echoing off the tile. I clamp my hand over my mouth and let the tears fall onto the marble surface below me.

I can't believe I wasn't there. I'm so godddamn selfish.

Last night, I was so caught up in needing what Landon could give me that I didn't even realize I had turned off my ringer. I cut myself off from my daughter when she needed me. Mom was always there with us. Every minute of every day, she was *there* for whatever any of us ever needed. She committed her life to us. Like a mother *should*.

This can't happen again. Ever. I didn't even think about Angel *once* last night after Landon started touching me, after we broke down all those barriers between us and came together truly as lovers. It was like I completely forgot the most important thing in my life. I'm such a terrible mother. And person.

I tug my clothes on with shaking hands and take a moment to splash some cold water on my face. When I raise my head and meet my reflection in the mirror, I want to smash it into a million pieces to destroy the image of the woman there.

Instead, I dig in my pocket for my lipstick and write a message for Landon across the reflective surface.

Maybe it's the coward's way out of this.

Maybe it's selfish.

I guess that would make sense, since that's what I am.

I'm sorry. I can't.

Four bright red words taunt me from the mirror.

What the hell happened?

Last night was...everything. Everything I've been waiting for. Everything I never thought I would want again.

Our talk was the catharsis she needed and it opened the door to the connection I knew was there, that she was feeling too.

So, what happened between us falling asleep and her leaving that caused this response?

Was it because I told her I love her?

I hadn't planned on making the confession. They aren't words that get tossed around lightly, especially by me, and after everything we said to each other, I knew she had already been through a tremendous emotional upheaval. But I couldn't deny anymore that I've been feeling it. Slowly falling in love with her, with every smile, every laugh, every tear, every touch, and every kiss.

I brace my hands on the counter and drop my head down, picturing her face when I said those words.

No. That can't be it.

She may not be in a place where she's capable of returning that statement, but she didn't run last night, and she didn't look terrified. Confused, yes. Overwhelmed, definitely. But not scared, and not enough to make her disappear.

So, what in the everloving fuck happened?

The words I found scrawled on the mirror when I woke alone echo in my head even though I'm trying so hard not to look at them again.

If she thinks, for one second, that I'm about to let her go that easily, that scribbling these words on the mirror is going to be enough for me to turn my back on her, then she has another thing coming. We can't let our own inadequacies and hang-ups get in the way of being together and being happy. We both deserve to be happy.

Whatever bullshit in her mind that snuck up and reared its ugly head will get sent straight back to Hell. We worked too hard to get to what happened last night. She had an epiphany, and so did I. The thought of her rejecting this, us, me...it's just too much to bear. My chest aches just considering it, and I reach up and absently rub at it.

No. It's not ending like this.

I shove off the counter and stride back into the bedroom. My silent phone mocks me from my nightstand. No voicemails. No texts. No messages whatsoever from her.

My hand shakes from the fear Storm has gotten lost in her head again. I press the call button, and it goes straight to her voicemail.

"Hi, you've reached the voicemail of Storm Matthews."

I hang up. I can't listen to her voice, especially when I know she probably won't even listen to my message anyway.

The only way this is going to work is if I see her in person. Getting through to her will be easier when she's looking me in the eye. It will be so much harder for her to give me whatever bullshit excuse she has for why she left this message when she can't just hang up.

My fingers fly over the keyboard to send a text to her.

<Baby, I don't know what happened. I'm not letting you walk away. We need to talk. You at least owe me that.>

I delete the last sentence.

No. She doesn't owe me anything.

If this really isn't what she wants, then I have to let her go. But I don't believe for a second this *isn't* what she wants. Last night proved that. Something happened between then and now. It must have. We were in such a good place. Exactly where we needed to be to explore where this could go, what we could actually be if we aren't fighting against ourselves all the time.

We need time to figure this out.

I send out the message as it is and wait. After five minutes of no reply, I force myself back in the bathroom for a shower. Those damn soul-crushing words taunt me over my reflection. I grab a towel and wipe them away the best I can, but I only smear the red all over the mirror.

Better than seeing the words again, though.

There's no time for proper clean up right now. Today is the meeting at the site with Savage and Gabe. I can't be late. Storm hadn't planned on being there, but I had hoped she would show up. Another chance to confront her demons at the site and prove to herself how much stronger she is.

Now, I'm sure she won't come. She'll be avoiding me like the plague. She won't come to me; I'll just have to go to her.

I jump in the shower and let it run scalding hot, trying not to think about what a fucked-up morning I've had, and by the time I pull up in front of the Hawkeye Club THREE construction site, Gabe's car is already sitting outside.

It's still so strange to me to be here knowing what happened, the lives that were lost. Savage, Gabe, and Storm made the decision to rebuild here as a fuck you to Dom and as a memorial to both Ben and Caleb. They didn't want the evil acts of the Abellos to change their plans, and now the building is even further along than it was when the fire occurred.

The completed exterior is stunning. The Gothic architecture makes it appear like it belongs in an old part of New Orleans, housing some hoity-toity family as opposed to a strip club. Savage and Gabe have always gone out of their way to try to keep their businesses as upscale as possible, and that's certainly been done here. Storm's design, coupled with a few ideas I've added inside, have created an absolutely perfect environment for patrons *and* the staff.

Today's walk-through is more to confirm that everything is on schedule and they're happy with the progress than it is to address any real issues. This shouldn't take long, which is good. I don't think I'll be able to concentrate when all I want to do is drive over to Storm's and tell her what a huge mistake she's making.

I slide out of my car and race up and into the building. Savage and Gabe are near where the main bar area will be, examining some of the equipment. "Hey guys, sorry I'm a little bit late."

Gabe glances down at his watch. "It's okay, man. You're right on time. No problem at all."

Savage narrows his eyes on me. "Are you all right?"

"Yeah, why?"

He examines me for a moment, his dark eyes narrowing. "You just look a little flustered. Is something wrong?"

Shit. Talk about awkward.

"Yes, Savage something is wrong. I've been fucking your sister for weeks and last night, she finally let me make love to her then she ran for the hills this morning."

I'm sure that conversation would go well. Savage is known for his short temper, and I don't want to be on the other end of it. We haven't spent much time together, just a few meetings and that awkward Hawke family dinner, so it's hard to anticipate how bad a beating I would receive if he knew the truth. The dude is huge though, and from what I've been told, very capable of kicking someone's ass. Plus, he has his own personal assassin at his side.

So, this isn't the time to come clean.

"No. Everything's fine." I shake my head and plaster on my best fake smile. I hope that sounded more convincing to them than it had to my own ears. I've never been a very good liar. In fact, I suck at it.

A tiny smile tugs at the corner of Gabe's mouth. He turns to Savage. "Don't you think it's time we end all the pretense?"

What the hell is he talking about?

I flick my gaze between them. "What pretense?"

Gabe's deep laugh fills the empty, cavernous space. "Landon, you haven't been around for very long, so you may not know this, but there are very few secrets between the Hawkes, and even fewer among sisters. Skye told me about you and Storm weeks ago, at least, her suspicion. And she confirmed it after a conversation she had with Dani and Storm after a recent family dinner."

Well, damn.

Here I thought she was doing her best to keep things hidden, and I was going along with it, but the whole time, her sister knew. And she told Gabe, who then told Savage, who probably told everybody else who didn't know in a sick game of Hawke family telephone...

I don't know what to say. Savage stares at me with icy hard eyes, and Gabe's smug little smirk doesn't tell me much of anything.

"I'll bet money the reason you look so flustered today has something do with my sister." Savage's words are cold and harsh. "If you so much as lay a hand on her in any way, I swear to God, I'll kill you and then Gabe will kill you again after I'm done."

I hold up my hands in defense. "Whoa. Guys, I have no intention of ever hurting Storm." If there were ever a time to come clean, I guess this is it. Any result would be better than the alternative, which appears to be getting my ass kicked. "I love her."

Silence permeates the space. And I can almost feel Ben's presence settling over us. I give them a moment to process it. Neither look particularly surprised, and neither says anything.

"She's the one who is getting all hung up in her head about stuff and is pushing me away. I just need to figure out a way to get through to her. I thought I had done that last night, but she was gone this morning with nothing more than basically a dear John letter written on my mirror in her lipstick."

Gabe shakes his head with a little chuckle. "Storm can be quite dramatic."

Savage sighs and offers me what I think is supposed to be a sympathetic smile. "I know what happened."

"What do you mean?"

"I know what happened that made her leave. Angel was with our mom last night, and she got real sick. Mom had to take her to emergency room, and she couldn't get a hold of Storm. I'm sure she woke up, saw messages, realized what happened, and now she feels guilty that she wasn't there."

Son of a bitch.

I'm sure that's exactly what happened. Storm is letting her guilt over things she can't control get in the way of her happiness again. She takes on and carries around so much burden that isn't meant for her.

No fucking way that's going to continue.

Gabe slaps me on the back. "You want some friendly advice?"

I snort out a laugh and nod. I'll take *any* advice at this point, friendly or not. Storm was never going to be easy. That's one of the things that drew me to her, but I never anticipated the whiplash I'd receive from being with her.

Savage chuckles and gives Gabe a knowing look. "My sister is always going to put Angelina first."

I nod my agreement. "She should."

"Yes, she should, but she's going to continue to do it at the expense of her own happiness. She already feels like she's failed Angel since Ben died. She's not going to do anything that makes her feel like that's going to continue."

Gabe sighs and crosses his arms over his huge chest. "You need to get through to her and make her see that her happiness is just as important as Angel's. If you don't, you're going to lose her."

That won't happen.

I'll figure this out. I'll figure out a way to get her to *see.*

twenty-five

I sniffle over the plans laid out on the drafting table. The same ones I've been staring at for almost an hour without touching them. A single tear drops onto the plans, and I swipe at my eyes to keep from ruining them.

After my flight from Landon's this morning, everything has gone wrong.

Angel still has a fever and couldn't go to school, but I had too much to do here at work to stay home with her.

Mom fail #8,567.

If Dani hadn't been able to take her today, I'm not sure what I would've done because I can't afford not to be at work right now, and with Mom tied up with friends in from out of town, that means my go-to babysitter is MIA.

On top of that, three different clients want revisions on plans I thought we had finalized, so I'm going to have to spend time I don't have revising them and re-presenting them to clients who were apparently not happy with my prior work.

I can't blame them, I guess. The spark my designs have always had seems to be missing lately. It's hard to let your creative juices flow when everything in your world is falling apart.

But now isn't the time to dwell on all the ways I've fucked this up so badly—with Angel, with work, with Landon. It's the time to buckle down and get shit done.

All the work does have *one* benefit. It keeps me from spending every single second dwelling on what happened with Landon last night. Not that it's not constantly on my mind. It's just that instead of *every* second, it's *every other* that's consumed with visions of our tangled limbs and echoes of the words we said to each other...and especially those three little ones he said to me.

The ones I had internally begged him not to say. The ones I haven't said to anyone but Ben. The ones I'm glad I didn't say back. I wasn't ready, and now, it's so much better they were never uttered.

This is a moment of weakness I can't afford. I *have* to work. Tears can wait until later.

I force my eyes to focus on the plans—the straight lines, the curves, every minute detail that needs to be exact for it to remain standing. The things the clients are relying on me to have perfect. I press the pencil to the paper when a knock at the door has me jerking around.

Marcy stands in the jam with a small box in her hands. She's an amazing assistant, and I couldn't live without her. Seeing the gift only reminds me how much I need to get her something to say thank you for all she's done while I've been MIA. "This was just dropped off for you."

What the heck?

I set the pencil down and turn to face her fully. "Who is it from?"

She shrugs and glances down at it. "I don't know. It was a delivery service. There's a card on the top, though."

Odd.

It's not my birthday, and there's no other reason someone should be sending me something.

I cross over to her and take the small, lightweight box from her hand while flashing her a smile. "Thank you."

"No problem." With a smile, she turns and then disappears back down the hallway toward the reception area.

The white box with the red bow is innocuous enough. But, my spine tingles with unease. Unexpected gifts. It wouldn't normally rattle me, but the fact that things have been so quiet after the strange incidents has any little thing becoming more suspicious.

But the handwriting where my name is scrawled on the envelope attached has me releasing a sigh.

Landon.

I would know that handwriting anywhere. And I was stupid to think he was just going to let me walk away without another word. That what I wrote on that mirror would be enough to keep him away.

This gift is probably only the beginning.

I wander over to my desk tugging at the bow and drop into my chair. I set the box down and tear open the envelope.

Storm,

I know why you left this morning. I know why you think you had to. I saw this quote a while back, and it made me think of you. Now seemed like the right time for you to read it. We'll talk soon.

Love, Landon.

Tears sting my eyes as I set the card on the desk and lift the box cover. An immediately recognizable turquoise box sits inside with another white bow tied around it.

My hand shakes as I pull it out and tug off the bow. I take a deep breath and flip open the top.

A simple thick silver wrist cuff sits inside.

It's beautiful. And simple. And very me.

I pick it up and turn it over.

The engraving on the inside of the cuff has the tears bursting free and my heart practically exploding in my chest.

Grief never ends, but it changes. It is a passage, not a place to stay.

Grief is not a sign of weakness nor a lack of faith: it is the price of love.

The words slice through me like a razor and straight to the heart of everything I've been feeling this last month. And the six months before that.

Grief is a really fucked-up thing and a bad bedfellow. It strangles you. It makes you second-guess everything you know to be true and overlook that which *could* be.

I will never get over losing Ben. It's impossible.

He was my first love. My husband. Angelina's father. My life for so damn long.

But Landon's right. Opening myself up to that kind of loss again is just the price I have to pay for love. Opening myself up to *him* means subjecting myself to the possibility of losing him the same way I lost Ben.

And maybe there is no appropriate amount of time to grieve or to reach the point where we're capable of loving again. Maybe Ben sent me Landon because he knew how badly I needed to get up and start over. He knew how badly I needed help getting back on my feet.

Yet, I've done nothing but push Landon away. Even after last night, even after what he said, what happened, instead of waking him up to tell him what was going on this morning and letting him comfort me, let him help me...I ran.

It feels like all I'm doing is running from him. And that's so unfair.

Then he goes and does something like this. Sends me this. These words.

He actually fucking understands. Which shouldn't surprise me at all, not with everything he's said.

Whatever happened in Chicago has turned him into an incredibly insightful and compassionate person, if he wasn't before. I don't know his entire past, and I don't need to. It created the man he is today, a man who has it in him to give so much love, so much empathy to me without asking for anything in return except for me to just give it a chance.

I slip the cuff onto my wrist and twist it back and forth, watching it glint under the overhead lights.

No matter what happens with Landon, this stays on.

It's the reminder I need to keep moving forward, at my own pace.

The cue ball strikes the eight ball and sends it ricocheting across the table and into the corner pocket.

I grin over my shoulder at Chris. "Two to one. Pay up."

He shakes his head and grabs the rack off the wall. "No way. Best out of five."

Wishful thinking.

Chris knows he's not nearly as good as I am at pool, yet he continues to make these bets and fork over his hard-earned cash despite getting his ass handed to him repeatedly.

"If you really want to lose more money, that's fine. Double the bet, though."

I don't need the money, and more games would actually be good. More distraction. More of *something* to concentrate on instead of wondering what Storm thought of my gift.

It was perfect. At least, I think it was.

The famous quote from Elizabeth the First struck me hard with its truth.

Grief doesn't have a timeline, and Storm can't keep beating herself up for feeling something for me in what she thinks is too soon after Ben's death, nor should she feel guilty for still loving her husband and missing him. I will never expect that to go away, just like what happened to me will always shape who I am. It's made me appreciate Storm even more. Because there's absolutely nothing fake about her.

Chris starts racking the balls, but he keeps tossing glances over at me.

"What?"

"Nothing. Just wondering why you were so eager to go out tonight. And why you're on your fifth beer already. You seem... stressed about something. More than usual."

That's certainly the truth. Hours in the pool earlier tonight didn't help, but a few cold ones and a couple games of pool usually provide some relief. But not tonight.

There's too much of a weight on my shoulders and too much pressure in my chest.

Too much on my mind.

The entire Hawke clan knows what's going on. There's really no reason not to tell Chris everything at this point. Other than the whole "I'm sleeping with my boss, your business partner, who was married to your dead best friend" thing.

I take a swig of my beer and sigh. "I've been sleeping with Storm."

"Shit." He pauses and leans against the opposite end of the table. His eyes bore into mine. The anger there is something I haven't seen in years. "Seriously? I thought we had that talk about what a bad idea it was to get involved with her."

"We did." I shrug and take another drink. "I just didn't listen."

He sighs and turns to grab his beer off the ledge next to the pool table. "Sounds like I'm going to need a drink for this."

Probably.

I lean against the wall while he takes a drink. Then he narrows his eyes on me. "So what happened?"

"Storm happened."

He snorts. "I warned you."

"I know you did. But there was something about her. I couldn't get her out of my head. I thought we could do the friends with benefits thing, since she clearly wasn't looking for something more but..."

One of his pale eyebrows rises. "But what? Aww, shit. You fell in love with her, didn't you?"

"When you say it like that, it sounds like a really bad thing."

"Isn't it? Jesus, Landon. After what Candace did to you. After what you went through, why would you want to get involved with anyone, let alone someone who has as much baggage as Storm?"

He says it like I had a choice. There was no choice. Something drew me to her from the beginning. Sucked in by that very sadness that weighs her down so often. Then once I got to know her, got to experience her passion for her family, for Angelina, for her work, it was like falling down a rabbit hole I couldn't climb out of.

"It wasn't planned, Chris. It just happened. For both of us."

His eyes widen. "Both of you?"

"I think so."

He shakes his head and takes another sip of his beer. "That doesn't sound very definitive."

"I guess it's not. She's definitely been fighting her feelings for me, and last night, something happened that set us back after we had just taken a tremendous step forward. I'm just not sure what to do about it now."

"Have you tried to talk to her?"

I shake my head. "Not really. I called but didn't leave a voicemail. And I sent a gift today."

He wanders around the table until he can lean back against it directly in front of me. "I don't want to know the details. They're none of my business. But here's what I'll tell you about Storm from the time I've spent with her, and from what Ben has told me." He pauses and considers me for a moment. "If you aren't in this one hundred percent, you need to back away now. Leave it alone. Leave her alone. I'll pull you off all the projects she has a hand in."

"No, I don't want to do that."

"It's not about what you want, Landon, it's about what's best for Storm. She's a passionate woman who loves with her entire heart. My guess is that's precisely what's been causing issues between the two of you. She was with Ben for a *long* time, and the two of them were happy as hell. She will forever be comparing you to him and their relationship, whether she does it intentionally or not. Are you prepared to live with another man in your relationship? Does she even know about what happened in Chicago?"

So many heavy statements there. Complicated questions to unravel. But the ultimate answer comes quickly.

"I'm ready for whatever it takes to be with her, if that's what she wants."

"So, she knows about Candace?"

Shit.

"Not really."

He snorts. "Not really? What the hell does that mean? Either she knows or she doesn't."

"She doesn't. She knows *something* happened and that it drove me to leave Chicago and come here. But that's all. I didn't want to tell her until things are resolved with Candace, or before I knew she actually wanted to pursue something more with me."

"And you don't see a problem with essentially lying to the woman you claim to now love about your past?"

Asshole.

"It's not lying. I'm just not telling her everything right away."

He chuckles and downs the rest of his beer. "Yeah, I'm sure she'll see it that way when you come clean."

She will. I have faith that no matter what ends up happening in my future with Storm, she will understand why I never told her the entire truth. Why I had to keep it from her.

"It may be a non-issue if I can't figure out how to get Storm to listen to reason."

He reaches around me to set his empty bottle on the ledge to my left. "Give her space. Give her time. I may not know a lot about women, but I know enough about Storm. Forcing things and pushing her when she's not ready will only get you pushed further away."

Well, hell.

That's no help. Gabe and Savage tell me not to let her push me away, and Chris tells me to give her space.

Just when I thought things couldn't get more confusing.

"I'll figure it out. I have to."

He slaps me on the shoulder and walks back around to where his cue leans against the far side of the table. "I hope you do. Just remember, she's your boss and my partner. So, don't fuck it up."

Gee, thanks.

twenty-six

The clock reads 5:30, but it feels more like 10:30. It's just been one of those days.

I inspect the cuff for the hundredth time since Landon sent it yesterday. The words scrawled on the inside are almost alive. Like I can feel them against my skin, telling me I need to make a choice about which direction my life will go. And that it needs to happen soon.

The phone on my desk buzzes. "Storm, I'm gonna take off."

I press the speaker button. "Okay, Marcy. See you tomorrow."

"Are you staying late?"

I sigh and check the clock again, as if it's suddenly rotated back an hour in the last five minutes. "Unfortunately, yes. I have a new client coming in in about ten minutes."

"Oh, I don't have that on my calendar."

"I know. He called earlier today when you were out at lunch. I told him he could come in tonight because he said it was somewhat urgent, and I can't afford to turn away any new business right now."

No matter how badly I want to go home and crawl into bed with Angel for a movie marathon and ice cream.

Any new client is an influx of money I will need for Angel's college and anything else that may come up. Ben did well, and so did I, and there was also his life insurance, but it's not as much as everyone thinks. I still need to have a steady stream of clients to keep living the way we do and keep Angelina out of debt when she's older and wants to pursue her own studies.

"Okay, do you want me to stay?" Concern laces her voice, but she doesn't need to worry.

Saint has been watching me like a hawk and nothing has happened. Whatever the threat was—if there even was one—seems long gone.

"No. I'll be fine."

"Okay, see you tomorrow."

Probably another day I'll be swamped under piles of projects and stuck here late.

Footsteps sound on the tile floor in the hallway, and I watch the door. It has to be my new client. Hopefully someone with a major job that will give me an influx of cash to help compensate for the clients I've lost.

Thank God, he's punctual.

It means I may still get out of here at a somewhat reasonable hour. Maybe I can pick up dinner on my way home.

I rise from my desk to greet him; a tall, broad-shouldered man in an impeccably tailored black suit enters my office.

His dark hair and even darker eyes are far too familiar. And not just because I saw them watching me from behind the mask at the party the night I met Landon. This man shares his father's eyes. In fact, he's the spitting image of what I remember Dom looking like when I was a child. If he hadn't been wearing a mask that night, if I hadn't been absorbed in my dance with Landon, I may have made the connection then.

Luca Abello, the prodigal son. He's back and standing three feet away from me.

My heart races. I'm completely alone here. Saint isn't even outside. I told him I'd call before I was going to leave work tonight. There was no reason to suspect anyone who would be a threat would just waltz right in.

It would take two seconds for him to pull a weapon and end me, just like Dom tried to do to Stone. "What the hell are you doing here?"

Luca moves toward my desk, his strong, solid form looming over me, and I instinctively slide open the drawer and reach my hand down to where I keep my gun. I curl my fingers around the grip. Gabe taught me how to use this thing, and I won't hesitate to if needed.

The son of the man who ruined my life holds up his hand and offers a small smile. "Relax, Storm. I'm just here to talk."

Is he fucking kidding me?

"Talk? What the hell is there to talk about? Your father already killed my husband and tried to destroy just about every member of my family. What? Are you here to finish the job?"

The fact that Luca is back in town does not bode well for any of us.

He was at the party. And shit...the dark-haired man who was at the aquarium when I was there with the girls and Angelina...

Things start clicking into place.

The dark sedan following me that I thought was my protection detail from Gabe and Savage. The slashed tires. The slaughtered cat clearly meant to intimidate me.

Luca has been sending a message. I just didn't know who it was from until now.

Savage and Gabe have heard nothing from him. After Dom's death, they thought he might show up, but after months of no sign of him, we all assumed he wasn't coming. He's been gone from New Orleans for twenty years. If his own father's death didn't draw him home, we thought nothing would.

Underestimating a Hawke never ends well. The same can be said about the Abellos. That's been proven again and again over the last few years, to the detriment of all the Hawkes. And that's apparently what we've done. Underestimated a very lethal man.

The man whose father brought us all so much pain folds his hands together in front of him, looking completely professional and innocuous, as if this is a typical business meeting and we're cordial colleagues who may grab a drink together when we're done.

I know just how dangerous he is, though. Dom, who was like a second father, was nothing like he appeared to be when he was with us. It was all an elaborate act, a stage show designed to keep us in the dark about who and what he really was. And when that curtain came down, exposing the rancid truth, it shook the world of all the Hawkes in a way we can never recover from. His son is no different. This is a charade. A smoke-screen.

"I understand your distress, Storm. But all I can do is apologize for my father's actions."

Apologize? Fucking apologize?

"Don't you dare." I pull the gun from the drawer and point it at him. "Don't you dare give me your bullshit platitudes. He murdered my *husband!* Took my daughter's father from her! How fucking *dare* you come here? Get the hell out and stay away from me and my family."

My hand shakes. I re-center the nose of the gun on his chest. If I need to shoot the fucker, you better believe it will be the entire magazine center mass, just like Gabe taught me. "If I suspect for even a second that you're still following me or anyone else, I swear to God, I will fucking kill you myself."

He holds up his hands again and backs away from the desk a few steps. Those dark eyes hold no fear, though.

The asshole doesn't believe I'll do it. He thinks it's an empty threat.

"Storm, I'm not a threat to you or anyone else. I just came to—"

"Get the hell out!"

The elevator opens onto the floor that houses Storm's office. The eerie silence that greets me is a bit unnerving. It's weird being here after hours when there's usually so much activity, but I know she's still here. Her car is in the parking lot, and given how stressed-out she's been about work, she's probably staying late to get ahead.

I've tried to stay away. Follow Chris' advice and give her some space. But every second, every minute, every damn hour since I woke and found her note on the mirror has been agony.

I need to talk to her. I can't leave things the way they ended. The longer I let this go on, the further she's going to revert back to the Storm she was before we talked, before she came totally clean with me. Hiding has become a reflex to her, a way to shut out anything and anyone who could ever hurt her again.

She's not going to run or hide from me, though.

I've worked way too hard to make her accept the truth to let her get away now.

I barely make it past the reception desk when Storm's voice reaches me from down the hallway.

"Get the hell out!"

What's going on?

My feet pound on the tile as I race down the hallway toward her office. A large man in a dark suit backs out of her office with his hands raised. He stops in the doorway and turns his head to glance at me briefly before returning his attention to whatever is happening inside.

I slide to a stop a few steps away and eye him up and down. "Who the hell are you? What's going on?"

He takes two more steps back into the hallway, and before I can even think to grab him, he turns on his heel and strides toward the elevator.

Wait!

I know that guy. Steele. I met him at the party.

What the hell is he doing here?

Two more steps bring me to the door, and I peer into Storm's office.

Jesus Christ!

Storm stands behind her desk with a gun pointed at the doorway, where I now wait holding my breath. Whatever Steele was doing here, it wasn't anything good.

"Storm, baby, what the hell is going on? Who the hell was that man?"

Her entire body vibrates, and the hand holding the gun shakes. She lowers it and sets it on her desk. Once it's down, I finally feel safe enough to glance back at the man making his way down the hallway. He doesn't even pause or look back.

I rush over to her and pull her in my arms. "Storm, tell me what's happening."

She heaves out a sob and clutches to me. Her arms wrap around my neck, and she buries her face into my chest. "Luca Abello."

Holy fucking shit.

He must be Dom's son, though I never knew he had one. Given how shaken up Storm is, I have no doubt the man is just as dangerous as his father and threatened her.

"Call Savage and Gabe. Tell them what happened and go straight to their place."

Her head snaps up as I pull away from her. "What? Where are you going?"

I rush toward the door and turn back to her. I don't want to leave her like this, but I have to. "Call Savage. I'll be there soon as I can."

She's probably pissed, but I don't have time to argue with her about this. I rush off down the hallway as fast as I can and make my way to the stairwell. Three flights will be faster by foot than waiting for the elevator to come back up.

Every step down feels like it takes an hour, even taking them two or three at a time.

What was that fucker doing in Storm's office?

I swear to God, if he threatened her...I'll fucking kill him.

The metal door at the bottom of the stairs appears, and I slam into it at full force, ignoring the fire alarm siren that blares in the building. My feet hit the pavement just in time to hear a car engine start.

A black Mercedes backs out of the spot halfway down the lot and turns away from me. There aren't any other cars moving out here, so that has to be him.

Shit. The black sedan that's been following her. Where the hell is Saint?

My car roars to life, thanks to the remote start, and I slide into the driver's seat and throw it into gear before I even put on my seatbelt. I can't lose sight of him. I'll never find him once he hits one of the busier streets. Not at this time of day with the traffic.

He stops at the stop sign down the road and turns onto Canal Street. I slam the pedal to the floor to catch up and take the turn. I don't even care if the fucker knows I'm following him. He's got some real fucking balls showing up at Storm's work and confronting her.

Her slashed tires and the dead cat pop into my head. That had to be him sending a warning.

Well, it's about time I sent him one.

He pulls up in front of the Ritz-Carlton and stops at the valet stand. Two cars separate us. I don't want to lose him when he gets inside the hotel. A valet in a red coat steps forward and opens his door for him, and Luca climbs from his car and heads straight to the hotel lobby without looking back.

Shit. I can't lose sight of him.

I climb from my car and wave over the other valet who was just about to approach the car behind Luca's. "Look, man, I'm running late. Do you mind if I just leave my keys?"

"It's cool. What's your last name?"

"McCabe."

"Are you staying with us, Mr. McCabe?"

"No, just meeting someone. Actually, I shouldn't be very long."

He rips off a ticket and hands it to me. "Okay, no problem."

I hardly hear his words as I take off toward the lobby. The revolving door spits me out in time to see Luca step into an elevator.

Son of a bitch!

The door closes behind him before I can try to get in. Not that I'm really sure what I would do if I were in an enclosed elevator car with the son of a mafia don who murdered my girlfriend's husband, but I would have figured it out.

I step back and watch it climb. It stops on the fifth floor.

Please God, let him be the only one on that elevator.

There's no way to know if that's his floor or if someone else was in there and got off. I just have to take a chance. There's no other option.

I press the call button and enter the elevator car next to the one Luca just used. The fire of hatred burns in my chest along with my lungs from having run. I guess swimming hasn't kept me in as good of shape as I thought.

A ride in an elevator has never felt so agonizingly slow before. I can't scrub the vision of Storm sobbing with that damn gun in her shaking hand from my head.

When I get my hands on this asshole, he's going to regret ever knowing the Hawkes.

The ding alerting me I've reached the fifth floor jerks me back to the task at hand. I need to be alert. Prepared for whatever I might find when this door opens.

I step out and survey to my left—a deserted hallway.

Shit.

Turning my head to the right, I fear finding the same, but instead, my heart stalls in my chest.

Luca Abello leans against the door jamb of a room halfway down the hall, looking casual and unconcerned with his feet crossed over each other.

His eyes meet mine, and he offers me a grin before pushing himself off and holding the door open. "Well, are you coming in?"

twenty-seven

$\mathcal{I}$ should probably climb back into the elevator and walk away. The fact that he clearly knew I was following him and is inviting me into his hotel room is likely a bad sign for my life expectancy.

But I can't just walk away, not after he threatened Storm. Not without knowing why he's here and why he's doing this to her.

My steps eat up the distance to his room. A tiny smirk tilts the corner of his lips as he holds the door open for me to enter in front of him. Giving a mobster my back seems like another really fucking bad idea, but I don't have any choice.

I half-expect him to slip a *garotte* around my neck the moment the door closes behind me, but instead, he brushes past me and walks over to a small bar area in his suite. He holds up a decanter of amber liquid. "You want a drink?"

Is this guy for real? He can't be serious.

"No. I'm good."

He shrugs and points to a chair that likely costs as much as my car. "Then take a seat."

Luca is pretty nonchalant for someone who was just threatened at gunpoint and then followed to his hotel room by a virtual stranger.

"Don't you want to know why I'm here?"

He grabs a tumbler and pours the liquid into it before he turns to face me. "I'm pretty confident I know why you're here, Landon."

Heat spreads up the back of my neck, but it's not from embarrassment. It's from knowing I just charged into the lion's den with no weapon, and while he was expecting me. He's one step ahead and has been since the night he watched me dance with Storm at the party. He's been watching her, watching *us* this entire time.

"What makes you so confident of that?"

One shoulder rises and falls nonchalantly. "I do my homework."

"You mean you've been stalking Storm."

His brow furrows. "Stalk is a strong word. I've been observing her, yes."

"And threatening her."

He shakes his head, his mouth set in a firm line. "No. I've never threatened Storm, and I never would."

I scoff and push to my feet. I don't like being at a disadvantage by sitting. Luca's a big man, built like a fighter, and on top of that, there's no doubt he has weapons in here somewhere. Probably more than one on him. "I find that very hard to believe considering you slashed her tires and killed the damn cat on her porch."

Luca's dark eyes narrow on me. "That is all very disturbing, but I had nothing to do with those incidents."

Bullshit.

The words sound sincere enough, but someone who comes from his kind of family is bound to be a master manipulator and liar. It's no mere coincidence he reappeared at the same time this all started with Storm. "Why have you been following Storm? Why did you stop at her office tonight?"

He swirls his drink in the glass before taking a sip. A moment passes, and he closes his eyes, savoring what is no doubt a very expensive Scotch. "I've been back in town off and on since my father's death. I've been trying to salvage what's left of his legitimate businesses."

I bark out a laugh and shake my head. "Yeah, right. Like Dom had anything legitimate going on."

A tiny grin tugs at his lips, and he nods. "I'll admit, my father had some unscrupulous business behaviors."

That's the understatement of the fucking year.

I won't say it out loud though, because this guy is just as likely to pull a gun on me and unload it as his father was.

"But he was also a brilliant businessman. Not everything he had his hands in was dirty."

That may very well be true. I haven't spent much time learning about Dom. Most of what I know comes from what Chris told me and the bits and pieces I've picked up from the Hawkes. But it's enough to know he was two-faced, rotten to the core, and dangerous as fuck.

"Why bother? I didn't even know you existed until today. Clearly, you weren't close to him."

He shakes his head, and something that looks an awful lot like disappointment crosses over his dark eyes. "No, I wasn't. My mother left with me when I was about ten and went back to Jersey, where her parents were. That's where I've been since, for the most part."

"Why come back here?" I clench my hands at my sides. There can only be one reason he's here—to get revenge for his father's death. That much is clear.

Luca stares off for a moment, contemplating his answer. "This may sound asinine, but even though I knew I would never win my father's approval in life, part of me hopes that now that he's dead, maybe I can. Maybe I can salvage the family name."

I can't stop the laugh that bubbles out of my chest, even though it's a tremendous risk to my life to let it out. "Salvage the family name? You've got to be fucking kidding me." I wave my hand at him. "Your father was a mob boss. He murdered people. Lots of people. Including a Hawke employee, and Storm's husband." I suck in a deep breath to at least try to calm my anger. Flying at this guy with fists raised probably won't end well for me. "Storm, someone whom he thought of and treated like a daughter. He was capable of doing that to her, so I can imagine what he did to other people. If Gabe hadn't finally ended him, he eventually would have been put away for life. There's no salvaging that."

My verbal diarrhea wasn't just stupid. It was also dangerous. I don't know why I can't keep my mouth shut here, but this guy is really pissing me off. I can't seem to hold it back, even if that's in my best interest.

His dark eyes watch me carefully. Their depths hold so many emotions, it's impossible to tell what he's thinking. "You may be right, but I have to try."

"What does any of this have to do with Storm and the Hawkes?"

He stares down into his drink for several minutes, long enough I think he may not answer me. When he finally looks up, there's something unexpected in his gaze.

Regret? Pain?

"I grew up with the Hawkes. Those kids were my best friends until I moved. They were more like brothers and sisters or cousins than family friends." He sighs and rubs his free hand over his jaw. "If I had known what my father was doing to them, I would've done whatever I could to intervene and stop him."

I want to challenge him on that, but he starts up before I have a chance to speak.

"But I turned a blind eye to who I was and didn't care what he was doing. I can't deny that I'm an Abello. My mother legally changed my name to her maiden name to try to remove me from his life and his business. I started going by Steele, a nickname I earned in middle school. That's a funny story that I won't go into. Mom didn't want me to have anything to do with my father or his connections to the outfit in Jersey. But that didn't stop them from approaching me."

So, he's connected to the mob up there too.

Fucking great.

I can't say I'm shocked. When you're born into that life, even if you remove yourself from it—or are removed by force like his mom did with him—you can never really escape who you are at your core. What blood runs through your veins.

"I learned the business. My father's business. And they somehow managed to keep him in the dark about it. He never knew what I was doing. He never wanted to know. All he did was send a check to my mom every month until she died." He takes another drink from his glass and stares at it for a moment. "The Hawkes are the only family I have left. And even though I've been gone for twenty years, it doesn't mean I forgot them or how good they were to me, or how much I love them. I need you to help me convince them about my good intentions."

Shit.

That's the last thing I him expected to say.

Why the hell does he think I would help him?

He's the son of the man who killed Ben. He decimated Storm's life.

He drinks his Scotch while he waits for my response. I want to lash out at him for suggesting something so fucking stupid. Yet, this guy doesn't sound like a cold-blooded killer. He sounds more like a little, lost boy searching for someone to love him.

But looks can be deceiving and words can be lies.

"I'm sorry, Luca, but I'm having a really hard time believing that you have nothing but good intentions when you're here to take over your father's business. Especially when all these things have been happening to Storm."

A sardonic grin tugs at the corners of his mouth. "I'm not going to lie and say I won't potentially return to some of my father's less scrupulous business dealings, but it's been over six months. Others have stepped in and established themselves already. My goal is to try to resurrect legitimate businesses, and if the other ones happen to come with it," he shrugs, "so be it." He downs the rest of his drink and sets the tumbler on the bar behind him. "Returning here would certainly be a much easier process if I knew the Hawkes were okay. And I can assist you in looking into the events plaguing Storm."

Jesus Christ...

"Is that why you've been following Storm? To see if she's okay?"

He nods almost imperceptibly.

No fucking way.

"She's *not* okay. Your father burned her husband alive! He destroyed Savage and Gabe's business. He tried to kill Savage's wife. Storm is most definitely *not* okay. None of them are."

I don't dare mention the miscarriage. That's something that will remain between me and Storm if and until she decides to disclose it to the Hawkes. But I sure would like to throw that in this fucker's face too. To make him *really* see the cost of what his father has done.

His eyes darken even more, and he shakes his head. "I know. Please give me the opportunity to talk to them, to explain why I'm here and how sorry I am for everything my father did. I need someone to convince them to at least hear me out."

Well, shit. Why the fuck does it have to be me?

Where the hell is he?

I pace the length of Savage and Dani's living room for the millionth time in the last two hours. My nails have dug holes in my palms, and I swear, the clock has been moving backward instead of forward while I wait to hear from Landon.

Why the hell did Landon go after him? Does he have a fucking death wish?

Running out after Luca Abello is like agreeing to go home from the gay bar with Dahmer. Only at least with Luca, you already know he's dangerous.

I take a deep breath and try to contain the frustrated scream that's crawling its way up my throat.

Keep your shit together, Storm.

Angel is in the next room. She doesn't need to see me melting down...again. Her giggle trickles down the hallway, relieving a little of the tension tightening my chest.

Thank God Savage and Gabe are distracting her with the movie back in the theater room while I stand out here, trying not to go completely insane.

He's been gone too long. He should have called or been here by now.

Should I call the cops?

A sharp knock on the door has me jerking my head in that direction.

Landon?

My feet can't get me to the door fast enough, and I fling it open.

Oh, thank God!

Without thinking, I launch myself at him, and he catches me, burying his face against my neck. The warm flutter of his breath against my skin makes my heart beat again.

I pull back and smack his shoulder. "Don't you ever do that to me again. Do you have any idea how worried I've been?" I was more than worried. I was absolutely terrified and was losing my shit.

There's no way I can tell him that, though. I shouldn't even be reacting like this. I need to distance myself from him. I can't get sucked back into his vortex. I need to concentrate on being a better mom and getting my life back on track. He's a distraction, and I need to get everything else in line before I can decide where we really stand.

Being a mom has to come first.

Even if it does shatter what's left of my heart.

I push away from him and turn toward the living room so he won't see the distress I've been feeling since the moment he left me alone in my office. He follows me into the condo. I take a deep breath and turn to face him. "What happened with Luca?"

He looks around. "Where is everybody? It's probably easier if I tell this to everyone at once."

He's right. And having other people in the room will give me a much-needed buffer. I can't trust what I'm feeling, and I don't want to confuse Landon even more.

"I'll go grab Savage and Gabe. Dani is trying to get Kennedy down."

Landon nods, and I head down the hallway toward the theater room. Angelina sprawls with her head on a pillow in Savage's lap and her feet up on Gabe's. Princess sits curled on her chest, snoring lightly.

God, I love these guys.

She needs a father figure with Ben gone, and they've stepped up more than I could ever have anticipated to be more than uncles to her.

I catch Gabe's eye, and he nods his understanding. "Angel, Uncle Savage and I have to go out to talk to your mom for a couple minutes. Stay here and finish the movie with Princess."

Angel pops her head up and peers over at me. A grin spreads across her tiny face. "Momma, are you going to watch with me?"

"I'll come back as soon as we're done. I promise."

She pouts but drops back down onto the couch and allows Savage and Gabe to disentangle themselves from her. I turn back to the hallway and wait for them to join me. Just as Savage appears, the door to Kennedy's room opens and Dani slips out and closes the door gently behind her.

Dani spots us in the hallway. "What's going on? Is he back?"

I nod, and everyone follows me into the living room.

Every second Landon was gone, I ran through everything that's happened over the last month in my head. It's so obvious now what was happening. That all this was Luca.

Why couldn't we see it?

Landon stands in front of the fireplace, examining the photos on the mantle. Everyone settles into the couches and chairs, and he rotates to face us.

This is far too reminiscent of what happened here only seven months ago, when Stone came clean about what he did, what Dom did, everything that had gone down. The day Gabe killed Dom, and the day after my entire life went up in flames.

A cold shiver rocks my body, but I try to ignore it. If I dwell on that day, I won't be able to focus on the current threat.

"I spoke with Luca."

His words have a sobering effect on everyone. The tension in the room intensifies to an almost uncomfortable level, but no one speaks. We all just wait.

Landon shoves a hand into his hair and shifts uncomfortably. "He is adamant he's not behind the tire slashing or the dead cat, but he does admit he's been following Storm."

I knew it.

Savage growls. "Why the hell should we believe him? He's admitting to *stalking* her!"

Landon holds up his hands protectively. "I know. He said he just wanted to make sure she was okay. He claims that he's here to take over his father's *legitimate* businesses and re-establish the Abello name. And he swears he is no threat to anyone and wants to be friends, like you all were as children."

Gabe scoffs and leans forward to rest his elbows on his knees. "You've got to be fucking kidding me. Does he really think we're that stupid? That we're just going to take his word that he's this great guy with the best of intentions?"

I feel sorry for Landon. He's only the messenger here, but Savage and Gabe are going to tear him apart.

Dani shifts in her seat and glances to Savage before she speaks. "Look, I'm not saying we embrace him with open arms and believe every word he says, but for the record, Dom *did* have a lot of legitimate businesses. I found dozens of them when I was researching my story. It's entirely possible Luca did come here with good intentions."

Savage looks like he's about to argue with her, when Landon clears his throat. "Um, there's more, kind of. He told me he was involved with the mob in Jersey and that if the opportunity presents itself, he wouldn't be against getting back into some of his father's less scrupulous businesses either. So, I certainly don't think he's squeaky clean."

No fucking shit.

I don't care if his mother removed him from Dom's clutches at ten; he was exposed to that life. He knew what his father did. He had to. You don't walk away from growing up like that and go on to be a damn saint.

Gabe stands and paces behind the couch. "What do you think? What sort of feeling did you get from him?"

The fact that Gabe trusts Landon enough to ask his opinion on this speaks volumes. Gabe doesn't trust anyone, yet Landon has somehow managed to form a bond with him, with Savage too. One that happened so damn fast. Just like how he worked his way into my heart in what felt like an instant.

Landon sighs. "Honestly? I think he's dangerous, but...I don't think he's dangerous to any of *you*. He seemed to really want to rekindle the friendship you all had as children. He said, and I quote, 'the Hawkes are the only family I have left.'"

I jerk to my feet, anger burning in my chest. "Fuck that! He may not have been directly responsible for what his father did, but he's here with no qualms about starting the business back up, the very business that Dom used as a justification for killing Ben.

I'm not about to let that man into my life or the life of my daughter."

"I'm not saying you should." Landon takes a step toward me. "I'm just telling you the vibe I got from him. I think you all should meet with him in person and hear him out. Then you can make your own decisions."

Even thinking about being in the same room as that man has my blood curdling, but Landon may have a point. Luca may not go away until we've given him the chance to talk to us. As long as we do it on home turf, where we can be assured of our safety, it may be the only way to get rid of the Abellos from our lives permanently.

I turn to Savage and Gabe. "Let's schedule a meeting. We'll do it at the club. We can control it there. Let's hear him out and then sending him packing."

Savage growls. Gabe clenches his hands into fists at his sides, and Dani flicks her gaze between the two of them.

It's abundantly clear they don't agree with the course of action, but I know they'll defer to me in the end. One thing that's become evident over the last seven months is, everyone wants to please the grieving widow. It's annoying at times, to have them all think I need to be handled with kid gloves and given undue deference, but there are definitely times it plays in my favor. Like now.

After a moment, Savage gives Gabe a look, one I'm sure they've exchanged a thousand times over the years, and then he nods his agreement to me. Dani remains suspiciously silent, giving me the belief she's actually on-board with the plan and doesn't want to say anything that might set Savage off.

"Mom! Are you coming?" Angel's voice carries down the hallway.

"I need to go." I move to brush past Landon, but his arm snakes out around my waist, halting my progress.

Those bourbon eyes I've lost myself in so many times beg me to stay. "Storm, we need to talk."

I can't. Not now. Maybe not ever. Maybe it isn't fair to him to leave things this way, but it's time I made a choice. My daughter's happiness and well-being have to trump my own, at least for the foreseeable future.

"I'm sorry. I can't."

I didn't intend to repeat the words I left scrawled on his mirror. Those are just the ones that came out. He recoils almost as if I slapped him and releases his hold on me.

Walking away from him and down the hallway sends red hot agony shooting through my chest, but I force each foot in front of the other.

This is for the best.

twenty-eight

"**Y**ou look like you could use a drink."

I've only been sitting at the bar at The Hawkeye Club for less than a minute. When I came in, there was no one behind the bar, but somehow, this big guy with arms the size of tree trunks managed to sneak up and stand right in front of me without me even realizing it. He must've come from the back or something.

"Actually, I could probably use two or three."

He chuckles, a deep, low sound that vibrates from his enormous chest, and plants his palms on the bar. "What's your poison?"

"A beer sounds good. IPA."

"You got it." He steps back and reaches into the bar and comes out with a brown bottle and a frosted glass. The lid pops off easily, and I wave off the glass so he hands the bottle to me. His brown eyes never leave me. "Only two things put that look on a man's face. The first is your dog dying. The second is a woman. So, which is it?"

Well, damn!

A light chuckle flows from my chest. His insight is spot on. The last time I felt like this was a different woman, one Barry still hasn't managed to find, and the time before that was when Scooter died when I was twelve. "Is it that obvious?"

He grins and nods at me. There's a depth of intelligence and understanding in his eyes. He's probably heard a thousand sob stories in here over the years. "It is. Even to a big gay fucker like me."

I practically choke on my beer. "Excuse me?"

Did I hear that right?

"You're gay?"

I turn and examine all the beautiful waitresses and naked girls shaking their stuff on the stage. This is the last place I'd expect to find a gay man bartending.

"Sure am." He winks at me playfully.

In another type of bar, that would be interpreted a completely different way. But I know he's just messing with me. "What are you doing working in a place like this?"

He laughs as I scan the room again. "I've been working for Gabe and Savage since they opened this place. Back then, I wasn't so comfortable with people knowing my sexuality, and I thought working here would be the perfect front." He shakes his head with a smile. "I thought I was so damn smart, but they saw right through me. They let me go on pretending for a long time, too. I'm Byron, by the way." He holds out a hand to me.

"Landon."

"I know."

"What do you mean you know?"

The sly grin spreads across his face. "There are very few secrets with the Hawkes, and at this point, I'm basically family. I wasn't here when you came to meet with Savage and Gabe last time, but I hear things. So, I can assume your need for alcohol is caused by the oldest Hawke sister."

I take a long pull of my beer and fiddle with the wrapper. "You could say that."

He sighs and leans against the bar. "She's been through a lot. She has a lot of baggage. Takes a real man to deal with all that."

I snort and shake my head. Baggage is something we both carry, but I've been trying to cut the line on mine. To fully move on from it and leave it in the past. Storm, on the other hand, seems intent to let it drag her down. "Believe me, I know. And I want to make us work. But..."

One of his dark eyebrows rises. "She's fighting you?"

I bark a humorless laugh. "That would be the understatement of the century."

One of his massive shoulders rises and falls. "It would surprise me if she went down easily. The Hawkes all have a fuck-load of fight in them."

His words couldn't be more true. She's fighting me at every turn, and I have no idea what to do. Do I keep pushing, keep forcing her to see what's right there in front of her? I'm terrified of doing that. I could lose her forever.

"Look, Landon, do you want my advice?"

I throw up my hands. Everyone has advice. None of it the same. "At this point, it can't hurt."

He leans in closer so I can hear him over the bass of the song that just started. "Don't let her shut down. I've seen her change completely since Ben died. She's closed off to all of us. She barely comes in here anymore when she used to be here a couple times a week to either meet with the guys or just hang out here at the bar with me and sometimes Skye. But she likes you, and that means a lot. Make her see that. Do whatever it takes."

Do whatever it takes.

"Thanks, man. I appreciate the advice...and the beer."

"Anytime, brother. But if you want to avoid your troubles, you might not want to look to your left."

Of course, my head immediately turns to find the source of all my agony standing just inside the door of the club chatting with the bouncer. When they're done, her eyes meet mine. Her steps falter for a second. Then she regains control of herself and nods toward me and Byron before she makes her way to the elevator on the far side of the room without a glance back.

I twist on my stool to watch her.

She gives us her back while she waits, but when she climbs into the car, she has to face us. Her eyes hold mine as the doors slide closed. There's longing there, that dark swirling pull that drew me to her in the first place. And that gives me a glimmer of hope. But the fear and regret lingering along with that make my heart ache.

"I didn't know she would be here tonight." I turn back to Byron.

"She's meeting with Savage, Gabe, and Luca."

Holy shit.

When I left Savage's the other night, there still wasn't any plan, and a lot of tension over whether to meet with him or not still existed between the Hawkes. It wasn't my place to give any further opinion on it. It was awkward enough being in the middle of the family and Luca. The only reason he used me as an envoy was he knew they would never let him near them otherwise.

"They're actually meeting with him?"

He frowns and nods, the tension visible in his tightened jaw. "Gabe gave me the rundown of what happened. Apparently, there's been quite a bit of debate over the last couple days about it. But yeah, he finally decided that it's probably best to sit down. I think Stone is coming too."

That would make sense. Not only is Stone a lawyer but he also worked for Luca's father. He knows more about that family and their workings than any of the Hawkes. The way they think. What makes them tick.

Even with the guys there to protect her, the thought of Storm being in the same room as Luca again makes my blood heat in my veins, and I clench my hand around the bottle.

Luca said he's not behind the things happening to Storm, but I'm not sure I totally buy it. Who else would be trying to scare Storm? The tires, the cat, the car following her? It's all sending a message. One that's pretty loud and clear.

That man has evil in his blood. He can talk peace and love all he wants, but as they say, a tiger can't change his stripes.

Even one who wears a fancy suit.

The front door of the club swings open, and the man himself

appears in a suit that probably costs more than I make in a month. The bouncer at the door gives him a dirty look but lets him in.

Luca strolls over to the bar casually, like he doesn't have a care in the world, when really, he's here because he's the son of evil incarnate and has been stalking my woman.

My clenched jaw starts to hurt, and I have to physically keep myself from making a scene at the club. They invited him here. It's not my place to get involved. I glance over at Byron but find that his face has ashened like he's seen a ghost. His immense, hulking presence seems to have deflated in an instant.

Luca's sly smile at Byron hints at him being the source of Byron's distress, but he doesn't address him. He leans against the bar next to me. "Landon, I didn't know you were going to be at the meeting."

"I didn't even know about it. I just came for drink." I tip my bottle toward him, and he nods.

"Where are they?"

Byron shakes his head, seeming to snap out of whatever daze had consumed him, clears his throat, and nods toward the elevator. "Upstairs. Savage's office. Take the elevator. First door on your left. I'll call up to let them know you're here."

Not that he needs to. Just from looking at the plans for the club, I know Gabe and Savage have cameras just about everywhere. I'm sure they already know he's here.

Luca nods and taps the top of the bar. "Thanks." He winks at Byron before he turns and strides toward the elevator.

What the hell is that about?

I rotate back to find Byron scowling at the retreating back of the young mobster. He grunts and grabs the phone from behind the bar. "Yeah, he's here."

His eyes flick over to mine. "Yeah, okay. Thanks." The phone returns to the receiver. "Savage says if you want to join them, go ahead."

Part of me thinks I should be there. I want to hear what he has to say, but this is a family thing. I shouldn't be butting into it any more than I already have. It's only deepened the chasm between me and Storm, and the last thing I need is another reason for her to try to push me away.

The front door opens again, and Saint's massive shoulders block out any light from outside as he steps in. He says something to the bouncer who points to the elevator. Saint nods at him then glances over at us. He tosses another nod our way then walks off toward the back of the club.

He's been Storm's shadow, but I know he feels bad about Luca getting into her office. It wasn't his fault. There was no reason to think Storm wasn't safe and sound while she was at work. He must have followed her here and waited outside for Luca to show.

They don't need me in that meeting. There's plenty of testosterone up there and Saint and several other people down here.

"I think I'll stay here and have another beer."

Byron nods and pops the top off another one for me. "That may be the wisest choice, man. You don't want to be in the middle of anything involving that many Hawkes in one room."

I snort-laugh as I bring the beer up to my mouth. "I know, man. I've been to Sunday family dinner."

Savage's office has always been home turf. Anytime things go down, this is the place we convene. But tonight, something feels... off. I don't know what it is, but waiting for Luca to arrive, I can't shake the chill or goose bumps spreading across my skin.

I rub my arms and finger the cuff on my wrist while I pace between the couches in the seating area. Maybe some of my unease is due to the unexpected run-in with Landon. Well, not run-in, more like drive-by. I should have gone over and said something. Anything.

But what the hell do I say?

I'm sorry I ran? I'm sorry I changed my mind in the blink of an eye? I'm sorry I almost told you I love you? I'm sorry I broke your heart? I'm sorry just seems so...empty and not even what I want to say at all.

Savage's phone rings, and he answers while Gabe and I stop and stare at him. "Good. I see Landon is here too. Tell him to join us if he wants."

What? What the hell is he doing?

This is Hawke business, and the *last* thing Landon is, is a Hawke. He can't be. If we let him into this family, it means letting him into my heart fully. And I can't do that. Not now, maybe not ever.

It kills me to think I may never be in a place to give him what he's offering me in return, but it's the harsh reality of my life.

The ding of the elevator reaching the floor echoes ominously down the hallway. One tiny little bell acting as a harbinger of danger.

Another shudder moves through me, and I wrap my arms around myself even tighter.

Savage waves me over. "Storm, come stand behind the desk by me."

Gabe sits on the corner of the desk and crosses his arms over his broad chest.

I thought Stone was coming too, but no one's heard from him in a couple of hours. There's no time to wait for him now. Luca's here, and there's no delaying this conversation any longer. Even though we've only known he's back for a few days, it's been a long time coming. None of us have heard from him since he left two decades ago, and we have no idea what he's been up to except what little Landon was able to reveal. With all the threats, the stalking, all of it—this needed to happen.

Footsteps on the wood floor move closer to the door, and then he's at the jamb, looking crisp and sinister in a form-fitting Italian silk suit. A slick smile spreads across his face as he steps into the office, and he opens his arms wide.

"The Hawkes. It's so lovely to see you again. Savage, Gabe, Storm. Where are Stone and Skye?"

Neither Savage nor Gabe move to embrace the man who was once their childhood best friend. This isn't that boy. That boy died when he moved away. His mother worked so hard to rip him from the clutches of Dom, but apparently, the apple didn't far fall from that diseased tree.

When he realizes neither are going to embrace him and no one is going to answer his question about Stone and Skye, he lets his arms fall to his sides and approaches us. He motions to one of the leather chairs facing Savage's desk. "Shall I take a seat?"

Savage shifts forward in his chair and straightens his back. "If you'd like. But you won't be here long."

A low chuckle falls from Luca's lips as he lowers himself into the chair and crosses his ankle over his knee. "I doubt that. We have so much to catch up on and talk about."

Smug fucker.

The elevator dings again, and everyone's heads turn toward the door. Heavy footsteps move toward us, and Stone rushes into the office with Landon behind him.

Shit. What's he doing up here?

I was not prepared to see him today. The few seconds I had to look into his eyes downstairs were hard enough. But now, in this enclosed space, it's unavoidable.

Landon scans the group until he finds me. He gives a pathetic half-smile and moves to the far side of the room near Gabe.

Whether he's intentionally putting distance between us or not, it's both appreciated and agonizing.

Stone lowers himself into the vacant chair next to Luca. "Sorry I'm late. I'll explain later."

I don't really care why Stone is late. I care why Landon is here. This isn't his problem to deal with. It's ours. His presence makes it impossible for me to focus. I keep drifting my focus to him when I should be concentrating on the threat in the room.

Luca casts a grin around the room at everyone. "Let's get back to business, shall we?" When no one responds, he drops his foot back to the ground and sits up straight. "I understand the reluctance of all of you to embrace me during this homecoming, but I think you have somehow established the wrong idea of why I'm here."

"Oh really?" Gabe snorts and leans forward slightly, towering over Luca. "You've been stalking Storm, you've been making threats to her, and from what Landon tells us, you've also taken over Dom's business. That seems pretty clear from where we sit."

The man who was once such a soft-spoken and polite boy leans forward and holds out his hands. "And you have it all wrong. I did follow Storm, yes. But it wasn't for any sinister or nefarious purposes. Whether you believe it or not, I wanted to ensure she and her daughter were okay after what happened. I wanted to witness for myself how she was doing, what her life was like, before I approached any of you to let you know I was back." His dark eyes find mine, and I force myself not to look away. I can't show any fear. "But I absolutely had *nothing* to do with anything that's happened to Storm, just like I told Landon."

Bullshit.

"I don't believe you, and neither does anyone else in this room." Savage's growl fills the room. "Every bad thing that has happened to this family in the last few years has been a direct result of the actions of an Abello. You come back into town, and suddenly more bad things occur. You expect us to think that's some coincidence?"

Savage nailed it. Luca's explanation doesn't make sense when all these strange things have been happening.

Who else could possibly want to hurt me?

"I don't expect anything, Savage. I understand your reluctance. I understand your mistrust. All I can do is come here with an open heart and with honest words and hope you'll believe me." While he maintains a stony expression, his eyes war with emotion.

He really wants us to believe him. He *needs* us to believe him. I'm not sure why. Maybe the past we all share means more to him than I thought. But that doesn't mean I can take what he's saying at face value.

Stone, who has been surprisingly quiet up to now, shifts in his seat to face Luca. His hands clench into fists on the armrests. "I knew your father better than anyone in this room. At least, I thought I did. He was more of a father to me than my own, and I believed him, I believed *in* him. That trust brought nothing but pain to everyone I care about. So, I'm not willing to offer you that same trust."

Luca shakes his head and sighs. "I know, Stone. And I truly am sorry for everything my father did to you, to the Hawkes. When I found out what happened, I was devastated." He sucks in a breath and lowers his head down slightly. "You all were like family to me before my mother took me to Jersey. Maybe you don't know this, but my father and I never had the best relationship. He didn't feel like I was capable of living up to his greatness. He thought I was a failure, and he never fought my mom taking me because he wanted nothing to do with me, with what I was."

What I was?

That's an odd choice of words. We all wait for him to explain further, but instead, he drops his head into his hands and shoves them back through his perfectly styled hair.

Stone clears his throat to break the tension in the room. "I knew your relationship with him was basically non-existent. Which is why your sudden desire to return here to take over his businesses is even more surprising and suspicious to me, to all of us."

Especially coupled with the whole stalking, slicing, and disemboweling going on...

I'd love to say the words, but I know it's best to let Stone take the reins right now. He did know Dom best, and he's the one who deals with criminals on a daily basis. That should mean he knows how to read people, and how to get what he wants from them. Dom may have pulled the wool over his eyes, but he won't let Luca do the same.

I'm confident of that. No matter what tension may still exist between us, I do trust Stone.

Luca raises his head and surveys the faces of everyone in the room. When his eyes land on me, I squirm under his assessment. "I won't lie and say I'm not taking over Dom's businesses. I am. But, most of them are completely legitimate. That's easy enough for you to check, if Stone doesn't already know."

He looks over to baby brother, and Stone nods his agreement.

"I know it sounds insane, especially given the way my father treated me, but I want to regain my name, my birthright. I've been living as someone else for far too long. Part of that includes his businesses. There may be some illegal things happening. I won't lie about that, but have no doubt, I am *not* my father. I don't hurt people. I'm not a thug."

Gabe stands, rising to his towering height. "Thug or not, you're a gangster. You prey on the weak. Maybe *you* don't hurt people, but no one here believes your goons wouldn't. That's not something the Hawkes can embrace."

Luca rises to his feet too, and every person in the room tenses. The two men stare each other down—one a Ranger who could kill the other in a millisecond with just his hands, the other, the son of Satan who is probably packing at least two weapons on him and has an army of goons at his disposal.

Then a smile appears on Luca's face, and he steps backward, away from Gabe and toward the open door. "I didn't come here for a fight. I came to make my peace and plead my case. I'm here to stay, whether you like it or not. We can be friends, or we can be enemies. I'd prefer the former, but if you would rather the latter, that can be arranged too. You let me know what you want to do."

He turns and disappears down the hallway before I even have a chance to fully register his words.

What the fuck?

When they finally process in my head, I turn to Savage. "Was that a threat?"

He clenches his hands together on the desk and nods. "I think it was."

twenty-nine

hat the hell did I just witness?

Coming up here with Stone was a *bad* idea. Terrible. Horrible. I have no business being in this room right now. There was more tension and animosity here in the last twenty minutes than I've ever felt in my life. And given what went down with Dad, that's saying a lot.

I thought I knew what betrayal was. I thought I understood pain. I thought I had a grasp on what Storm has been going through. But this...this is all just...

Fuck.

Gabe turns to face Savage and Storm, and I'm left lingering at the side of the room—the interloper. The big man who is so lethal shakes his head. "What do you want to do?"

Savage sighs and leans back. He glances up at Storm, who turns to me. Those eyes have told me a thousand things over the last several weeks. They've looked at me with lust, anger, confusion, and even love. But right now, I'm not sure what they're saying.

She's lost. She's just as lost as she was the night she ran from me at the party. Only now, she's looking to *me* to be the one who finds her.

Three other men in this room have been rocks for her for her entire life, but she's not looking at them. She's looking at *me.*

Holy shit.

This is it. This is the moment. This is where I have to take that epic leap without a goddamn parachute.

My heart thunders in my chest. Blood rushes in my ears,

drowning out the noise of the music below my feet. I step forward until I'm standing between the chairs facing the desk, where I can see everyone.

All eyes focus on me. It's like being under a fucking microscope, where all my flaws are exposed for them to see.

I clear my throat and try to steady my shaking hands before I start. "I know I'm not a Hawke. I haven't been affected by what Dom did the way you all have. But I *have* been affected. Because of Storm."

She raises a shaky hand to bat away a tear that trickles down her cheek, then reaches down to twist the cuff on her wrist. She's still wearing it. That's says more than words can.

Take the fucking leap, Landon.

"I love Storm. And the only thing I want in this entire world is to be with her, to love her, and to protect her and Angel, to be everything they need. I know I can't replace Ben. That's not what I'm talking about. But the problem is, what Dom did has made it impossible for Storm to admit she loves me too, that I am what she wants. So, I *do* have a stake in all this."

I expect a round of vigorous objections from the Hawke men, but instead, I get a round of nods of approval.

Jesus Christ. What's happening here?

It feels like some weird initiation into a club I didn't know existed or that I wanted to be a member of. Still, no one says anything, they all just stare at me, waiting for me to make my point. And they may not be so eager to embrace me when I have my final say.

"I do have a stake in this, but I am also an outsider for all intents and purposes. I can view this with some objectivity that I think you all lack. I don't mean that as an insult. It's just impossible to look at everything and not be blinded by what happened."

Savage grunts. "I don't disagree with that."

Really?

They're the first words anyone has uttered, and the fact he's agreeing with me buoys my strength to go forward.

"I believe him when he says he didn't slash Storm's tires or kill the cat. It's not his style. If he wanted her gone, she'd be dead. What's there to threaten her about? Dom is dead and gone. There's no threat to Luca right now, not from the Hawkes, and especially not from Storm."

If they ask why I'm so confident about my belief, I don't think I can give them a more detailed explanation. It's more of a gut feeling. Luca is dangerous; there's no doubt about that. But whether he's dangerous to *us* is a different question entirely, and the answer to that just seems to be no.

Gabe looks over his shoulder, and his shrewd gaze meets mine. "I actually agree with him." He turns back to Savage and Storm and leans forward to place his palms on the desk. "Of course, my first reaction was to blame Luca. It was all of our reactions, and I think it was warranted given everything that's happened. But Landon's logic rings true here. We can't be blinded by our hatred for Dom and what he did. Luca isn't Dom. We need to think clearly about this because if it's not Luca, then there's another threat out there."

Which is exactly why my stomach is churning like a waterspout and my heart is thundering in my chest.

Storm has already lived through Hell. To have to watch her back, live in fear, would be too much for her. For anyone, really. She doesn't deserve any of this.

Savage frowns and nods. "I agree. This wasn't Luca. I'm not saying we should discount him as a threat or turn our attention away from him, but he's not the one threatening Storm."

The chair Stone's been sitting in creaks as he rises to his feet. "I agree, too. This doesn't feel like Luca threatening her."

"Then who is?" Her question comes out soft, her voice shaky. I stand helpless as her bottom lip quivers and tears shimmer in her eyes. "What the hell did I do? Who could I possibly have pissed off enough for them to have done that to Mittens?"

I want to go to her. I want to take her in my arms and cocoon her from all the vile things in this world that could hurt her and Angel, but I know how much she hates to appear weak, even in front of her brothers.

The fact that she looked to *me* in this is monumental. I don't want to do anything that could undo any progress I may have made with her. Going to her and highlighting her weakness could very possibly do just that. So, rather than go to her, I curl my hands into fists at my sides. "You can't think of anyone you've had a disagreement with? Anyone at all?"

She shakes her head and gives a mirthless laugh. "No. I mean, I barely left the house for six months. How the hell could I have pissed someone off enough for them to do this?"

I shove a hand into my hair and run through the timeline of everything that's happened. We've already eliminated Storm being followed by Luca as being connected, so that just leaves the slashed tires and the cat. "It started around the time you went back to work."

Her blue eyes widen. "You're right."

Stone exchanges a look with Savage and Gabe. "Jealous competitor? Someone who was benefiting from her being out of commission and didn't want her coming back?"

Savage taps his fist against the top of the desk. "It's definitely possible. Storm, put together a list of anyone you can think of who benefited from you being gone. Maybe people who took over some of your projects. Give them to Gabe. He'll look into it."

The man who is as much a Hawke as any of them even without Hawke blood nods. "I will, and in the meantime, I don't want you and Angelina alone. I know you have a security system at your house, but you almost never arm it, and even with it, it only alerts you to an intruder. You would still need to wait for help to arrive. I'm not risking that. You need to come stay with me and Skye or Savage and Dani."

Her dark hair swirls around her head as she shakes it. "No. I'm not going into hiding. I'm not leaving my own home."

There's the fire I've been waiting for.

Gabe holds up his hand. "I understand how you feel, Storm, but this is for your own safety and Angel's."

"I'll stay with them." The words come out before I really think them through. I should have asked her if it was okay, if she wants me there, but I want to be the one. I need to know for myself that she's safe.

Not that I have the kind of experience Gabe does, but I know how to handle a gun and know how to protect my woman. If she even is that anymore.

Savage shakes his head and holds up a hand to silence Storm. She shuts her open mouth and presses her lips together, clearly annoyed at her brother's command. "No. Whoever this is knows where she lives. It's not safe there no matter who stays with her. But she and Angel will go to your place. No one will connect her with it. It will be safe."

My heart swells at the thought of having Storm and Angel with me. I can't help but imagine it permanently. What would it be like to wake up next to her every morning? To rush to get Angel ready and off to school? To snuggle into bed with Storm every night? To be able to roll over and touch her...love her anytime I want?

God, I want that so badly.

Storm scowls and glowers at her brothers and Gabe before her eyes finally settle on me. The anger there burns across the blue. "I don't like it, leaving my house, taking Angel from the only home she's ever known, but I also know arguing with you assholes won't get me anywhere. I'll go."

Her words slice through me like a blade to the chest. The reticence, the surrender...this isn't what she wants. She doesn't *want* to be with me. She's only accepting this as a necessity for the time being.

I cough to clear the tightness from my throat and turn away from everyone as I head toward the door. They can't see the unshed tears forming in my eyes. They can't see how fucking weak I am when I'm supposed to be able to protect their sister and niece. "Storm, meet me at your house to get your things."

The words are tossed over my shoulder without a look back.

There's no reason to anyway.

Shit. Shit. Shit.

That look in Landon's eyes. The one I put there. It's been there far too many times recently because of me. And I had to go and do it again.

Stop crushing that man!

He stood up and said something he knew we wouldn't like. He spoke up in front of Savage, Gabe, and Stone. That takes guts. It was so damn brave. And I practically begged him to do it by looking to him for help.

He disappears out the door, and my chest tightens around my aching heart.

I can't let him go like that. If he leaves this building believing I don't want to be with him, I'll lose him forever. The uncertainty I've let eat away at me has made me into what I despise—a woman who jerks around the man who loves her. I'm not going to lose him.

Too much has already been lost.

God, I've been so fucking stupid.

He's willing to risk his life to protect me and Angel, and I have been pushing him away because I won't risk my heart again. It was destroyed. Gone. Obliterated. Nothing more than ashes. But not anymore. It beats again. I *feel* again.

That man is the sole reason. And I have to go after him.

I race around Savage's desk and out the door after Landon.

The hallway is dim, and the floor vibrates with the bass from below me.

Until the day I die, I'll never forget how he looks at this instant—forearm leaning against the wall beside the elevator, head dropped against it, eyes clenched closed, tears on his cheeks.

What have I done?

He looks...broken.

Is that what I look like to him?

A shell of a human being?

A shadow of myself?

I swallow through the giant knot in my throat and brush away a tear threatening to run down my cheek. "Landon?"

His head snaps up, and his eyes meet mine. They're always so playful, so full of that spark of life and humor. It's what's always drawn me to him. But now, they're clouded by something.

Anguish.

I recognize it. It stares back at me from the mirror every single day. Or it did...until Landon.

How could I have been so blind?

Every moment we spent together. Every laugh he managed to pull from deep inside me. Every crooked, sly smile and grin he gave. Every touch. Every kiss. Every whispered word. They all made me love him. Despite my heroic efforts to keep him at bay and to find excuses to run, just like I did *again* the other night when I found out Angel was sick, he still made his way past my defenses.

Thank God he did.

The few feet that separate us in the hallway might as well be a million miles. Every step I take can't bring me closer to him fast enough.

He turns and closes the space between us, opening his arms to me. I launch myself at him, tangling my arms around his neck and clinging to him as his arms tighten around my waist.

I bury my face against his neck. "I'm so sorry. I never meant—"

"Shh." His hot breath floats across my skin, and he presses a kiss behind my ear. "Don't apologize. You can't help the way you feel…"

I pull my head back and take his face between my hands. "No, you don't understand. I want to be with you. I *need* to be with you. I'm just stubborn and—"

His lips are on mine, stealing my breath and the rest of my words.

Stupid. I was going to say stupid.

The kiss is everything. Everything we've been dancing around and holding back and keeping inside for so damn long. I pour my soul into it, into him, unyielding in my need to show him how much I love him and need him. I can't imagine another day apart. No matter what the challenges, we have to face them together. Opening up to him means the potential for pain, but it also means having a partner—someone to help shoulder the load, someone to help me raise Angelina, someone to support me in every single way.

When he moves away and drops his forehead to mine, his hot breath flutters over my lips. "There are some things I need to tell you. About Chicago."

I know Landon has secrets. We all do. But nothing he can tell me will change how I feel about him, about us. Not anymore. I know who he is at his core. He is strength. He is loyalty. He is the man who has managed to pick up the shattered pieces of a heart I didn't think existed anymore and put them back together. "It can wait. Let's go get my stuff and pick up Angel from my mom's. We can talk tonight."

We have all the time in the world.

He nods and presses another tender kiss to my lips. I want more, so much more, but I let him pull away. He reaches over and presses the call button for the elevator. The doors slide open, and he tugs me in with him, keeping his arm wrapped around me.

The first time he held me, on that dance floor at the party, creeps into my mind as we descend. Of all the futures I could have imagined then, none of them involved me being here with Landon right now. I'd love to say things kept us apart, but the only thing doing that has been me and my inability to let go of Ben and my own guilt.

Ben Matthews was my everything, and I don't intend to ever let go of the love I have for him or the memories of what we shared. But being happy, being with Landon, it isn't a slight on what I had with Ben. He would want me to live my life. He would want this. I know that deep down even as the thought tears my heart open and brings fresh tears to my eyes.

I love you, Ben. I always will.

Landon uses his fingers to pull my chin up. "You okay?"

The door dings and opens to the main club level. Bass vibrates the air around us, and Buckcherry's "Crazy Bitch" filters into the elevator cab.

"Yeah, I am now."

He kisses my forehead, and hand-in-hand, we step out into the din of the club. Byron gives us a nod and a knowing grin as we pass the bar.

Saint approaches from the back and rushes over to us. "Are you going with her?"

Landon nods and wraps his arm around my shoulder. "I got her, man. Thank you."

I snuggle deeper into him and offer Saint a quick wave good-bye.

When we hit the parking lot, Landon stops me. "Go straight home. I'll follow you. Pack only what you guys absolutely need, and then we'll go get Angelina."

"You're sure you're ready to take two women into your bachelor pad?"

He grins down at me. "Storm, that place has never been a bachelor pad. It's just been waiting for you and Angel to make it more than an empty place where I sleep."

My heart swells with his words. They're true. I can see it in his eyes. He would never lie to me. Ever. "Then let's go get my stuff."

I lean up to kiss him before I slide into my car and start the engine.

This meeting didn't go anything like I had anticipated. Apparently, the Hawkes are giving Luca a pass, at least for now. And instead of heading home alone again, I'm finally going to get what I want.

God, just let whatever the hell is going on end, already.

Let me be happy.

thirty

*S*torm's neighborhood sits relatively deserted now that night has fully fallen. Streetlights illuminate small round patches on the asphalt and sidewalks, but the houses and yards are mostly cloaked in darkness.

I've only been over in this area once or twice since moving here, and I never paid much attention other than the night I came over to deal with the cat, but I can see how someone could relatively easily slip between houses and yards unseen. Not very many have spotlights or flood lights, and it seems like the neighbors keep to themselves for the most part.

We need to get the girls out of here until we figure out what's going on. This is for the best.

Storm turns into her driveway and shuts off her car. She climbs out as I pull up at the curb. My fingers find the handle to jump out and join her when the ring of my phone breaks the silence in the car.

Shit.

I retrieve it to check the caller. Barry.

Dammit. This can't wait.

Especially now, with Storm waiting to talk to me about my past tonight. I need to know where things stand.

I shove the door open. "I have to take this phone call. Go in and start packing. I'll be right behind you."

She waves her understanding and heads up to unlock the front door.

I slide back into the driver's seat and pull the door closed before I answer. "Barry. What do you have for me?"

"Nothing you're going to like."

Fuck. Why can't this man ever just do what he says he will?

"What is it?"

He shuffles some papers around and clears his throat. "She left Chicago three weeks ago, maybe earlier."

That isn't a huge shock. The fact that no one could find her and no one had heard from her either meant she was dead and undiscovered somewhere, or she had left town for some reason or another. Although, it's not like her not to tell someone if she were going on a vacation or to visit someone out of town.

Something is definitely off. And off doesn't bode well.

"What did your guy find?"

"Well, she stayed in St. Louis for one night at a Holiday Inn. Then she disappears for a few days, then reappears in Memphis where she stays for a couple days before we lost track of her."

St. Louis and Memphis.

What the hell are you doing? Where could you possibly be heading...

When it hits me, it's like a ton of bricks dropping directly on my chest. My breath seizes and I cough to regain some air. "Barry, were the hotels, the other places she stopped along Highway 55?"

Every mile of my drive from Chicago to New Orleans was a blur. City after city. Town after town. Truck stop after truck stop. I didn't talk to anyone. I did nothing more than sleep, drive, pump gas, and occasionally eat.

But those cities...it's too much to be a coincidence.

"Uh, let me bring up a map real quick and check."

The tapping of a keyboard hits my ears, and Barry mumbles something to himself about technology. I'm sure he usually has a secretary or assistant to do this kind of shit for him if his investigator doesn't. I guess I am making him work for his big paycheck.

I clench my hands around the steering wheel. "Barry? What does it say?" My attempt to steady my voice fails, and it comes out wavering and full of unease.

"The hotels are definitely on Highway 55, or right off them within a couple miles."

Son of an everloving bitch.

"She was heading here."

Barry grunts. "Huh? Why do you think that? I thought she didn't know where you were."

I shake my head and drop my forehead against the steering wheel. "She didn't. At least, I never told her. But there are a hundred ways she could have found out. My brother could have said something to my dad. He could have told her. She could have somehow found out from the office since they mailed me my stuff."

My gut churns, and my palms are suddenly wet and clammy.

The old life is catching up with the new one. And I have no fucking clue what to do about it. It never once crossed my mind that Candace would show up here. She was firmly planted in Chicago, firmly planted in the past.

"Well, damn. You might be right, Landon. She was definitely heading south. You can't think of any other reason she could have been going that way?"

She doesn't know anyone down south. No one I know of, anyway. And despite the fact that she was clearly hiding things and keeping secrets, I think I would know if there was someone she would go to down here.

"No. It's me."

Son of a bitch.

I should have known. I should have anticipated this. She's not the type to just let things go. To just let *me* go. For weeks, she tried to talk, tried to convince me to work things out, to forgive her. She was relentless. Why did I think she would just stop because I left?

"She was coming for *me*. The only question is, where is she now?"

"I'm sending my investigator down there. It's the only way he's going to be able to track her. In the meantime, you may want to reconsider your stance about talking to your father. He may know something."

Jesus, not Barry too.

"Not happening, Barry."

"Hear me out. If there's any chance he knows where Candace is and what she's doing, don't you think it's worth sucking up your pride for two minutes to find out?"

It's not about pride. My pride was destroyed by his treachery and deceit. It's a matter of principle. That man doesn't deserve to breathe, so there's no way I'm begging him for help.

Things are good with Storm. Bringing him and my past into it will only ruin what we have. I need to take care of this without him. If I can get the Candace situation settled, I can fully and finally be with Storm.

"You want this done and over with, don't you, Landon?"

I growl and tighten my grip on the phone. "Of course, I do. What a stupid question."

"Then do whatever you have to do to end it." Barry hangs up before I can respond.

Do whatever you have to do to end it.

Isn't that what I have been doing? Trying to end that life?

I left. I started over here. I have Barry to handle all the loose ends.

Then again, maybe he's right.

I drop my forehead against the steering wheel and grip my phone in my hand. "Maybe I should call him."

He may be the only one who knows where Candace went and why. The man is a self-centered, arrogant asshole, but I only need to ask him one question. It's not like I'd be calling to chit-chat and catch up on old times.

Not that there were that many to remember in the first place.

Suck it up for two minutes, Landon.

I drag my head back up and cast a glance at Storm's house before I turn my attention to my phone. Calling this number again feels like stabbing myself in the back, like twisting the blade deeper and deeper into my own spine.

The excruciating pain of defeat radiates out into my limbs as I press "send" to connect the call. Every ring only forces the knife deeper, reminding me of what he did, of why I left in the first place.

"Son?"

One word, but it's enough to steal the breath from my lungs and make me wish I'd smashed my phone the hundred times I've wanted to. Somehow, I managed to find my voice. "Don't call me that."

"I'm glad you called. I've wanted to—"

"No." I can't bear to hear another excuse or empty apology from this man. There have been far too many over the years, especially recently. "I didn't call for your apologies or bullshit. I only have one question. Do you know where Candace is?"

Deafening silence greets my question.

He doesn't want to admit he's been talking to her. It only solidifies his guilt in all this. Not that the man feels any, but he should. No jury in the world would convict me for killing him for what he did.

And he knows it.

I suck in a deep breath and wrap my free hand around the steering wheel to ground myself. My voice rises despite my best attempt to keep my anger and agitation at bay. "Do you know where she is?"

He clears his throat, and the sound brings me back to seeing him there...

Fuck.

I clench my eyes closed and shake my head.

"I know she left Chicago. She wanted to talk to you, to explain..."

Like there's anything to explain.

I slam my palm against the dashboard. "How the fuck does she know where I am?"

He releases a sigh, and I can almost see him kicking back in his leather office chair, cigar in his mouth and a grimace on his lips. "She talked with the office. Eileen told her she shipped some of your stuff to New Orleans."

Shit.

I scrub my free hand over my face. So much for employee loyalty. I guess I never explicitly told Eileen not to reveal where I was going to anyone, but I would think, given the circumstances, it would be obvious.

Apparently not.

The best laid plans...

"You need to talk to her, Landon. Hear her out. She was really upset—"

"*She* was really upset? Did you really just say that to me?" I slam my palm against the wheel again and fight the urge to punch the window. "No, I don't have to do *anything* except be done with you and with her. This conversation is over. You are dead to me."

I end the call and drop my head back against the headrest. He was, of course, completely unapologetic. It wasn't unexpected, but it still stings.

At least the call garnered some important information. I confirmed she's in New Orleans. Now, I just have to find Candace and end this so I can move forward with Storm.

And that starts tonight with getting her to my place and safe and explaining what I can about Candace.

I don't want to leave this house, the house Ben built for us where we had our perfect little family. But I don't have a choice. The door clicks shut behind me, and I flip on the entryway light.

My chest tightens, and I bite back the sob threatening to crawl up my throat.

Don't cry, Storm. This isn't forever.

Two suitcases. That's all I am going to bring. Just enough to get us through a couple days at Landon's. I refuse to believe I can never come back here. Whatever's going on will get sorted out sooner or later. It's just a waiting game.

I've waited a long time to get my life back together. A few more days won't hurt that, especially when I'll be spending them with Landon. Being safe in his arms, knowing he loves me and accepts all the baggage that comes with me, is more than I could have ever dreamed of, more than I ever thought possible after losing Ben.

It will be good for Angelina to have a chance to get to know him better. He's about to become a more permanent fixture in my life, and she's going to have to adjust to having him around. I will too.

Shit. Where are the suitcases?

They haven't been used in a long time, so they're probably in the back hall closet. I circle through the dining room as a shortcut to the hallway. The closet door sticks a little, and I give it a hard yank. Something falls to the ground after hitting my head hard enough to probably leave a bump.

"Ouch! Shit!"

Tears blur my vision, and it's not because of the dull throb on my head. Ben's motorcycle helmet rocks gently on the hallway floor. He never rode that monstrosity after college. It's been sitting collecting dust in the garage for years, but he refused to sell it, or just get rid of this dang thing. Some sentimental tie to his college days when he was young and dumb enough to enjoy it.

I pick up the helmet to shove it back into the closet above the suitcases.

Footsteps from the living room float down the hall.

About time.

"Hey, Landon, can you help me get these suitcases out?" I don't need more crap tumbling down on me trying to get these suckers. I tug on the handle of the suitcase while holding up the shit piled on top of it with the other hand. "Landon?"

What the hell?

With an annoyed grunt, I lean my head around the door to see what the hell he's doing instead of helping me with this.

Only the hallway is empty.

Footsteps.

Banging.

And...

What is that smell?

Sharp.

Acrid.

Chemical.

It tickles my nose as I approach the living room. "Landon? What is that smell?"

I turn the corner and stop in my tracks.

What the hell?

The diminutive blonde holding the gasoline can gives me an awkward half-smile. "Sorry. Not Landon."

Holy shit.

Blood freezes in my veins as I take her and the room in. The once gray couch appears almost black, having clearly been doused in the gasoline. Or maybe paint thinner, given the bottle at her feet.

Streaks of liquid mar the walls too, and my eyes drift to a bottle of lighter fluid near the corner of the coffee table.

Jesus Christ...

Fumes burn my nostrils and eyes, and I let out a hacking cough.

"Who the hell are you?" My shaky voice does nothing to hide the fear coursing through my body. This woman's intentions are clear, even before she drops the can and reaches into her pocket.

This can't be happening.

Visions of the fire engulfing THREE flash before my eyes. Heat. Thick black smoke. Ashes.

My worst nightmare. I clutch at my stomach while surveying the room for anything I can use to stop her.

Don't lose your shit, Storm.

I can't fall apart right now. Only a clear head will help in this situation.

She stands casually, like the gun in her hand at her side she just pulled from her coat doesn't have the power to end me in a split-second.

Do I know her?

My mind races to make the connection. Work? Angel's school? The Club?

No.

I would remember this woman. She's beautiful, in that plastic Barbie doll way that screams high-maintenance, but her disheveled clothing suggests something else entirely. Stained jeans. Wrinkled white blouse. A men's jacket that's way too big for her.

Unstable.

The word screams at me in my head. This woman is not all there.

"Who are you? Why are you in my house?"

Even with my heart racing and hand shaking, I know what I need.

My gun. I have to get to my gun.

But it's locked in the bedroom nightstand, and I would need to turn my back on her to try to get to the stairs to get to it. There's no way to know if she has the balls to fire that weapon or not. The fact that she's already doused the living room in every flammable liquid she could find in the house doesn't bode well, though. There's a plan here, even if it isn't a rational one. A gun and flames. Two ways to really cause some major fucking damage.

Motherfuck.

Her forehead furrows, and she reaches up and scratches the side of her head with the barrel of the gun. "Who am I?"

"Yes, who are you?" Annoyance tightens my voice, and I struggle to keep it at bay. If I set her off, there may be no way out of this.

One of her slim shoulders rises and falls slowly, as if the act of shrugging takes too much energy from her. "I'm Candace."

Candace.

Doesn't ring a bell.

I'm confident I don't know her.

Who the hell is this woman?

If Gabe has taught me anything, it's to stay calm in a situation like this. Don't antagonize her. Let her talk. Figure out what she wants and how to give it to her before things get ugly.

Do. Not. Panic.

Get to the door if possible. Get to the gun if possible. Stay fucking calm.

I push away the thoughts of the fire that stole Ben from me. The desire to scream and curl into a ball and pretend none of this is happening has to be banished for me to concentrate on ending this without a bullet or a blaze.

"Well, Candace, you need to leave."

Her hair swings around her head as she shakes it. "Can't. Not without him."

Him?

That's what she wants. It's not something; it's someone.

Who is she talking about? Ben? He's the only one who's ever lived in this house.

It doesn't make any sense, and this woman is clearly unstable, which makes her even more dangerous. You can't reason with crazy. At least, I don't think you can. If I can't reason with her, I need to get past her, to the front door, or, I need to suck up my courage and go for my gun.

Either move poses a huge risk. Not to mention, Landon's right outside. It's only a matter of time before he comes in. Unless...

Oh, God...

What if she hurt him? What if she—

The front door flies open.

"Hey, Storm? Where are—"

Landon's words die when he sees us. The lips that have kissed me a thousand times open, and he gasps for air. Wide, confused bourbon eyes flick between us and over the room, taking in the damage Candace has already done with all the flammable liquids. He's no doubt deciphered her intent the same as I did.

Candace jumps slightly and turns her head toward the door and Landon. I could rush her, but if the gun goes off, I'm toast. Or even worse, she could point it at him.

It should be a relief, Landon being here, but the thought of him being in danger makes it impossible for his presence to comfort me.

I can't lose him.

We *just* figured this shit out. It can't end like this. God can't possibly hate me that much.

Landon's eyes roam over the blonde and then flick to me. Terror fills their depths, mixed with confusion and something else.

"Candace, what are you doing here? Storm, are you okay?"

What? He knows her?

That's what it was...recognition. Whoever Candace is, she's connected to Landon. This has nothing to do with Ben.

Him is Landon.

She's here for *him*, which makes me a target at worst and expendable at best. Whoever she is, she's someone from his past.

Who is she to him? What does she want?

I should have asked him about Chicago. I should have pushed him to tell me what happened, to tell me everything. If I knew what their history was, maybe I could help talk her down and neutralize the threat. As it stands, I'm at the mercy of a mad woman with a gun in a house rigged to burn. This old place will go up fast. The ancient wood and all the wood sealers plus the accelerants she's added...it's a recipe for another raging inferno.

Candace focuses her attention on Landon. Her hazy eyes seem to have trouble focusing, and a tiny smile curls the corner of her lips, sending icy tendrils of fear through me.

Oh, God, no. Please don't hurt him.

Blood thunders in my ears, and shaky legs bring me a step, then two closer to her. She glances over at me, her cold, cloudy eyes locking with mine, and I freeze.

Those eyes don't belong to someone who's rational. Those eyes scream *crazy as fuck.*

But she's seemingly content that I'll stay put because she turns back to Landon. "I came for you. You wouldn't talk to me. You wouldn't let me explain."

Explain what? Who the hell is this woman to him?

Maybe it's a bad idea to ask, but I have to know what and who I'm dealing with here. "Landon? What is she talking about? Who is she?"

A low, humorless chuckle comes from the woman. It's so Hannibal Lectoresque, it makes my skin crawl. "Seems Landon's been keeping some secrets from you. I'm his wife."

Wife?

Acid crawls up my throat, and my lunch threatens to make a reappearance. She must be joking. Landon isn't married. He can't be...

Landon holds out his hand and takes a step toward her. "Candace, give me the gun."

No! Stay back.

My gaze bounces between them as I hold my breath. Every inch he moves toward her makes it easier for her to hit him with a bullet if she wants to. It brings him closer to danger. Closer to doing something that will take him from me.

Candace shakes her head and points the gun at him. "Not until you hear me out."

My vision blurs, and my chest tightens again. I can't seem to suck in any air.

Oh God, please...

He holds up his hands, and his wide eyes move to meet mine. Terror mixes with something else...an apology? If she really is his wife, he certainly owes me one. And a *massive* explanation. "Okay, tell me what you came here to say."

She nods slightly and slowly lowers the gun to her side again.

Thank God.

I take a deep breath and try to steady my shaking hands by clasping my arms. What the hell else am I supposed to do? She listens to him. That much is clear. I need to let him take the wheel here. Otherwise...

No. I can't think about any other possibility.

Landon takes a step toward her with his hand out, and this time, she lets him close the distance.

"I don't want to hurt you, Landon..." Her voice wavers, and tears trickle down her pale cheeks. Then before he can even react, she's facing me, with the barrel pointed at my chest. "But this woman, this whore, she ruined everything."

I did what?

Her hand shakes, making the gun bob up and down.

I thought I knew what terror was. Seeing the club burning, knowing Ben and Caleb were inside...I thought that was it. As bad as it could get. But having that gun pointed at me is something else entirely.

Every muscle in my body stiffens, and I take a single step back. This cannot be how I die. This cannot be how it ends. I look to Landon, desperate for that connection, to see the love there one last time if this is it. To know we've finally made it to where I don't have to say the words out loud for him to know.

Landon steps toward her again. "No, Candace. Everything that happened was because of your own choices. I didn't force you to sleep with him, and she sure as hell didn't either."

A single tear trickles down her pale cheek. Her hand shakes more violently, and I take a step backward until I hit the wall next to the opening to the hallway. She turns her head to regard Landon, who keeps glancing at me out of the corner of his eye. "Yes, you did. You were always so busy at work. You never paid any attention to me. I was so lonely."

He scoffs. "And you thought the best way to deal with your loneliness was to sleep with my father?"

She flinches, and I cringe away from the uncontrolled weapon in her hands and at Landon's words.

His father? Holy shit.

It explains so much. Why he left Chicago. Why he came to New Orleans. Why when we first met, he wanted nothing to do with any sort of attachments or connections to anyone. The reaction he had to questions about his father at our family dinner.

His own father and his wife...

What kind of fucked-up father must he be to do that?

And why didn't he ever tell me he was married? He had all the time in the world to come clean. I did...eventually. Though he did have to force it out of me.

If we make it out of this, he and I are having a very long conversation.

Candace scoffs and shakes her head. "Why does it matter who it was, Landon? You still drove me to do it."

The anger and pain lacing her voice slices through me. Even though I can't understand her actions, the very real agony this woman is suffering is apparent. I feel for her as a human being, even if she is here with malicious intent. Her logic is incredibly flawed here, but it's clear she's had some sort of a mental break. Nothing Ben could have done would have driven me to another man's arms. And this...is just so messed up.

Landon's eyes meet mine over her shoulder, and they're screaming at me, begging me to understand. I don't have time to sort through how I feel about him not telling me about Candace and what happened right now. My focus is getting both of us out of here alive.

He returns his attention to her and nods. "You're right, Candace. I was wrong. I neglected you. I forced you to make that decision. I'm sorry I didn't let you explain. But I understand now."

What the hell is he doing?

Those bourbon eyes plead with me again. He takes several quick steps, closing the distance between them. She whirls before he can reach her, gun raised. It ends poised only inches from his chest.

Any breath I had in my lungs rushes out. I slap my hand over my mouth to hold in the scream threatening to slip out.

No. No. No.

Please no.

I can't lose him. I can't do this. Not again.

Candace sobs and wipes the snot from under her nose with the sleeve of her jacket. Probably Landon's jacket. "You don't mean that. You're just saying that now because I'm the one with the gun and all the power."

He shakes his head and moves his hand toward the gun. She shoves it into his chest. "You'll never take me back. Not now that you have *her.*"

The gun swings around and onto me. There's nowhere to run.

Landon pulls his hand away, giving her a little space. "That's not true, baby. I love you."

The words drive an ice pick straight to my heart, but the flick of his eyes over to me tells me he doesn't mean it. Not that I would have believed it. Not after what we shared. He's just trying to do whatever it takes to talk her down.

I have to ignore the tightening in my chest and the burn in my eyes to focus on what's happening.

Landon's words seem to have the desired effect. She turns her back to me completely and lowers the gun. Her shoulders slump forward and relax. A whisper-silent voice slips from her lips. "Do you really mean that?"

He steps forward and extends his hand. "Yeah, baby, I do. Just give me the gun and we can work this all out."

Her shoulders shake. She's going to give in...

Thank God.

thirty-one

*M*y hand shakes as I reach toward the gun. Candace never exhibited any mental health issues before, but she's definitely not all there now. The light and warmth that was always in her eyes is gone, replaced by a glossy, empty stare and shimmering tears.

This isn't Candace.

Even though what she did was unfathomable and unforgiveable, she's not a bad person. She's not the person who brings a gun and points it at someone.

At least, she wasn't.

Something has changed. Something has snapped. Me walking in on her with Dad was a catastrophic shock to my system, but the aftermath affected her too. I left her. Left the condo. Left our lives together without a word to her except to stay the fuck away from me. I've had Barry trying to serve her with the divorce papers so we can end things legally, but other than that, I cut her off completely after almost five years together.

I'm all she had other than her vapid socialite friends, the gym, and the damn salon. She didn't work. She never graduated from college. She was a trophy wife, plain and simple. She was easy and didn't ask for much other than money, which I was more than capable of providing for her. The sex was always good, but she's right, I started working more and spending less time with her.

Still, nothing can excuse or explain what she did. What Dad did. Unless she was already in some sort of mental downward spiral. It would be just like the old man to see her crumbling, see her vulnerability and step in to take advantage. It's what he does best.

This woman isn't one I know, but I have to try to get through to her to keep this from escalating any further. So I can get her some damn help.

Candace's lip trembles, and the barrel of the gun shifts away from my chest. A deep breath and a single step bring me closer to her. I don't dare look at Storm, even though I'm dying to see her eyes and make sure she's still okay.

The moment I walked in the door and saw Candace with the gun pointed at her, my entire world stopped, along with my heart. After everything Storm's been through, I've now brought this down on her, brought this danger to her door.

I can't let anything happen to her.

"Candace, give me the gun. We can talk about this."

Mere inches separate my fingers from the gun. This close, the trembling of her arm is unmistakable. So is the fear and confusion in her eyes. She doesn't want to be doing this, but something inside her has changed—morphed her into this shell of who she once was.

Before I can even register what's happening, Candace moves away from me and turns, and the gun is no longer pointed at me, it's aimed directly at Storm.

"No!" Storm recoils and takes two steps back with her arms raised. "Candace. Stop. You don't want to do this. You don't need to do this."

I want to rush at Candace, knock that damn thing out of her hand. But any sudden movement could make her shoot. I can't risk her shooting Storm.

Candace's disheveled hair swings around her as she shakes her head. She glances over at me. The calm that was there momentarily before, when she thought I would come back to her, is gone, replaced with malice and something dark and evil. "I'm sorry, Landon. But until she's gone, I can't know for sure that you'll come back to me."

Christ, she's totally lost it.

My eyes sting with tears welling there. What the fuck happened to get us here? A place where my former love and current one are face to face, one threatening to end the other? It's like some fucked-up Jerry Springer episode only instead of a riotous studio audience, they have me standing here shaking.

Storm seems to sense the same predicament I see. I can't lunge at Candace without putting Storm at risk. Those blue eyes I love so much meet mine, and she shakes her head a little. She doesn't want me to do anything. I don't know what she's thinking or planning, but whatever it is, she better act fast. The longer this drags out, the higher the chance someone isn't walking away from it.

Storm takes a step toward Candace.

What the fuck is she doing?

My heart pounds so hard, it may burst free from my chest. Blood rushes in my ears. She can't do this. She can't risk her life like this.

I step forward but Storm raises a hand, stopping me in my tracks.

"Listen, Candace. I don't know you, and you don't know me…"

She scoffs at Storm and the gun wavers, sending my heart into overdrive. "Oh, I know more than enough about you. You're the slut who stole my husband. I've been watching you. I've seen you two together. Seen you sneak off to his place. You snatched him right out from under me. You took any chance I had at getting him back. You took everything."

Somehow, Storm manages to blow off the comment and remain calm.

Christ.

She somehow found that inner strength I always knew was

there to pull herself together enough to confront this. It makes me love her even more.

Storm lowers her voice and shakes her head. "I know that's what you think, but I didn't steal anything. It was stolen from me. My husband, my daughter's father, he was taken from us by a very bad man."

I expect Candace to respond, but instead, she just stares at Storm, as if waiting for her to continue. Storm's eyes flit over to mine before she takes another step toward Candace.

"I know what it's like to lose everything, Candace. I know how *you* feel. But, you can get it back. Landon is right here. He's safe, and alive, and willing to take you back."

Her voice is level when she says it, but I know saying that had to hurt.

Ouch.

Those words sting more than they should. I know she's only saying it to calm Candace, but all the same, they're like a knife to my heart, just like I'm sure hearing me tell Candace I love her felt for Storm.

Candace shakes her head, and her eyes drift to me. "He won't. Not when you're in the picture."

She's right. But even if I'd never met Storm, reconciliation would have been out of the question. You don't forget something like that. You can't forgive something like that. And now that I've had space. Time to think. Time to reflect on what I shared with Candace...I can see it for what it was. I settled.

I loved her in my own way, but it was nothing compared to what I share with Storm. It was superficial. She was fun and beautiful. Light and airy. Ease and contentment.

Storm is dark and stunning. Deep and emotional. And she will never, ever be easy. She's everything I need. What I've always needed, I just never knew it.

"He's not mine, Candace. He's yours. But if you hurt me, do you really think he's going to be so willing to open his arms to you? Do you think you have any chance with him if you're in prison?"

Something in Storm's words seems to touch Candace. Her arm slowly lowers to her side, and tears stream down her face. She stares at Storm for several long moments.

This is my chance.

Two steps close the distance between me and Candace, and I pull the gun from her hand. She lets out a sob and collapses onto the floor.

I shove the gun into my jacket pocket and turn to Storm. Her bottom lip quivers before a strangled sob comes out. I rush over and pull her into my arms. She buries her face against me. Hot tears trickle down my skin and soak my shirt.

"I'm so sorry, Storm."

What else can I say?

No words exist to convey how much I regret bringing this into her life.

She cries against me, and her arms tighten around my neck. For the first time since I walked in the door and saw Candace, I relax and the vise wrapped around my heart finally releases, allowing me to take a deep breath.

Her scent invades my lungs, mingled with the acrid smell of the gasoline and other accelerants Candace doused the room in, and I pull back and take her face in my hands. Tears shimmer in her eyes and flow down her pale skin. I brush them away with my thumbs, but I can't erase the pain in her gaze.

I have so much explaining to do...so much she doesn't understand.

"I knew it." The whispered words from Candace send ice through my veins despite the warmth of having Storm safe in my arms.

I release Storm and turn to face Candace, who's no longer in a crumpled heap on the floor. She stands a few feet away, between the couch and the coffee table. Out of reach. Physically and emotionally.

Her entire body vibrates, and she reaches into her pocket with a shaky hand. "I knew you were lying. I never should have trusted you."

Shit.

My first inclination had been to get to Storm. Candace wasn't a threat anymore. It was a bad idea to let her see us embracing. But it's okay. I have the gun.

Everything's okay.

"Candace, let's go outside and talk some more."

She shakes her head and pulls something small and metal from her pocket. "There's no point in talking anymore." She raises her hand.

Fuck.

A lighter. My lighter. The one I kept in the study at the condo we shared together for when I wanted to enjoy the occasional cigar.

The scent of the gasoline and other flammables becomes ten times stronger. I've been so focused on de-escalating the incident with the gun, the fact she had prepared to light the place wasn't even my concern.

Her thumb flips back the cover and hovers over the tiny metal wheel that could spell our doom.

This can't happen.

I hold up my hand. "No, Candace. You don't want to do this."

Those lifeless eyes meet mine, and she flicks her finger.

"No!" I lunge to grab it, but it's too late.

The lighter falls from her hand onto the couch. A wall of heat and flame slams into me almost instantly, pushing me back from any hope of grabbing her.

Fuck!

"Landon!"

Storm's scream drags my attention away from the inferno for a split-second. She tugs at my arm, and we both retreat as the flames blaze across the furniture, over the floors, up the walls, and engulf Candace.

They consume the room and her so fast, there's no hope to save either. Her screams as she crumbles to the floor in a fireball echo in my ears with the roaring of the flames that have engulfed her.

We have to get out of here.

If I try to get Candace out, I'll never make it. I grab Storm's arm and drag her toward the front door, the heat licking at our backs.

Fresh air rushes in as we bolt out. It feeds the inferno. Flames flow through the open door after us, and I haul Storm away from the house and out onto the street.

Holy shit.

Candace...

It's gone. Everything.

"Fire...inside..." Landon's panicked words into his phone barely register as I watch flames and smoke billow from the open front door.

How can this be happening again? Why? What the hell did I ever do to God or Karma or whoever controls the damn universe to deserve this?

Tears cloud my vision as the smoke burns my eyes, and I stumble back to the curb before I drop to the cool cement. My entire body shakes, and I wrap my arms around my legs and drop my face into my knees.

I can't catch my breath. I suck in air, but my chest just burns and tightens. My head swims, and I cough violently trying to get some damn oxygen.

Landon collapses next to me. "I'm so sorry, Storm." He wraps his arm around me, and I bury my face against his neck with my eyes squeezed shut.

If I don't look at it, it's not real.

If I don't look, then I haven't lost everything...all of Ben's things, our photos, the house we shared that he rebuilt with his own hands.

I don't care about my stuff. Stuff can be replaced. Those things can't.

"I didn't mean for any of this to happen." Landon's words are hoarse, barely audible, and the unmistakable quiver of tears reveals he's on the edge of breaking down.

That edge I'm so close to as well.

But, I can't. I won't. If I do, I'll never come back from it.

"On a scale of zero to *I want to throw you back into that fire,* how mad are you?"

I pull my head up and glance up at him before returning my attention to the house.

There's no doubt, I should be furious. He got involved with me while he's still married. He didn't tell me he's married. His psycho wife slashed my tires, killed my cat, and tried to kill me. And she burned the house Ben put so much time and effort into making perfect for us.

Who knows how much damage will be done to the house and our things by the time the fire is out. I may never get any of it back. If it's all gone, if we have to start over again, I don't even know how to begin.

Yet, for some reason, I'm not furious. I'm not even angry. I'm just...exhausted.

Bone-deep.

There's no fight left in me for anything or against anyone.

Even if it may be deserved.

I shake my head slowly. "I'm not mad."

He tugs me against him and buries his face against my hair. "I'm so, so sorry, Storm."

"I know you are."

Landon is so compassionate, so caring, I have no doubt he's being torn apart inside by what's happened—to me and to Candace.

God...

She was his *wife*. He loved her. Who knows how long they were together? What sort of relationship they had? Even though things went bad, there had to have been good times. There was love there...at some point.

Even though he loves *me* now, it's only human for him to be in shock and grieving what just happened to her.

I've been there...watching something...someone...I love burn.

"I'm so sorry about Candace."

He pulls away and a hiccupped sob comes from his throat. "I don't know what happened, Storm. That wasn't the woman I married. That wasn't the woman I knew before the whole thing with my dad."

"What do you think happened?"

His shoulders rise and fall. "I don't have a fucking clue."

He's in shock. I've been there. I understand it. I'm close to that point myself, watching another fire take what's mine again.

Sirens in the distance send my heart racing.

Maybe they can save something.

Candace is gone. There's no doubt about that with the way the flames engulfed her.

That's part of why I can't be mad at him. He lost her. No matter what their history was, watching someone you once cared for that deeply about die that way is beyond traumatic. If I had actually seen Ben engulfed in those flames...

My stomach turns, and I clamp my hand over my mouth to

stop the sob.

A woman rushes up to us. One of the neighbors.

"Are you okay? Is anyone inside?"

I shake my head and swallow against the dryness in my throat. "We're fine. There's someone in there, but it's too late to do anything for her."

The words bring a sob from Landon and bring fresh tears to my eyes. Despite what she did, Candace was still a human being. She was still someone he loved once. Someone who deserved love. And now, she's gone. Lost to some break in her mind. Lost to actions controlled by jealousy.

It shouldn't have happened.

If she had been rational, it wouldn't have. Though, I guess nothing is rational when it comes to love. You fall, and you keep falling. But sometimes, you hit rock bottom. That's what happened to her. He couldn't have anticipated it. No one could.

I press my lips against his cheek. "You didn't know any of this would happen. You didn't tell me about Candace when you came here because you weren't looking for a relationship. You weren't looking for anything and neither was I."

God, how fast things have changed.

It's been a whirlwind. But a good one. One I needed. One Angelina needed. One we *all* needed.

"There was no reason to open up about something like that, just like I didn't open up to you about Ben's death and losing the baby. You would've told me."

There's no need for him to be worrying about how I'm reacting to the revelations about his past when he's just seen that past burn alive.

He pulls away from me and shoves his hands through his hair. Tears streak his cheeks. His head shakes from side to side listlessly. "I just...I don't know how everything went so wrong."

Because that's how life goes. Things go wrong. People make bad choices. Those choices snowball.

Stone made a choice when he was a child that had catastrophic ramifications twenty years later. He couldn't have known. He never intended any of it. But it happened, all the same.

Landon's in the same boat. I can't blame him for any of it.

"I was trying to serve her with divorce papers, but she kept dodging my lawyer and then she disappeared. I never would have guessed she would come here looking for me. I thought she understood we were over."

I sigh and capture his hand with mine. "How long were you together?"

He heaves out a shaky breath and turns his wet, red eyes to meet mine. "Are you sure you want to hear all this right now?"

"You're right. It can wait."

I've been through too much to let anything get in the way of my happiness. There's nothing he can tell me now that will change what I want or how I feel. It only cements for me that this is right. He is right. For me. For Angelina.

Neighbors rush out along the street and stop in the periphery, watching the inferno engulf my life...again.

He brushes his fingers across my cheek and turns my face to his. His teary eyes ask the question even before the words leave his mouth. "What do we do now?"

The mirthless laugh claws up my throat, mixing with my tears, and I return my focus to the house as a fire truck comes to a stop in front of us. "I guess Angel and I will be staying with you longer than we had planned."

Losing the house feels almost like losing Ben again, but this time, it's different. My eyes drift to the cuff still wrapped around my wrist.

This time, I have Landon to rely on, to hold on to, to help pull me up from the darkness sure to creep in. And that's okay. I can admit I need the help now. More than ever.

Landon squeezes my hand. "As long as I'm with you and

Angelina, I don't care where we are. My place. A new place. We'll figure it out."

Firemen rush out of the truck and toward the hydrant. One approaches us at the curb.

"Are you all right? Did everyone get out?"

Landon chokes back a sob, and I rise to my feet. "We're fine, but there's a woman inside. Candace. She was the one who started the fire. There were accelerants. She was engulfed quickly. There was nothing we could do."

"How long has the fire been going?"

It feels like hours, but I've lost any sense of time since the moment I saw her standing in my living room with that gun. "Maybe ten minutes?"

He nods and races off, yelling something to the other fire-fighters who are already releasing water onto the house.

Flames lick up the front from the blown-out windows and smoke pours from every possible opening. They're too late.

It's all gone.

Angel and I will be starting over again.

But this time...

I turn back to Landon, and he rises from the curb, swiping at his eyes.

...this time...I won't be alone. Not anymore. Not ever.

He steps up to me and tugs me into his strong, warm arms. "I love you, Storm. And I promise, things will only get better from here. They *can* only get better."

My tears soak his shirt, and the smoke in the fabric invades my lungs with every sob. "I love you, too."

I want to believe his words. I want them to be true. But life constantly throws curveballs. I know that more than anyone.

There was a time I would let this break me, but I won't. I can't.

Like a phoenix, I rose from the ashes once. I can do it again. I can rebuild my life.

With Landon.

epilogue

FIVE MONTHS LATER

*C*hris scans the main stage room at THREE before returning his attention to me. "I think everything turned out pretty brilliant, don't you?"

The club looks outstanding. Exactly what I had envisioned all those months ago when I first laid eyes on the plans. It really is something to be proud of and in awe of.

How could it not be when Storm designed it?

"Yeah. It's pretty perfect." I take a swig of my beer and watch the bartender and a few of the servers scurry around behind the bar to get things ready for the grand opening.

Chris smacks me on the shoulder. "You and your girl did good."

Pride swells my chest. "I wish I had *anything* to do with it, but this was all Storm. I just put the plans into motion to ensure her vision was realized."

She managed to push through and get it done despite all the reasons it never should have been completed. Between the fire and living on edge because of the uncertain Luca situation, things were a little up in the air. But it's complete. It even got done without her stepping foot in here again. Through phone calls and pictures, she managed to make sure everything was finished to her exacting standards. Even after losing the house and almost everything in it, she only allowed a slight delay before she insisted we push forward. She really is incredible.

He clinks his beer bottle against mine. "Well, you still got it built."

I chuckle and take a swig of my beer. "It would have been done whether I was here or not. You would have just been really fucking busy handling things yourself."

"Don't be so sure." He shakes his head and leans back against the bar. "I think you working this project is the best thing that could have happened."

A laugh slips from my lips. "Bullshit. If you had known what would happen between me and Storm, you never would have brought me on." I very vividly remember the warning he gave me when he first had an inkling I was interested in her, and the reaction he had when I came clean and told him we were sleeping together and things were going less than swimmingly.

He grins. "Yeah, you're probably right, but I never could have anticipated how it would end."

Neither could we.

No one could. Except maybe God or whatever all-seeing power is out there.

Who would have thought two broken people who wanted nothing more than a sexual outlet could find everything they've been looking for and exactly what they need to put their lives back together?

We're perfect together, the ultimate team—professionally and personally. And even though we've already had a lot of hard times, we've managed to establish something that no one's ever going to be able to break apart. Two totally broken people reassembled into one unbreakable unit.

"I'm going to go check on her. You want to come?"

Chris shakes his head. "No, I want to stay in here to make sure the staff doesn't need any help with anything and maybe have another beer."

I down the last of my beer and set the empty on the bar before exiting the club.

Cool late afternoon air and fading light hit me. The Hawke clan filters around the parking lot. Antonia—ever the matriarch —and Nora stand with Stone to my left, cooing over baby Isaac while Dani, Skye, and Caroline try to wrangle Kennedy and Angelina where they play in the little grassy area in the center of the lot. Savage and Gabe are talking with a local news anchor who's doing a story on the club opening.

It takes me a moment to find Storm. She stands at the far edge of the street, well back from the building, staring up at the finished product.

The breeze whips up around her, sending her dark mane swirling around her face. She reaches up and brushes it back behind her ear as I approach.

Christ. Even after all this time, every time I see her, she takes my breath away.

Just like the first time I laid eyes on her at the party, her dark beauty calls me toward her. She turns her head to acknowledge me, and I wrap my arms around her from behind and place a kiss on her temple. "You doing okay?"

It's a loaded question, especially today. But I've learned to keep asking, even if she fights me, even if she doesn't want to answer. Sometimes Storm needs a push to open up and a reminder she doesn't need to face everything alone.

She sucks in an unsteady breath and nods. "I think so. I've managed to keep the tears back since we left the cemetery."

I still can't believe they chose today for the grand opening. The one-year anniversary of Ben's death.

Not to mention, it was Storm's idea. She said she didn't want the day to be about sadness; she wanted it to have a happy connection too. So, after we went to mass and visited the cemetery this morning, the rest of the day has been dedicated to getting ready for the launch of THREE.

It undoubtedly has helped take her mind off what happened

a year ago today. Though, I think she'd be okay even without this. She's come so far in the last couple months. We've come so far. Farther than I ever imagined possible. We've built a life together, a future.

The ring that's been hiding in my office for the last month will cement that future. I'm just waiting for the right time. But there's no doubt in my mind it's what I want and that it's what she wants.

I squeeze her tightly, and she wraps her arms up around mine and sighs. "I'm so proud of you for doing this."

She snort-laughs and looks back at me. "What? Not falling apart?"

I grin down at her. "You can fall apart, you know. I meant completing the project despite everything."

A smile tugs at her lips. "You really think Savage and Gabe would have let me get away with not finishing it?"

"Good point."

She returns her focus to the club and the Hawkes mingling around. For better or for worse, they are family—hers and mine. I may never be a Hawke in name, but I'm forever tied to them by my love for Storm and Angel.

After Candace's betrayal, I never thought I'd want a relationship again let alone to get married, but Storm and Angel have completely changed my life. Storm opened my heart to real love in a real relationship where two wounded people come together to help heal each other.

I loved Candace, I truly did, but it wasn't this. It was more superficial. We didn't share the same connection or the same depth of emotion and maybe we never could because I hadn't suffered that loss. Maybe that's what made Storm and me perfect for each other in the first place. If it weren't for what Candace did, I may never have found Storm. I may never have found this. I would be going on with my life in Chicago thinking I was happy when what I was doing was living life barely content.

Now I know what happiness is.

I squeeze her again, and she turns partially in my arms to peer up at me. "What about you? Are you doing okay?" She raises an eyebrow at me.

I plant a kiss on her lips. "Why wouldn't I be?"

She shrugs. "I don't know. This whole thing is emotional for the entire family and I know you didn't know Ben, but after everything we've been through, I feel like you did."

"I do too."

There's a strange camaraderie with her dead husband. A special club that only he and I have ever been in. The Loving Storm and Being Loved By Storm Club, and it's fucking amazing to be president of it. Because when she finally accepted she loved me, that she needed me, that we could be so much to each other, she gave me everything.

I got my ready-made family. And while I can never replace Ben as Angel's father, I can be there for her and let her know I'll always do anything and everything to protect her and her mother and to be there for whatever they could ever need.

Lately, that's been finalizing the renovations and rebuilding of the house. But it should only be another few months before we can move back in there—another decision we made together, mostly for Angel's benefit. Even though it will be a little strange living in the house Ben essentially built for Storm, this version is all my hands. This version is ours.

And we're going to live in it without fear. While things with Luca are still dicey and full of a whole lot of uncertainty, we aren't letting his vague threat control our lives. If and when anything happens, we'll deal with the fall-out then.

Skye approaches and stands next to us to look at the building. "Hey, guys. Mom is leaving with Nora, Dani, Caroline, and the kids. Nora, Dani, and Caroline are coming back later."

Angelina waves at us from across the parking lot as she climbs in the car. "Bye, Mommy!"

Storm and I wave good-bye to her, and I blow a kiss to Antonia before she slides in and starts up the engine.

Skye turns to us and nods at me. "Can I talk to my sister for a second?"

I don't want to let her out of my arms, but Storm and Skye probably need to talk more than Storm needs me here at this moment. Sometimes, there are things you can only say to your sister. And something tells me, this is something for family.

The Hawkes are an unbreakable team. I may never forgive Dad for what he did, but I have Chris and I have the Hawkes. You create your own family sometimes.

I press a kiss to Storm's temple. "I'm going to head back inside. You'll be okay?"

She nods and smiles at me. "I will."

And I know she means it.

She will be okay. We all will. It just took us a long time to get here.

Skye takes Landon's place and wraps me up in her arms, burying her face in my hair. "Are you really okay? You don't look okay."

When Landon asked just a moment ago, I had been okay, but Skye's arms around me unleashes something I didn't even know I've been holding back. The weight of everything that's resting on this date finally falls on me.

I cover my mouth to catch my sob and shake my head. "I thought I was."

This morning was hard. The cemetery. I've been there a hundred times since he died, but today, it was different. Knowing only a year ago he was home in bed with me, tangled in my arms...thinking back to the day I lost him. Standing there staring at the tomb that holds him forever. I couldn't hold it back anymore.

Skye grabbed Angelina from me and gave me the opportunity to drop to my knees and place my forehead against the cool marble where his name is engraved. I don't know how long I knelt there, but it felt like forever until I felt strong, warm arms wrap around me and pull me from the ground.

Landon is always there, lifting me up when I need it and supporting me through anything that may come.

I thought after this morning's breakdown, I'd be okay. But the current blubbering mess I'm devolving into proves me wrong.

She squeezes me tighter. "It's only been a year. You have every right to cry and scream and be upset. It doesn't diminish everything you've accomplished, everything you've worked through in the last year. You're the strongest of any of us. You always have been."

It sure as hell doesn't feel that way.

Sometimes, it feels like one tiny step forward followed by a giant leap back with where I am at processing everything that's happened. Not just losing Ben, but finding Landon, then having to watch Candace almost kill us and then destroy the house. It would be a lot for anyone. Logically, I know that. But I just wish I was able to handle things a little better while maintaining the outward appearance of having my shit together. I know I fail at that most of the time.

Like now.

Skye sighs and rests her chin against my shoulder. "People think it's Savage because he stepped up when Dad died and how he recreated his life after the accident, or that it's me because I lost Star and managed to stay sane...kind of...or Stone because of what he's overcome after what Dom did, but it's always been you. If I had lost Gabe when he was shot, I don't really think I would still be breathing."

Her words go straight to my heart, and my chest aches, because I know that feeling all too well. "There were days when I didn't want to keep breathing, Skye. There were days I wished I could stop."

She shakes me a little, then squeezes tighter. "But you *didn't*. I know we all pushed you, but it wasn't because we didn't think you could do it on your own. It was because we saw that you needed a reminder of who you are. There was never a question you were strong enough. You just needed a little kick in the ass."

A laugh escapes despite the utter lack of humor I feel. It releases some of the tension that's been winding up in me since I woke in Landon's arms this morning. Even that...his warm, comforting touch, wasn't enough to keep it at bay today.

Kick in the ass is right.

They literally dragged me kicking and screaming from the dark hole I dug myself into. They and Landon.

Skye waves toward the building. "You did that. Ben would be so proud of you for finishing the project, for choosing today of all days for the grand opening."

I let out a mirthless chuckle, swiping at my tears. "I'm starting to think maybe picking today was a mistake."

She shakes her head. "You feel that way right now but you did the right thing by turning this day into something happy. Cry now if you need to, but you know the tears are going to stop, and you know it's going to get better."

Skye doesn't often offer deep words of wisdom. It's not that she's not intelligent or deeply loving, she just spent so long pushing everyone away and lashing out that she rarely steps from behind her claws.

She's right, of course.

That's one thing I *have* learned since Landon came into my life. The pain is very real, and it always will be. I'll never get over losing Ben. It will be a part of me as long as I live, and he'll always own a massive part of my heart. But the tears dry, and the guilt at moving on fades more and more every day.

It's only been the blink of an eye in the grand scheme of things, yet, Landon opened my heart. He did that for me even though neither of us wanted it, even though neither of us expected it and were blindsided.

It was a force too strong to ignore, and we were stupid for fighting it. Finally giving in and accepting what we were to each other helped me free that last little bit of shame that had been keeping me from really living.

Skye releases me as Savage, Gabe, and Stone approach and join us.

Savage wraps his hand around my forearm and squeezes. "You all right?"

I laugh and place my hand on top of his. "I will be."

And I know it's true.

Just like Savage rebuilt his life with Dani. He found love and acceptance and has a beautiful, doting wife and daughter. Just like Skye and Gabe fought through their own guilt and anguish to find each other. They have what they both need and are completely content to just be *them,* no matter what anyone else thinks. Just like Stone and Nora faced their demons and forgave. They're building a family with Isaac and learning that their pasts are just that—in the past. Just like the rest of the Hawkes, I will be okay.

We all stare up at the building that is so much more than a strip club. It's so much more than we could ever explain to anyone even if we tried.

After everything this family has been through—Dad's death, the accident and losing Star, Gabe almost dying, Stone discovering what he did and the pain he unleashed, the fire and losing Ben, the vague threat Luca leveled on us that still lingers—there are a lot of people who would be broken, who would be so shattered by what life has thrown at them that they would cave.

There are so many people who would've just given up, who would have said, "well that's it." People who would never believe anything good would happen again, that they could ever truly *live* again.

But not us. Not the Hawkes.

We all moved forward in our own way and at our own pace. We all found a way to live with the loss and the pain. A way to take it day by day and just keep breathing and rebuilding.

We will always continue to rise, because Hawkes will always soar.

———

If you enjoyed *Building Storm*, check out the other books in the series and stay tuned for more from the Hawke family. *Tainted Saint* is coming March 19, 2019 and is available for preorder now: books2read.com/TaintedSaint

Savage Collision
Books2read.com/SavageCollision

Tortured Skye
books2read.com/Tortured-Skye

Stone Sober
books2read.com/StoneSober

Building Storm
books2read.com/BuildingStorm

Tainted Saint
www.books2read.com/TaintedSaint

Steele Resolve
www.books2read.com/SteeleResolve

Sign up for Gwyn's newsletter to stay up to date on releases: www.gwynmcnamee.com/newsletter

ABOUT THE AUTHOR

Gwyn McNamee is an attorney, writer, wife, and mother (to one human baby and two fur babies). Originally from the Midwest, Gwyn relocated to her husband's home town of Las Vegas in 2015 and is enjoying her respite from the cold and snow. Gwyn has been writing down her crazy stories and ideas for years and finally decided to share them with the world. She loves to write stories with a bit of suspense and action mingled with romance and heat.

When she isn't either writing or voraciously devouring any books she can get her hands on, Gwyn is busy adding to her tattoo collection, golfing, and stirring up trouble with her perfect mix of sweetness and sarcasm (usually while wearing heels).

Gwyn loves to hear from her readers. Here is where you can find her:

Website: http://www.gwynmcnamee.com/

Facebook: https://www.facebook.com/AuthorGwynMcNamee/

FB Reader Group: https://www.facebook.com/groups/1667380963540655/

Newsletter: www.gwynmcnamee.com/newsletter

Twitter: https://twitter.com/GwynMcNamee

Instagram: https://www.instagram.com/gwynmcnamee

Bookbub: https://www.bookbub.com/authors/gwynmcnamee

OTHER WORKS BY GWYN MCNAMEE

The Hawke Family Series

Savage Collision (The Hawke Family - Book One)

He's everything she didn't know she wanted. She's everything he thought he could never have.

The last thing I expect when I walk into The Hawkeye Club is to fall head over heels in lust. It's supposed to be a rescue mission. I have to get my baby sister off the pole, into some clothes, and out of the grasp of the pussy peddler who somehow manipulated her into stripping. But the moment I see Savage Hawke and verbally spar with him, my ability to remain rational flies out the window and my libido takes center stage. I've never wanted a relationship—my time is better spent focusing on taking down the scum running this city—but what I want and what I need are apparently two different things.

Danika Eriksson storms into my office in her high heels and on her high horse. Her holier-than-thou attitude and accusations should offend me, but instead, I can't get her out of my head or my heart. Her incomparable drive, take-no prisoners attitude, and blatant honesty captivate me and hold me prisoner. I should steer clear, but my self-preservation instinct is apparently dead—which is exactly what our relationship will be once she knows everything. It's only a matter of time.

The truth doesn't always set you free. Sometimes, it just royally screws you.

AVAILABLE NOW AT ALL RETAILERS:

books2read.com/SavageCollision

Tortured Skye (The Hawke Family - Book Two)

She's always been off-limits. He's always just out of reach.

Falling in love with Gabe Anderson was as easy as breathing. Fighting my feelings for my brother's best friend was agonizingly hard. I never imagined giving in to my desire for him would cause such a destructive ripple effect. That kiss was my grasp at a lifeline—something, anything to hold me steady in my crumbling life. Now, I have to suffer with the fallout while trying to convince him it's all worth the consequences.

Guilt overwhelms me—over what I've done, the lives I've taken, and more than anything, over my feelings for Skye Hawke. Craving my best friend's little sister is insanely self-destructive. It never should have happened, but since the moment she kissed me, I haven't been able to get her out of my mind. If I take what I want, I risk losing everything. If I don't, I'll lose her and a piece of myself. The raging storm threatening to rain down on the city is nothing compared to the one that will come from my decision.

Love can be torture, but sometimes, love is the only thing that can save you.

AVAILABLE NOW AT ALL RETAILERS:

Books2read.com/Tortured-Skye

Stone Sober (The Hawke Family - Book Three)

She's innocent and sweet. He's dark and depraved.

Stone Hawke is precisely the kind of man women are warned about—handsome, intelligent, arrogant, and intricately entangled with some dangerous people. I should stay away, but he manages to strip my soul bare with just a look and dominates my thoughts. Bad decisions are in my past. My life is (mostly) on track, even if it is no longer the one to medical school. I can't allow myself to cave to the fierce pull and ardent attraction I feel toward the youngest Hawke.

Nora Eriksson is off-limits, and not just because she's my brother's employee and sister-in-law. Despite the fact she's stripping at The Hawkeye Club, she has an innocent and pure heart. Normally, the only thing that appeals to me about innocence is the opportunity to taint it. But not when it comes to Nora. I can't expose her to the filth permeating my life. There are too many things I can't control, things completely out of my hands. She doesn't deserve any of it, but the power she holds over me is stronger than any addiction.

The hardest battles we fight are often with ourselves, but only through defeating our own demons can we find true peace.

AVAILABLE NOW AT ALL RETAILERS:

books2read.com/StoneSober

Building Storm (The Hawke Family - Book Four)

She hasn't been living. He's looking for a way to forget it all.

My life went up in flames. All I'm left with is my daughter and ashes. The simple act of breathing is so excruciating, there are days I wish I could stop altogether. So I have no business being at the party, and I definitely shouldn't be in the arms of the handsome stranger. When his lips meet mine, he breathes life into me for the first time since the day the inferno disintegrated my world. But loving again isn't in the cards, and there are even greater dangers to face than trying to keep Landon McCabe out of my heart.

Running is my only option. I have to get away from Chicago and the betrayal that shattered my world. I need a new life-one without attachments. The vibrancy of New Orleans convinces me it's possible to start over. Yet in all the excitement of a new city, it's Storm Hawke's dark, sad beauty that draws me in. She isn't looking for love, and we both need a hot, sweaty release without feelings getting involved. But even the best laid plans fail, and life can leave you burned.

Love can build, and love can destroy. But in the end, love is what raises you from the ashes.

Tainted Saint (The Hawke Family - Book Five)

He's searching for absolution. She wants her happily ever after.

Solomon Clarke goes by Saint, though he's anything but. After lusting for him from afar, the masquerade party affords me the anonymity to pursue that attraction without worrying about the fall-out of hooking-up with the bouncer from the Hawkeye Club. From the second he lays his eyes and hands on me, I'm helpless to resist him. Even burying myself in a dangerous investigation can't erase the memory of our combustible connection and one night together. The only problem... he has no idea who I am.

Caroline Brooks thinks I don't see her watching me, the way her eyes rake over me with appreciation. But I've noticed, and the party is the perfect opportunity to unleash the desire I've kept reined in for so damn long. It also sets off a series of events no one sees coming. Events that leave those I love hurting because of my failures. While the guilt eats away at my soul, Caroline continues to weigh on my heart. That woman may be the death of me, but oh, what a way to go.

Life isn't always clean, and sometimes, it takes a saint to do the dirty work.

Steele Resolve (The Hawke Family - Book Six)

For one man, power is king. For the other, loyalty reigns.

Mob boss Luca "Steele" Abello isn't just dangerous—he's lethal. A master manipulator, liar, and user, no one should trust a word that comes out of his mouth. Yet, I can't get him out of my head. The time we spent together before I knew his true identity is seared into my brain. His touch. His voice. They haunt my every waking hour and occupy my dreams. So does my guilt. I'm literally sleeping with the enemy and betraying the only family I've ever had. When I come clean, it will be the end of me.

Byron Harris is a distraction I can't afford. I never should have let it go beyond that first night, but I couldn't stay away. Even when I learned who he was, when the *only* option was to end things, I kept going back, risking his life and mine to continue our indiscretion. The truth of what I am could get us both killed, but being with the man who's such an integral part of the Hawke family is even more terrifying. The only people I've ever cared about are on opposing sides, and I'm the rift that could end their friendship forever.

Love is a battlefield isn't just a saying, for some, it's a reality.

AVAILABLE AT ALL RETAILERS:

The Slip Series (Romantic Comedy)

Dickslip (A Scandalous Slip Story #1)

One wardrobe malfunction. Two lives forever changed.

Playing in a star-studded charity basketball game should be fun, and it is, until I literally go balls out to show up my arch nemesis. When I dive for the basketball and my junk slips out of my gym shorts, I know my life and career are over. There's no way the network can keep my kids' show on the air after I've exposed myself to millions of people. I don't know how Andy, the new CEO, can go to bat for me with such passion. I also never anticipate how hot she looks in a pair of high heels.

Rafe's dickslip has made my new job even more stressful. It's hard enough being a woman in a man's world without dealing with sex organs being publicly displayed when someone is representing the company. But he's an asset to the network, not to mention hot as hell. I can barely keep my eyes off him or his crotch during our meetings. Defending him to the board puts my ass on the line as much as his, but it's worth it. So is risking my job to fulfill the fantasies I've had about him since he first set foot in my office.

Things may have started out bad, but... some accidents have happy endings.

Nipslip (A Scandalous Slip Story #2)

One nipple. A world of problems.

I own the runway. Until my nipple pops out of my dress during New York Fashion Week and it suddenly owns me. Being called a worthless gutter slut by a fuming designer is the least of my problems. My career is swirling around the toilet like the other models' lunches. Until smoking hot Tate Decker steps in with a crazy idea about how his magazine can maybe salvage my livelihood.

It's less than two feet in front of me. Perfect and perky and pink. And the woman it's attached to looks absolutely horrified. I need to help her, and not just because she's beautiful and has a perfect rack. Using my position in the industry to expose the volatile nature of our business puts my career in jeopardy in an attempt to save Riley's. I'm willing to risk that, but falling for her isn't part of the plan.

When love and tits are involved... Things can get slippery.

AVAILABLE NOW AT ALL RETAILERS:

www.Books2read.com/Nipslip

Beaver Blunder (A Scandalous Slip Story #3)

One brief mistake. A world of hurt.

No panties. No problem. At least until I slip on the wet floor and go heels over head in front of my colleagues and half the courthouse. Returning to consciousness can't be more awkward, until I find out who my sexy, argumentative, and bossy knight in shining armor really is. My career may not survive my beaver blunder, and my heart might not survive Owen Grant.

Madeline Ryan tumbles into my life on a wave of perfume and public embarrassment. She falls and exposes herself in front of me, and I find myself falling for her despite the fact she fights me every chance she gets. Being a woman in a good ol' boy profession demands a certain brashness, but it definitely has me thinking, maybe litigators shouldn't be lovers.

With stressful jobs and big attitudes, going commando has never been so freeing.

AVAILABLE NOW AT ALL RETAILERS:

www.Books2read.com/BeaverBlunder

Made in the USA
Columbia, SC
06 August 2019